UNFAITHFUL

J.L. Butler trained as a lawyer and journalist. She lives in London with her husband and son. J.L. Butler is the pseudonym for *Sunday Times* bestselling author, Tasmina Perry.

Unfaithful

J.L. BUTLER

HarperCollins*Publishers*

HarperCollins*Publishers* Ltd
1 London Bridge Street,
London SE1 9GF

www.harpercollins.co.uk

HarperCollins*Publishers*
1st Floor, Watermarque Building, Ringsend Road
Dublin 4, Ireland

First published by HarperCollins*Publishers* 2022
This paperback edition published 2022

1

A catalogue record for this book is available from the British Library

ISBN: 978-0-00-826247-1

This novel is entirely a work of fiction.
The names, characters and incidents portrayed in it are
the work of the author's imagination. Any resemblance to
actual persons, living or dead, events or localities is
entirely coincidental.

Set in Sabon by Palimpsest Book Production Ltd, Falkirk, Stirlingshire

Printed and Bound in the UK using 100% Renewable Electricity at CPI Group (UK) Ltd

MIX
Paper from
responsible sources
FSC™ C007454

This book is produced from independently certified FSC™ paper
to ensure responsible forest management.

For more information visit: www.harpercollins.co.uk/green

This one is for my agent Eugenie Furniss

Prologue

The card is typed, the gift carefully selected. I touch the box one last time as I wrap it in brown paper; crisp, but anonymous. I dab the stamps with a damp sponge – just a precaution should things become complicated, and press down hard. Hard enough to cut off air.

I will find a remote postbox from which to send it, push my gift into its hungry scarlet mouth, the address delicately printed.

I know where you live, Rachel; of course I do. I know everything about you. What scent you wear, where you buy your lingerie – those flimsy things – who you're thinking about when you put them on . . .

Which brings me back to your present. So apt. Just what the doctor ordered, in fact. I'm imagining your sweet face as you pick it up, eager to see what's inside. You'll touch it with those long, slim fingers, wondering if it's another pointless something you've ordered online, another handbag or trinket you will hardly ever wear. Is it?

Why, no.

When you see my gift, your headlight eyes will flare; those pale pink lips will curl. You might even cry out, pushing away. What *is* this? Who would do such a thing?

1

Me. Me, me, *me*.

It's always me, Rachel. Always just me.

Deep down, I think you know that. Just as you know that the gift is completely perfect. The best gifts come from people who understand us, don't they? From people who know what's best.

Because in your heart of hearts, you know you've strayed. Inside, you're still a good girl, Rachel. I don't know what made you forget it. I don't know what made you lose yourself in those tangled, knotted lies.

I wonder if you regret what you have done? I wonder if you hate me by now? That's the last thing I want. Or is it?

We both know it's not that simple. My feelings are complicated. They are like a hard stone sitting inside my chest. Impervious, strong, cold in the winter, blazing hot in the sun.

Enough chat. I need to move. I need to catch the post if your gift is going to arrive by the weekend.

And you know what? When it arrives?

I don't think you'll tell anyone.

In fact, I'm willing

To

Bet

Your

Life.

Chapter 1

My watch was fast. I tapped a nail against the glass, but it kept moving. The second hand was jumping ahead, I was sure of it, over-eager, hyperactive. Pause, flick. Pause, flick, like a goose-step, legs kicked forward too smartly, charging forward too quickly.

I looked around the university car park, at all the inter-changeable 4x4s with their interchangeable boots open just like ours, all unloading their suitcases and boxes of pots and pans, vital lifelines in the halls of residence, supplied by heartbroken parents sending their beloved children off into the world, and I wondered if they all felt the same pain that I did. The same sense of everything coming to an end with the final sweep of a stopwatch.

Did Dylan, my daughter, feel it too? Probably not. My only child loitering at the kerb, hooded eyes looking down at her suitcase, bruised and scuffed, with a tufted pink wool pom-pom tied around the handle, a relic of our family holiday to Ibiza a few weeks earlier.

And from ten paces, I could almost read her mind: 'why is my suitcase so scruffy?' That was what she was thinking. 'Why did Mum not buy me a new one for such a big day?' And, as my husband Robert paced and muttered into his phone across the road, 'why are my parents so embarrassing?'

'We should have hired a van,' said Robert, pocketing his phone, then hoisting another bag from the car, dropping it on the tarmac. Dylan winced; that one was important. It had her laptop and a magpie's nest of chargers and dongles inside. Twenty-first-century magic. Oh, and the handwritten diary she thought I didn't know about.

'Dad, be careful,' said Dylan. It was meant as a complaint, the casual way teenagers express their constant displeasure with their 'lame' elders, but today it was different. Softer, more affectionate. Gentle eye-rolling, feigned irritation. Maybe even Dylan, armour-plated by hormones, still felt the tug of that wire-taut cord as it stretched between us.

'Come on,' said Robert, all gruff bonhomie, 'let's get you inside. It looks like rain.'

We all looked up at the sky, each hunching our shoulders against weather yet to come.

Dylan smiled but I could hear her breath stutter as my husband locked the car. It felt strange to watch my daughter in the final moments of our family life. People tended to remember their days at uni as fun, carefree and hedonistic, a brief, perfect shadow world between being a child and the realities of responsibility, mortgages and wrinkles. But today, on the cusp of this idealized adult life, no one looked like they were having any fun. The new students drifting through the corridors looked awkward, anxious, torn between wanting us to leave so they could get on with being adults and not wanting us to go because then they would finally be on their own. A gold-plated portcullis poised to drop.

Her room was on the second floor. It was small, but at least she didn't have to share it with anyone, and it had a view of the lake which was the centrepiece of the university's sprawling halls of residence campus. As Dylan unpacked the assortment of bags and cases that had made the journey from home, I helped her put them away.

'Are you sure you know how to use that?' I said as she pulled a new steam iron out of a banker's box.

'Mum, it's not my first time with an electrical appliance,' she sighed. 'Besides, I can't imagine I'll be doing much ironing.'

'Not when there's so much partying to do,' said Robert, nudging her, always playing good cop.

'Exactly. I'm a student now,' she grinned.

'So that's what we're paying thirty thousand pounds in tuition for,' I said, also trying to be light-hearted, but I was afraid it came across as a telling-off.

'Where do you want these posters putting up?' Robert added, tapping the end of a cardboard tube.

'It's fine Dad. Leave it. I'll do it later.'

I wanted it to go on forever, the banter and the small-talk but a knock at the door told me it wouldn't.

A soap-pink face framed by a mop of curls peered into the room.

'Hello,' said the girl. 'I'm Amy. I've just moved in next door.'

Amy was from Shrewsbury, doing 'Mech Eng', whatever that was. She reported that 'a group of them' were heading down to the bar, then shrugged apologetically, realizing too late that perhaps her new neighbour's parents might not approve. Amy was the jolly, sensible sort you hoped would be your daughter's next-door pal, but I still couldn't help feel a pang of resentment that Amy was cutting in on our party of three. The door closed and Dylan gave a shy grin.

'I should probably go and check it out before everyone makes lifelong friends and I'm left in the cold.'

My eyes met Robert's and he gave a quick nod. This was it then. The moment. The one thing I had been dreading for the past twelve months.

'We don't want you getting left out,' said Robert, slipping his hand into mine. Reassurance, or restraint.

Tears pooled in my eyes and I wasn't sure a stubborn blink

could get rid of them. Instead, I stepped forward and hugged Dylan. Robert, still attached, joined in like a family chain gang.

'Guys . . .' said Dylan, wriggling under us. 'This is Birmingham. I'm not going to the moon. I'll be back most weekends.'

I caught my husband's eye again. We both knew that wasn't true. We were close as a family, but Dylan had always been independent. Even at seven, she had been asking how old she had to be before she could get her own flat.

Robert's phone rang.

He swore, scrabbling in his pocket for his phone. 'Sorry, got to take this,' he said, holding up a finger. 'Back in a mo.'

I was grateful for my moment alone with Dylan and pulled my daughter close again, taking a deep breath through my nose and holding it in. I've always known my daughter's smell: a faint smell of cotton fabric softener I'd always used for our laundry and that pear shampoo she likes. But now – suddenly – it didn't feel quite so familiar. My daughter smelled new, different, as if she had suddenly shed a skin. I wanted to learn it, drink it in, never let go. Just a tick, just another, hold onto my baby just another minute longer.

'We're going to miss you so much.' I said. 'So, so much.'

I'd spent half the previous night awake, crying silently into my pillow, but I was determined not to let my daughter see how upset I was now.

Dylan pulled back, putting on that half-adult scolding face.

'You can Skype and WhatsApp me.'

'I hate WhatsApp.'

'You are such a dinosaur.'

I tried to smile.

'Maybe, but I do remember uni. It's tough.'

I was talking about myself, of course. I hadn't found university easy at all. I was earnest, intense, and I thought, poetic. I was, in hindsight, just annoying and lonely. I found the coursework difficult too, just managing to keep my head above water, scraping across the finishing line of Finals with a low 2:2 and an inferiority complex.

But Dylan wasn't like me. She had a fierce mind and despite her health problems, had breezed through her A levels with a string of As.

'I know you'll be fine, but if anything's wrong, just call – okay?'

'I'm more worried about you,' said Dylan, looking at me directly.

I looked at her, taken aback.

'Me?'

'You do know there's more to life than Zumba and reading about other people's children on Facebook, don't you?'

I managed a weak laugh.

'I do, yes.'

'Just make sure you keep busy, okay?'

'Aren't I the one supposed to be giving you advice?'

Robert walked back in and touched my shoulder.

'I can hear the noise from the bar from the corridor. I think it's our cue to leave.'

I looked back at Dylan.

'Are you sure you don't want us to take you out for dinner?'

'Mum . . .'

She flashed a look at her father for support.

'We're going,' he smiled. 'Just text us later to let us know things are okay?'

'I will. And don't worry, I'll be fine.'

And it was only then, in that moment, I realized that was exactly what I feared the most.

Chapter 2

A late shower made the road black, wet and shiny, reflecting the moon's face back at us. We sat in silence, no cars passing, apparently alone; just us and the haze of the slip road.

'Why didn't we sort out staying over?' I said, finally glancing across at Robert as we slid onto the M6. 'I mean, there are plenty of nice boutique hotels in Birmingham. We could have made a night of it.'

My voice sounded glassy, like the treble had been turned up too far.

'You mean we should have stayed in the area in case Dylan needed us,' said Robert, glancing over, his smile teasing me.

'You're suggesting we're above spying on our only child.'

Robert laughed.

'Despite that being a bit creepy, how do you propose we do that?'

'Can't we track her phone or something?'

'Ignoring the fact that Dylan is about a hundred times more tech-savvy than us, I'm not sure it would help. She'd only have to be within fifty feet of a nightclub and you'd be panicking she's on drugs.'

I returned a soft snort. After twenty years of marriage, he could read my internal Autocue.

'She needs to stand on her own two feet, Rachel,' said Robert more softly. 'If there's anything wrong, she knows where we are and by now, I'm sure about a dozen new friends are hanging on her every word. She's probably forgotten about us already. Dilly's never had trouble getting stuck in, remember her first day at nursery?'

I did. Dylan was four and I'd left her for half an hour – twenty-nine minutes longer than we had ever been apart before. I'd gone to the new joiners' coffee morning in the school dining hall, but before I went home, I'd returned to the nursery block, pressed my face up against the glass, expecting to see my daughter shuffling aimlessly around the classroom. Instead, she was sitting on a plastic chair in the Wendy House, with a queue of tiny children lined up in front of her. When I'd asked her about it later, she had said they'd all been waiting for the chance to 'meet the queen'.

I nodded, feeling teary again. To the outside world, Dylan was a leader, the life and soul of the party. So much so, it was easy to forget the wobble in our lives just a couple of years earlier.

Anorexia. Even now I couldn't even say the word, let alone admit it had once consumed our life. I had put Dylan's meagre appetite down to the stress of GCSEs. I didn't know that her periods had stopped or that she'd lost over a stone in weight from her already slim frame. I still woke up in the middle of the night, asking myself how could I not have noticed any of it: the baggy jumpers in summer, the excessive chewing, all that crap about how 'I stuffed myself at lunch', the significance of her long daily runs.

And although it could have been worse – officially she had an OSFED, or 'other specified feeding or eating disorder', rather than full-blown anorexia – it still felt too difficult for me to let her go, to let her slip away from my watch.

Robert reached across and squeezed my hand. He knew what I was thinking; how could he not?

'Rach, she's okay.'

'How can you be so sure?'

'She's fine. She looks great, she eats more than we do, she's happy . . .'

'How do you ever really know that?'

He turned back to the road. There was no answer to that question.

'It's just us now, huh?'

We'd been talking about it for years, that mythical point in time 'when Dylan leaves home'. All the things we'd do, all the places we would go: a summer in Africa, the sabbatical in Rome. We were going to travel, and learn new things – sculpture, Mandarin, Tai Chi. But now it was here, I didn't want anything other than our old routine.

'It's not too late, you know,' he said.

'For what?' My voice lifted a notch. Was my husband actually proposing we had another child? I'd thought about it a lot lately. At forty-seven I was technically not too old, the window for being a mum again was ajar, just a sliver, just enough to let the wind stir the dust. But still, I felt a quiver of panic.

'Finding a hotel, getting some dinner . . .'

I was tired just thinking about an impromptu mini-break and everything that involved; food, wine and the routine sex that neither of us really wanted. I just wanted to get home, even if it was an empty house full of ghosts.

'So that's a no?' he said, disappointed. Perhaps I was wrong about the sex.

'We should just get back,' I said, putting a consolatory hand on his knee.

We sank back into silence as I watched the motorway lights flip over us. Light, then dark. Light, then dark, the lump in my chest constant as I played back a rush of random memories of Dylan, like those highlight compilations they played when a reality TV contestant was evicted from their fake house or jungle. I could see the little girl who scoured every beach for oysters, hoping to find a pearl, the child who built her own writing den at the bottom of our garden, where she'd disappear for hours with her notebooks and survival kit stuffed with sweets, cuddly toys and torches. I turned to the window to hide my glistening eyes from Robert.

The streetlights had gone now, our headlights cutting into the gathering night, and I knew it was time. Time for the conversation I'd been rehearsing for weeks.

'You know I've been thinking,' I said, trying to keep my tone light, my eyes fixed on the scarlet glow of the taillights ahead. 'About going back to work.'

'Work?' he said, turning on some music.

'You know I put my career on hold when Dylan came along,' I said, trying not to rush the script. 'But it was never meant to be permanent, was it? I was only ever meant to stay at home until Dilly went to school. But it didn't work out like that.'

Even now, it was hard to believe where the time had gone. Once Dylan had started school, we'd decided that I needed to be around just for the first few years to be there for parents' evenings, supervising homework and ferrying her to clubs and play-dates. But then I needed to see her through the eleven plus, then getting her GCSEs . . .

I stopped myself, slightly ashamed at the drab, linear description of my life. Was that it? A wedding, a baby, then a series of coffee mornings and taxi runs? Had my existence on the planet been measured in bake sales? I wasn't exactly sure if we'd ever actually 'agreed' that I would stay home to look after Dylan, but that's what had happened. Eighteen years, gone by in a blink.

'And now, well. She doesn't need me anymore. I'm freed up for other things,' I said, my voice cracking slightly.

'What about Bill and Iris?' said Robert glancing across.

I looked at him, not sure I'd heard correctly. Bill and Iris? I hadn't expected Robert to greet my idea of going back to work with whoops of excitement. My husband looked good for his age, and had a wardrobe of expensive clothes that reflected his position as CEO of a property firm, a mover and shaker around the capital. But deep down, Robert Reeves was still a traditional, conservative man. I knew he liked the status quo, Him as the striver, the provider, me as the home-maker, sweeping out the cave. No, that wasn't fair. But neither had he ever suggested I go back to work. And anyway, what did our elderly neighbours have to do with any of this?

Eight years ago, when we had moved into Robert's dream house in Highgate, we knew we had 'arrived'. My husband's property business was flying, the market was booming and Highgate Village had felt like a jump to another level from our previous home in Crouch End. The house we designed and built was beautiful: modernist, open plan, all glass and steel. We had fantasized that our neighbours would be preten-tious novelists or avant-garde architects, only half-joking when we said we'd be sucked into a world of dinner parties where the hosts wore polo necks and thick-rimmed spectacles. That hadn't happened. Instead, we got Bill and Iris.

Bill was ninety – or rather, he was ninety now. Back then, he'd seemed older. Mostly deaf and partially sighted, Bill had shuffled around on that first day to loudly complain about the moving van blocking his drive. I could sympathize: the two years we'd spent on the building project before we moved in probably hadn't endeared us to them. Iris was two years older than her husband and in the late stages of Alzheimer's. We had the impression that in her earlier life, Iris had been a formidable woman. She certainly had plenty of opinions when she spoke up.

'Bill and Iris?' I repeated. 'Haven't you spent the last few years telling me I was wasting my time on them?'

'I never said that. I know how much they rely on you.'

That much was true. About three years earlier I'd made the mistake of stepping in to help them. I say a mistake, I was glad to assist – ordering their supermarket deliveries, running them to the odd hospital appointment. At first it had felt good to take some responsibility, but there had been a slow creep of more and more requests and now, without really planning it, I had taken on the role of de facto daughter.

'I need to cut the cord, Robert,' I said as firmly as I could.

'Cut the cord?'

'I'm practically their full-time carer.'

'I think that's an exaggeration.'

'How do you know?' My frustration was rising. 'You're not at home most of the day. You don't know how much I do and how much they expect me to do.'

'Come on, Rach, they're nice people.'

'That's not the point,' I snapped.

He let that hang in the air for a moment, as if he was thinking.

'Maybe you need to speak to what's-his-name, their nephew John? Maybe you could suggest they pay you?'

'We can't ask for money.'

'I don't see why not. You are literally saving them thousands, hundreds of thousands of pounds keeping them out of a home. One of the guys at work was telling me that he'd worked out it would be cheaper to house his mum at Claridges than the care place she's currently at.'

'I can't, Robert,' I said, not wanting to back down now. 'Anyway, going back to work is a win-win. I start to use my brain again, and I can back off from Bill and Iris. It's awkward otherwise.'

'But what would you do?' Robert said.

His question irritated me, but still, there was a chink of hope, the possibility I was winning him round.

'What I used to do. Publishing.'

He gave a cynical glance.

'I think a lot has changed a lot since you left.'

He wasn't trying to be unkind but still I bristled.

'What's that supposed to mean?'

'The world's changed, Rach. Twenty years ago, people bought hardback books. No one had even heard of an eBook back then. Now it's all digital and audio, and all those supermarket promotions you used to do? I mean, does anyone even go to the supermarket anymore?'

'People still want great stories, well told, and I was always good at finding those.'

I hated the sound of my voice, the begging tone. And I hated the very idea I needed my husband's permission to do something I wanted this much.

'We'll talk about it later,' he said.

'Later? How about now?' I said, pushing back.

'I'm tired. It's been a long day and we're feeling emotional as it is.'

'Robert . . .'

'No, Rach. Please, not now.'

He glanced across and I knew that look. The matter was settled and he had made his decision. I turned back to the dark window, biting my tongue, biding my time. The world had changed; he was right about that. But I had to change too.

Chapter 3

The house was quiet. So quiet I could hear the tick-tick of pipes cooling and the press of the wind on the floor-to-ceiling glass. I knew the exact timings of aeroplanes passing overhead – every ninety seconds – and a car pulling up in the street got me dashing straight to the window. That first week, I could tell you exactly who had a delivery and who used Uber. It hadn't been like that when Dylan was in the house, when she had been constantly playing music, watching videos at top volume or chatting to me about whatever random thought popped into her head. Even when she'd gone out – and once she'd turned sixteen Dilly seemed to be out most of the time – the house still felt different. It felt lived in. But now, it was as if her leaving had sucked all the warmth out of our home, like when you returned from a winter break having forgotten to leave the heating on and the building felt cold to its core. I felt like that too. Empty, neglected, alone.

If I was being completely honest, I knew that feeling lonely had begun way before we'd packed our daughter's suitcases and the obligatory pot plant into the car and headed for the M6.

Robert worked away from home a lot. In any given week, he could be in Singapore, New York or Dubai; global centres of money where he would drum up finance or meet new clients. At the beginning, I always used to be busy too, my life full of people, right from the moment that Dylan had been born. Baby music classes, NCT reunions, swimming lessons, the cult of the new motherhood, new friends bonded by reflux and wet wipes. As she got older there were coffees and gossip about catchment areas and the nursery playground. And once Dilly went to school, to her all-girls prep just off the high street – Robert had been very clear she would be privately educated – my friendship circle grew still. The school gate was the hub and I threw myself into it all – class-repping, volunteering at the summer fair, the PTA and cheering from the side-lines at the hockey and lacrosse matches. There were the weekly coffee mornings in the various village cafés or at the homes of the mums who had a remodel to show off. It was a real-life community and although I was not naturally a loud or gregarious person, I found myself right at the very heart of it.

But somewhere it stopped. Perhaps when Dylan went up to senior school and somehow the parents didn't knit together, or didn't seem to need the reassurance of a group. There was no daily chit-chat at the gates because the girls walked to school or took the bus. Or maybe everyone had enough friends by then. Was friendship like a computer hard drive? At some point it simply said it was 'full'.

It didn't matter at first. There was the old crowd to run with, go to spinning class with, to have lunch. But slowly, that friendship group shrank too. Trudy and Jake were the first to move. Competition for school places was fierce and they literally had to move to the other side of London to get their daughter Tilly into a school that they deemed up to scratch. Others had tired of London life, or realized that for the price of their three-bed terrace they could live like kings outside of the M25 – garden-less homes in Archway swapped for mini manor houses in Kent or mortgage-free cottages by the sea. There was no chance of us joining the exodus –

Robert's business was doing well and he needed to be in striking distance of Zone One. Plus, we loved Highgate and we loved the house. Or Robert did, anyway.

I looked around now and sighed. Sometimes, I thought he loved the house more than he loved me.

Building Swain's House had been Robert's dream.

After three years of looking, waiting, the perfect plot had finally come up in a secluded part of the Village. A 1920s detached had been pulled down and in its place, we built a tribute to the Modernist design that my husband so loved. The open plan space was a series of smooth lines built from granite, concrete and cedar wood. From the top two floors there were views over the cemetery, each room decorated in natural shades to complement the cool grey English skies. Every room smelled of Jo Malone, and underfloor heating kept them warm. We had a cinema in the basement, and a glass retracting roof in our en-suite. It was a world away from the small Belfast semi in which I had grown up. It had everything we could need, but nothing that I wanted.

I pulled my wrap tighter and picked up the phone that was on the kitchen table. I clicked onto Instagram, ignored my feed and went straight to Dylan's page. My heart contracted as I saw my daughter's silly, smiling profile photo and her new life in a grid of pictures. A fresh-faced selfie by the lake on the halls of residence campus, a gaggle of girls next to the university clock tower, a row of empty pint glasses on a bar. Nothing new since the last time I'd looked two hours earlier, but even so, it made me feel emotional. The photos were a lifeline to my daughter, but also a reminder that I was now locked out of her world.

Emotion bubbled in my chest and I told myself to get a grip.

She was my daughter. I wanted her to go to university, have fun, meet new friends. And although I missed being part of her life so fiercely, my whole body felt hollowed out, a

17

shell, like one of Robert's building projects, I couldn't hold her back because of my own neediness.

I clicked off Instagram but I didn't let go of the phone. Instead, I scrolled to messages, past all the contacts I never seemed to see or speak to anymore. Serena's was one of the few numbers I knew off by heart.

Still on for today?

I put the mobile back on the breakfast bar and looked at it, waiting for the incoming ping. I began to get restless, panicked, wondering how else I could fill the day if my friend was going to blow me out at the last minute.

But finally, Serena replied.

See you at one. Usual place.

I smiled with relief and I began to get ready.

Even mid-week, Joules was packed, so I was lucky to grab one of the tables by the window facing the street. I slumped down and tried one of those deep-breathing exercises in a vain attempt to reduce my spiking stress levels. An hour agonizing over the right wardrobe and make-up – not too formal, not too loungewear – half an hour grinding my way into town, and the fifteen-minute walk to the tube. How had I done it every day?

Because that was eighteen years ago, I reminded myself, looking around the bar at the bright young twenty-somethings. Eighteen years and six months, actually, as I was heavily pregnant with Dylan when they finally dragged me out of the office. The men and women laughing and chatting in Joules looked much the same though: younger, of course, but that same slightly smug look of upwardly mobile media professionals. Sometimes it seemed like yesterday since I was among them, lunching agents and sales reps, but mostly it felt as if I dreamed it.

A handsome twenty-something walked through the door and waved in my direction. I tried to place him but he wasn't familiar. He was too young to be a former colleague, too old to be one of Dylan's friends. I gave a non-committal half-smile not wanting to seem rude, but as he looked straight through me and I heard the sound of a chair scrape behind me, and the sound of happy media air-kissing, I realized that the wave was not meant for me.

My embarrassment was salvaged by the chirp of a text: B there in ten. S x

I ordered a silver chai, the latest thing, according to *Vogue* – or was it *Tatler*? – either way, I wanted to fit in here, desperately wanted to reconnect with this lifestyle, this place. Joules was a Soho institution, it had been the hang-out for the media crowd since Berwick Street and Golden Square had become the centre of creative London in the Eighties and Nineties boom. I'd only seen the tail end of all that, but I'd been a part of it – the gentle hum of lunchtime gossip and office politics moans, the talk of weekends in the Cotswolds or Paris, plans for after-work drinks at The Atlantic bar or yoga classes at some hip, new gym, the idea of which seemed so cutting-edge back then.

I didn't want to be invisible anymore. I wanted to feel alive. I wanted to belong. I wanted to be part of this scene once more, so much that I could feel the weight of longing pressing on my chest.

'Sweets, how are you?' said Serena, rushing in and dipping for an air-kiss. 'Have you been waiting ages? Got tied up in some marketing nonsense.' She rolled her eyes in that 'you know how it is' expression and she was right, I did. Or rather, I could still remember those brightly lit boardrooms with glass tables and cantilever chairs, the crisp shirts, the take-out coffee, Mont Blanc pens twisted in smooth fingers slick with hand-cream. At the time, those meetings had seemed a grind, but right now? Just the memory was making my heart beat harder.

'So, how's work?' I asked. 'Are you snowed under?'

'Oh, you know. Comme ci, comme ça. The industry's going to hell in a handcart, as usual.'

She leaned forward and whispered. 'Although between you and me, sales are up 12 per cent year on year in our division, so I'm safe for a few months anyway.'

I smiled. Typical Serena: indiscreet, but with an undercurrent of 'me, me, me'.

She was still one of my closest friends despite it. We had started working at Edelman, one of Bloomsbury's smallest but most prestigious publishing houses in those Nineties glory days when London's medialand was pulsing. Serena got her job via a well-connected godparent, I'd seen an advertisement for an editorial assistant in the Monday *Guardian* media pages and miraculously had said all the right things at interview. Twenty-plus years on, our close-knit little company had been folded into BCC, a giant global media concern, and Serena was now a top editor at their biggest commercial imprint, shuttling between London, New York and Frankfurt. And her authors were no longer the type who won critical praise but hardly sold anything, they were the bestsellers – blockbusting thrillers and big-name romances by world renowned authors.

'So, what's the big book I should be reading?' I asked, sipping my silver chai.

Serena waved a vague hand.

'I'm definitely the wrong person to ask; I never read.'

'You never read?' I laughed.

'Not if I can help it.'

'Aren't books your business?' I smiled.

She glanced up from the menu. 'Rach, there's not enough time in the day to read all the submissions that come in, let alone the ones that actually make it to print.'

She lowered her voice.

'Besides, it's all about IP these days. No one really cares about the words anymore. It's the idea, the pithy little concept we can sell on to Netflix.'

Serena had always been prone to these sorts of pronounce-ments: splashy headlines with an undercurrent of insider knowledge. Usually I shrugged them off, but today, I was all ears. I was about to ask for more details, but Serena leaned across and laid a hand over mine.

'And how are you holding up?' she said with a sympathetic tilt of the head. 'Dylan off to uni and everything?'

'I can't believe she's gone,' I sighed. 'All those things I took for granted,' I said, staring out of the window, lost for a moment. 'The things I complained about. The attitude, the bickering and demands for attention. "Mum, can you test me on my biology, can you give me a lift to Hampstead?"' I did a fair impression of Dylan and Serena laughed.

'You miss being a taxi service?'

I didn't want to admit how crushed I'd been feeling over the past week. How every afternoon, at about the time Dylan used to come home from school, I'd become so mournful that I would cry. How I would sometimes say her name out loud, to pretend that she was just out of sight in her room, or how I'd lie on her bed, like a cat stretched out in the sun, remembering all the good times we'd had as a family, only to curl up in a ball, sobbing when I realized that those days were over.

'I miss everything,' I said simply.

She nodded, but I wasn't quite sure she understood. Serena wasn't an empty nester yet, although her twin boys Max and Christian were boarders at Charterhouse, so she did have some idea.

'Darling, the holidays come around quickly,' said Serena, summoning the waiter. 'No sooner have the boys gone to school then they are back again. Honestly, I like to think of it as the best of both worlds.'

I bit my tongue. I knew that Max and Chris still came home most weekends and family holidays – skiing and winter sun breaks were all already planned. There was an ominous feeling to our summer vacation this year; Dylan accompanied us to the Ibizan finca on the west coast of the island. I couldn't fault the villa, which had views over Es Vedra, but Dylan seemed restless, finding any excuse to sunbathe or head out to a bar.

I had mentioned a girls-only shopping trip to New York a few weeks earlier and she did perk up at that one, but really, I guessed it was the best I could hope for. At eighteen they were gone. Gone. I was sure that Ibiza family holiday had been our last.

'And how's Robert?'

I did my best to focus on Serena.

'Working like a lunatic,' I shrugged. 'I've hardly seen him since the holiday, to be honest.'

'But look at how well he's doing.'

There was a slight reservation to her tone.

Serena was old school money. She'd always respected wealth, believing that it was useful to pay for private schools and parties and upkeep of the country house. But the likes of her parents' – the Cotswolds hunting set – were sniffy about the Euro and Arab billionaires who sunk their spare change into Robert's projects and by reflection, our success was not quite kosher.

'It's so good to get out of the house though,' I said, forcing myself to think positively. 'You know I wonder,' I said, allowing myself to think aloud. 'Now Dylan's has gone, maybe we should even move further into town.'

Serena looked sceptical.

'Would Robert ever sell Highgate?'

She knew how much our house meant to my husband. It was influenced by the great American architect Frank Lloyd Wright. During the planning of the house, Robert sat along-side his architect for months and even made a week-long research trip to Illinois to see the great master's work. I'm sure it was one upside of Dylan's departure for him – to see his house as the show home he had always envisioned, now the detritus of teenage life had gone.

'Maybe he'd move,' I said. 'If it was another project.'

'Perhaps you should suggest it to him. He could certainly find the right property.'

That bit was true. Robert spent his life finding and developing properties, mainly in central London for super-wealthy clients with very specific and expensive needs. If anyone could find a suitable property in Chelsea or Marylebone, it was Robert. And it could be just the thing to focus his mind back on the family. On me.

Serena looked at me with sympathy.

'You don't look terribly convinced,' she said.

'It wouldn't fly. Robert's been talking about moving out, not in. A country pile, somewhere for the weekend.'

'Come to the Cotswolds,' she grinned.

'I'm sure it's lovely, but I want to feel more connected, not isolated.

The waiter took our order. Two chicken salads. Two diet Cokes. No wine although I desperately felt like it. Not in front of Serena. I was here to look serious.

I took a deep breath.

'What I really want is to get back to work.'

There was an uplift to Serena's brow, as I knew there would be. I thought of Robert's reaction – 'the world's changed, Rach' – by which he had meant it had changed beyond my recognition and skillset. But I knew I could still do it.

'Look, I know I've been out of the game for years, but I still know books, and I'm still good with organization and handling people. I'm behind on the tech stuff, obviously, but I'm a fast learner and I'm keen . . .'

Serena was holding up both hands, a smile on her lips.

'Alright, alright,' she said. 'You don't need to convince me.'

My shoulders dropped with relief. I had spent weeks – no,

months – rehearsing this conversation in my head and had expected to have to argue much harder to get Serena onside.

'Thank you,' I said, my voice soft and quiet. 'I need this. Dylan leaving – it's just hit me hard. She's only just gone and already I feel driftless. Robert's so busy it doesn't seem to have affected him, and that only makes me feel worse.'

I gulped hard, surprised by my honesty. Serena was one of my oldest friends but she was also one of the toughest. She rarely showed any vulnerability herself – and as her friend, you avoided revealing your own frailties.

'How soon were you thinking of starting?'

Her very matter-of-factness gave me a shot of confidence.

'The moment something comes up.'

Serena looked thoughtful.

'Something might be going at Edelman. Ginny Lane – editor in the literary fiction division – is pregnant. I say pregnant, but she had the baby a few days ago. It came at twenty-eight weeks can you believe. Baby's fine but it's left the team on the back-foot.'

'Won't they just get by without her?

Even when I was there – back in the Nineties glory days – when an editor went on maternity leave their workload, their authors were just spread around the team until they came back. Unless, like me, they didn't.

Serena shook her head. 'No – they've got to get someone in. We've just launched a new imprint – Emerald – and three Edelman editors have moved across. It's left them too stretched.'

'It sounds perfect,' I said, allowing myself to feel giddy. Edelman was where I started, where I'd spent all of my working life. By the time I'd left I was a respected editor with a huge word-of-mouth hit under my belt. I was someone, not a no one.

'Of course, it's not my division,' she added. 'You'd need to convince Ian.'

'Ian?'

'Ian Sinclair. MD at Edelman. I think you'd left by the time he arrived. Can be prickly, snobbish, but if you get him onside . . .'

Serena looked at me and gave a sly smile.

'What are you doing on Wednesday night?'

I shook my head. I still hadn't taken a breath.

'How do you fancy going to a party?'

Chapter 4

Robert's overnight bag was packed and standing by the front door when I came downstairs. His silver Rinowa – the perfect cabin size roll-on, a Christmas gift from three years ago – was as familiar a sight in our front hall as Dylan's Converse trainers used to be. As long as I'd known him, he was always away on business, but his latest project – the redevelopment of a Grade 1 listed mansion in Regent's Park into twenty-four super-prime apartments – was keeping him busier than ever. This month alone he had been to Moscow for a week and Abu Dhabi for three days. Usually, before Dylan had gone, I wouldn't give a second thought to my husband going away, because the truth was, I enjoyed it. I liked cooking Dilly's favourite suppers while she did her homework on the break-fast bar. I liked baking – chocolate cakes and key lime pies – without the pressure of everything being scrupulously cleared up before my husband, ever the neat freak came home. I liked curling up in the media room with my daughter and binge-watching *Friends*, enjoying the nostalgia of one of my favourite shows, secretly thrilled that Dylan loved it as much as I did. I even joked that we were like Joey and Chandler in our matching La-Z-Boy chairs and when Robert had installed deluxe velvet recliners, it wasn't too far from the truth.

But now I hated the thought of him going away. The house seemed bigger, darker, when I was the only person in it. I hated locking up the house at night, turning off the television and climbing into our cavernous emperor sized bed alone. I hated the way the regular noises of our home seemed louder and more sinister – the distant bark of a fox in the cemetery seemed wolf-like without Robert or Dylan in the house, even the soft gurgle of the boiler sounded otherworldly. And although I told myself that our home was safe, secured with a state of the alarm security system, my imagination had gone into overdrive about what could happen to Swain's House – gas explosion, armed raiders, spectral invasions – and how I would deal with it alone. Most of all, it was a reminder that Dylan was not there to keep me company. Sometimes I wondered if, in recent years, I had been looking after her, or she had been looking after me.

Robert was flipping through his phone, elbows resting on the granite tops, when I walked into the kitchen.

He was wearing his favourite bespoke suit, the first made-to-measure he'd ever ordered when he'd pulled off a big deal a few years ago, and the blue shirt that always made him look like he had a tan, even in winter. My husband was a handsome man, with dark eyes like two chips of coal, and symmetrical features. He was not model good-looking, but he was the model of success, so much so that he reminded me of the watch adverts, where you were saving your investment for another generation.

'I made you coffee,' he said, glancing up. 'Had a new blend just delivered. Limited edition. It's good.'

'I can smell those shades of morello cherry already,' I smiled, eyeing the cup. It was a standing joke between us that he could pick out the subtleties in any coffee where I thought it all tasted exactly the same. Given the choice, I would still go for a strong mug of builder's tea, but Robert was so proud of our state-of-the-art drinks machine, I tried to join in with his fun.

'Where are you off to today?' I asked, taking a sip.

'Paris.'

'I can't keep up,' I said, perching on the bar stool beside him.

'Neither can I.'

I fumbled round for something to say. It was something that was happening to me a lot lately, especially with my husband. I'd just run out of conversation.

'What have you got on?' I asked finally. 'In Paris, I mean.'

He shrugged. 'Back to back appointments all afternoon, some big dinner for the mayor tonight and lunch tomorrow with an interesting Kuwaiti.'

'You mean rich.'

'A potential investor.'

He smiled, not even trying to hide his excitement. This was what my husband lived for. The deal. He loved making contacts and sniffing out interest. He loved the back and forth of negotiation, the competition of beating others to a prize. I'd seen him minutes after closing a big transaction and he'd be giddy, high, as if he'd actually been loaded full of class A drugs. I'm not sure if it's because the professional success validates him – Robert didn't go to university and you don't have to dig very deep to know he has a slight chip on his shoulder because of it – or because he just loves business, in a way that actors have to act or an artist feels lost without a paintbrush in their hand.

'Any chance of you nipping into Fauchon?'

Fauchon eclairs were Dylan's absolute favourites and although I tried to curb my sweet tooth, I loved it when he brought a box home. It sugared the pill that he was having a big, busy life while I stayed at home.

'I'll see what I can do.'

His phone beeped before he could reply and as he stood up and slipped on his jacket, I felt the swell of panic at the thought of being left alone again.

'Car's here,' he muttered.

He stepped across and gave me a peck on the cheek. 'What are your plans?'

He hadn't noticed that I'd had my hair cut and coloured the day before, or if he had, he hadn't said anything.

I'd been meaning to tell him about my lunch with Serena all week, but there had never seemed to be the right moment. I certainly hadn't mentioned the party.

'I'm meeting Serena later. 'We're going to the launch of BCC's new thriller imprint,' I said as lightly as I could.

I wasn't ready to tell him about a potential job opportunity just yet. After all, it would probably come to nothing.

'A big night out?'

'Hardly. You know how book launches go: half an hour of canapés and chat, speech from the publisher, clap-clap, everyone goes home.'

'Sounds more fun than the reception I've got to go to tonight at the Hotel De Ville,' he smiled.

'I wish you weren't going,' I said honestly.

He pulled the cuffs of his shirt below his jacket.

'It's only one night.'

I picked at a loose cuticle around my nail and it stung as it ripped away from my skin.

'I was thinking . . .' I hesitated before I continued. 'Maybe we should get a cat.'

'A cat.'

I looked up at him.

'Cute, fluffy things. Can be selfish, prone to wandering, highly independent.'

'We've already got one teenager,' he grinned.

'Come on, what do you think?'

'Rach, I've got hives just thinking about it.'

'Since when have you have a cat allergy?'

'You remember what I was like when I went around to the Fishers' house. Sooky the Persian was almost the death of me.'

'His name was Sooty, she's Burmese and your itchy eye was hay-fever.'

I stopped and reminded myself I didn't really want a pet either. It was just something that someone on Mumsnet had suggested when I had typed 'empty-nest' and 'lonely' into a forum, but I thought it was at least worth a discussion.

Robert's face softened in sympathy.

'It's not always going to be like this.'

'I know.'

I wasn't convinced. My husband seemed to be working harder and harder, not slowly taking his foot off the gas. And why should he? He wasn't even fifty and according to last month's issue of the *Property Gazette* – Robert had been the cover star and it was now framed and hung up in our guest loo – his latest development, Regent Place, was going to catapult him into the highest tier of developers. Who was going to give up when they had only just arrived?

He took a step towards me.

'Maybe next time, you can come? I've got an overnighter in Milan in a couple of weeks if you fancied it. I can get Petra to sort something out. Opera, ballet, your call. Maybe we could get in at La Scala.'

I knew he'd prefer to take a client out to watch AC Milan but I appreciated the offer.

There had been a time, many years before, just after we had married, that I'd loved joining Robert on a business trip. It wasn't Moscow or Dubai in those days, but Manchester, Newcastle, Glasgow. I had my own big, busy career back then, but Fridays were my days for lunching agents or authors and I'd sometimes slip off early after those meetings, catch the train to wherever Robert was having his, and we'd have a meal in the city's best restaurants, keeping an eye on the price of drinks, but nevertheless wanting to spoil ourselves. We'd walk back to a hotel we couldn't quite afford, have sex in the room, in the shower or on one particularly risqué occasion in the loos by the ground floor bar. We'd sleep in late, order breakfast in bed, make love all over again, then wind back to London feeling happy, successful and in love.

Yet more recently, I'd spent a trip to New York shuffling around Bloomingdale for three hours on my own, waiting for Robert to come out of endless meetings, worrying that I was so far away from home, away from Dylan – even though she was on a school trip to Florence.

But maybe next time we'd have more luck.

'I'd better shoot. The car's waiting. Say hi to Serena for me,' he said, disturbing me from my thoughts. 'We should do something soon.'

I was going to reply but Robert had gone, padding into the hall, looking for his shoes.

'Back tomorrow evening?' he said as I heard the front door open.

No goodbye. I hurried out into the hall, just as the door clicked shut. And I stood there, listening to the car's engine until it faded and was gone.

I felt the butterflies flutter up in my stomach as I pushed through the glass door into Soho's Ham Yard Hotel. The party was in the basement, a fashionable open space with an orange juice machine that ran from floor to ceiling, a bar that stretched across the entire room and a cinema annexe which was set up for a presentation for the new imprint.

I hovered at the top of the stairs, looking down on the party, and tried to locate Serena, but even with this bird's-eye view she was nowhere to be seen. My hand clenched around my handbag strap, nails digging into my palm and as I took a deep breath, I told myself I could do this.

After all, this used to be my life. Book parties just like this one, where the crowd was a moveable feast of new names and faces and the wine flowed freely. Back then, the tightness in my chest was anticipation, the notion that anything could happen. I'd always had the feeling that I would meet my future husband at a book launch; it seemed so impossibly romantic. I had in fact met Robert in Po Na Na's, a Moroccan-themed club on the Kings Road, but I still felt my stomach fizz at the sight of a crowd.

'Found you!'

I jumped as I felt a hand on my shoulder and turned to see Serena grinning at me.

'What are you doing, creeping around up here?'

'Looking for you,' I smiled.

I followed my friend into the bowels of the party as she filled me in about the new imprint, which had been set up to capitalize on the interest in historical thrillers.

The launch title was *Darkest Night: a Clint Porter novel*. The eponymous Hollywood noir hero was apparently one of the biggest characters in detective fiction – so much so, that the author, a shy former policeman named Liam Grey, barely got a mention on the cover.

'People love Clint,' whispered Serena, sipping a blood-red cocktail designed to match the book's scarlet jacket. 'He's a legend. Can you believe we managed to poach him from Transworld? This is the twelfth book, all of them bestsellers, all of them practically identical, but that's what people want these days. Reliability. If they're going to spend ten quid, they want to know what they're getting.'

I nodded, smiling. Half an hour in, this was already the best night out I could remember in ages. I loved the spectacle: the cinema screen was showing a stylish-looking French film noir – apparently the Clint Porter character was a fan – there were gorgeous waiters dressed in Porter's trademark bowling shirt and best of all, there were crowds of dressed-up media people mingling and chatting and having important conversations. I desperately wanted to be part of this again. I was never the life and soul of any party but I always enjoyed the events and the glamorous trimmings that came with being part of media London.

To think, when Robert was away, I'd usually just be polishing off a bottle of wine on my own, watching Netflix.

'You know, you should speak to Elizabeth Martin,' said Serena, nodding at a tall woman across the room. 'She's head of commercial fiction at Upstream, that new publishing offshoot of Coney Pictures. Very clever, they actually want to own 360 IP – novels, podcasts, movies. We should definitely pick her brains.'

I nodded. That was the other thing I was loving about the party: I adored all this shop-talk, seeing how things worked on the inside, how things had changed and how they had stayed the same.

Serena waved towards a short, stocky man in a hound-stooth jacket. 'Ian!' she cried. 'I thought you'd never show up. Now the party can start.'

One hand still on the man's shoulder, Serena turned to me. 'Rachel, this is Ian Sinclair . . .'

He was fifty-something, with a bald head and thick black-rimmed spectacles with pale blue tinted lenses that matched his shirt. He looked eccentric enough to seem interesting but just enough aloof to convey that his job was important.

'Ian, this is Rachel who I mentioned for Ginny's cover.'

'So, when can we expect you in the office?' he asked, taking a tiny sip of red wine.

'I can come for a coffee anytime,' I offered.

'Coffee? What for?'

Ian looked confused,

'To talk about my experience.'

He was frowning now. I'd had one chance and it looked like I'd blown it.

'I assume you're Rachel Reeves, as in editor of David Becker's five-million-copy-selling *This is Your Life* Rachel Reeves.'

I nodded and grabbed a fortifying glass of prosecco from a waiter. I took too big a sip and liquid dribbled on my chin.

'You know David was one of our authors when I was over at Random House,' said Ian crisply. 'We didn't renew his contact. Then before we knew it, he'd moved over to Edelman, to you, and he had a number one bestseller on his hands.'

'It was a great book . . .'

'I hated you for about six weeks twenty years ago when that bloody book hogged the *Sunday Times* top slot for an entire summer and none of our titles could get a look in.'

Ian paused and lowered his voice. 'I heard you sent it back to the author three times before he got it just so.'

I was amazed that Ian knew my work, amazed at how gossip got out so accurately. Everything Ian was saying was true. I'd always been a fan of Becker's work but the novel he had written out of contract wasn't quite there and it had taken six months of revisions to make the story and characters and dialogue sing like I knew they could.

'Rachel, I don't need to see your CV or meet for a coffee, I just need to know how soon you can start. Thankfully Ginny's little baby is fine, but honestly, we've been left in the lurch and I need someone in to cover her list immediately. When Serena recommended someone who was immediately available and highly experienced the only thing I had to ask was, are you in?'

'Yes . . . I'm in.' I felt a surge of confidence that I hadn't felt in years. 'I can start on Monday for however long you need me.'

'Good. That's sorted then,' he said, already signalling to someone over my shoulder. 'Drop me an email tomorrow and I'll put you in touch with HR. Let them sort out such vulgarities as money . . .'

I was shell-shocked.

'Have I just got the job?' I whispered to Serena.

My friend looked as surprised as I was.

'Your reputation obviously precedes you,' she said with a slight rise of her brow.

My hands were shaking. I was elated and just a little bit scared.

'Congratulations,' said Serena, slipping an arm across my shoulder. 'I think this calls for another drink.'

I tipped back almost the entire glass of prosecco and turned to look at my friend.

All I had to do now was break it to my husband.

Chapter 5

By 8.30 p.m. the room was thinning out, people drifting off to bars or waiting for Addison Lee taxis. I, on the other hand, didn't ever want to leave. I was dizzy on the events of the night, high on the sudden possibilities of life. I had a job! A real life job! More than that, I had my dream job, working in publishing, right at the heart of things in swinging London. I couldn't see Serena anywhere, but assumed she had left, given that she'd been complaining about an 8 a.m. breakfast meeting the next day at The Wolseley. But I was loitering, soaking up the last of the atmosphere – and the cocktails – practically floating on a cloud. Finally, reluctantly, I realized I'd have to leave when the waiters began closing the bar.

'Rachel?'

I turned, expecting to see Ian, as he was the only man I knew at the party.

'Rachel Reeves?'

The man who had spoken was tall, even featured and wearing dark trousers and a white shirt. I was definitely a little drunk and it took a full second before I looked through his features, back to what they once were, and recognized him. It was another moment after that before I replied.

'Chris Hannah?' I gasped. 'Is that you?'

Of course it was him. Chris Hannah. My university . . . what was he? Sweetheart? Saviour? Disappointment?

We'd had one of those whirlwind relationships you can only manage when you're very young: intense, deeply felt, punctuated with stupid rows and make-up sex, love letters and childish imagined jealousy. I suppose the truth was it had burned too hot to last, and eventually it – we – came apart at the seams. Certainly, he was one of those romantic regrets, one of those guys who occasionally popped into your head and made you wonder 'what if . . .'

We exchanged an air-kiss, my cheek grazing across the stubble on his chin. I felt something pass between us but dismissed it as static from his facial hair.

'I can't believe it's you,' he said, still looking at me.

I laughed. 'It's been a long time.'

'Twenty-five years,' he said without skipping a beat to count them.

'More,' I said.

He paused before he said anything. He didn't look me up and down but I knew that he was taking me all in.

'You've cut your hair.'

'Yesterday.'

'Other than that, you haven't changed a bit.'

I blushed, feeling self-conscious in the slim-fitting silk dress I had bought especially for the party.

'You're being kind.'

'I'm being honest.'

He hadn't changed either but I didn't want to say it out loud. Chris Hannah was gorgeous – then and now. Dark hair with a hint of curl, bright green eyes framed with black lashes, full lips and sharp cheekbones. Back in the day he had a moodiness that stopped him being too pretty, now it was the craggy lines of life lived that prevented a movie star handsomeness, like a teen idol who had returned to the big screen after years of rehab, more worn-in, human and attractive.

His expression was deadly serious, no hint of flirtation or amusement and there was that split second – that moment when we could have said our goodbyes and moved on.

But we didn't. I didn't want to.

'What are you doing here?' he said in a tumble of words.

'At a book publishing party,' I said, thumbing back to the room. I tried not to look at him too hard. Part of me was still annoyed that he was still so good-looking.

'Are you a writer?'

I laughed and looked down, flattered but embarrassed.

'No, no. I used to work with writers a lot, but this was a social thing. Sort of.'

'Sort of?'

'It's the launch of a new publishing company. I came to hustle for a job,' I said, not even noticing how easy it still was to talk to him.

'Did it work?'

I laughed again, a loud, nervous laugh.

'It did. I've just been offered an editor's position. To start Monday. I still can't quite believe it.'

'That's excellent, congratulations.'

There was an authenticity to his words that I hadn't quite felt from Serena, whose obvious surprise at my job offer had rubbed the edge off her good wishes.

But Chris was smiling broadly and his grin made me feel even happier, like a balloon filling with more air. He had always been good like that, always positive and encouraging. One of life's enthusiasts.

'What's the book?' he said, looking at what I was carrying.

I held it out to show him.

'The new Clint Porter novel? Liam Grey's great. Like Raymond Chandler on acid.'

I should have guessed that he knew about Clint Porter. Chris had always been a massive bookworm. I could picture his tiny student bedroom now, tatty, well-thumbed novels piled up in every dusty corner. It was hard not to contrast it to the first time I had seen Robert's bedroom, where one book – Branson's autobiography – and a couple of CDs sat lonely on the windowsill. I felt guilty making the comparison.

'You can take it,' I said without thinking. 'I only took it because I can't resist a freebie.'

'Then you should keep it.'

'Don't be silly, it's yours,' I pressed.

'Okay, but only if you let me buy you a drink.'

I wanted to. I felt happy, valued, clever. I wanted to carry on drinking, and celebrate Ian Sinclair's offer, especially as the person offering to clink glasses was someone whose company I had always loved. But despite the number of glasses of prosecco I'd had at the party, I was still sober enough to know that I should resist.

'I should probably be off,' I said.

'I'll only keep you for one. We've got to toast your new job.'

It sounded as good enough an excuse as any, but still, I hesitated.

'You deserve it,' pressed Chris and I knew he was right.

I thought about my husband, in Paris at his dinner at the Hotel De Ville. There was nothing waiting for me back at the house except silence. 'Okay,' I said, not wanting the night to end.

The hotel bar was packed. Chris made some quip about not getting served until midnight and ushered me out onto the street. I was expecting the night air to be cold, and to slap against my cheeks. But there was a softness to it that I hadn't really noticed on the journey into town, and suddenly it was as if the evening was prickling with magic and promise.

'Have you eaten anything?'

I shook my head.

'How about Chinese?' he asked, and despite the ripple of danger, registering inside me like a distant rumble of thunder, I found myself saying yes.

*

'So, what were you doing before this job?'

Tell me about your life. That's what he was saying. And his expression said something else: 'I'm interested in you'.

I shifted uncomfortably in my chair, glad that we'd skipped the bar at the Ham Yard Hotel for somewhere more discreet, a dark little restaurant in Chinatown with just a door and an orange lantern festooned window that overlooked the street. It had been Chris's suggestion – he had always known the best places. I'd been keen to leave Ham Yard Hotel as I hadn't wanted to be seen, even by colleagues who didn't even know me yet. But, here, in a corner booth, where the diners were mostly Chinese, I didn't just feel safe, it was as if we had been transported to a back street of Shanghai or Kowloon.

'I supposed I've just been raising my daughter,' I said, feeling my cheeks flush the colour of the plastic cherry blossom in the vase on top of the fish tank.

'I read a quote once that a mother is always a working mother,' said Chris, sipping his sake.

It felt good to have my efforts appreciated. Usually, I had to be apologetic to so many of Robert's crowd: the accomplished couples who had his and hers high-flying jobs – architectural practices they managed to juggle with four children or design firms that had offices in five capital cities.

What do you do, they used to ask me in the years after Dylan was born and they'd make all the right noises when I said that I looked after our daughter, but then would glaze over when I'd tell them about Caterpillar Music, baby signing classes or the squeeze for nursery school places in London.

'How old is she?' he asked.

'Eighteen,' I said. 'She's just gone to university, Birmingham, studying English and philosophy.'

'She must be smart, just like her mum.'

'Dylan's way smarter than me.'

'Dylan – like the poet?'

Another in-reference.

I'd always imagined college boys to be dreamy intellectuals. But almost all of them were interested in beer and sex and sport. Chris was different. Chris Hannah loved little known indie bands with lots of guitars and poignant lyrics. He liked Mexican films and art house cinemas and even looked like a French auteur with his chunky boots and old jeans that always had a paperback in his back pocket. He wrote reams of verse which he sang to the strum of the battered guitar he kept in his student bedroom in Hallgarth Street.

'You'll be amazing.'

I focused back on the conversation and realized he was talking about my job. I hadn't actually accepted anything yet, and I knew I had to have that conversation with Robert. I had always had trouble with confidence, always needed someone else to help me say 'yes'. And tonight, it seemed as though it was Chris Hannah's turn to do the job. Just like it used to be.

'So, what about you, Chris? What have you been up to? Where do you work and why were you at Ham Yard?'

'Soho and meeting a client. Prospective client. He'd just left and I was about the leave Ham Yard when I saw you.'

'How did it go?'

'Not sure. It doesn't matter. My night perked up as soon as he left.'

There was a definite flirtation there now but I tried to ignore it. Besides, I didn't want to linger on his business affairs too long. I'd left university with a decent degree but Chris, despite his smarts, hadn't. Twenty-five years later, I still blamed myself for that, although from the sharpness of his shirt I could tell he wasn't doing too badly, despite everything that had happened. That gave me some consolation.

One drink led to another and we must have had six or seven courses, each one more delicious than the next – hot and crispy salt and pepper squid, honey chicken and ribs that fell of the bone and left thick, sweet sauce smeared on our fingertips.

It was all accompanied with laughter, as we remembered the old times, the glorious mid-Nineties which suddenly seemed to be a golden era, in the way that baby boomers talked about the Sixties, everything sounding just a little more glamorous and fun than I had previously remembered it. I told him about my time in publishing and it felt good telling him – and reminding myself – about my professional successes. We talked a little about our life now although I didn't dwell on my day-to-day, those mundane, unproductive hours that yielded nothing but the slow hollowing out of my soul.

Chris told him how he had managed to 'soldier on' after university without me, setting up a corporate hospitality company, 'deathly dull, obviously'. How he had a flat south of the river, and still nursed a secret obsession with Nineties hair metal. I listened for a reference to a wife or a girlfriend, but I didn't ask specifically. And while I had mentioned Dylan, I hadn't talked about Robert. I didn't need to ask myself why. And Chris didn't ask, presumably for the same reason.

'So how does it feel being an empty nester?'

'Oh God, don't start me off,' I said, clutching my forehead. 'I'll get all maudlin.'

'I know what will sort that out,' he smiled.

'You do? What?'

'Vodka.'

I laughed. 'Vodka?'

Chris nodded solemnly. 'Scientifically proven to dispel all miserable thoughts and to make you want to dance on tables. Seriously, it's nature's version of Prozac.'

'Isn't that tequila?'

He see-sawed his hand back and forth and spilt my glass of wine which bled dark red over the scarlet tablecloth.

As I tried to mop it up with a handful of napkins, I didn't even notice Chris get the bill.

'Let's get out of here,' he laughed and I agreed.

I had no idea what time it was. I didn't even want to look.

I felt like a bubble on a breeze and I didn't want anything to pop.

'Do you think the 42 Club is still there?'

We'd had a few mini-breaks to London when we were going out, getting the National Express to Victoria to escape the small-town life of Durham. Back then, the capital had been as exotic as Paris or Rome. We'd stayed up all night wandering the streets, drinking coffee in Bar Italia and finding dive bars in back-streets where we could drag the evening out a little longer. 42 was one of our favourites. A knock-off Ronnie Scott's with no admission fee and rumour had it – the occasional lock in, I couldn't tell you what music we had heard there – whether it had been a solo saxophonist or a twelve-piece band – I could only remembering us kissing in a dark corner, not caring if we had work to prepare for tutorials or whether our youth hostel had a curfew.

The club was still there, on a snicket off Dean Street. Now it charged twelve pounds to get in. Chris paid for both our admissions and I bought us two beers even though I hadn't drunk lager in years.

In the corner of my eye I saw the gaze of an attractive brunette linger on Chris. I turned quickly and led us to the back of the club.

The booths were still there too, but they were taken. We stood again the back wall, the floor tacky under our feet, and swayed to the sound of a bossa nova. For a moment I closed my eyes, feeling young again. I actually felt lighter as I moved in time to the music, as if I was an exotic feather being carried on a tropical breeze.

'Remind me how we met,' I said, opening my eyes. Of course, I knew but I wanted to see what he remembered.

'Can't you remember?'

'Lots of uni just disappeared in a fog of alcohol.'

'You'll be saying that tomorrow,' he laughed as he carried

on watching the band, focusing just a little too hard on the stage.

'It was that house party on Church Street,' he said finally.

'That's right,' I nodded. In my loneliest days, I spent a long time thinking about that night, although I wasn't going to admit that now.

It had been someone's twenty-first. It was winter, cold and dark but I'd still gone outside to escape the people and noise. I'd found a swing hanging from a crab apple tree at the bottom of the garden, sat down and looked back at the house at the silhouettes and the glowing windows, realizing that I didn't really belong to that crowd.

I'd been about to go home when I'd seen the orange light of a cigarette coming towards me. It was Chris. He'd let me share his Marlborough Light, I offered him the bottle of warm wine I had squirreled away outside. We were together for the next six months almost to the exclusion of everyone else. I'd gone to Durham to get away from my past but that night in the garden, I was convinced I had found my future.

'Why did it take us so long to meet? We were on the same course for two years . . .'

If I sounded needy, I didn't care.

'I saw you at Freshers but you were too pretty to talk to.'

'Me?' I laughed, not wanting to admit how good it was to hear it. These days, I would look into the mirror, and just see my soft, sagging jowl and forehead scored with lines; pretty and its suggestion of youth and beauty was not a word I'd use to describe myself and it was hard to believe it ever had.

'Same girl,' he said, taking a swig of beer, still not looking at me. 'It was a big year group, different tutor groups. It took me a long time to pluck up the courage. You always looked so beautiful and aloof.'

Aloof. Was that how he interpreted my loneliness?

He put his bottle of beer down on the sticky carpet. When he stood up, his hand brushed against mine. I didn't move it away.

'Why did we finish?' He looked at me this time and his question hit me like a punch in the guts.

'We were young.'

'You went travelling and didn't come back.'

I didn't want to tell him the whole truth. I knew it would hurt him.

'I shouldn't have gone. You were one of the good ones,' was the most I was prepared to say.

'Where's Robert tonight?'

Looking back, I knew that my answer was the moment that changed everything.

'Paris,' I said, hardly daring to breathe.

'What do you think of the band?'

I knew I was walking closer and closer to the edge.

'They sound a bit samey after a few songs,' I replied, daring myself to take another step forward.

'What now?'

As he said the words something in my world shifted. A big, red light was flashing in my head but I didn't care. It was as if I had shed a skin, as if I had suddenly become someone else. A more exciting and glamorous version of myself.

'Let's just be young again,' I said as he took my hand and we left the club.

The hotel was two streets away from the 42 Club. I was vaguely aware of it; I read the broadsheet travel supplements religiously, always dreaming of mini-breaks we never seemed to take anymore and remembered reading about this place, often cited as one of London's most romantic places to stay. Rumour had it that Oscar Wilde once lived here.

Perhaps I should have felt cheap turning up with just my coat and handbag but I was too drunk and high on the thrill and adrenaline of it all to care.

I hung back in the tiny reception area while Chris filled in some paperwork. The front door swung open and I turned, my heart thumping as if I was about to get caught out, but it was only the wind.

I followed him up some rickety stairs to a room on the second floor.

'Did you have a reservation already?' I asked as he unlocked the door with a big brass key. I'd noticed that check in was unusually seamless for two people who had just walked in off the streets and felt just giddy enough to ask.

He turned around and our faces were only inches apart.

'I might have phoned ahead,' he admitted with that sexy half-smile I loved.

'When?' I whispered, knowing I was at the point of no turning back.

'Somewhere between margaritas and dim sum.' He kissed me softly on the lips.

'Cocky.' I closed my eyes enjoying the sensation of his velvety soft skin on mine.

'We'll see.'

I had a split second to take in the details of the room – four-poster bed with grey velvet swags and claw-foot bath by the window – but Chris was kissing me again before I could notice anything else. He took off his jacket and unzipped my dress, letting it fall to the ground. My underwear wasn't my best. It was a long time since I had bothered with uncomfortable scraps of lace. But it didn't matter. I felt beautiful and alive as he planted tiny kisses on my shoulder, moving down my spine. Although the sensation of his lips on my skin felt electric it was as if it wasn't quite happening to me. Instead, I was a femme fatale in an edgy, erotic movie that I was only watching, not playing the leading lady.

I shivered as he rolled my knickers over my hips taking his mouth down to the dark crease between my buttocks and then licked each mound of flesh. I stepped out of the puddle of silk and turned around where he buried his face in my unwaxed pubic hair.

I felt so strong and vital standing there in just my high heels and bra. I tipped my head back then pushed my palms down my body until my fingers were in his hair and I felt the shape of his skull.

His mouth came north, and we kissed again, passionate, primal, greedy. I kicked off my heels and he unclipped my bra. I wasn't sure if I could wait. I fumbled at his shirt buttons as he unfastened his belt, my heart thumping hard. We stumbled onto the bed and he started kissing every inch of me. I flipped onto my back and he came between my thighs, his mouth swooping down to stroke my belly before taking each nipple one at a time in his mouth.

They were hard and ripe by the time he got there and I groaned as his warm mouth savoured me. I cupped my breast trying to give him more of me to taste.

I moaned over and over.

We couldn't wait any longer and when he pushed inside me, I screamed out loud.

It was slower, sweeter the second time. He kissed me everywhere and I never wanted it to stop. I was consumed with the need for sex and the feeling of being desired. At some point we dozed off and at some point, we woke up and fucked again. We did it every way we could think of – nothing was too intimate or off-limits – the only thing that mattered was our connection and the exquisite feeling of being inside one another. I supposed I was still drunk – on alcohol and other emotions I didn't quite understand or at least dwell on. I supposed I didn't think it would have any consequences. Looking back, I don't think I had ever been more wrong.

Chapter 6

He was still asleep when I woke up.

I closed my eyes again and snapped them open just to make sure the whole thing hadn't been a dream, but Chris Hannah was in bed next to me and we were naked. I could smell him and as my tongue touched the top of my lips, I could still taste him.

Despite my thumping head, I could only think of one thing. My husband, who I knew, at this very moment, would be waking up in a hotel bed not dissimilar to this one. Years ago, I'd taken the decision that when Robert went away on business for days on end, all I could do was trust him. But sometimes, when he was away, when my mind wandered and imagined him with an escort or a client who had become something more, I wondered what infidelity would feel like, imagined how I'd react if I smelled another woman's perfume on his shirt when he came home, or found a stray blonde hair in his suitcase, the realization that he'd had an affair. But I'd never once imagined what it would be like if I was the one being unfaithful. And now I knew.

I lay still, unable to move, unable to believe what I had done. I was married. Happily married. As happy as it was possible to be after twenty years. Just a few weeks before I'd done a quiz in a women's magazine *How good is your marriage?* It was the sort of magazine I didn't usually buy but always found quite inspiring when I did pick it up, enjoying the features of fifty-something women who had turned their lives around with kitchen table businesses or mindfulness. I'd given honest responses, admitting that we hardly had sex or many shared interests, but still, my answers to the quiz questions concluded that I had a solid, loving relationship.

Slowly, quietly, I sat up and swung my legs around, trying to plan my next move. My naked body was cold, spot-lit in a shaft of pale light coming into the room.

I heard him stir behind me, but didn't look round, hoping he would settle back down so I could escape unnoticed. Instead, I felt the feathery touch of a finger running down my back. I froze again, but it was impossible to deny its pleasure. I closed my eyes and inhaled the sensation trying to capture it in my mind for when it had gone.

'I should go,' I said, my eyes still fixed forward.

'Are you sure?'

I didn't want to leave but I couldn't tell him that or even admit it to myself.

Finally, I turned around to look at him. He looked crumpled around the edges but sexy as hell – I almost had the urge to take out my phone and photograph him.

'Stay,' he said touching my hip. 'I don't think we get kicked out until eleven.

'Don't you have a job to go to?' I laughed, trying to lighten the mood.

'The beauty of being my own boss.'

He smiled. I'd loved that smile. Lazy, naughty, full of promise of fun things. It felt out of place now like a misaligned tooth.

I'd heard of the French Exit – the discreet slipping away from a party without saying farewell – but given that was no longer an option, I wondered what was the best way to get out of this. My tea-dress was on the floor, just a few feet away from the bed. Like summoning up the courage to submerge my shoulders in the cold water of a swimming pool, I took a breath in readiness to stand up.

I didn't need to turn around to know he was watching me, taking in my nakedness.

Bending down, I scooped up my dress and knickers and clutched them to my chest, wondering where I should put them on.

'You are so beautiful,' he said and I shivered.

I looked down and laughed nervously. Robert used to tell me that all the time when we were first married. When we still used to date and I'd get dressed up to go for dinner or a walk in the park. But I hadn't felt beautiful for a long time and Robert no longer said it. I took a moment to enjoy the compliment.

'It's definitely time to go,' I said and went into the bathroom, closing the door behind me. I had no idea where my bra was. I couldn't bear the shame of going back into the bedroom to hunt for it; instead, I slipped my dress over my head, splashed my face with cold water and tucked my hair behind my ears in a bid for some sort of propriety.

There was no toothpaste, nothing to hide the taste of him. I filled a glass with water and gargled but it was no good. My pale, guilty reflection stared back at me in the square mirror about the sink. Despite a quick wash, last night's make-up clung stubbornly to my face. I rubbed a bar of soap in my hand, and scrubbed my skin.

My hand paused on the door handle before I opened it. Chris was dressed and sitting on the bed when I went back into the room.

'There's a great place for breakfast around the corner.'

I didn't need to reply. He knew my answer was no.

My bag was on the chair near the door. I went to collect it and Chris stood up, knowing it was time to say goodbye.

We stood a few feet apart and just looked at each other. It was suddenly awkward.

'So, where's Edelman based?'

'Aldwych. By Waterloo Bridge.'

'I'm in Covent Garden a lot.'

'Chris, I don't usually do things like this . . .'

'Neither do I.'

We both fell silent.

'We should at least talk about it.'

'I think it might just make it worse.'

'What? Saying how we feel?'

'I'm married,' I replied with an unexpected touch of steel.

I thought he might challenge me, question how happy my marriage was when I had spent the whole night having sex with someone other than my husband, but he didn't say anything, and I was grateful.

Instead, he stepped towards me. I flinched at first but then I let him put his arms round my waist. He was tall enough to rest his chin on the top of my head, and as I relaxed against him, it felt so familiar it was as if we were back in his tiny bed-sit in Durham, when nothing mattered but being together.

I wondered if he felt it too, as I heard him sigh, sad and regretful.

He didn't make a move to kiss me and somewhere deep inside, I felt disappointment mix with my shame.

'I should go.'

'Do you have to?'

I stayed there another few seconds, enjoying the moment, feeling his heat press against my skin, and then I pulled away knowing I couldn't waver any longer.

'I've got your number,' he said slowly. 'I can WhatsApp you later.'

It sounded so sleazy.

'That's what my daughter says. But as I tell her, technology defeats me.'

'What are you really saying, Rach? I shouldn't call?'

It was his turn to sound casual but I knew him too well to know what he was really thinking.

'I think it's probably best for everyone if you didn't,' I said.

'Goodbye Chris,' I whispered as I opened the door. I put my head down and I padded down the stairs and didn't look up until I hailed a cab on Frith Street to take me home.

Chapter 7

I was careful not to slam the taxi's heavy door as I got out. Our house was only overlooked by Iris and Bill's and although Bill was half blind and Iris didn't often even know the time of day, I still wanted to slip into the house as discreetly as possible.

My hands trembled as I slid the key in the lock of our front door.

I closed it behind me and for once, since Dylan had left home, I was grateful for the quiet that filled our house.

As I took off my jacket, loose change fell out of the pocket and clattered to the poured concrete but I didn't stop to pick it up. Instead I went straight upstairs, tearing off my dress before I'd got to the bathroom, where I kicked off yesterday's knickers.

Naked, I could still smell him on my skin, stale and heavy. I turned on the shower as hot as I could stand and stepped inside, using my most perfumed body wash to scrub myself, hoping to lose myself in the scent of Turkish rose. I must have been under the water for ten or fifteen minutes, until my skin started to wither and the water began to run cold.

Shivering, I stepped onto the slate tile and wrapped myself with a towel, squeezing the excess water out of my hair.

The sight of my pants on the white tiles repulsed me. I kicked them into a corner and went straight to the dressing room. I picked out fresh underwear – big cotton pants and bra, the sort I used for the gym – then a T-shirt and jogging pants, not tight Lululemons that showed off every curve but old, baggy leggings I'd earmarked for gardening. I sat in front of the mirror, pulled my damp hair back in a band and glimpsed at my reflection. The plain, bare-faced, sexless woman who looked back at me reminded me of a mugshot. 'Highgate Woman Charged With Murder.'

In the bedroom I climbed under the duvet, and got immediately out again, smoothing down the covers so it looked freshly made. My damp hair made a dark circle on the pillow case so I fetched the hairdryer and blasted it with heat until it faded. In the en-suite, I picked up yesterday's clothes and went to the laundry room, slamming the washing-machine door on the evidence, feeling relief as the drum began to turn. Back in the kitchen I lit a candle to get rid of any lingering alien scent, and hung my jacket under a waxy old Barbour by the back door, methodical, and shamefully cunning, in my attempts to cover my tracks.

Only then did I boil the kettle to make some camomile tea, perching on a stool to sip it.

I picked up my bag, pulled out my phone and scrolled to messages, honest enough with myself to know what I was looking for.

A message from Chris – a 'goodbye, you're beautiful', or 'it was the most amazing night of my life'. But there was nothing but a text from my phone provider telling me my allowance had been refreshed.

Instead, I clicked on an MMS I'd received the night before. A picture of me holding up two fortune cookies as earrings. We'd laughed so hard when Chris had taken a picture and I had felt so funny, interesting, sexy. Giddy, drunk, I'd begged him to send me the photo and had given him my mobile number. Last night, it had been funny, this morning it was incriminating.

Proof of last night. Proof of the invisible crack in my marriage.

But still. Still, the text was all that I had left to connect me to Chris Hannah. I wasn't sure if I could find him again on LinkedIn and he'd been vague about his place of work. Not sure I was quite ready to let him go, I pressed create contact and typed Southern Electric into Details. Message saved.

The front door opened and then slammed shut. I jumped. Throwing my phone back into my bag, I got up.

'Robert . . .'

I watched my husband putting his smart, silver case down in its usual spot.

He grinned as he slipped off his jacket.

'Who did you think it was?'

'You gave me a fright.'

'Sorry.'

He pecked me on the cheek, then rubbed his chin as if he was tired.

'Aren't you supposed to be in Paris?'

'My lunch was cancelled so I caught an earlier Eurostar. I was going to text you but I thought I'd give you a surprise.'

He handed over a box. I felt ashamed when I saw it was from Fauchon.

'Eclairs.'

I couldn't bear to look at him.

'Just as you were going to the gym,' he said clocking my T-shirt and leggings.

He smiled and I felt horrible.

'Yoga can wait.'

As I beamed back at him, I caught myself. It had begun. White lies to my husband had started.

'You should still go. I've arranged to go and view a site

in Hampstead in an hour so I'll be going back out in ten minutes. I just thought I'd drop the case off.'

Robert noticed the coins on the floor. He bent down to pick them up and put them on the table piled up on top of each other.

'So how was your night out?'

I focused hard on making us a cup of coffee, but I didn't need coffee. I needed fresh air.

'I've been offered a job,' I said, my back turned away from him.

I was dreading telling him but suddenly it felt like a lifeline to normality.

'A job?'

There was the same note of surprise that I'd heard in Serena's voice.

'An editor's position at Edelman. I ran into Ian Sinclair, their MD at the launch. He's a friend from the old days.'

It was another lie, but what was one more?

'He said they were looking for some maternity cover. Asked if I'd be interested.' I had to stop myself from babbling.

'He offered you a job? Just like that?'

He didn't sound convinced and I felt my back stiffen, annoyance this time, not my guilty conscience.

'Robert, I'm not exactly a novice. Serena had already recommended me and they need someone quickly. Plus, Ian is a big fan of the work I did on *This is Your Life*.'

'Which was twenty years ago.'

That really did wind me up.

'Thanks for the vote of confidence.'

'I didn't mean it like that . . .'

He paused and took the coffee I'd made him.

'So, you're going to take it.'

It wasn't a question.

'It's not the most left-field suggestion, Robert. It's what I used to do . . .'

'Is it full-time?'

'I have to discuss that. But it's only until the editor comes back from maternity leave, although her baby is a preemie so it might take longer than normal.'

'When are you supposed to start?' he asked.

'Next week, I think.'

'*Next week?*'

He paused as if to collect himself, to sift through the facts and think everything through.

Nothing my husband did was ever ill-considered. That's where we differed. I had always been more impulsive.

'Well?'

My voice had a tight little snap. I wasn't going to ask for his permission to take the job but I expected more support than he was offering. When we were first married, Robert had been the first to push me towards promotion, like an athlete's pacemaker. Our careers had been on an equal footing back then. We cheered each other's successes and plotted how we could achieve more of them. But something had changed.

'It's great you've just walked into a job . . .'

'But . . .'

I willed myself to stop being so chippy.

'It's just that our life works,' he said more carefully. 'I make a great living, we have a beautiful home, you have time, money to do what you want. We don't want the wheels to come off just because you're feeling a bit lonely because Dylan's left home. Do you even remember how shitty that daily commute into town is?'

'This isn't about being lonely,' I said, frowning. 'This is about feeling that my life has no meaning anymore. No point.'

'You can't go around saying that or people will think you need a therapist, not a part-time job.' He said it with a soft sigh as if he was dealing with a particularly difficult and dramatic teenager.

'Don't you want me to be happy?' I managed to say.

I was angry, frustrated disappointed, unable to stop comparing the reaction I had received from Chris Hannah about my job offer to my husband. Chris was pleased for me. He wanted to see me smile. He wanted to make me smile.

'Rach, all I want is to make you happy,' said Robert, stepping towards me.

It took a lot to make my husband emotional but he looked genuinely upset about how he had made me feel.

I wanted him to hold me. To tell me that everything was going to be alright. But still, I wanted to get out of there.

'I'm going to the gym,' I muttered.

'Rachel, please.'

And as I heard my clothes go around and round in the washing machine, I wondered how I had just done that. Laundered away my own indiscretions and made my husband feel guilty.

Chapter 8

I sat in Iris and Bill's living room, a cup and saucer balanced on my lap, trying not to let it rattle. It was my first day at Edelman and I'd been nervous from the moment I had woken up. I could have done with starting the day with some light meditation or Pilates – at least a leisurely breakfast with my husband or a phone call to Dylan who I rang or text at least once a day. Instead, I was at my neighbours'.

I glanced again at the ornate clock tick-tocking away on the mantelpiece. It was only five to eight: the carer was due at eight. I would be fine if I could get to the station by half past, plenty of time to get into London, even this early on a Monday.

I told myself to calm down. After all, I should be feeling good about this. Arranging a carer for Bill and Iris meant I could get away from here, away from Highgate: it meant a step towards my new life. But still, it felt as if there was a black cloud hanging over the room.

'What's his name again?' asked Bill, sitting upright in his chair, white stick clutched across his knees.

'Nathan, Nathan Deer,' I said patiently. 'The lady from the agency said he's very nice.'

'Hmm,' said Iris. I wasn't sure if that was scepticism or if she was having trouble following the conversation. Most of the time, it was hard to tell.

'We don't need a carer,' said Bill, as if he was translating for his wife. 'We're alright on our own.'

I didn't like to point out that they hadn't exactly been on their own for the past couple of years, because they'd had me to do the endless list of jobs

'Nathan's not going to interfere,' I said instead, leaning over to speak into Bill's better left ear. 'He's just going to come by to make sure you're alright and help around the house.'

I looked at the clock again. I hoped this guy wasn't going to be late. Bill was very exacting when it came to his schedule. He always seemed to know what time Robert or I had left or arrived home and if you said you would 'pop by around three', you'd better not come at five past.

Iris's head twitched as the doorbell rang, and Bill caught the movement. Being partially deaf, Iris was his early-warning system; she was dotty, but her basic functions were fine.

'Should you get that?'

John, Bill's only nephew, a sixty-something dentist from Torquay, stood by the fireplace with his arms crossed. He'd been useless from the moment I had contacted him on Thursday afternoon to let him know that I would no longer available to help Bill and Iris and that they should, without question, recruit someone to assist them. He was obviously annoyed as well, no doubt at the thought of his reduction of inheritance once a carer had been employed, but had reluctantly agreed to come and oversee the handover process.

I went into the hall, smoothing down my skirt. It was ridiculous: I wasn't auditioning here, I was escaping. I was only their neighbour, I reminded myself. They needed a professional.

With a deep breath, I opened the door. And standing there was a man in his early twenties, wearing a navy polo shirt and chinos. I don't know what I'd been expecting – something else – scrubs or at least something more clinical looking.

'Mrs Reeves? I'm Nathan Deer.'

'That's me,' I said. 'Do come inside. We've been waiting.'

I led him into the front room, trying my best to ignore Bill's glare.

The younger man immediately stepped across to Bill and formally offered him a hand. 'Sir, it's a pleasure to meet you,' he said, meeting his eye. Slightly reluctantly, Bill shook it.

'And you must be Mrs Neville,' said Nathan, crossing to Iris. The old woman didn't reply, instead she looked up at him and smiled, which I took to be a positive sign.

'So, you have been doing this kind of work for a long time?' I asked politely.

'Almost five years,' said Nathan. 'I joined the agency straight from school. I had a uni place to study nursing but, you know, studying is expensive. I thought I should get straight into the workplace.'

'Are you familiar with the area?'

'I just live in Finsbury Park.'

'Excellent,' I said relieved at how well it was all going. 'So, who wants tea?'

Bill frowned and cupped a hand to one ear. I watched Nathan raise his hands, smoothly moving them, tapping his palm and pointing to his face, finally acting out a man sipping from a cup.

'You can sign?' I said, taken aback.

'A little.'

He was getting better by the minute.

Bill got out of his chair and started padding to the kitchen. 'I'll make it,' he grunted. 'And I don't need sign language.'

I made reassurances that I would return after work and it was Nathan, and not John, who followed me to the door.

'You don't need to worry,' said Nathan reassuringly. 'I've

been through all this before. Old people hate change, but they get over it once you start waiting on them hand and foot.'

I laughed with relief. He seemed exactly what Bill and Iris needed.

'Has the agency briefed you on their conditions?'

Nathan nodded.

'Bill has low vision. His visual impairment is a result of glaucoma and diabetic retinopathy. He also has moderate hearing loss. Iris has Alzheimer's. She has good days and bad days with regular episodes of sundowning.'

'Sundowning?' He made it sound like a cocktail hour which was exactly what I needed.

'Confusion, anxiety, hallucinations, wanderings. There are various things we can do to manage it like avoiding over-stimulation from the TV and radio.'

'You know your stuff,' I said, impressed.

'I've done this before.'

'Thank you, I said, putting a grateful, complicit hand on his shoulder. 'John will answer any questions you've got and if you need anything you have my mobile number.'

'Sure, but I think I'll be fine – as long as we can find the teabags.'

Truthfully, I'd been grateful for the distraction of organizing Iris and Bill's care arrangements in such a short space of time as it had stopped me from dwelling on my night with Chris Hannah, but as I walked down the hill towards the tube, I couldn't help but think about him again.

It'd been four days since I had seen him. Four days since we had sex. Made love? Was there a difference? I had no idea. What I did know was that the guilt of our one-night stand had been an acid burn in the pit of my stomach. It wasn't just the disgust at my lies and behaviour that made me uncomfortable in my own skin, but the temptation to see my old flame again.

The rawness of the memory of our night at the hotel had softened. I no longer squirmed when I thought of myself checking into a hotel without a bag, or picking my clothes off the floor, but I had tasted the drug. I couldn't forget the electric current of my leg brushing against his under the table of the Chinese restaurant, the swell of desire when he first held my fingers, the sugary heat of his breath on my neck as he told me I was beautiful. It was the small things that I craved about that night, not the sex that made me scream out loud and I felt empty and deprived without them.

He hadn't contacted me. I didn't know why. I thought he might have sent some tentative, exploratory text on Friday or Saturday, but there had been nothing and I wasn't sure if I was more relieved or annoyed. I was certainly hurt and disappointed. Despite my hasty retreat from the hotel, it still felt like rejection. Chris Hannah wasn't someone to hide his feelings. He'd suggested the drinks, dinner and the hotel, done all the running. But it was becoming increasingly clear that it had just been a drunken, nostalgia-soaked shag.

Edelman and the rest of the BCC publishing group were housed in a wedding cake of a building by Somerset House near the river. A wholesome brunette wearing washed-out dungarees met me in reception and made me feel old and overdressed in my silk blouse and pencil skirt. She introduced herself as Lydia, Ian Sinclair's assistant, and took me to the fourth floor, where Edelman shared a floor with the company's cookery and wellness imprint.

When I'd last worked here, when the company was still located in a double fronted townhouse just off Tottenham Court Road that was now luxury apartments, editors had their own separate offices dotted around the building, which varied in size according to their seniority. But here the office was open-plan and my cubicle, which looked the same as everybody else's, was right in the heart of the space.

I sat down on the ergonomic chair, and took my diary and pen out of my bag, breathing out slowly as I acclimatized. The years rolled back and I remembered my first day at Edelman all those years ago. I'd felt a fraud then and I felt a fraud now.

'Hello.'

A woman with a sharp red bob, thick framed glasses and a stud in the curve of her nose, turned around from her cubicle behind me.

'Hello. Vicky Knight. Marketing. You must be Rachel.'

She was another twenty-something. I hadn't felt this old since I went to a lunchtime screening of *The Second Best Exotic Marigold Hotel* at the Everyman Hampstead.

'Good to meet you,' I said, extending my hand.

'So where have you come from?'

I hesitated. 'North London.'

'I mean, where did you work before?'

'I used to work here. But it was a long time ago,' I replied, not wanting to admit that I had been a stay-at-home mother. Vicky was wearing a T-shirt with 'Fierce' emblazoned across the front and although she didn't look particularly fierce, I felt sure that she would take a dim view that I hadn't been working for the past eighteen years.

'I've been freelancing since then,' I added.

'Rachel?'

I looked up and saw Lydia again.

'Conference. In the boardroom.'

Back in the old days, the editorial weekly catch-up meeting had always been on Tuesdays as our MD, Henry Elmont, had a weekend house in the country and often only straggled in late on a Monday afternoon. Things had been so civilized then. Long lunches with agents, half-day Fridays during the summer that meant we could drift off to a riverside bar and stay there until the sun set over the Thames.

Lydia pointed me in the right direction as I gathered my

diary and notebook and joined the stream of editorial staff trooping down towards the boardroom.

They seemed a happy, laid-back team. Yet, I was far from relaxed.

Robert had been right. From the very little I had seen and heard, it was not just the dress code, and the meeting time and the location of the BCC offices that had changed. Twenty years ago, a marketing campaign for a new book involved posters on the tube, adverts in magazines and maybe some sort of promo event. Now it was all social media and wooing bookstagrammers. I'd read a lot of books over the past eighteen years, but had never read a book blog before yesterday and had been running to catch up. I hoped to God no one asked me anything at this conference or I might throw up.

'Good morning team,' said Ian, sweeping into the room and taking the chair at the head of the table. Today he was wearing a dogtooth jacket. He definitely thought he was Andy Warhol. I was grateful for his arrival because it meant I was no longer the oldest person in the room.

'For those of you who have yet to meet her, this is Rachel Reeves' he said, addressing the staff. 'She has been in publishing longer than some of you have been alive and what she doesn't know about books, you could fit in one of your tweets. She's looking after Ginny's list until she comes back.'

I was mortified to be singled out, but buoyed by Ian's glowing words, even though they alluded to my middle-age. I managed to raise my hand with a weak wave and a mutter of hellos followed.

'Speaking of which, I hope you've all come filled with inspiration for the new Jemima Finch campaign. Rachel – Jemima is one of Ginny's authors but given her importance to the company, I will personally be looking after her until Ginny returns. However, I would be very grateful if you could give me a hand on the day-to-day . . . yes?'

'Of course.'

At least I knew who Jemima Finch was. The latest big name in historical fiction, she'd scored a hit with *Cage of Iron*, a saga following the life of Elizabeth of Scotland, wife of Robert the Bruce. Clocking that she was one of Edelman's authors, I'd skim-read it over the weekend and there was little to it beyond descriptions of feasts and people getting locked in towers. Although enjoyable, I found the story not particularly different from the other historical dramas in this sector and wondered how it was possible to get a sequel to stand-out in this crowded part of the market. Ian looked around the room, but no one met his eye.

'No?' he said. 'No promotional ideas from anyone?'

'We definitely have a review going in *Good House-keeping* . . .' began a girl with thick, horn-rimmed glasses.

'Good start. What else?'

'We're just finalizing the blog tour . . .' someone else began.

I glanced around the table at the anxious faces. I knew immediately what sort of boss Ian Sinclair was – tough and exacting. Clearly no one wanted to upset him and so no one had spoken up before. Getting it wrong was obviously as bad as saying nothing at all.

'How about you, Rachel?'

I looked up at the mention of my name, but it took a moment to grasp the idea that Ian was actually talking to me; I had assumed there was another Rachel in the room.

'Me?'

I tried to smile back, but my face wasn't responding. Why was he picking on the new girl? A sudden thought hit me: was this why he'd so quickly agreed to have Serena's novice friend join his team? So he could humiliate me and fire me as an example to the others?

I tried to pull myself together.

'Obviously I'm new to the team but I can speak as a reader . . .'

Ian offered an encouraging nod.

'I'm guessing that Jemima's audience is older. Not fifty-plus, but sixty or seventy-plus. It's an older demographic than we think, like television viewership.'

I waited for someone around the table to contradict me but they didn't.

'This is Jemima's second novel. That's a tough sell. She's not an interesting debut and I guess all the best think-pieces on Elizabeth of Scotland herself have been written.'

I saw the girl in the glasses nod and it gave me the confidence to continue.

'If it's harder to build heat around the book, maybe we should build it up around Jemima herself. I googled her at the weekend and she's fascinating. She went from a tough secondary modern to Cambridge, became an accountant, and then stopped to have children. She didn't start writing until she was sixty but her first book was an international number one bestseller. She's inspirational and she looks amazing – that white bob and those red glasses. She's older but she's strong. She's the new Mary Beard. Creating interest in Jemima, creates fans of her and creates interest in the books.'

My mouth was dry when I'd finished. I had no idea if I was talking complete rubbish but I had certainly meant what I'd said and it had felt exhilarating to think on my feet and be listened to.

'I liked what you said in there,' said Ian after we'd finished. He leaned in closer to say it as if it was a secret. 'Fleming, Wodehouse, Colette . . . back in the days authors were like Madonna – one name required – today no one knows who wrote their favourite novel.'

'I quite like the sound of Jemima,' I replied, proud and happy. Having spent the last two weeks feeling wretched and stupid, I enjoyed the sensation. 'I'm really looking forward to working with her.'

Ian's cubicle was beyond mine and he walked me past my

desk where there was a huge bouquet of flowers waiting for me – a riot of sunflowers, iris and soft violet roses hand-tied with tissue paper and stylish jute string.

'Someone's been a good girl,' said Vicky, swivelling around in her chair. 'They must have cost a fortune.'

I saw Ian's brow lift just a fraction in surprise, or possibly disdain, and he disappeared back to his corner without another word.

I looked at the flowers, then back to her. 'They're for me?'

'Apparently.'

There was an envelope hidden between the foliage addressed to me.

I pulled out the card and there were just two words written on it. *Good Luck.* I turned it around, looking for the name, but there was nothing.

It was an incredibly tasteful arrangement and Robert's taste to a tee – from the pale lilac of the roses to the fashionable brown card and envelope.

I felt guilt and then a pang of affection for my husband. He hadn't disguised his preference that I stayed at home, but now I had taken the job, it felt like a flag wave of support.

'How's it going?'

I spun round feeling two firm hands on my shoulders.

'Serena!'

'I told Lydia to call me the moment you got out of your meeting. My gosh – are these yours?' she said, pressing her nose against the roses. 'They're heavenly. From Robert?'

'Who else?'

'They're gorgeous, although I have to say, I'm not sure he's been very political on your first day. Every woman in the office is going to be mad jealous. Flowers like these are going to have you hated before you've even started.'

I shuddered to think I could be the sort of person that people hated. I never tried to rock any boat, always tried to be polite, helpful and unshowy. Growing up in Belfast, during the Troubles, did that to you. When you grew up surrounded by tension, when you saw soldiers on the street, you learned to put your head down just to get by.

I had always tried to do what was right. I never wanted to be disliked.

'Alan and I thought you and Robert should come to us next weekend. We can celebrate all this. A fabulous job, a husband who buys you such gorgeous flowers. Just to think you were dreading being an empty nester. It's starting to look like a glorious new beginning.'

Chapter 9

Dylan sent me a text at lunchtime wishing me luck, with two whole rows of emoji smiley faces, and my heart felt as if it would combust with joy. I often wondered if my daughter was paying any attention when I called her. Generally, I was lucky to get a snatched few minutes of chat between lectures or drinks at the Guild, and I was never convinced she was listening to what I had to say. But not only had she been listening when I'd told her about my new job, she'd actually remembered and let me know that she'd remembered.

For the first time since my daughter had left, I felt a little sparkle of hope that my new life was going to be okay. My night with Chris Hannah had almost derailed it, but in the few hours I had been an employee of Edelman, the memory of him, was fading like footprints on the shore, washed away by an incoming tide.

Buoyed by Dylan's text, Robert's flowers and a general sense of relief that I wasn't completely out of my depth being back at work, my first day sped by, as I worked out how I was going to be occupied for the next three months. I'd been allocated a dozen authors who were all in various stages of the publishing cycle. Most of them were months off delivering their manuscripts – they were the low-maintenance writers on my list that needed very little attention, perhaps some promotion of their backlist titles, or some hand-holding if they were having trouble with the plot. Three authors were coming up to launch, which meant that I had marketing and press campaigns to oversee, and another couple were about to deliver. That meant actual editing – going through the manuscript line by line, seeing if the story actually worked, noting where it dipped or felt rushed, highlighting points where it could be improved, helping the writer tease out the very best novel they had in them.

That was the bit I loved most, the bit I had always been good at. I had always loved stories. From a young age, the world of books swept me out of the shadow of sectarian violence in my hometown into new worlds. I hated it when a book finished; we couldn't afford many new ones and the library was quite a trek. Instead I used to read my favourite novels again, worked out what I would have done differently, how the author could have created a sequel.

It had never been the foundation for my own glittering writing career – I'd never had the confidence to put pen to paper, and at university I found it difficult to craft essays that reflected my understanding of the play or poem we had been studying. But editing was something I could do and it made me feel good.

By six, almost everyone had gone home. I could see the muted glow of a desk-lamp coming from Ian's cubicle. Nancy, one of the publishing directors was in a meeting room taking a call from America but beyond that it was very still.

'You're going to have to get a cab home with those,' said Vicky buttoning up her coat. She was off to birthday drinks, on a Monday night, but looked at me like my mother.

I smiled again at my flowers. Robert had always been good at buying gifts. Although they were generally of the expensive variety – jewellery, handbags, perfume from the big-name brands – rather than small thoughtful tokens, they always made me feel special, and today's blooms had been particularly welcome.

I switched off my computer, gathered up the bouquet and struggled down in the lift, muttering 'sorry, sorry,' as I stabbed people with thorns or dropped lilac petals in my wake.

Outside the building, I looked up and down the road. It had been pouring down all afternoon and the still-damp black tarmac reflected the streetlights, like shimmering balls of golden wool. In the distance, I could see a cab with its light miraculously lit and I raised my arm. I'd have to bite the bullet on the crippling fare back to North London: there was no way I could take this mini-Kew on public transport.

'Reeves.'

I turned, jumping at the voice behind me, but immediately recognized the grin.

'Chris.' My stomach galloped. Excitement, guilt, nerves. I wasn't sure which. 'What the hell are you doing here?'

He looked more casual today than at the Ham Yard Hotel, in chinos, a sweatshirt over a blue denim shirt and a corduroy jacket the colour of golden syrup. I'd seen plenty of Robert's friends wear clothes like this but none of them looked like Steve McQueen.

He pulled the collar up on his jacket as a thin dribble of rain fell from the moody skies.

'I had a meeting on The Strand,' he said. 'I was just walking to Waterloo.'

It seemed convenient but plausible. The taxi had stopped but pulled away again when I lowered my arm.

'How's the new job?' said Chris after a few moments. His green eyes were fixed on me. He could do that – make you feel as if you were the only thing in the world that mattered.

'I'm enjoying it. The team are nice, I have some great authors to look after. The boss might be tricky but thankfully he seems to quite like me.'

'No surprise there,' replied Chris. 'You'll probably have his job within the year.'

'I don't know about that.'

We both fell silent. I felt a cold river wind brush the back of my neck and shivered.

'Do you like the flowers?'

It suddenly dawned on me who had sent them.

'They're from you?'

He nodded.

'They're beautiful,' I said nervously.

'I'm glad you liked them.'

Aware that I was still in full view of the office building. I looked up and down the road again, but only saw occupied taxis hiss past. I didn't want to just stand there feeling slightly wrong-footed. What was Chris Hannah doing here? It was one thing to send me flowers, but quite another to be waiting for me in the dark.

'I just wanted to wish you luck.'

In the low light I looked for some traces of colour in his cheeks. But there was none. He looked completely unbothered by the slight creepiness of the gesture.

'I'm sorry. I didn't realize. I thought they were from . . .'

I didn't finish the sentence.

Without asking, we started walking. I just wanted to get away from Edelman's watchful glare.

'I'm going to Waterloo,' I said quickly.

'Can I tempt you with the American Bar? Whisky sours at six-thirty on a Monday night might seem decadent, but given that you're celebrating your first day at work I think it's entirely appropriate.'

'Chris. I can't go to the Savoy. I have to get home.'

'Do you want me to hold them?' he asked, motioning to the flowers.

I shook my head in a tight little movement.

'I probably shouldn't have sent them.'

'It was really kind of you,' I said, wanting to dump them in the river.

'I lied,' he said, stopping in his tracks.

I turned and stood still.

'Lied?'

'I did have a meeting on the Strand but I did a detour to see if I could catch you.'

I was glad he'd at least admitted it, but it put me on edge. I was flattered certainly, even thrilled – I still found him as attractive as I had the moment I had seen him at Ham Yard. There had been a reason I had been checking my texts more often than usual all weekend, hoping for some missive from him even though I wasn't sure if I would act on it. He made me feel desired as I desired him in return. Chris Hannah stirred all sorts of things inside me that I had thought had been extinguished.

But still, still, I knew it was dangerous.

As I took a step towards him the wind caught my breath. 'If you wanted to meet me, why didn't you just send me a message?' I said, brushing my hair away from my face.

'I figured if I did, you'd have politely rejected me.'

'You'd have been right,' I said, unable to resist a tiny smile.

Chris pushed his hands in his pockets and gave me that grin. I swear, whatever he actually did for a living he was wasted. He deserved a spotlight, a stage.

His smile faded.

'We shouldn't have left it how we did, on Thursday.'

'What were we supposed to do, Chris? I'm married.'

'We could at least talk about it.'

'There's nothing to talk about

'We've got plenty to talk about. That's the problem.'

I didn't reply, because he was right. I'd loved work – bouncing my idea around the conference table and getting listened to. But it hadn't been like Thursday when Chris had made me feel like the most interesting person in the world.

'I tried not to text or call, but we're adults Rach. We can't have the most incredible night together and then carry on with our lives as if it never happened.

'Chris, I can't . . .' I could hear the weakness in my voice. What did I want? I'd spent the past few days trying to convince myself that our one-night stand hadn't happened. I'd even quietly disposed of the underwear I had worn that evening because it was too much of a reminder. But still . . . standing here in the dark, I couldn't deny the adrenaline that was ripping through my veins.

I looked away from him, looked for courage in the glory of the 360-degree view of London's majesty, St Paul's to the left, the House of Parliament and the London Eye to the right, the river, grey and oily like fish scales, shimmering in the lights of London. It was one of my favourite views anywhere in the world, one of the most romantic. In a movie he would have kissed me right here. But this wasn't a Richard Curtis film.

'We can take it as slowly as you want it to,' said Chris carefully. 'But I think we owe it to ourselves to try.'

'We don't owe ourselves anything,' I said too sharply. I softened my tone. 'Look, Robert came home early on Thursday.'

Saying my husband's name out loud gave me focus.

'He caught an earlier Eurostar and almost caught me in the clothes from the night before. I just can't do it again.'

'Why not? Your daughter has left home. The only person you owe anything to is yourself. Think about what you want, and what is going to make you happy in ten, twenty years from now.'

'You were my first love,' I said honestly. 'But our moment . . . it came and went.'

'Tell me you didn't enjoy it.'

'I did enjoy it but that's not the point.'

'Are you happy with Robert?'

It was the second time he had said my husband's name. He'd mentioned it at the jazz club, but looking back, I didn't remember telling him what it was.

'I'm not sure you are.'

The comment rankled.

'You know nothing about my life or my relationship, so please don't make assumptions.'

'Rachel, please.'

'Chris, I'm married . . .' I said with more feeling.

'You're not the only one with a reason not to be here.'

His words had a bite, and a memory dislodged, something that happened so long ago I could barely remember it but he let that thread of conversation drop.

'Have you been as happy with him in the past year as you were with me on Thursday evening?'

For a moment, we were back there. Back in the hotel room, his tongue running along my neck, his fingers twisting in my hair, electrified with desire. I could admit to myself that I didn't regret it but I knew there couldn't be a repeat performance.

'I've been married to Robert for twenty years. He is the father of my child. We have a great life and I don't want to lose it. Not for anything, or anyone. So you ask me if I'm happy – I am. You ask me if I love my husband – I do.'

I expected him to look at me with hatred and I wouldn't have blamed him. I had just told him how selfish I was. How I wanted the stable, comfortable marriage to the rich, successful man, after the excitement of a one-night stand with my handsome old flame. I expected him to hate me for my selfishness, my lack of control, the way I had been careless with his feeling as the expense of my own desire.

Instead, he lifted his hand to my face and pressed it softly against my cheek. I looked away from him, to avoid the intensity of his gaze. I still wasn't sure if this should be goodbye.

Traffic was building up on the bridge. A taxi had stopped on the opposite lane and I could see a man's face in the side window. Just a glimpse, then it was gone. Bald head, glasses, the curved shoulder of a tailored jacket.

The spell was broken.

I flinched and glanced back at the cab, but it had pulled away into the night.

'What's wrong?' he said. He always knew me.

'Nothing,' I muttered. 'I just thought I saw my boss.'

I wasn't sure it was Ian Sinclair. But still, I had to get out of there.

'You should take these,' I said, pressing the flowers into this grasp. 'I'm not sure how I could explain them to my husband.'

I put my hand out for a taxi and one stopped almost immediately.

'Please don't call or come to the office again,' I said, although my voice got caught on the breeze.

'Highgate,' I said, slamming the door as quickly as I could and as it sped away, I didn't even look back.

Chapter 10

I pushed through the door of Le Circe, one of Mayfair's smartest restaurants, startling the man at the desk. 'Mrs Reeves,' I said breathlessly, slipping off my coat. 'My husband booked the table.'

The maître d' ran a finger down the list in front of him, 'Mr Reeves, party of four. Seven-thirty?'

The final word had a slight upward inflection, a question: *either I wrote it down wrong or you're very late.*

I tried to catch my breath as we threaded through the tables, slipping my coat off as we went. It was something closer to eight o'clock, but there was no point now telling myself I should have left the office earlier. I'd very little choice when Ian Sinclair had said that he wanted to 'thrash out' the plans for a tube poster campaign for one of our authors. I could hardly walk out as the meeting ran on and on, not in my first week anyway, and how was I supposed to know that a demonstration in Trafalgar Square meant that a ten-minute taxi ride across town took over half an hour.

'Sorry I'm so late,' I said to my husband as I quickly slid into my seat. 'I left the office at quarter past and got a cab, but there's some sort of demo by the fountain, they were only letting three cars past at a time.'

I smiled apologetically at the other couple at our table but without looking at him, I could tell that Robert was miffed by my late arrival. I didn't blame him. He'd told me that morning 'don't be late'. He'd said it jokingly, but I knew he wanted the meeting to go well.

'No problem, happens all the time these days,' smiled the woman across from me. She was quite beautiful with a small, fine-boned head, like an upholstered skull.

She flashed me a smile that was meant to put me at ease, but instead made me feel completely inadequate.

'Rachel, this is Elena and Max,' said my husband with an introductory gesture.

'Elena. Lovely to meet you.'

I turned my attention to the equally good-looking man to her left.

'Max, I've heard a lot about you.'

It was true. Robert didn't talk much to me about work, but I knew about Max Miskov, who my husband had met at the MIPIM property expo in Cannes three years earlier. I wasn't sure what he did exactly – some hybrid of banker and business adviser from what I could make out. It was through Max that Robert had been introduced to Elena Dimitrov, a socialite from Moscow money. Elena wanted to open a gallery – a cultural centre for the mind and soul was how she'd pitched it to Robert, and he had spent twelve months hunting down the right premises with exhibition retail and event space, eventually settling on an old warehouse in Vauxhall which had just the right amount of edge and proximity to Damien Hirst's Newport Street gallery to make it fashionable.

'Robert was just telling me you've started at Edelman.'

Max spoke as he had his glass refilled by the sommelier. I quickly clocked the label – Chateau Margeaux – and knew that my husband was pulling all the stops out. A bottle like that in a place like Le Circe came with a four-figure price tag. I felt another pang of regret for being late.

'That's right,' I nodded. 'It's my first week although I worked there for many years before I had our daughter.'

'Do you know Henry Golding?' Max replied.

'He was my first boss,' I said, taking my own sip of claret.

'I was at Harrow with his son.'

I grinned, grateful to find some common ground.

'I think Henry went there too. It's where he met Emmet Brand the author.'

'I've heard this story,' said Max, raising a finger. 'They were flatmates in Bloomsbury. Henry had just started at Edelman when he found Emmet's half-written manuscript on the kitchen table and bought it for five hundred pounds. It won a Pulitzer.'

'And within five years Henry was the youngest ever publisher in the company's two-hundred-year history.

Robert squeezed my knee under the table and I knew that my late arrival had been forgiven. I was well aware of my role at dinners like this. To charm, to flatter, to smooth the way for whatever development Robert was trying to finance with his wealthy clients. Be interesting, but passive, don't upstage the main act.

I didn't find these situations easy, but lifted by my connection with Max, I told them about Emmet Brand's new novel and in return I found out that Max shared a flat with another author, Kevin Shriver, at Cambridge. On her part, Elena revealed that she had just bought a magazine, which I assumed was a single copy purchased from Selfridges, or wherever wealthy people shopped, until I realized she'd bought the actual publishing company.

Throughout the conversation I tried to work Max and Elena out. I'd been a little nervous when my husband had told me that his latest venture was with wealthy Russians. I read the papers, heard about oligarchs and the influx of money from Eastern Europe and wasn't sure that I wanted my husband involved in any of it, however judgemental that made me feel.

Yet it wasn't clear whether Max was Russian at all. His patrician looks and public-school education were blue-chip British. And Elena was fashionable rather than flashy – her grey leather dress and sharp Perspex necklace was more edgy London designer than opulent Muscovite chic. *Just Robert's type*, I thought to myself with quiet panic. Knowing how easily things could happen.

'Max has just moved to Hampstead,' said Robert as the waiter cleared our main courses.

My husband had a sonorous voice and I was aware that we were attracting attention.

'I don't know what North London has got that Knightsbridge hasn't,' said Elena.

'Green spaces. I run,' he said, turning his attention back to me.

'I run too,' I replied. 'There are some great trails on the Heath and proper tracks at Parliament Hill and Regent's Park.'

'You should send me the details.'

'I'll send you the links. How is the gallery coming along?' I asked, turning to Elena

'I'm in contact with such wonderful artists. Obviously finding the right gallerist or curator is going to take time. I have someone perfect in mind from the Gagosian in New York. But I can't even start formal conversations before I know when the build is completed.'

'Structurally, we'll be finished within three months,' said Robert with confidence. 'My meeting in Paris with Peter Armand Associates went well last week. It's a real coup to have them on board. It's difficult to get on the waiting list let alone have Peter himself overseeing the work.'

I felt something shift in my personal space at the mention of Paris. I'd tried hard to push Chris to the back of my mind since our meeting on Waterloo Bridge, keeping busy, not wanting my mind to stray, but I could have done without any mention of the trip that had taken Robert out of the country and assisted my infidelity.

My husband had moved on the conversation, to price per square foot in Knightsbridge but I could feel the heat pool around my neck, and my hand tremble as it held the thin stem of my glass.

I began to watch people on the other table to compose myself. The second date couple to my right, the Japanese tourists bent over the menus to my left. And then I froze. A face in the crowd, dark hair, a sheen of stubble over square jaw.

My stomach clenched and my breath caught in my dry throat like fabric against Velcro.

He was here.

Chris Hannah was here. In Le Circe.

I looked across the restaurant again and he was still looking at me.

'Rachel, are you alright?'

My high-necked black dress seemed to tighten around my throat. I felt dizzy, as the earth was moving under the chair.

I looked up; Max was peering at me with concern.

'I'm fine,' I whispered.

I wasn't. I was hot.

I reached for my tumbler of water but caught the rim of my wine goblet. I watched almost in slow motion as the glass tilted, then fell, spilling claret across the white tablecloth – straight towards Elena. With a strangled cry, she jerked backwards, her chair flying.

'Jesus, Rachel!' hissed Robert.

I looked at him, then back towards Chris. Only it wasn't Chris. The man was looking towards our table, towards the commotion, and it was just some young waiter with dark hair. Not Chris. Not even close.

'Excuse me.' I mumbled something about the ladies' room and ran outside, past the maître d' and a queue of people waiting to get in. I look a gulp of fresh air and closed my eyes, oblivious to the dark street around me.

I thought I had finally put Chris Hannah behind me. I thought I had managed to shut him out of my thoughts. I no longer saw my discarded clothes on the floor when I shut my eyes.

It was another few moments before I felt a hand on my shoulder.

'Rachel.'

It was as if I had regained consciousness and looked up to see my husband. At first his voice was muffled as if I was listening to him through water.

'Are you okay? What's going on?'

I blinked, swallowed.

'Nothing,' I said, hearing my voice shake.

'That wasn't nothing,' said Robert with alarm.

'I just had a funny turn . . .'

'Are you ill?'

I shook my head.

'I don't know. I don't know what happened in there.'

'Rachel, Elena is an important investor. She is connected, influential. I can't put a foot wrong. *We* can't put a foot wrong.'

He didn't sound angry, just frustrated and anxious. I didn't blame him. There were dozens of high-end developers in London, all of them looking for money and backers who seemed increasingly demanding and cautious with their money.

'I'm sorry,' I said, feeling emotional.

For a second he didn't reply.

'Are you sure you're alright?'

He put his arm across my shoulders, his voice softer this time, more concerned. I couldn't look him in the eye. I felt sick, sick with guilt and the dead weight of deceit that I had been carrying all week. I just wanted to offload the truth. Here in the cold night air, I want to tell him, tell Robert what

I had done and wipe the slate clean. But how could I? How could I tell him that I'd fucked another man while he was trying to secure interior designers in Paris?

I didn't want to lie to my husband anymore but I couldn't tell him the truth.

'It's just been a busy week. It's been harder than I thought.'

'We can leave.'

'I thought the plan was to go to 5 Hertford Street?'

Robert shook his head.

'We don't have to. We should get you home. I can talk to Max tomorrow.'

'Don't be silly. They are important clients. You can't bail just because I'm knackered. You go.'

'Are you sure?' he said a bit too soon.

I nodded. 'But I'm not sure I can go back in there. I'm so embarrassed. Elena's dress.'

'It's leather. It'll wipe clean.'

He gave a little laugh and I joined in, the solidarity between us warming my skin. I'd been given a reprieve and didn't want to mess it up.

He pulled me closer and the tenderness of his gesture surprised me, but I settled into him, enjoying the faint smell of aftershave on his shirt. We had so few of these moments lately. Moments when we shared a private joke, when it felt like me and him against the world, like it had been twenty years ago when we first married and I used to sell the free books I'd been given at work to buy our groceries and Robert would blag leftover paint from interior designers so we could spruce up our tiny Holloway Road flat, a little haven for two. We were Robert and Rachel, two young soldiers in the foothills of life, on our journey through life, with little swords and shields but feeling powerful through the presence of each other.

'Feel better?' he asked.

I nodded.

He pulled away and looked at me.

'I know you've been dreading Dylan leaving and I know it isn't easy for you when I'm away so much. But I'm doing this for us, you do know that, don't you? Deals like Regent Place, clients like Elena, nights out like this. We do it so one day we won't have to.'

'Aren't we there yet?' I looked up at him. 'Because I always thought that when Dylan left home, when it was just us, we could travel the world and go on adventures. Or just stay at home and make great food and enjoy one another's company. I thought we could just relax and enjoy life, enjoy what we've worked so hard for.'

'You've just started a job,' he pointed out.

'Only because you are never around and I need something to do. I need to fill my life, Robert. Yes, I've had a great week at Edelman and I think it's going to be fun, but I'd much rather be painting in Florence with my husband, or seeing Machu Picchu or taking bikes out on a random Tuesday and having a picnic by the Serpentine, knowing there was nothing to rush back for, no back to back meetings. No investor dinners. Just me and you.'

'Soon,' he said. 'When Regent Place is sold, that's the game changer for us. All those things that you've always wanted to do, we'll be able to do them. Soon.'

Chapter 11

I apologized, of course. Elena was gracious about the spill. She didn't seem bothered about her dress, and she actually seemed more concerned about my wellbeing. I claimed I had contracted a food bug from a badly washed take-away salad and made my excuses when Max and Robert suggested they 'push on through' to the club.

Elena's driver was waiting for her outside the restaurant. She was going to Belgravia and offered me a lift. Although I was tempted to ride in her sleek black Bentley, I let Robert hail me a cab and I rolled through the neon night of London feeling light-headed and a little sick.

I put my head against the glass, enjoying the coolness against my temple. I had no idea what had brought on that rush of blood in the restaurant? In hindsight, the dark-haired man hadn't really looked very much like Chris. So what had tipped me over the edge? Had my guilt-laden mind created a crisis to punish me? Or had I really wanted to see Chris so badly, I conjured him out of thin air? I dismissed that thought as quick as it had come. What mattered was that it wasn't Chris Hannah I'd seen in Le Circe. He hadn't followed me, wasn't waiting in the shadows. It had just been a waiter. That's all. Things were settling, life was getting back on track.

It was gone ten o'clock by the time I got back to Highgate. The security light flashed on as I walked towards the front door, and for a moment, I flinched in its white phosphorous glow, which fixed me to the floor like a convict trying to escape jail.

I groped around my handbag for my keys but I couldn't find them. Trying not to panic, I glanced over at Bill and Iris. They had a spare set but the lights were all off.

I pulled out my purse, and make-up bag to see better, but the bag was unzipped and my cosmetics fell out onto the porch.

I swore as I crouched down to scoop them up. The top had come off my Tom Ford lipstick and the deep coral tip was speckled with dust and dirt from the cement floor. I winced as my tights snagged on a rough pebble. At least I found my keys and I relaxed as I let myself into the house.

I shut the door behind me and locked it.

Compared to the buzzy atmosphere of the restaurant, our home felt cold and empty. Dylan had only been gone two weeks, but already it was starting to look different than when she lived here, like one of Robert's empty shells before the interior designers came along with their velvet cushions and wallpaper swatches. There were so few remnants of our daughter here now. Her pink phone on the dining room table, kayak-sized trainers, scarves, books, hair bobbles and make-up that were usually littered around like breadcrumbs were gone. Dylan gave our house warmth. She made it as much like a home as our last place – a three-storey terrace in Crouch End, a naturally cosy place, with parquet floors, sash windows and a sweet-smelling arch of honeysuckle over the red shiny door. Sometimes you could even hear pigeons cooing in the loft, which lulled me to sleep when I sat in the bedroom bay window to read.

Swain's House was nothing like the old place and without Dylan's presence, it was cool, grey and ordered. It was Robert's world now and that's what made me nervous.

I switched on a lamp and stepped out of my shoes. In the kitchen I filled a glass with ice cubes from the dispenser and went upstairs.

I kept a bottle of gin in a hat box in the dressing room. It was expensive stuff from a Devon distillery that reminded me of summer holidays: sailing, swimming and long walks down lanes trimmed with buttercups and cow parsley. It was good enough to drink neat so I poured three fingers worth into the glass and took a sip enjoying the sharp, burning sensation on my tongue.

Gin always made me feel good. I'd once read that it used to be called the opium of the people and I could see why. Gin relaxed me and took the edge off my boredom and anxieties. It gave me something to do on the empty afternoons and helped me cope when things seemed to get on top of me. I'd been trying to drink less lately, and at least my job at Edelman cut down on my daytime drinking. It was a good thing. Although it all seemed to be more socially acceptable these days – you couldn't move for books, cards and tea-towels plastered with prosecco lovers and G&T addict memes – I could still recognize that I was drinking too much, that it wasn't as funny or empowering as the humorous paraphernalia was suggesting.

Robert didn't know about my gin habit either, and I wasn't sure he'd like it.

But tonight, I needed a drink. My mind was still whirring and I knew I wouldn't be able to drop off, not straight away.

I stood at the window of our bedroom and looked out into the distance, towards the cemetery which was just a dark space and outline of trees, black on black, in front of me. Friends always asked if our proximity to the graves of Highgate was spooky, but that wasn't the reason it sometimes put me on edge. The tombs and headstones were a reminder of lives lived, the infinite number of things that human beings can achieve and sometimes the very sight of them made me question the way my own life had plateaued. However, there was a calm to this part of London that soothed me.

I stared at my reflection, pale and rigid, my arms pulled closed to my chest as I cradled my drink. I glanced away after just a second – it was still hard to look myself in the eye.

Our curtains closed electronically. I flicked a switch and the window hummed as the drapes pulled together, blocking out the blackness outside. I knocked back the gin, washed out the glass in the sink and dressed for bed in a camisole and shorts. I turned off the bedroom lights, leaving on a reading lamp, got my phone out of my bag and climbed under the duvet.

Earlier in the year, I'd tried to cut down on my bedtime internet habit. I knew it wasn't good, allowing myself to get sucked into a rabbit hole of Instagram or the *Daily Mail*, letting the blue light of the phone, the excitement of other people's lives or the doom-mongering of the tabloids keep me alert, so I set myself a rule. No phone after 10 p.m. For a few months, I'd kept to my promise, but recently I'd needed it again. My mind was too busy to sleep, and I knew there was no point lying there in the dark, eyes wide open, thoughts tossing around like a rowboat at sea.

My phone was flashing to indicate a message. There was a text from Robert checking I was home, and one from Serena inviting us to their place in Oxfordshire the following weekend. A third text was from a number I didn't recognize but I clicked on the message box. There were three words on the screen:

I saw you

I had no idea what it meant but I was immediately on edge. I read it a second time and forced myself to think. Who had seen me – and when?

Had the message been fired off without finishing it. I saw you at Le Circe! Was that what it had really meant to say or had I received a text meant for someone else? I didn't know and I didn't like it.

My thoughts circled round to Chris Hannah and the room seemed to dim. I thought I'd seen him in Le Circe, but I'd been wrong. And yet, what if he had been there? Instead of my imagination playing tricks on me, conquering up some Banquo's ghost in a Mayfair restaurant, could the text have been from him? After all, he had my number.

I saw you

My throat felt thick as an idea took hold. Why would he have been in Le Circe anyway? Had he waited for me outside work again? Had he decided to follow me, to trail me in a taxi, and watched me get out on Dover St? The restaurant was busy but not full. He could easily have got a table, observed us, see me leave alone.

My chest seemed to contract, my heart pumping hard as I realized what it meant if he had been in Le Circe and had sent me a text to let me know.

'Stop it,' I said out loud, tossing the phone on the duvet, telling myself I was being ridiculous, that my overactive imagination was simply a side effect of working back in the world of fiction.

I pressed my thumbs hard against the bone above my brows, a technique I'd once learned at a mindfulness class, then lay back on the pillow forcing myself to relax. I stared at the ceiling, watching the Alexander Calder mobile above our bed twist silently as if it were moving in time with my breathe. The installation was Robert's pride and joy, the most valuable item in our house by far. When he'd bought it, I'd gone mad at him for spending so much, unmollified by his claims that it would only appreciate in value. But now, I was content to let it soothe me, lull me back into a calm with its soft, slow kinetic motion that bounced pale shadows onto the ceiling.

My eyelids were growing heavy, the gin was kicking in.

I turned the light off and tried to settle my thoughts.

I imagined my diaphragm moving up and down.

Tightening, relaxing. In, out, in out.

I thought about cats and dogs. A pet would be good. A pet was what we needed around the house. Not a soft, fluffy thing I had first imagined, but a hunter, something with bark – and bite.

In, out, in out.

I could hear the soft patter of rain on the window and the wind pick up through the trees, a soft swoosh like a distant waterfall.

There were other noises too – animals in the cemetery, no doubt: foxes, badgers and owls. My mind wandered to what they might be doing in there. Prowling, digging, watching.

Stop it.

And then I heard something else. The noise was so slight I thought I might have imagined it but it got louder, easier to make out. The scuffle of leather against stone. Footsteps. Footsteps outside at the front of the house. I was awake, alert again.

It was possible that it was Robert arriving home but it would have been a very short stay at 5 Hertford St and besides, I hadn't heard the grumble of a taxi pulling up outside.

I sat up and I peered through the darkness towards the door. It was slightly ajar but the crack was illuminated, soft and grey, from a stronger light source from downstairs, not the soft hall light I'd left on for Robert's arrival but the white glow from the security light, which meant that something – or someone – had triggered it.

The house had an alarm system but I hadn't turned it on.

Another sound. Metal crunching in the lock, the turning of a key. A ripple of cold ran around my body. I turned on the lamp as I heard the front door open and then close. I grabbed my phone which was still where I'd thrown it.

I saw you

It would have been easy for him to follow me in a taxi. Easy to wait outside until the lights were all off.

'Hello.'

I tried to call out but my voice was strangled in my throat. Someone was inside the house now; I could hear them in the hall. My breath had quickened, Sweat gathered in my palms.

I got out of the bed, toes clawing into the carpet and hit contacts, ready to dial Robert.

I didn't know whether to shut the bedroom room or swing it open. The footsteps came up the stairs now, fast, agile. I pressed 'call' but it went straight to voicemail.

I was frozen to the spot. My eyes darted around the room, looking for something, anything, but my bedroom door swung open before I could make a decision what to do next.

I screamed out loud. So did the intruder.

And it was only then, amid two high-pitched curdles, that I saw it was my daughter Dylan.

Chapter 12

I woke up aware of a heavy arm lying across my abdomen. I shifted position and the body next to me made a sound – a deep guttural sound of a still-tired person waking up.

'Guess who's here,' I said turning to my half-asleep husband.

He opened one eye and grunted.

'Who?'

'Dilly,' I smiled. 'She came back last night, before you got home.'

'Dylan's back?'

He sat back on the pillow and stretched, bending his elbows and putting his hands behind his neck. I admired the soft ripple of his stomach muscles and the small brown discs of his nipples. I couldn't deny that my husband kept in good condition. That famous Paul Newman quote, 'Why go out for hamburger when you can have steak at home?' popped into my mind but I squashed it like a gnat.

'Did she tell you she was coming?'

I shook my head.

'No. She's didn't get here 'til about ten-thirty. I was in bed. She scared the bloody living daylights out of me.'

The sleep in my voice kept my tone soft and casual, but

93

I was awake enough to know that I shouldn't tell my husband how frightened I had been. I thought I had better bring it up in case Dylan mentioned my screaming.

Robert rubbed his eyes and then opened them wide as if he was stretching his face. His dark hair was messy. For a split second he reminded me of Chris. Perhaps I had a type and I didn't even know it.

'I didn't think we'd see her until Christmas,' he said, sitting up.

'Maybe she misses us.'

'And here's me thinking we were going to have Saturday morning to ourselves,' he said, leaning over to plant a tender kiss on my lips.

'We should all go out for brunch,' I said more briskly.

Robert rolled away from me like a teenager slapped down.

'I doubt she'll be up before midday.'

I got out of my bed and put on my silk robe, a gift from Robert from a recent trip to Dubai.

I tied the belt firmly around my waist and went to sit back on the edge of the bed next to my husband.

'Is it a bit weird?'

'Is what weird?' He yawned.

'Dylan coming home. After two weeks.'

Robert laughed.

'It's not weird. It's perfectly normal. I'm sure the halls of residence campus are half empty this weekend.'

He seemed to find Dylan's arrival inconsequential, even funny, but for me it definitely rang alarm bells.

'I think it's strange. Coming back so soon. What if she's not made any friends? What if she has, and they're horrible?' I said, my mind racing.

'Honey, it takes weeks to settle in. I don't blame her for feeling a bit homesick, do you?'

It was easy to imagine myself in her position. I'd never really settled into university life, not even after three years.

'Besides it's more likely she's spent her allowance already and has just come back to butter us up for a top up.'

I nodded, feeling better. Robert was always good at re-assuring me.

'So how was last night?' I asked after another minute.

He slipped his hand between the fold of my gown and stroked my pubic hair.

I pushed my thighs closer together but it just encouraged him.

'Come back to bed,' he said in a low voice.

I really wasn't in the mood.

Truth was, I hadn't been in the mood since Chris Hannah. I didn't want to be touched, not by anyone. It didn't feel right.

I ignored him by standing up.

'Are you sure Elena forgives me? About her dress.'

Robert pushed back the duvet and got out of bed.

'They thought you were great,' he said, opening the curtains with the remote control. 'In fact, seeing as the weather is going to be good this weekend I've invited them round. For a barbeque.'

'Today?'

'Elena flies to Moscow this morning but Max is coming. With his girlfriend. He's keen to see the house.'

I looked surprised.

'Girlfriend? I thought he was with Elena.'

'Strictly business,' he smiled. 'I think her tastes run richer than Max. Besides, she's married.'

I was glad to hear it.

'We should invite Bill and Iris,' I decided on the spot. 'To the barbeque. And Nathan too if he's working today. We should catch up on how it's all gone this week.'

'Great idea. We should check on them. Besides, isn't Iris from Russia?'

'Germany.'

'I'm going for a run. I told Max to come for around four o'clock so we'd better make sure we've got something to give them.'

Dylan came shopping with me to Hampstead without too much resistance.

We wound our way around the village buying Gloucestershire Old Spot sausages from the butcher's on Heath Street, brioche buns from the bakery run by the friendly Turkish couple and relish from the deli where you needed a mortgage to buy a cheese wheel. It all cost twice what it would in the supermarket, but it was a sunny afternoon and I loved the atmosphere of the narrow leafy streets. Most of all, I loved spending time with my daughter. At one point she let me link my arm through hers as we crossed the road, and I sighed with happiness feeling her close again. And although the dynamic had definitely changed between us – I could feel it, see it, when I glimpsed ourselves in a shop window, Dylan walking just a little taller, holding her chin a little higher, no longer a mother out shopping with child, but two women enjoying the freedom of the weekend – I felt like I had gone back in time, back to how it used to be.

Dylan went to Waterstones to buy some notebooks for college and I went to the florist for some flowers for the house.

As the florist wrapped the tulips in brown paper, I looked over the road towards a pavement café where a solitary man was reading his newspaper over a coffee. I wondered what Chris was doing, who he was spending his Saturday afternoon with. Was he also in one of London's cafés, or running down the street in headphones filling time, pretending he wasn't lonely?

'Want me to take those?'

I spun round and saw Dylan.

'Thank you,' I shuttered.

'You looked deep in thought.'

'Just thinking of the menu for tonight,' I lied, hurrying back towards the car.

'Why are we having this barbeque again?' said Dylan as she helped me load the boot.

'I think Dad is buttering up a client.'

'Does he know I've gone vegan?' she asked, picking up a £12 steak from the top of the shopping bag and then putting it back.

I looked at the groceries in dismay. We had packets of sausages, burgers and halloumi cheese – way too much for eight people, without one going meat and dairy free.

'We'll just have to do you a salad,' I said, slipping into the driver's seat and starting the engine.

'Don't bother. I won't be eating.'

'Why not?'

'I'm going out.'

I drove home the long way, down the quiet back streets.

We'd always had our best chats in the car. It was why I had never really minded over the years, being the unpaid taxi service. The confines of the vehicle became the confessional booth.

'So where are you going?' I asked, choosing my moment.

'Bella's off to Chile on Monday,' said Dylan, looking up from her phone. 'The Operation Raleigh thing. She's having a big going away party at The Flask tonight'

'That's why you've come back?'

Robert and I had purposefully not discussed Dylan's return when she had woken up at midday as my husband had predicted but this seemed like my opportunity.

'Yeah,' she replied without much enthusiasm.

Various scenarios about her return home had been swirling round my head since her surprise arrival. I imagined her lonely in her small halls of residence bedroom, those early acquaintances from Freshers weekend having not quite taken hold and converted into genuine friendships. I imagined her sitting on her own in the lecture theatre, I imagined her being as homesick as I had been for so long at university.

'Why didn't you tell us you were coming back?'

'I wasn't sure I was. But Bella is one of my best mates, and there's nothing much happening at halls this weekend, so I thought what the hell. Cost me forty quid though,' she said with a light-hearted grimace. 'I'm getting the coach next time.'

'You know, I thought you were a burglar when you crept in last night,' I said, glancing across. 'It was late. Next time maybe you could just send us a text saying what time you're coming.'

'Soz,' she shrugged. 'I was supposed to stay at Bella's but I decided to come home at the last minute. I thought you'd be pleased to see me.'

'Of course I was pleased to see you.' I said it a little too enthusiastically – the last thing I wanted her to feel was unwelcome. I wanted her to come home every weekend, although I knew that was too much to ask for.

'Why didn't you end up staying with Bella?' I said this more cautiously. I knew how it was with teenagers. You had to tread carefully when you were getting them to open up. It was like being a ranger on the wide-open plain approaching wildlife, knowing that one false move could send them scampering back into the undergrowth.

'I met her in the pub but she'd met some bloke at the bar. I felt a bit of a gooseberry so I left.'

She tied her hair up with a scrunchie that had been fastened around her wrists.

There was no reason not to believe her.

'So you're enjoying it?'

'Uni? Yeah.'

She didn't sound convinced.

'Course good?'

'We haven't done much work. Not yet.'

'What are the people like?'

'Great. Really nice.'

'Your tutors.'

'They seem alright.'

'What's Birmingham like? Nightlife, shops . . .'

'Mum, what's with all these questions?'

'I'm just interested.'

'Look. I'm enjoying it.' She looked over with a softer, mischievous smile. 'More to the point, what have you been up to other than missing me?'

An image popped in my head unbidden. A hotel room in Soho. Taking Chris Hannah's cock into my mouth and letting him come inside me.

'Working,' I said, squeezing some water on the windscreen.

'Lots of long liquid lunches in Soho.'

'Those days are long gone in the publishing industry.' I laughed nervously.

'One of the senior common room members is an American Literature lecturer. I told her that you worked for Edelman and she was so excited. In fact she's got a couple of third years who are after some work experience and I said you might be able to swing it . . .'

'I'm sure . . .' I said, suddenly eager to please. The good mother, the perfect wife.

'You're the best,' she grinned and I felt a deep sense of shame.

Chapter 13

'Where've you been?' Robert was actually cleaning when we arrived home. Dylan vanished upstairs and I loaded the meat, still wrapped in greaseproof paper, into the fridge.

'Sorry it took ages, but we were having a lovely time.'

I watched him scrub a stain from the granite worktop. 'Good look,' I smiled at his yellow gloves.

'I try.'

He threw the cloth in the sink and snapped off the Marigolds. So did you get to the bottom of her visit?'

'Bella Davies is having a party in Hampstead tonight,' I said, lowering my voice. 'She's going away to Chile. Sounds like it's a farewell party and she is one of Dilly's best mates.'

Robert looked relieved. 'I told you there'd be a simple explanation.'

'And she's gone vegan.'

'Along with half the world.'

'Did you think she looks thin?'

'She looked the same as she did when we dropped her off two weeks ago.'

'She felt thin. When I gave her a hug this morning.'

'Honey, you've got to stop worrying,' he said, washing his hands at the sink, then drying them with a tea-towel.

'But she said she didn't want to eat tonight.'

He leaned back again the island.

'Rach, come on, I thought you were getting over all this. You have a job now, Dylan's come home for the weekend. All is good. You've got to stop fretting or you will drive yourself mad.'

I looked up at my husband, resentful of his cool, calm personality.

'You don't understand.'

'Of course I understand. She's my daughter too.'

I wasn't sure he did. Robert was part of our family unit but he was very much the third wheel. He had missed so much of Dylan growing up – I worked out once that, spending at least one or two nights a week away from home, he'd not been there for almost a fifth of our daughter's life. His bond just couldn't have been as tight. Dylan did not grow inside him. Had never relied on him for milk, food, for lifts to school or help with homework. It was no wonder that Dylan's departure to university hardly seemed to have touched the sides in Robert's world. Why he didn't seem to understand my grief.

We hadn't entertained for ages. When Dylan was younger, when we still lived in Crouch End, we'd invite school gate families round for a bring-a-dish lunch or meet them at Kenwood House for coffee, cake and long walks with the kids around Hampstead Heath.

But today, I felt nervous. Nervous enough for a drink although Robert wouldn't approve of me starting so early.

Robert disappeared into the wine cellar and returned with three dusty bottles of his special occasion claret that he left on the countertop, waiting to be admired, before he went outside to fire up the barbeque as I started to make the food.

Somewhere over the years I had become a good cook. A really good one, I could admit to myself now.

I made a big bowl of salad, with tomatoes the colour of kumquats, big squares of crumbly feta cheese, lentils and green beans. Chicken breasts were marinated in a spicy flavoured sauce I had perfected and although I did not have time to make fresh rolls – the proofing process alone ruled out any spontaneous bread making, I could make impressive pats of artisan butters from double cream churned in an old water bottle.

I'd planned a pavlova, cobbling together enough eggs that morning to make a crown of meringue which had slowly baked while we were shopping. All it needed was to be filled with berries and delicious thick freshly whipped cream.

Bill, Iris and Nathan arrived first. Bill was in a suit, Iris had painted her lips in a bright red, which matched the crepe dress that hung off her tiny, bird-like frame. Nathan was in the same polo shirt and chinos that I had seen him in on his first day of work. He was cleanly shaven and I could smell the tang of a cheap, musky deodorant even from a distance.

'We're not early are we?' said Bill as he came in.

They were twenty minutes early but they were obviously excited – Bill and Iris anyway. It was hard to feel anything but affection.

Nathan handed over a box of Ferrero Rocher. His choice, I gathered, a hastily bought gift from the newsagent. I thanked him warmly and put them to one side for future re-gifting and poured them a drink.

'It's a lovely house,' muttered Iris, looking around. 'Does it still have an outside loo?'

She mentioned the outside loo on many occasions and I still hadn't got to the bottom of what it was she was remembering.

'No,' I smiled. 'Although Robert wants to build a studio in the garden. For yoga.'

'I used to be able to stand on my head.'

'You'll have to show us later, Iris,' I laughed as Bill handed me his white stick.

'Can you put this somewhere?

'Are you sure you don't need it?'

'I'm sure,' he said gruffly.

I knew he hated his cane, especially since it had been upgraded to one with an additional red band to indicate his hearing loss.

'I can see,' he grumbled time and time again.

Nathan stood back as if he was taking it all in. I realized how difficult it must be for him, being an outsider in rich, new circles like these.

I'd felt that unease for the entire time I had been at Durham. I'd applied because the city looked quiet and pretty, but I hadn't realized that so many of the students there would be nothing like me. They wore signets rings and the air of privilege, and all seemed to know each other from other places – boarding schools, point-to-point racing and Oxbridge interviews. I remember, during Freshers Week, sitting by the river in a big group and the boy to my left, a beautiful thing with long floppy air and an elegant *Brideshead Revisited* recline, asked me where I came from. 'Belfast,' I told him. 'How unfortunate for you,' he replied. I hated him from that moment on and never felt entirely comfortable at college again.

I offered Nathan a beer.

'So how's it going?'

'Good, I think.'

'How many hours are you doing.'

He opened the can with a hiss.

'I'm working eight 'til five at the moment. The agency sends someone for an hour in the evening, just to help get them into bed, make sure everything is switched off.'

'Are they behaving?'

We shared a smile. I liked Nathan – felt as if I could trust him.

'I have to keep reminding Iris I'm not a butler,' he grinned and I laughed back.

Max arrived a couple of minutes later. There were hasty introductions to his girlfriend Chloe who was very pretty with long auburn curls that fell to her waist. Her dress came to mid-calf where it almost met the top of her lace-up boots. She was a trainee solicitor at one of the magic circle law firms which meant that she was smart. She looked more like one of Dylan's friends than part of Max's fast, cosmopolitan circle.

By the time I went back into the kitchen Robert and Max were drinking beers by the barbeque and Chloe had joined Nathan, Bill and Iris at the garden table, shaded by the bough of our Canadian maple tree. Nathan was making them laugh even though Iris had that look on her face that suggested she didn't quite know what he was talking about.

It wasn't a big gathering, but it was enough to make me feel part of something. I saw Robert glance over to the group and as he smiled back at me, I knew that he felt it too.

As long as I'd known him, Robert had been alone. His father had died when he was ten or eleven, his mother passed away in his mid-twenties. There was an older brother, David but they weren't close. He lived in Malaysia now, having drifted over a few years earlier, strapped for cash, and had a wife and family out there. We'd only seen him once in the past ten years on the way back from a holiday in Langkawi. I knew that Robert missed him, but he liked making money more; there was little time in Robert's life for anything other than work, and carving out sibling time – diving together in Mabul Island or meeting halfway in Dubai – was not a priority.

But still, I knew how much family meant to him, and I understood his loyalties to Bill and Iris.

Only Dylan was missing from our group but when she joined us a few minutes later, I almost didn't recognize her. She'd changed out of her sweatpants and hoodie into tight high-waisted jeans and a pale pink T-shirt that hung off one shoulder to show she was not wearing a bra.

Two weeks had made my daughter not quite a stranger but certainly someone that didn't seem entirely familiar. She was sexy, like a Sixties Parisian starlet, all innocent, doe-eyed beauty that is irresistible to men. She looked how I had felt that night with Chris Hannah. Ripe and ready for sex.

I saw Max had noticed it too and felt my back stiffen.

'Dilly. Come and help me make the salad,' I said, leading Dylan back inside once she had made her introductions.

'I thought you wanted me to be sociable,' she said when we were in the kitchen.

'I do. But I need help pulling this lot together.'

I didn't want to start lying to my daughter too but suddenly I wanted to protect her.

'Who's that?' she said, looking out onto the patio where Robert was ignoring the demands of the barbeque in favour of chatting to Max.

'One of Dad's clients,' I muttered, glad to see Nathan approach the grill to flip the burgers.

I gave Dylan the strawberries to hull as I sliced and scooped the passionfruit.

'So come on, how's the job? Working with anyone famous?'

'No one that you would know. But I love it.'

Dylan cocked her head to one side. 'Do you ever regret it? Giving it up?'

I didn't want to tell the truth. That sometimes, often, when I was in the grip of loneliness, I wanted to be back at work so badly, that I would spend hours scouring *The Bookseller* or *Publishers Weekly*, just pretending I still had a job. I didn't want her to think that I made the wrong choices for her.

'I had eighteen amazing years at home, looking after you,

and now I get to do all the other things I didn't do. You can have it all, just not at the same time.'

She wasn't listening to me.

'Shit. I've got strawberry juice on my T-shirt,' said Dylan shaking her hands in the air.

'Quickly. Sponge it down or it will stain,' I instructed.

Our kitchen was not set up for the messy spoils of family life – everything was clean and kept away behind sleek German units. Dylan looked around for a cloth but when she couldn't immediately find one, ran upstairs to change.

I carried on cutting through the thick, dark purple corrugated crust of the passionfruit, wanting to complete the pudding quickly so I could get back outside where I wasn't sure everything was under control. The barbeque was flaming and Iris kept bending down as if she was limbering up to show off her headstand.

I scooped the yellow juice out with a tablespoon and put it in a bowl ready to pour over the berries. The seeds looked so good, glistening in their tangy golden liquid, I started to slice another couple of passionfruit.

When Dylan came running back down the stairs, she was still in the same T-shirt smeared with red.

'Your phone was ringing. It was on the bed. It's Southern Electric.'

I noticed her bemused expression just before I felt the pain of the knife slicing through my finger. I winced in pain but tried to ignore it.

'Hand it to me,' I snapped.

'Mum, your finger is bleeding.'

I ended the call and scarlet drops dripped onto the screen. My finger was throbbing. Dylan handed me a tea-towel and I wrapped it around my hand.

'You've wrapped the phone up too,' she laughed.

'I'd better go and get a plaster,' I said, eager to get away.

Out of the corner of eye I could see Robert looking back

at the house. I ran upstairs, breathing deeply, trying to squeeze some air into my lungs.

I unwrapped my hand and pressed my fingers against the wound like a fleshy tourniquet.

I rubbed the blood off the phone and switched it to silent before jamming it into my pocket. I ran my finger under the tap watching the blood stain the water then dapple the sink in pale pink puddles.

'Are you okay?' Dylan was standing in the doorframe.

'I'm so bloody clumsy.'

Dylan reached up to the medicine cabinet and got out some Savlon and a plaster.

'Come here.'

She wrapped the latex carefully around my fingertips as I had done for her so many times.

'Why is Southern Electric calling you?' she said, concentrating hard.

'No idea,' I said, looking down. 'It's probably a cold call.' I looked up. 'Did they say anything?'

'No. I passed them over to you.'

My whole body almost shivered in relief.

She paused. 'I thought they came from call centres. Why did the company name come up on your phone?'

'I don't know,' I said, trying to think on my feet. 'Actually, I did ring them last week. I'm thinking of having a smart meter installed. It's probably their London office.'

'It's a bit keen calling you on a Saturday afternoon.'

'They must want the business,' I said, trying to stop my hand from shaking.

Dylan didn't look convinced but she seemed content to let it drop. I wasn't sure what surprised or infuriated me the most. That I was lying to my daughter or Chris Hannah had called me on a Saturday evening.

Dylan wrapped the thin strip of plaster around my throbbing finger.

'I think this calls for alcohol.'

'Wine. Wine always helps.' I nodded.

Dylan disappeared. I pushed the bathroom door closed and I pulled the phone out of my pocket.

Nausea rose in my throat. Why did I want to press return call and hear his voice at the other end of the phone. I wanted to make a plan to see him again, to go somewhere loud and hot and sweaty where we could drink and laugh and dance. I wanted to wear tight jeans and a T-shirt that fell off the shoulder he kept trying to kiss. I wanted him to take me outside, to a quiet back street and press me against a wall, and push his fingers into me. All I wanted at that moment, was him.

Instead, I sat on the edge of the loo seat and scrolled to messages. Contact. Southern Electric.

I am at a family party. Please don't call.

The phone sat cradled in my shaking palm.

The white tiled walls of our bathroom made it seem like a cell. My finger was still smarting. Blood seethed through the plaster. Punishment.

There was a gentle knock at the door and I stood up to open it.

Dylan handed me a glass of rose and I smiled gratefully.

'Are you okay?' Her eyes were shrewd and questioning, like her father's.

'I'm fine,' I replied unconvincingly.

'Are you coming back down to the party?" she asked, touching my elbow to usher me down. 'Everyone is missing you.'

'I'll be there in a minute,' I said, hanging back.

I thought of my husband and daughter outside. I thought about the life we had built for ourselves and however much I wanted to see Chris again, I wasn't brave enough to bet that he was the love of my life.

I knew that my text wasn't enough to stop him. To stop me.

I'd never blocked a number before. It didn't take me long to work out how to do it. And when the job was done, I went back into the fresh autumn evening to join my family and friends outside.

Chapter 14

'So, can I take that coffee machine?'

'Which coffee machine?' I said, looking up from the Sunday papers.

'The one in the cupboard. The one we never use.'

I folded *The Times* and went over to Dylan's rucksack by the door. It was the size of China. She seemed to be going back to Birmingham with at least three times the amount of stuff she had arrived with on Friday night, but lugging a heavy load back on the train wasn't what concerned me.

'What do you want it for?' I asked as casually as I could.

A distant alarm bell had sounded in the back of my mind, a semi-forgotten conversation with a fellow parent I had once met at an eating disorder support group. Her daughter had been diagnosed with anorexia, and she was a font of information. She'd told me how anorexics often loaded up on free calorie drinks to make them feel full – soda water, tea and diet drinks. Coffee was a particular favourite. It was a diuretic, an appetite suppressant and a stimulant, giving a nutrient-depleted body the energy boost it craved.

'Dunno. Thought it be might be cool to have one in my room.'

'Why? What's wrong with a kettle?'

Dylan was already rummaging around the cupboard in a frantic fashion pulling out bags-for-life and long forgotten spiralizers.

'Got any of those capsules?' she called over her shoulder.

'No, we ran out,' I said, not wanting to be distracted, 'Dylan, wait, we need to discuss this.'

'Discuss what?' said Robert, running down the stairs in his gym-gear. He had a big bag slung over his left shoulder and looked as if he was off to rob a bank.

'Mum doesn't want me to take the old coffee machine,' said Dylan with a downturned mouth.

'Why not?' asked Robert. 'It'll be like Starbucks in her room. She'll be the most popular girl in halls by Christmas.'

'Told you,' said Dylan, giving her father a peck on the cheek.

Robert helped her load the machine into a heavy-duty shopper as I stood watching them, arms folded, feeling shut out. I knew it was wrong to feel competitive, but I guessed most parents would secretly admit to it. Who doesn't want to be the most loved, found the funniest and the coolest in the eyes of their child?

But in our house, I felt as if I had the strongest claim. Robert didn't know Dylan's favourite TV show or her comfiest pair of jeans. He didn't know that she preferred dark to milk hot chocolate or coconut lip balm to cherry. He didn't know half the names of her friends, let alone those of her countless teddy bears or the tiny figures that still lived in the doll's house in the corner of her room. I doubted he really knew our daughter at all, and yet the way they shared a joke, or tossed a quip at each other and caught it every time, suggested it didn't really matter that he hadn't put the hours in. And for that I felt the ripple of resentment.

'Come on, Dils. I'll give you a lift to Euston,' said Robert grabbing his wallet.

'I'll take her . . .' I offered.

'Don't be daft,' replied Robert. 'Thought I'd go climbing on the way back.'

'Again?'

It was another thing that Robert had taken up over the past year alongside yoga and cycling. There was a club with some of London's best walls in Archway and he'd bought all the kit – rucksacks, ropes, harnesses, special shoes and shorts. There had been some loose talk of an expedition to the Alps which I wasn't happy about at all. Robert was the sort to head to the Matterhorn from a standing start and not even see the risks. My daughter had already left home but at least she came back.

'Let's go, grandad,' said Dylan ending the debate. 'My train leaves in forty minutes. Can you order me some capsules and send them?'

Robert gave me a kiss on the cheek and said he'd be back in a couple of hours. He must have felt my resistance, detected that I was feeling left out, because he stopped and looked me straight in the eyes just like he used to do at the beginning of our marriage.

'Maybe you can come one time?' he offered.

I hated feeling suspicious and needy so I just waved my hand and laughed.

'Climbing? The odd Zumba or yoga lesson is about as far as I go.'

'Good point. I forgot you haven't got a head for heights.'

We both smiled at the shared memory we didn't have to articulate.

Paris. The night he'd proposed to me. He'd got down on one knee on the Place du Trocadero, and afterwards we'd gone for drinks at the bar at Jules Verne, the famous restaurant up the Eiffel Tower, to celebrate. We'd had a table window and too many glasses of champagne. Vertigo, happiness and alcohol collided – Robert had needed the help of three waiters to get me down – and out. But he'd managed it, protected me from the worst of my alcoholic indulgences by stroking my head in a taxi all the way back to our hotel. I knew then that I had done the right thing saying yes to this man.

'Have fun,' I whispered and went to give my daughter a big squeeze goodbye.

I stood at the door watching Robert reverse out of the drive and watched them until they only left a trail of vapour behind.

That wasn't so bad, I told myself when the door had shut behind them. We'd said our most difficult goodbye. If she came back as regularly as this, I could get by.

The evenings were already beginning to draw in and although the weekend had seen cloudless cornflower skies, there was the crisp chill of incoming winter in the air. Without lights, the kitchen seemed cold and grey, and in the twilight, gloom seemed to press at the windows.

The dishwasher had finished its run. I put the crockery away and the clank of the plates as I put them in the cupboard seemed to echo off the walls.

Dylan's return had taken me back to my old life and made me seen how much comfort there had been in it.

I'd loved making pancakes for the three of us that morning, listening to Dylan natter about the party she had been to the night before. I'd even loved entertaining, making food, the easy talk with Nathan, Max and Chloe and the satisfaction that Iris and Bill had obviously enjoyed themselves. Iris had been particularly lucid and for her, I knew good days were rare.

But although Dylan's return had restored some stability to my world, now I was alone again, darker thoughts began to creep back into my consciousness. Alone in a house that felt violated. Yes, Chris Hannah's phone call had given me a quick thrill but it had been short-lived. He had come into my home, almost spoken to my daughter. That had crossed a line in the sand and had put me on edge. Now I was alone I could allow myself to be angry.

How dare he, I thought, pouring a tumbler of water and tossing it down my throat. Did he know me so little he might have thought I might be turned on by his casual intrusion, enjoy the danger, the adrenaline of him stepping so far into my world.

I was not that girl.

Stop it, I told myself. Things were good. Things were on an upwards curve.

I had a job and Dylan was enjoying college. As for the coffee machine – Robert was probably right. It was just a social thing, a cool thing.

Tomorrow was the beginning of another week and it would be a completely fresh start. Chris Hannah had been a blip, a wrinkle in the transition to my new life. Teething problems.

That called for a drink.

There was still some good wine left over from the party. I poured myself a large glass, and went upstairs to the bedroom. We only had one study in the house and that was Robert's on the top floor. At some point I would have to find a place to work, but for now I retrieved my laptop from the drawer of my bedside cabinet and sat cross-legged on the duvet.

I had work to do – looking over a marketing plan and writing the blurb for a gothic mystery writer who was launching in eBook in December – but first there was Facebook.

Here's the thing about being a book editor. You feel invisible. You could spend months working on a manuscript, your magic wand polishing a book so much so that it could be transformed from mediocre to bestseller. And yet it was only your name that appeared in the acknowledgements that recognized your contribution, even if, especially if, it was your best work. Most of the time I liked it that way. I had never been a showy person. The job satisfaction and the pay cheque had been enough, unlike Serena who loved singing her achievements from the rooftops. But now I felt ready again to join the social media world to tell the world I had done something.

I hadn't been on Facebook for weeks. Before Dylan went away, I was on it all the time – I was a reader, a watcher, rather than someone who relived their whole life post-by-post. My contributions were likes and the occasional comment, giving the humblebraggers what they wanted, because most of the time I felt as if I didn't have anything to say. Nothing beyond the odd recommendation of a book or the discovery of something noteworthy like a charcoal latte.

But now I had something to shout about. Now seemed liked the perfect time, my excuse, to reconnect with my NCT friends, Tasha and Natalie and Jo and the crew from the school gate.

To tell them about my new job editing authors they'd have heard of, working a stone's throw from Covent Garden where I went shopping at lunchtime and bought macarons from Ladurée, lipsticks from MAC and old books from the little shops on Cecil Court.

This was the new me. Not the stay-at-home mum who had nothing to talk about but running and Zumba. Not the lonely housewife who was vain and foolish enough to have a one-night stand with a college sweetheart.

I logged on and started scrolling through other people's news. A former Edelman colleague had just had her wisdom teeth removed, someone else was at a spa. Janice, our neighbour in Crouch End, was after a pet-friendly Cornwall cottage recommendation. There were lots of people venting their continued anger about politicians, pictures of dogs on beaches and Serena was on there too sharing a link to a Scottish Castle she said she had her eye on. I also had a friend request.

Jemma Kwan. It took me a moment to recollect the name but then realized it was a quiet girl from the art department at Edelman.

I pressed confirm and hopped back onto the news feed. I scrolled back days and then when I had plucked up the courage, I wrote something next to my profile picture

What's on your mind . . .

Back in the world of books and editing this major talent.

It wasn't worthy of Seinfeld but I uploaded a photo of *Cage of Gold* and within a few seconds I had received a couple of thumbs up.

I knew the psychology behind social media. How it was designed to give you little rush of dopamine and it worked. I was on a high.

I followed the link to Serena's dream Scottish castle which had a salmon smokery and a bothy, thinking about how sociable my friend was, how she often complained that the Cotswolds was too far out and didn't think she would last two minutes in remote, lonely Highlands, no matter how good the bragging rights for owning a castle. I hopped over to the *Daily Mail*, a travel website and then circled back round to Facebook to see if anyone else had something to say about my job.

Tasha had put a smiley face in the comments box and it looked like I had a message.

I was surprised when it was from Jemma Kwan.

At first, I thought it was spam.

You are embarrassing.

I frowned. That was weird. It was definitely rude.

There was still some wine left in my glass on the bedside table. I stretched over to pick it up and tipped the lot down my neck.

I read the message again. Why on earth did Jemma Kwan think I was embarrassing? I didn't know much about my colleague except she was a junior designer in the art department. Had I done something wrong? Had I upset her in some way?

I rubbed my chin, wondering if I should ignore it or respond and went to the loo while I thought about it.

By the time I returned there was another message.

I didn't need to click on the box – I could already see it. You are a whore.

I snapped my laptop shut and froze. For a second it was as if I'd had a full body paralysis; not one muscle could relax or contract. My lungs expelled a jagged breath and my hands started to shake.

I told myself to calm down but I couldn't.

I stood up and paced around the room, settling by the window. I was in complete shock.

Jemma Kwan thought I was a whore. She didn't just think it, she'd said it, taken the time to message me and insult me.

Yes – I'd had sex with a man who wasn't my husband, which obviously wasn't great. But how did Jemma Kwan know and more to the point – why did she care?

With timid steps I went back to the bed and opened the laptop again. I couldn't pretend it hadn't happened. I clicked on her name but it was almost an empty page. She had no photos and no friends, even her profile picture was just an avatar. I wasn't tech-savvy at all, but it looked as if she had created this account just to troll.

I needed more wine, but the thought of going downstairs unnerved me – all those windows in our big glass house looking back at me like black eyes watching, judging.

There wasn't any logical explanation for what was happening but I was prepared to give it a go. One was the possibility that Jemma had seen me with Chris Hannah outside BCC house, deciphered the crackle of embarrassment and desire and had read the situation correctly. Perhaps she was religious or puritanical. Perhaps she was going through her own relationship break-up and somehow seeing me with flowers, with a man had sent her into a vindictive cycle.

Worse was the thought that Jemma actually knew Chris Hannah and she was jealous. It wasn't difficult to believe that she found him attractive, but surely Chris would have mentioned it if he knew someone who worked at Edelman.

My mind scrambled for another explanation why my new colleague would call me a whore, unless she had simply flipped.

The screen flickered and a third message arrived.

Don't think that you can hide.

My brain was like the spinning wheel on a computer screen – it simply couldn't cope with what it was seeing. Finally, I coughed out a breath.

'Why are you doing this to me?' I whispered.

My voice was small, a thin croak that barely escaped through my lips.

And there was the message I had been dreading more than anything ever since this nightmare had begun.

I'm going to tell.

Chapter 15

Jemma Kwan sat on the other side of the office, but from my cubicle, I could see the top of her head. She was just sitting there, staring at her computer screen, getting on with work like nothing had ever happened.

I had rehearsed what I was going to say to her most of last night as Robert had snored next to me and I had lied wide awake, eyes staring at the Alexander Calder mobile that hung above our bed wondering how to fix it.

There were three options. Never to return to Edelman, pretend it hadn't happened or simply to go and confront her.

Given that I was quite enjoying my job and I couldn't forget about the Facebook messages, I had decided on the latter.

I knew very little about Jemma Kwan and what motivated her but I'd always told Dylan that bullies lost their power the moment you stood up to them.

It was a bold course of action that carried the very real risk that my blackmailer would follow through with their threat and share my secret with the world, but as I ran through it in my head, I didn't see how else I could proceed. I couldn't stand this terrible not-knowing, I couldn't think of anything else until I had dealt with it.

I looked up sharply as Jemma stood and walked towards

the kitchen. This was my chance. At least there was a door on the staff kitchen; challenging Jemma in an open-plan office didn't seem like a particularly smart move, especially as it had crossed my mind in the paranoia of a sleepless night that Jemma Kwan might be innocent. Those messages had definitely come from a Facebook account with her name and posts and photographs, but it wouldn't have taken a huge amount of computer savvy to set up a fake account in Miss Kwan's name. Perhaps it was Jemma herself who had an enemy and I was the unwitting stooge.

I grabbed my phone and headed to the kitchen.

I could smell coffee and hear the gentle bubble of a boiling kettle from a few feet away.

'Hello,' she said, glancing up as I walked in. 'I was just making a drink. You want one?' She said it with eagerness, then wrinkled her nose and gestured with a teaspoon. 'It's instant, I know, but if you load it up with sugar like I do, it doesn't really matter.'

I blinked at her, frozen with indecision. She was either clueless or a cold-hearted psycho, but I needed to bring this to a head.

'Sure?' she asked, spoon poised halfway to the sugar jar.

I looked back towards the office to check no one else was heading to the kitchen and closed the door.

I could only spit the words out, the carefully rehearsed scripts I had drafted in my head deserting me like fake friends in a crisis.

'Jemma, did you send me a Facebook message last night?'

No reaction. Blank. Then a small frown – did I? – followed by a shake of the head.

'No. I was dead to the world by about half seven, I was convinced I was coming down with something, but it was gone by this morning.' She paused. 'Why?'

I clicked the Facebook app on my phone and turned it towards her.

'This is your page?'

She frowned again, black eyebrows meeting in a fine 'V'.

'Don't think so.' She looked up. 'I'm hardly ever on Facebook and I never update it.'

'Are you sure?'

She looked at it more closely.

'No, it's definitely not mine. It looks like a ghost page if you ask me.'

'Ghost page?'

'One that's never used. Why are you showing me this?'

'This page . . .' I began slowly. Jemma had to be twenty years younger than me but I felt no courage from my advantage of age or seniority. 'It sent me a friend request last night and a volley of messages.'

Jemma looked on edge, as if she was anticipating an accusation.

'What sort of messages?'

I still wasn't sure if I could trust her.

'Unpleasant stuff.'

'Like what?' she asked cautiously.

'Insults.'

I knew I might as well say it.

'Someone called me a whore.'

I felt my face flush. Jemma made a little gasp and put her hand to her mouth.

'That's horrible.'

She looked genuinely shocked.

'I had nothing to do with it,' she said, shaking her head for emphasis. Shock made way for worry and self-preservation. I could see her practically recalling Ian Sinclair's conference room speech word for word, about my years of experience and editorial wisdom. He conferred on me the status of office elder and Jemma looked as if she had no appetite to get on the wrong side of one.

'I just had to ask,' I said, backtracking quickly. 'It's just

121

weird that I've got messages from a Jemma Kwan within days of starting to work with one. I was worried that someone was trying to bully or implicate you.'

Now Jemma looked really worried.

'Oh God. What should I do?'

I almost smiled. Serena was constantly complaining about millennials and their self-obsession and I had to hand it to Jemma Kwan – she had switched the narrative around like a maestro.

'You should probably check your own account, just to make sure it's not been hacked. Think if you've upset anyone or given reason to do this.'

'This is my first job in publishing,' she said with panic in her voice. 'I've tried to be so nice to everyone. I don't think any of my friends would do anything like this. No way.' She was shaking her head.

'When you get to my age, you realize that you don't know what people are capable of.'

I could see Jemma's eyes welling with tears.

'I should go to HR, but I don't want to. All I want to do is make a good impression and if they think I'm some sort of stalker, that is going to look so bad and I'm on a three-month probation.'

I felt a maternal surge and stepped forward to give her a hug.

'Look, I'm sure it won't happen again.'

'It wasn't me; I promise.'

As I felt her shoulders tremble I knew she was wasn't lying.

'Rachel. Do you have a moment?

Ian Sinclair raised a finger aloft, just so much that I could see it above the screens of his cubicle.

I only just about heard him. My mind was elsewhere, mulling over my conversation with Jemma. I'd been so distracted I hadn't even got myself a coffee.

I took a deep breath and went to see him.

Ian's cubicle was bigger than everyone else's with a chair in one corner. His desk was scrupulously neat, with just an Anglepoise lamp, pen pot and notebook on the polished desktop.

'We were just discussing the Jemima French advertising campaign. Her agent is coming in tomorrow and we need to have something ready. She's pushing for tube posters but I don't think sixty-five-year-old women are commuting, do you? I want to know how to reach stay-at-home women and thought you might have some thoughts, hmm?'

Another time, I might have picked up on his casual remark, wondered if it was the real reason Ian Sinclair had hired me. It wasn't because of my publishing genius or adept editing of *This is Your Life*, but the simple fact that I was the affluent middle-aged reader and Ian Sinclair wanted to get into her mind.

'I agree that train and tube advertising might not be effective. I think the Jemima French reader or potential reader is more likely to read magazines or weekend supplements or watch television.'

'What about Facebook?'

I didn't want to be reminded of that.

'Yes, Facebook too,' I said, wishing I had a cold glass to press against my face. 'I did make some notes. I'll just go and get them.'

'No, no. I'll come down to your end. Obviously, we should include Vicky in the conversation.' He glanced at his ancient-looking watch. 'Say eleven o'clock? I just have a couple of calls to make.'

I scurried back to my desk and slammed myself into the chair. I could see Jemma Kwan back at her desk and wondered what she was thinking.

She was probably as panicked and paranoid as me.

I put my head down and didn't look up until I had reached my desk. I took the lid off my bottle of water looking from side to side as I sipped it.

The Edelman office seemed like a harmless enough place.

There was an industrious, intellectual hum like a college library but who knew what people were thinking in these booths dotted around the floor. Who was watching, waiting, hating?

I was certain that Jemma Kwan hadn't written those Facebook messages. But what I couldn't work out was whether something was trying to intimidate her – or me.

On its own, I might've just dismissed it. But there had also been the text that I had received on Friday.

I saw you

I didn't know who that was from either and although the most likely explanation was that it had been an unfinished message from someone not registered in my contacts, still, it had scared me.

There was no sign of Ian, and Vicky wasn't even at her desk. As I logged into Facebook my pulse was racing hard, slowing again when I saw there had been no new messages since Jemma's the day before.

That was something. I opened a new page and went to Twitter, typing in my password to get to my account. I was probably being as paranoid as Jemma Kwan but I just needed to check, make sure that whoever had contacted me on Facebook wasn't messaging me elsewhere.

The pale blue home page flooded my desktop. I scanned the text, not really knowing what I was looking for. Twitter was the social media feed I used the least, but I followed various celebrities, authors, comedians and media outlets for a mixture of breaking news and funnies. Today there was nothing unusual about the stream of tweets until I saw a blue dot at the top of the page. Notifications – sixty-five.

My finger hovered on my mouse before I clicked.

I read the first notification twice.

@rachelreeves5000 cock tease

It had been posted by someone called GastonLeRoux. I clicked on his profile and his profile picture was a white mask. He had four followers, he followed me, and had only joined Twitter that month. I knew immediately that it was a fake account but that didn't stop me clicking on the next dozen notifications that had been sent.

I felt my chest get tighter and tighter as if it was being gripped by a fist, as I read each one

@rachelreeves500 piece of filth

@rachelreeves500 hot bitch

@rachelreeves500 sweet pussy

@racehlreeves500 red hot

It went on and on. I fumbled about on my keyboard, searching for how to switch notifications off and block Gaston.

'Are you ready?'

I spun round on my chair when I heard a voice behind.

'Ian,' I said my voice trembling.

He was standing behind me with a notebook under his arm. He peered over my shoulder towards the screen.

'Twitter?'

I turned back towards my desk and managed to click it off.

'Are you on?'

'Sorry?' A rash was creeping around the base of my neck.

'Twitter,' repeated Ian. 'We encourage all staff to have an account. I believe Vicky has 14,000 followers. I've not reached those dizzy heights but Salman Rushdie has started following me.'

He looked back at the screen

'You can use it during office hours. So long as it's for work purposes, of course.'

'Of course,' I replied. 'I was just about to tweet about Jemima's appearance at the Birmingham Literary Fest.'

'Good. I must start following you so I can see the interaction.'

I smiled lamely although I felt as if I was about to vomit.

Chapter 16

I waited until mid-afternoon to text him. Chris Hannah had to be Gaston Leroux, whose name I had googled immediately and found out was the author of *The Phantom of the Opera*. At least, the white mask profile picture made sense, and although I'd never read the book or even seen the musical, I knew enough about the plot to know it was about unrequited love.

Having unblocked his number I spent half the afternoon deciding what to say.

I was angry, livid that someone was trying to intimidate me in this way, but I was apprehensive too. The night we had met, Chris had been smart, funny, considerate – all the things he used to be, all the things that had made me fall in love with him when I was twenty-one, all the things that had made me fall into bed with him at the hotel. But these Facebook messages and Twitter posts were not written by the Chris I thought I knew. They were dirty, vindictive and a little scary. They had not been particularly threatening yet – but I knew they had the potential to be. They indicated that some raw, unpredictable emotion had been triggered and I knew I had to tread carefully to try and diffuse any that could unfold. Finally, I opted for something simple.

Can we please discuss your tweets and messages? It's got
to stop.

His reply was almost immediate.

What tweets and messages?

I looked down at my phone and frowned. I typed back
furiously.

Twitter. Facebook. This isn't funny.

His reply was equally blunt.

I haven't sent you any messages.

I wasn't entirely sure why I decided to meet him. I was not
naturally a confrontational person – far from it. My default
setting was to yield in the face of any sort of resistance.

But Chris had always worn his heart on his sleeve, was
upfront with every thought, opinion and feeling. At college,
I gave him every piece of tutorial work for him to read and
we'd discuss it over red wine and big bowls of oven baked
chips in my bedroom. The first time I had ever given him one
of my essays to read he had told me it was brilliant which I'd
known wasn't true, not least because I had particularly struggled with the Chaucer module, but because he hadn't looked
at me once when he was muttering the words 'genius insight'.

I'd told him then he was a lousy liar and from that point
on, he had always given a fair critique of my work.

Twenty-five years later, I was sure I would be able to tell
if he was behind Jemma Kwan's fake messages and Gaston
Leroux's notifications.

I wanted to look him in the eye and then decide if he had
sent them and the only way to do that was to meet him.

I was prepared to meet him because I wanted to believe
that it wasn't him.

'Hello'

He was at a table in the corner when I got there, looking
down at his phone.

When he glanced up, he looked happy to see me and didn't take his eyes off me as I sat down.

'Let me get you a drink.'

'I'm not staying long.' I said, putting my handbag down but not taking off my coat.

'Shame. The food's good too, believe it or not.'

I'd arranged the rendezvous in the Golden Hart pub in the middle of the theatre district. I'd walked past it dozens of times it always seemed busy, full of tourists and men who looked like sales reps. It was within plain sight but precisely the sort of place that no one from Edelman would set foot in. It felt as safe a place to meet Chris Hannah as anywhere. I was sure it would be neutral territory for him too but perhaps I was wrong.

'I'm glad you wanted to meet up,' he said.

I looked at him, wondering if he was thick-skinned enough to believe this was an elicit assignation.

'I didn't,' I said bluntly.

'Then why are we here?'

'We need to talk,' I said, trying to switch into a forced work mode.

'You're pissed off.'

My tight expression said it all.

'Look, I know I shouldn't have called you Saturday,' he said, putting his phone away. 'I went to the pub to watch the match. I had a drink. Too many drinks. I was feeling sorry for myself and I wanted to speak to you. I didn't think it might be awkward. Obviously it was.'

'Awkward?' I said, lowering my voice. 'I was with my family, Chris. We were having a barbeque, my daughter picked up the phone.'

'I thought she was at college.'

'She came home.'

My face was getting warm. Chris looked more contrite.

'I shouldn't have done that. I'm really sorry. I sent you a text on Saturday to apologize.'

'I didn't get it.'

'That's weird.'

'No it's not,' I said looking away.

'What did you do? Block me?'

He'd said it as a joke but when he realized he was on the money, his expression hardened.

I had to get this over and done with.

'I've had some horrible Twitter and Facebook messages,' I said, my voice clipped.

'You mentioned. About what?'

For a second I was reminded of wide-eyed Jemma Kwan in the kitchen.

'Somebody impersonating a colleague at work sent me some unpleasant Facebook messages at the weekend. Someone called Gaston Leroux.'

'The French author.'

Of course he'd know.

'Not the real one. He's been tweeting insults about me,'

Saying it out loud made me realize how petty it sounded.

'Strong, sexual stuff,' I added.

He was on to me immediately.

'Hang on a minute. Is this why you wanted to meet? You think that *I* sent them.'

I was almost squirming in my chair.

'I never said that.'

'Really,' he said, pulling his whole body away from me. 'It's nice to know you have such a high opinion of me.'

I looked down with embarrassment. I was here to get a job done and couldn't stop now.

'Just look me in the eye, and tell me you didn't.'

Chris was shaking his head.

'I can't even believe you would think this.'

'What am I supposed to think?' I said, trying to keep as controlled as possible. 'Nothing like this has ever happened to me before. Then we have sex. You send me an expensive bunch of flowers, hang around outside my office, you called my phone over the weekend and when I block your number I start getting messages from a fake account calling me a whore, and disgusting tweets. I had a text suggesting I was being *watched*.'

'Do you really believe what you are accusing me of here?'

'Put yourself in my shoes,' I said, exasperated.

'I'm trying.'

'Then you'll know why it feels coincidental and weird.'

He looked at me and I could see his eyes were little black pin-pricks. I'd heard of pupils dilating when you were attracted to someone and I am sure that on the night of the Cole Porter book launch, ours had been the size of black holes. But in the low light of the pub they were tiny dark dots like the tips of sharp pencils piercing through crepe paper.

'What I know, Rachel, is that we've known each other a long time,' he said, his voice low and shimmering.

I held my ground. 'I know we have history, which is why I thought we should discuss it in person . . .'

'We were in love with each other once. I could have married you,' he said with more passion. 'So please spare me the lack of respect of blocking me or suggesting I'm some sort of stalker. The flowers might have looked a bit eager and I shouldn't have been the drunken dialler. But that's all I've done.'

'All?'

There was a petulance to my voice that reminded me of Dylan wanting the last word in an argument.

'I like you, Rachel. I've made that pretty clear. And forgive me for getting the wrong message, but when we have the most incredible night together, when your daughter's left home and you are finally free to make some decisions about the life you want live, and with who, then I'm going to give it a shot.'

'Don't bring my daughter into this,' I lashed back.

'Spare me the indignation, Rachel. I'm not the one who's married.'

'So, you're saying you didn't send the messages.'

I searched his face, looking for the tell.

'I did not send you any messages,' he said, pressing his palm on the table.

I didn't know. I couldn't read him anymore.

I felt another wave of anger. Anger at him, but most of all anger at myself for being weak and putting myself in this situation.

'If it was you, if you do it again, I will go straight to the police and I don't care how difficult it will make things for me.'

'I have every right to be pissed off with you,' he said, standing up and glowering at me. 'My whole life changed because of you but I'm not holding any grudges. Just don't make me out to be the bad guy here. Don't go blaming me for muscling in on your marriage. Or accuse me of harassment. You let me in. For the record, I haven't even got a Facebook account and even if I did, do you honestly think I'd make up a fake one to insult you. Strangely I've got better things to do with my time.'

He stood up and threw back the rest of his pint. He slammed it down on the table but as I scrambled out of my own chair he had already walked past the tourists and the men in suit trousers and shirts with the sleeves rolled up, and out of the pub. I caught a glimpse of his profile in the window, his expression stormy and stern, and as he disappeared out of view, I knew with a mix of panic and relief that I would never see him again.

Chapter 17

'In the kitchen.'

I was standing at the stove when I heard a low howl of wind as the front door opened and closed.

Even though I could not see him, I could picture my husband kick off his shoes, put his briefcase on the chair before softly padding into the heart of the house.

'What's all this?' he said, clearly bemused as he took in the places set on our long dining table, the candles and the open bottle of wine.

'I just felt like doing something special,' I said, wiping my hands on my apron.

Robert stepped over, dropping his keys on the breakfast bar. He bent to sniff at the pan I was stirring. 'Pasta with clams.'

'Your favourite,' I said, a little embarrassed. 'Or at least it used to be.'

He looked at me, his eyes sparkling with amusement, but also, I thought, a little genuine pleasure too.

'What's brought all this on?'

'Can't I just cook something nice for my husband?'

He inclined his head sceptically.

I turned back to the stove, grateful for the heat on my face from the bubbling pasta.

I told myself I hadn't just lied. I wanted to do this. I wanted to be a better wife. From the moment I had left the Golden Hart pub I had decided that I was going to wipe the slate clean, chalk my night with Chris down to misadventure, step into the second act of my marriage with purpose rather than try to manage it down like a sluggish career coasting towards retirement. As for the messages and the confusion of whether he had or hadn't sent them, as soon as I got home, I tried not to care. It was probably a bit much, threatening him with the police, but I was proud that I'd had the nerve to face him down. With a bit of luck, he would never contact me again.

The pasta was bubbling fiercely now, steam spiralled up the stainless-steel splashback in ribbons of silvery white smoke.

'How's work?'

'Good.'

He hardly ever said that. 'Fine' was usually the best I got, just like when I used to ask Dylan how her day at school at been. But when he said 'Good,' he was generally feeling king of the hill.

'When am I coming to see Regent Place then?' I asked, wiping my hands on my apron.

Other than Elena Dimitov's gallery, Robert had two big projects on the go. A vast stucco in Belgravia, which had been renovated from neglected shell to wow-home and was currently under offer, and Regent Place which was Robert's company's flagship development. Other than a hard hat visit six months earlier to see the site, I had only read a sales brochure for the project, which trumpeted floor-to-ceiling windows, views over Regent's Park and benefits of a luxury hotel: a concierge, gym, even an on-call Bentley service to shuttle residents around the city. It was the development my husband had been dreaming over ever since she had started his business renovating and flipping a flat in St John's Wood twenty years earlier. It would, without a doubt catapult him into the heavy hitting league of developers.

Privately I thought it was too big, too ambitious a project. I knew a little about how property finance worked – how developers used partners, investors, loans and money put down from off-plan deposits to pay for later stages of the build, and I had a horrible feeling that he was overextended and exposed.

'Rich people don't use their own money to get even richer,' he'd once told me on the odd occasion he had got very drunk. It brought little consolation.

'Come down whenever,' said Robert, retrieving a good bottle of red from the rack. 'You know we have someone interested in the penthouse already. At this rate, we'll have sold 50 per cent before they've even been officially released to market.'

I heard the gentle pop of a cork releasing from the bottle, the soft comforting glug of wine going into two glasses. There were few more romantic sounds than the slow rituals of two people about to spend time together.

'Wasn't sure I'd ever see you with a pinny on again,' he said as I felt a playful tug my apron string.

'Pinny?'

My voice lifted with pleasure. I was enjoying this. Lately, it was as if we were just orbiting around each other, Robert's sun to my moon so I was enjoying the shift to a more loving gear.

'That's what they're called, aren't they?'

I glanced over my shoulder. 'What's wrong with my pinny?' I challenged him, aware that I was flirting, flirting with my husband

'Now you're a career woman.'

I turned off the gas.

'You thought I'd start work and start burning my bras,' I said, hoping to sound sultry.

'I wouldn't mind seeing that.'

He stepped towards me threaded his arms around my neck, the back of his wrists connecting to my downy nape.

'The clams . . .' I said, resisting.

'I think they can wait a few moments,' he said, kissing me softly on the lips.

We kissed for at least a minute. I could hardly remember us ever doing that, could hardly remember the last time we'd even stood that close together.

He pushed his hand under the soft seam of my cashmere jumper and circled his palm across my breast, the lace cup of my bra brushing roughly over my nipple.

I groaned feeling tension leave my body.

'You like that?" whispered Robert.

I could think of nothing else but the pleasure beginning to pulse around my body.

I tipped my head and felt his breath on my neck and then we were kissing again.

The pasta was forgotten. We crossed the floor, locked together. I pulled my sweater over my head. Somehow my bra had already come off.

We were freewheeling, out of control.

Later, I wondered if my body was responding to my husband or if it was a release of pent-up sexual energy that had seen simmering under the surface for weeks.

He pushed me up against the table. His body was strong, firm from the climbing and cycling – an alpha body, unlike mine or Chris Hannah's. Bodies that have softened around the edges with age and lack of discipline.

I unbuttoned his shirt and unbuckled his belt. As my fingers raked through his chest hair, he pushed down his trousers, then fumbled with the zip of my skirt so it rustled to the ground.

I sat on the edge of the table and parted my legs as Robert came between them. He took his time, stroking a stripe of skin on the inside of my thighs.

I rolled my knickers over my hips and they slid off onto the floor.

I gripped the table with one hand and pushed the other down over my abdomen until it cupped my dark triangle of hair. Robert put his fingers on top of mine, finding the space between them as he slotted into me, moving back and forth, teasing me until I nearly came.

He pulled away and I grabbed the other edge of the table. I arched my back enjoying the cool air against my bare breasts. Robert pushed my legs further apart, a sweet stretch that made my hips tilt forward.

I lowered myself onto my elbows, moaning in delight as his face disappeared between my thighs.

I could feel him smell me and then taste me.

My spine connected with the cold tabletop and I shivered.

As I threw my arms about my head, my fingers hit something solid and I heard the sound of glass shattering on the concrete.

He sucked and licked with long, greedy laps, hands pressing my thighs out as wide as they could go. I was totally open and the pleasure was so sweet that I feel my core clench, my whole body contracting like a wound-up coil, trying to hold out, just a moment longer until the sweet release.

He flicked the small, sweet nub inside me with the tip of his tongue until it was as hard as a beach pebble. I circled my nipples with my palms, wanting every square inch of my body to feel the same stimulation. And when it came the waves of pleasure fired to every nerve ending making me cry out loud.

My breath slowed. Beads of sweat had collected between my breasts.

I turned my head to the side and touched my husband's hair affectionately. It was then that I saw a face at the blackness of bifold doors.

For a split-second moment, I was confused wondering if it was his reflection but then I realized that someone was stood outside watching us.

I screamed but Robert had already seen him too.

'What the fuck!' shouted Robert, scrambling to pull his trousers on.

I rolled off the table and grabbed my dress off the floor, clutching it to my chest to cover my nakedness.

But the figure had turned and run away. I could just make out the cream chinos in the darkness of the garden and I realized that it was Nathan Deer who had been watching us.

Chapter 18

Serena found it all hilarious.

'I can't believe he caught you at it,' she roared with laughter, handing me a glass of wine.

'Don't,' I said, instantly regretting I had told her. 'It was just awful. I saw this face staring at us and then I screamed and Robert went tearing out there. By the time I got to him, Robert had grabbed Nathan by the cuffs and had him pinned up against the water feature.'

'Sounds like he was asking for it.' Serena folded her legs under her on her vast velvet sofa.

I took a drink of my wine and shook my head.

'It was a horrible misunderstanding.'

'Misunderstanding!' snorted my best friend. 'He's a Peeping Tom.'

'I'm absolutely mortified but I don't think he's a pervert,' I said, having given it some thought. 'I'd told him at the barbeque that we sometimes can't hear the doorbell if we're in the kitchen and the TV is on, so if it was an emergency and he couldn't reach us, to come around and try knocking on the bifold at the back of the house.'

'Was it an emergency?' She raised her eyebrows to denote scepticism.

'Iris had one of her turns and he needed help to get her back into bed.'

Serena's brow didn't move.

'What?' I said looking at her over the rim of my glass. 'You think next door's carer popped round on the off-chance I'd be screwing my husband on the kitchen table?'

'He will now,' she grinned.

'Besides we weren't, actually, you know . . . shagging.'

'Well, what were you doing?'

I didn't say anything. My cheeks were flaming red. 'Other stuff . . .'

'He was going down on you,' she said quite matter-of-factly.

When I didn't reply she took it as an affirmative.

'You lucky cow. That would have been worth the embarrassment of the carer watching. I don't think Alan has gone down there this century.'

'Okay, I think we should change the subject,' I said, aware that our husbands were just outside, inspecting Alan's new man cave under the ancient oak tree in the Wilsons' garden.

Serena took another long slug of wine and giggled again.

'Come on, Rach. You do have to see the funny side of it.'

'Serena, I can barely face leaving the house.'

I took another gulp of wine and wondered whether I should tell Serena about the Facebook messages.

Coming here this weekend had reminded me what a good friend she was, how we clicked. Her confident head girl matter-of-factness was a foil to my reserve.

I wished I could tell her everything that was troubling me even though I had come here for one weekend to forget about it.

'What's going on in here?'

Alan, Serena's husband, popped his head around the door.

Alan was a commercial barrister, as jolly as their three golden retrievers that bounced around the slate flagstones of their hall. Our friends had been together almost the same length of time as I had been with Robert although they had left it just a couple of years later to have children.

'Nothing,' said Serena with a wave of her hand. 'I was just catching up on all the Edelman gossip.'

'Are you sure you don't want to come down to the club?' asked Alan, zipping up his jacket.

'Why on earth would we want to come down and watch you two play nine holes like two old golf WAGs?'

Serena clutched her wine glass to her chest and flashed me a conspiratorial glance.

'No, we're staying here, aren't we? We are going to make cocktails and cook dinner and eat it all ourselves if you're not back by six-thirty.'

'I am married to a very bossy woman,' grinned Alan as he threw his arm across Robert's shoulder.

'Sure you don't want to come?' Robert looked more serious than his friend.

'I hate golf.'

Serena went to wave them off and I curled up on the sofa, enjoying a few minutes of solitude. Serena and Alan's house was Robert's idea of a nightmare, a large, red-brick former rectory packed with original features like the vast fireplace in the kitchen and the leaded windows and beams, that Robert would have torn out and replaced with industrial steel in a heartbeat. But I had always loved it.

I felt safe in Serena's house. Besides its size it was always warm. The dogs were a big friendly presence in the house. Right now, I just wanted to be Serena.

'Do you realize, it's been over a year since I was last here?' I said when my friend came back into the room. 'I don't know where the time goes, or what I've done with the last twelve months.'

'The past is the past, my darling. Nothing you can do about it. But you're moving forward now, aren't you?'

Easy for Serena to say, the picture of relaxed success, her blonde hair piled loosely on her head, country casual in her grey jeans and white pullover and a long pendant that settled in the curve between her breasts. Even back in the old days, she'd oozed confidence and sophistication. No surprise she'd reached the dizzy heights of management and all the trappings that went with it.

I enjoyed the silence for a moment after they had gone.

'You know what we need?' said Serena.

'What?'

'Cake.'

'I'm trying to be low-carb.'

'Bollocks to that. I bought red velvet cupcakes.'

I followed my friend into her kitchen.

'Ian thinks you're fabulous, by the way. I was at a management event with him on Thursday and he literally couldn't stop talking about you.'

'That's good to hear,' I replied. I wasn't sure if I was still on some sort of probation.'

'So how are you enjoying it?'

'I feel a bit unsteady on my feet. But I love it. I'm hoping when Ginny comes back from maternity leave, I can move on to something else, so if you hear of anything, you must let me know.'

'Really, is that what you want?' she said opening a white cake box.

I looked at her, trying to hide my disappointment. I thought, more than anyone, Serena would understand why I wanted to be back in the cut and thrust of it all.

'It is,' I replied. 'I'm really enjoying it. I was bored out of my mind at home.'

'Don't you think you'll miss having the time to breathe?'

'Breathe?'

'Life always seems to be so busy. Busier than it's ever been.

I miss the opportunity to do nothing, not that I ever remember having it.'

I was about to say something, point out that I hadn't exactly been doing nothing for the past eighteen years, but I wanted to see where she was going with this.

'The time to have a run, meet a friend for coffee without the pressure of rushing back somewhere. Having my nails painted and knowing I could throw in a massage afterwards,' she said expansively, pushing a cupcake in my direction and taking a scarlet crumbly bite out of her own. 'Cooking, baking, when do I ever have time to do this,' she said pointing at the vast food processor in front her. I was surprised at her outburst.

'Serena, you love your job. You have the perfect life. You have the husband, the job, the friends . . .'

'Really?' she said more quietly. It was the first time in a long time I have heard her vulnerable.

'What's wrong?'

She shrugged. 'Look, I know why you wanted to come back to work. I get you were bored. But seriously, Rach, be careful what you wish for. Do you think I have anyone to pop out to coffee with, or for a yoga class? Most people I work with are fifteen years younger, and even if they're not, I'm the boss and that's just another boundary. Do you think they come up to my desk and ask me to come to Pret? Or go and see an exhibition at lunchtime even though three world-class galleries are within a ten-minute walk away? Am I invited to the birthday drinks down the pub, or the little gossips in the kitchen they think I don't know about? No. I don't get invited to any of it. And I work so hard, I don't have time to do it out of the office. Sometimes I look at your life, your old life, with all that time in it, and I think I would happily do a job swap.'

I couldn't believe that Serena felt alone too. That's what she was saying.

'At least you've got me now,' I smiled.

'Good things do come out of going out to parties, huh?' she nodded.

'They do indeed,' I said, trying not to think about the night in question she had just referenced.

Chapter 19

'Where are we going?'

Everything seemed to make me unsettled these days, even travelling on an unfamiliar road.

Robert glanced across at me with the hint of a smile on his lips.

'You'll see.'

I looked out of the window of the car, watching the hedge-rows and open fields of Oxfordshire zip past, trying to reign in my irritation. Robert knew that I disliked surprises; I far preferred buying my own birthday presents – at least that way you ended up with something you wanted.

As if reading my thoughts, he leaned over and touched my hand.

'Almost there. I think you'll like it.'

I doubted that. Robert was clearly enjoying the anticipation, but I just wanted to get home.

Just as I was beginning to relax at Serena's, more messages had come during the night.

Ever since Chris Hannah had called during the barbeque, I had kept my phone on silent mode, but that didn't stop texts from coming.

I'd found them in the morning.

Don't ignore me.
I want to see you.
I hate being ignored.
What are you doing?
I miss you.

There'd been about a dozen of them – all sent between 2 and 3 a.m.

Nothing threatening, probably sent under the influence of alcohol, but still, hard to ignore. It had certainly put an end to an enjoyable weekend in the countryside pretending everything was normal. Twice that morning Serena had asked me what was wrong and I'd blamed it on the hangover, and when pushed, on missing Dylan. That bit was true but not the real reason I felt as if I was standing in freezing cold water.

Robert turned off the winding B-road into a single-lane farm road, the hedges so high on either side, I quickly lost all sense of direction.

'Where the hell are we?' The track grew so narrow, the brambles that trimmed the road scratched against the windows.

'We're here,' he said, turning into a wide driveway flanked by tall stone gateposts.

Ahead was an avenue of tall, broad lime trees, their interlocking branches forming a canopy. In the spring or summer, I was sure it would be lovely, with dappled sunlight pushing through the leaves, but on a grey October morning, it was as if the trunks were squeezing us between them.

'Close your eyes,' said Robert, unable to keep the smile from his face.

'You know I hate surprises.'

'Indulge me,' he said.

I let out a low laugh, a little of his enthusiasm rubbing off and trying to join in with the fun; he put one hand over my eyes just as the avenue turned to the right.

'Wait for it, wait for it . . . now!'

I opened my eyes just as Robert pulled the car to a halt. We were parked at the top of a gently sloping drive that ran arrow-straight towards a honey stone manor house. There were four lines of tall leaded windows from top to bottom of the house, huge brick chimneys and deep gables. A double door had rusting ivy trailing around its edges. It was beautiful, like a classic English cottage built on a gigantic scale.

'Like it?' he grinned.

'It's gorgeous. But what are we doing here?'

Robert didn't seem to hear my question.

'It's called Marley Hall. Sir Edward Lutyens designed it,' he said, turning the car down the drive towards the house. 'A hundred acres of grounds, so big but manageable.'

'Manageable?' I said, trying to smile.

'There's a lake and a folly and a boat-house. There's even a walled garden at the back.'

I grinned sideways at him as he slipped into sales patter.

'Are you thinking of buying it?'

'It's not for sale.'

'Good,' I said with a sense of relief.

'Good?' he repeated, the smile dropping from his face.

'Oh, I don't mean I don't like it – I do, it's a beautiful place, but . . .'

'But what?'

'Well, I know it sounds silly, but I suppose I'm romantic about grand old houses like this. I want them to be loved and lived in as they were intended, not turned into apartments or country house hotels.'

'I couldn't agree more.'

I looked at him in surprise. That wasn't like Robert at all. Ever since I had known him, he'd talked of his dream of buying up an ancient pile and transforming it into a modern dwelling. Unlike most Parisians, Robert had always been a fan of the glass pyramid at the Louvre, that stark juxtaposition of the modern and the classical. And that had always been what Robert had yearned to do: take a lovely old house, leave the beautiful outside and bolt his beloved steel and glass to the inside, as if he were forcing the past and the future together in some crazed art project.

He parked the car and gestured for me to get out.

'Is it open? To the public, I mean?'

'To the public, no. But to us . . .' He pulled a hand from his pocket, holding up a set of keys.

He slotted a large key into the tall studded door and swung it inwards.

'Your private viewing,' he said, gesturing grandly.

I hesitated before I stepped inside. There was still part of me that believed this was not my world. Far from it.

'Go on,' said Robert, putting his hand in the small of my back.

'Look at that,' I said, stepping inside. Immediately in front of us was a wide wooden staircase lit from behind by stained glass windows, but there was none of the stuffiness of your standard stately home.

'Go and explore. That window is just the start of it.'

I walked through the double-height hallway into a series of reception rooms, all detailed with golden wood panels and coloured glasswork, then out into an amazing Arts and Crafts kitchen with a red-brick fireplace and oak cupboards, complimented by a sympathetic colour scheme of sage and terracotta. And beyond the leaded windows, there was a lovely view across a knot garden. There was a feeling of warmth and coziness even though it was clear from the dust whirling about the entrance hall that no one had actually lived here for a while.

I hadn't meant to go far, but I followed my nose, like a child in a fairy tale chasing the smell of freshly baked gingerbread through the forest. I went upstairs and saw bedroom after bedroom. It was all still furnished and although the

décor wasn't to my taste – the four posters were just a little
too grand, it was just idyllic.

I went all the way to the top of the house, where the tiny
bays all had window seats and sighed at the row of crammed
bookshelves that were up there. It was a dream reading room
and I imagined myself with a big club chair where I could
look out down the avenue of lime trees.

I was back on the first-floor landing looking out over the
ha-ha when I felt Robert come up behind me.

'There you are. I rang your phone but you didn't pick up.'

'It must be on silent,' I said quickly.

I felt on edge once more, but tried to relax the tension in
my face.

There was silence for a few seconds.

'So what do you think?'

I turned to look at my husband.

'I love it. But why are we here? Whose house it is?'

'Ours,' he said finally.

'You're kidding.'

Robert shook his head.

'I thought it wasn't on the market.'

'It was but now it isn't. My offer has been accepted. In
fact, we've just exchanged. Hence the keys,' he grinned. 'I get
some special treatment.'

Tears started to pool in my eyes. Robert's gesture was so
big, so full of love, that I couldn't help feeling traitorous. I
tried to blink them away but it just made me feel more
emotional.

'Rach, what's wrong?'

He looked shocked, upset.

'Don't you like it?'

'It's amazing,' I whispered. 'But it's just so big.'

I had to say something. I couldn't tell him the real reason
I was crying. Besides – it was true. The house was enormous.

'You mean so big for the two of us.'

It was an excuse to look away.

'You know Dylan has always wanted a fairytale castle. Now we've got one. Look, I thought we could stay in Highgate during the week and here during the weekend. Dylan will love all this space over the holidays. She can have parties, invite her friends. I know she loves the bright lights of London, but you know she's always fancied herself a princess.'

I wiped away my tears and Robert looked at me kindly.

'Look, I know I should have discussed it with you but you'd have tried to talk me out of it. But the thing is, we deserve this.'

It was the last thing I deserved.

'How much was it?'

'Cadogan House is about to complete. Business is good,' he said, avoiding the question. 'Besides, this is what we have worked our whole lives for. And before you think it's a bit remote, there's a Waitrose in Ellingham, Serena is only twenty minutes down the road and the train station is even closer. I've checked and it's an hour and twenty, door to door, to BCC should you decide to stay longer than the maternity leave.'

Robert took me in his arms and I rested my head on his shoulder.

'I love it,' I whispered. 'I love you.'

'Who'd have thought it? The girl from Belfast and a boy from the arse end of Dorset living in a place like this.'

'Just don't expect me to call you Lord.'

Robert pulled away, looking more serious.

'I know how things can get when your kids leave home. I know how people can drift apart and relationships get stale. I don't want that to happen to us. I want us to work. I want to be those two old people in the village still holding hands at ninety.'

'You want us to be Bill and Iris.'

'Something like that,' he said.

I'd often wondered if Robert thought about nothing but work, but he was clearly more intuitive than I thought. He too had felt the distance between us. But this, the house, felt like an opportunity to revive our marriage. It felt like the new start I needed.

I slid my hand in the back pocket of his jeans.

His body felt firm against my palm.

After Tuesday night, after the kitchen table, I wondered if this was our cue to have sex on the window seat, in the eaves of someone else's dream house. But we were content just to stand close to one another.

'You're sure we can afford it?'

The younger me had said exactly the same thing when we'd viewed our Crouch End house for the first time. I'd taken one look at the black and white porch tiles, and the back garden that had a pink potting shed and a dovecote and I was sold. I didn't think we could afford that house either but Robert had promised me he would work it out and he did, even though the house was about to go under offer. I wanted to tell that girl, the younger me, to tread carefully, and not to let her head get turned.

'Cadogan House is buying it for us.'

'I just don't want to you to have to keep working yourself into the ground for the rest of your life. I want us to be able to enjoy this.'

'When Regent Place is finished, sold, we are never going to have to worry about money again. I think the expression is, we have arrived.'

Chapter 20

By Monday, the euphoria and excitement about the new house had worn off and I had worked myself into a frenzy of worry, concerns much bigger than who was going to cut the lawns of Marley Hall. I was worried that Robert had overstretched us financially, worried that he'd spotted the fissures in our relationship and was using a second home to paper over the cracks, worried above all that I'd already messed it up beyond repair. Most of all I was worried that he knew.

Sick of staying in our cold, silent Highgate house, I decided to go for a run. Before Dylan left home, I used to run a lot – it helped fill the days and got me out of the house, but I hadn't been since I had started at Edelman.

My over-priced designer trainers were still sitting where I had left them in the porch from weeks ago, still caked in mud. I laced them up and screwed in my earphones, dialling up some cheesy pop on my iPhone.

The weather had turned cold which the *Daily Mail* head-lines were blaming on a Siberian wind blowing in from the east. But the icy breeze slapping against my cheeks felt good as I set off up towards Pond Square, then back down towards Parliament Hill where the rich housing stock gave way to the open grassland of Hampstead Heath. The thin mist had settled across the horizon, but the faster I ran, the grey cloud that had been following me for months seem to lift. For the first time in weeks, I felt good.

I followed the path through woodland and then out into the open next to Highgate Ponds, running, not jogging, pushing myself as hard as I could. When I could go no further, my lungs and heart screaming for respite, I stopped, hands on knees, air hooting in and out.

'Not . . . fit . . . enough . . .' I gasped to no one in particular as I reached the iron gate that guards the Ladies' Pond. Although I had lived in North London for almost twenty-five years it was a part of the Heath that I rarely came to. I'd always found the 'Men Not Allowed' sign a bit forbidding. Besides, I have never been a swimmer. I associated it with the run down municipal baths of Eighties Belfast, the smell of chlorine and the harsh cold as you struggled to dry yourself, shivering in paper thin towels, desperate to get out to the foyer where I was allowed a plastic cup of Bovril.

I took the shady path that led to the water trying to catch my breath. By the time I reached the meadow which flanked the edge of the pond I was ready for another run, but there was something tranquil and beautiful about the ponds that made me pause.

A sixty-something woman dressed in a rubber cap and a Speedo costume smiled as she pulled a towelling poncho over her pale, goose-pimpled body, as if in invitation to take a moment to enjoy the still of this part of the Heath.

I gave her a sheepish smile back, aware that my music was still playing, aware that she could probably hear it. I pulled my phone off the strap on my arm to click off the music.

When I yanked out my earphones, I could hear birdsong and the faint roar of London traffic behind the horizon.

I put my hands on my hips and took a minute to watch the handful of peaceful swimmers who were braving the chilly waters – dots of pink faces, plastic caps and radiating white ripples. I'd read enough blogs and magazine supplements to know that wild swimming was having a moment but I knew that these women were not here for the bragging rights of taking an October dip.

I've never had the guts to come swimming in the ponds and resolved to be braver, stronger in the summer. One day, I resolved, I would like to come for a wild swim on a chilly day just like today. I imagined my shoulders submerging and the pressures of life dissolving in the icy water. I imagined the clarity of thought one must feel when you could register nothing but the sharp needles of cold pressing against your skin.

I inhaled deeply with the satisfaction of a decision made. It wasn't the ripe smell of the countryside – more like rotting leaves and damp.

Despite my resolution to be more tough and daring, standing around in the cold was already starting to send my toes numb. Gearing myself up to start running again, I looked at my phone, to see how many steps I had already done.

As I looked down at the home screen, I saw the messages icon registering that I had a text.

Without thinking I glanced around, left to right before I read it. There was a row of unread messages that extended from the top to the bottom of the screen all from the same number.

I opened the oldest message first which had been sent thirty minutes earlier.

I want to see you.

On its own, it could have been harmless enough. A summons, and instruction to report for duty.

But there were more; each one increasingly intimate and all sent within minutes of each other.

I want to touch you.

I want to feel you

153

I want to taste you
I want to be inside you
I shook my head as my phone felt hot in my hand.

'Leave me alone,' I cried out loud as a picture message appeared in my inbox.

I clicked on it to enlarge the image and saw a photograph of a woman dressed in black and purple Lycra running. It was a picture of me.

For a moment, I stopped breathing. I had no idea when it was taken except that it was that morning.

A final text was incoming and I didn't even need to read it to know what it said.

I am watching you.

'Fuck you!' I screamed, the words choking deep in my throat. I threw my phone as far away from me as I could manage and it landed with a soft plop in the pond.

I saw one of the swimmers look up and then carry on carving through the water. A gust of wind blew past me, scooping up the copper leaves and tossing them around the meadow like a shower of pennies. I stood, motionless, watching the pool, watching the ripples subside from where my phone had disappeared into the murky water.

The phone was gone. But he wasn't.

I was cold. Cold to my bones. I shivered and looked from side to side, feeling afraid and exposed. I doubted the 'Men Not Allowed' sign would stop anyone determined from coming inside. The quiet of the ponds was suddenly too loud. Even the trees seemed to be whispering and the fierce lashings of wind were warning me to go home.

I turned around and started running. The sound of footsteps frightened me even though they were my own. I didn't stop until I was at Pond Square. Sweat dripped down my temples, my heart was racing. At the top of our street I had to slow down, afraid that I was going to be sick. I felt weak and stumbled over to a moss-covered bench. Wet seeped through the back of my leggings, but right then I didn't mind; if I didn't sit down, I'd fall down. I put my head in my hands and bent down over my knees, my fingers gripping the seat. I remembered reading somewhere that was what you were supposed to do if you felt faint, more oxygen getting to your brain or something, but it just made me feel sicker. I gagged, saliva drooling from my mouth in a silver trail.

I am watching you.

I hated Chris Hannah. I hated him.

I stood up and wiped my mouth. I began to walk back down Swain's Lane, quickly, with purpose, just as I had once been told at a self-defence class, passing Waterlow Park and the rear entrance to the cemetery, back towards the house.

I didn't stop. If eyes were watching me, I didn't want to linger.

The smell put me even more on edge. A rancid stench of rotting vegetables and vinegar; and what was that all over the road? Trash: crushed cartons and plastic wrappers and what looked like half a grapefruit squashed flat by a car tyre, trailing out of our driveway out onto the road.

'What the hell?'

Our security gate was half open which wasn't unusual – we often kept it open when it was refuse collection day.

I squeezed past the space into the yard and gasped at the mess.

Both of our recycling bins were lying on their sides beside my parked car; plastic cartons, tins, biscuit wrappers, magazines, soiled cleaning sponges and old bits of food hanging out of shredded bin liner were strewn across the drive.

'Shit,' I whispered looking at the mess. I was going to have to get rubber gloves and clean it all up, before we got rats.

Wind whipped up in the trees behind the house, a low howl that rattled through the skeleton of trunk and branches. I felt a speck of rain on my forehead and wiped it off with my hand. Wanting to get inside, I bent down to pick up the bin but stopped as I saw a piece of paper tucked in an empty aluminium can in neat roll. It looked white, cleaner than everything else and I thought that was strange. I pulled it out of the can and unfolded it as the rain began to get heavier. I gasped when I saw the one word, carefully typed on the shower dappled paper. The word SLAG.

Chapter 21

'Probably a fox. We're always getting loads of the little buggers coming through from the cemetery. Treat our garden like a bloody motorway.'

I nodded politely.

'I'm sure you're right, Bill,' I said, not having told him about the note. 'Just a fox.'

I didn't want to choose Bill's place as a refuge. The last thing I needed was to bump into Nathan Deer, who I'd been trying avoid him since the kitchen table incident, using the car where possible to slope out of the house, accepting lifts from Robert in the morning rather than walk past their house to the tube station. But I didn't want to go home.

I was too shaken to be on my own. I wanted someone blunt and straightforward to calm me down, and Bill's 'I remember the war,' gruffness always helped me put things into perspective.

'Where's Nathan?' I asked, putting my cup of tea down, on the old walnut coffee table, wanting to change the subject.

'What's that?'

Bill was hearing impaired, but if you were facing right towards him and came up close, he could also read your lips. I turned my position so that he could see me more fully.

'Nathan, isn't he supposed to be here?'

I'd been in the house a few minutes, long enough to make a pot of Earl Grey and I hadn't seen or heard their carer.

Bill frowned.

'Comes and goes as he pleases. He's like a bloody fox, that one. After Iris went to bed with a headache, he left. Something about his phone?' Bill shook his head. 'Glad to see the back of him. Better off alone.'

I gave a weak smile and refrained from pointing out that the fact that Bill had milk for tea and electricity to run the kettle were down to the carer making sure it happened. And without a carer, would Iris be able to lie down in her own bed in her own room? I suspected Bill knew that too. He was deaf, stiff and creaky in his limbs and he had something like thirty different medications to take at various times of the day – another strong reason for full-time help – but he was still sharp. I'd always had the slightly disconcerting feeling that Bill knew everything that was going on in the neighbourhood, from his habitual position sitting in his bow window.

'Bill, you and Iris are pretty switched on when it comes to things happening in the street, aren't you?'

'I know what time the postman comes, if that's what you mean.'

'Well, have you seen . . . anything unusual?'

'Unusual? How do you mean?'

'I mean anyone hanging around, watching the house. Maybe even driving past.'

'Like photographers? Paparazzi?' he said the word elaborately, as if he was showing off that he knew it. 'You think anyone would care about us?'

'No, but we're fairly isolated down the lane. Maybe if someone was thinking of burglary or something.'

His sight was poor but his eyes still looked shrewd.

'You think that's what the bins was? Someone on the rob who couldn't get into your house, so they smashed up the yard?'

'Maybe. I don't know,' I said, thinking about the spate of break-ins in the area over the past few months. One of Robert's friends who lived in Hampstead had recently installed panic buttons all over his house after intruders had smashed their way in while his wife was on the school run. Always one to embrace technology – Robert's super-prime developments had all the cutting-edge innovations including intelligent ovens that detected what type of food you were cooking and adjusted its setting accordingly and retina-scan entry – Robert had suggesting updating our security around the house, but at the time I had resisted. Dylan had already complained that our house was like Fort Knox when we had the gate over the drive installed. But now I wished I had taken my husband up on his offer.

'It wasn't that long ago I could tell you the colour and make of every car that drives up the road,' said Bill, shaking his head. 'Can't do much about the eyesight but the doctor wondered if I should consider cochlear implants. Said they've come a long way for us older people. General anaesthetic involved though, which I'm not sure about at all.'

I was too distracted to think about geriatric cochlear implants. I stood up and crossed to the window, pulling back the net curtains so I could see outside. You couldn't see our house from this angle, the wall and a tall sheet of thick privet hedge obscured it, although I knew it was possible to see some aspect of our house from some of the upstairs rooms

'Still thinking about those foxes?' said Bill after another moment.

I was too deep in thought to reply.

'I suppose it could have been Nathan,' he grunted.

I spun round.

'What could have been Nathan?'

'Tipping over your bins.' Bill hesitated. 'Iris heard him on the phone. Called your husband a rude name.'

'What name?'

Another pause.

'Dickhead.'

He said it deliberately as if he was describing something anatomical.

'When was this?'

'The other day.'

'Which day?' I pressed.

Bill waved a hand.

'I lose track of the time.'

'Please, Bill.'

Suddenly it was important for me to find out.

I am watching you.

Nathan Deer had been watching us that night on the kitchen table. Nathan had my number. He knew where I lived. Where I worked.

I am watching you.

I shook my head slowly. But it couldn't be him, could it? Not all of it, anyway. The messages started before he saw me naked.

In fact, they'd started coming before I'd even met Nathan. Or had they? I couldn't remember, couldn't get the timeline straight in my mind. Nothing fit together properly, nothing made any sense, but one thing was for sure, I couldn't keep on like this.

'Day after Iris fell out of bed. You know he never came back to our house that night. Went to get you and Robert for help getting Iris off the floor. But then scarpered. He's the one we should be cursing.'

I still prickled with embarrassment when I thought about that evening. But whatever my suspicions were about Nathan, I owed it to Bill and Iris to tell them the truth about it.

'We told him to go home,' I admitted. 'He had a little row with Robert. I knew Iris needed help and thought it would be easier if Robert and I came over and release Nathan finish his shift. He'd run into overtime anyway.'

'Argued about what?' said Bill, not missing a beat.

I shrugged.

'Nothing. Robert thought he was spying on us but he'd only come to the kitchen window to get our attention.'

No one said anything for another minute.

'He takes stuff, you know,' said Bill finally.

His face had lost his gruff expression. Instead, he looked a little meek. His change of demeanour put me on alert.

'Takes stuff? What sort of things?'

'Iris has lost a bracelet. Took one of my books, too.'

'A book? Why would he take a book?'

Bill had done his national service in the RAF; I had heard the same stories about his being stationed in Aden dozens of times. The experience hadn't been positive, but it had led to an interest in military aircraft and Bill had hundreds of books on the subject.

'Come see,' he said, groaning as he pushed up from his chair. He beckoned me to follow him to a bookcase in the hallway.

'You know what should be there? An operator's manual for the Hurricane. Original. From 1938, Battle of Britain time. Those things are worth a bloody fortune.'

'How much?'

'Fifty pounds, at least.'

I frowned, not wanting to argue the point, but it seemed to me that if Nathan really was a thief, he'd have chosen something more valuable.

'And Iris's jewellery? Are you sure she's lost it?'

'It's her short-term memory that's gone, not her eyesight.'

I nodded thoughtfully: again, I didn't want to rain on his parade, especially when Bill obviously believed his wife, but only last week Iris had complained that her 'best shoes' had been stolen and after an extensive search the shoes – her tartan slippers – were found safe and sound under her bed where she had left them.

'Can you talk to him?'

I didn't want to. I didn't want to see him again, especially not now.

'I will,' I said, knowing I had very little choice.

He hobbled back into the living room, taking a spot by the window. I followed him. His gaze was trained outwards into the street; his world shrunk to the ten yards he could see in either direction. I knew he couldn't hear me from this distance, but I kept talking because I needed to say it.

'I'm sorry I couldn't keep helping you Bill, but I needed to go and live my own life. But I know exactly how you feel. I've been a prisoner in my own home for so long, being nothing but a mother and wife, neither of which were needed anymore. Dylan had outgrown me, and Robert? He's the same, I suppose, but I felt like the light inside me was slowly going out, the air just got too thin. Which is why . . . why I did what I did. I needed to get out, I needed to spread my wings, although look what's happened. It's not exactly working out as I imagined. Someone hates me, and I'm not sure who it is and I don't know what to do.'

I took in a ragged breath, and pressed the tip of my finger into the corner of my eye to stop the escape of a tear.

Bill turned around and just looked at me.

'We all need help, Rachel. I know that. It's just sometimes we're just a little too scared of what it means to ask for it. But the strongest thing you can do is reach out.'

His expression was so wise and compassionate that I was hit by a wave of emotion. For a second it felt like that first dip in the Hampstead ponds, a cold and face-slapping truth, but then the realization that it wasn't as bad as I thought. It was absolutely exhilarating.

Chapter 22

My post was waiting for me on my desk when I got into the office. I took my coat off, hooked it over the back of my chair and flicked through the thick bundle, fastened together with an elastic band, passed a couple of thick white jiffy bags that no doubt contained books or manuscripts, passed letters, envelopes in a variety of colours and sizes, and pamphlets for industry events all across Europe.

Most of it was addressed to Ginny Lane. Apparently the postroom had been briefed from the day I got here that all her post should be directed to me, and I supposed that word hadn't quite filtered out yet that there was a new editor at Edelman to be targeted by agents, writers and marketeers, which kept a lid on post of my own.

There was one thing addressed to me. A postcard. The design was a cover of vintage Faber paperback – *Touch*, a selection of poems by the American poet Thom Gunn. The graphics of the title were on one side – black on orange in a font that reminded me of a Hitchcock movie. On the reserve side was the Faber logo in one corner and the name of jacket designer on the other. The rest of it was blank except for two words – '*hath the*' – floating around on the blank white space.

163

Heaviness pressed on my shoulders, panic fluttered in my belly, I was sinking into shifting sands, and I felt unsteady and dizzy.

'What's that?' said Vicky, looking over my shoulder.

It was the second postcard I had received in as many days. The first was a cover of another vintage Faber paperback Philip Larkins' *Girl in Winter*, which had been easier to dismiss as innocent. There had been just one word on the back of that card '*Thus*' and I had convinced myself that it was just a flyer or advert from a rival publishing company.

But now I knew the words were a message.

'Nothing,' I said, slipping the postcard into my hardback notebook but Vicky wouldn't let it go.

'I love those vintage book covers,' she said, letting me know what she had seen. 'My flatmate bought me a box of Penguin cards for my birthday. I mounted them all in a frame and they look amazing. I got so many likes on Instagram when I posted it.'

We were both called into the boardroom. I was glad. Vicky's wittering was white noise in my head and I just needed to throw myself into my work to forget about what was going on in my private life.

The weekly acquisitions meeting we had been summoned to attend was still one of the glaring differences between the editorial process now and when I had previously worked at the company. Back then, when I had fallen in love with a manuscript, whether it had come off the slush pile or had been pressed into my hands by an agent, I could generally get the nod to buy it pretty quickly. My long lunches with our MD to discuss the potential of a debut or brainstorm the reinvention of a more established author looking for a new publishing home was one of my favourite parts of the job. But from what I could see, twenty-first-century acquisition meetings were more a gladiator's arena where colleagues vied against each other – a publishing version of *Dragon's*

Den, where those with a confident pitch, a Hollywood-friendly concept and a snappy sound bite that the sales team loved could get the nod to sign a debut writer for a six-figure deal where others would be left empty handed.

I tried to concentrate as we spent an hour and a half talking in circles about whether psychological thrillers had reached saturation point. Jenny Pickles pitched a twisted literary horror set in Greenland, which the sales team thought was too much of a risk, although Kate Gregory had more luck with an Iraq war-set romance which she described as *The English Patient* meets *The Kite Runner*.

By midday I was getting tetchy, wondering if it would ever finish, but when Ian Sinclair reached for the biscuits – I had never seen him touch anything other than the bottle of Evian he kept on his desk – I knew it was a sign that the meeting was done.

'New acquisitions are our life-blood,' said Ian as his parting shot as everyone collected up their notebooks and pitch documents. 'Kate, Belinda, Georgina. Can you stay behind? Rachel, can you join us too?'

I hung back at the door until Ian beckoned me back into the room with two fingers.

We all sat back down and I wondered what he wanted. I glanced at my watched again – twelve-thirty. It was going to be tight if I was going to get to the appointment I had pencilled in for lunchtime and hoped whatever it was, was going to be quick.

'Simeon Averill.'

I looked up as Ian dropped the writer's latest book onto the table with a thump. 'Sir Simeon, has just delivered his new book, *The Joys of a Sorrowful Winter*, which, as you all probably know is the final one in his contract. Sir Simeon has had a very long and distinguished track record with this company. A Booker prize, the Prix Goncourt, ten million sales and a grand miscellany of awards and gongs. I accompanied him to Paris myself when he received his Commandeur de L'Ordre des Arts et des Lettres.'

He paused and steepled his fingers for dramatic effect.

'Unfortunately, Kate has heard on the grapevine that his agent has been sounding out other publishers for him to move to. And what does that mean for the company, hmm?'

'Is it such a bad thing?' offered Georgina, Edelman's publicity director leaning forward. 'The sales of his last two books haven't been great. I think he's seen as an old dinosaur and well, a bit of a lech. He was very inappropriate on Radio 2 last time he was on. I'm not sure they'll have him back.'

Ian didn't look impressed by her contribution to the conversation.

'Georgina, Sir Simeon has his faults but he is one of the literary greats. His books will be remembered one hundred years from now. He is a name. And the company big wigs like the prestige he brings us, so we have to hold onto him. So how do we do that?'

I noticed that Kate had gone red in the face.

In theory, Simeon Averill, 'Sir Simeon' as he insisted on being called since his recent elevation in this year's honours list, was one of Ian's authors – as Managing Director his job had moved away from day to day editing but he still liked to think of the company's biggest names as being on his list even though Kate did most of the hands-on work. In moments of glory, when an author had received a gong or a literary prize, Ian would claim the credit, but when a book had bombed or an author had jumped shipped Ian would lay the blame elsewhere.

'Sell more books,' said Belinda, our no-nonsense sales director.

'Belinda, Simeon and his agent will make the decision about whether to stay at Edelman or not in the next month. It is unlikely we will shift a significant amount of his novels in that time. What we need to recalibrate is his perception, given he has described us as . . . what . . .'

He looked at Kate to provide the answers.

'Useless pricks, I believe the expression was,' she said shuffling her papers.

As if he wanted us to understand the true gravity of the situation, he took a sharp inhalation of breath so we could hear the fresh air being sucked up through his nostrils.

'We need to impress him with the media campaign for *The Joys of a Sorrowful Winter*,' said Georgina with confidence.

Ian shook his head. 'He'll be signed to Random House by the time we can get a meeting in the diary to present to him. You know what Penelope his agent is like.'

There was a mumble of 'yes' and 'we know' around the room.

I cleared my voice to speak. I was the only one who hadn't contributed to the conversation, and although I wasn't exactly sure why I had been invited to this gathering of the most senior members of the team, I was flattered to be involved and I knew I had to say something.

'It seems to me, given the limited amount of time that we just need to love bomb him,' I offered.

'Love bomb?' said Ian suspiciously.

'Authors liked to be flattered. Money, fame, prizes, sales don't mean a great deal to the likes of literary lions like Simeon because he's had plenty of them, even if he hasn't had a hit since the Eighties. What he wants, what he needs, is to feel appreciated. He wants attention.'

'I did tell him that *Joys* was a ground-breaking piece of work. His best since *Nature's Feather*.'

'Ian, he wants public affirmation not just a few kind words over a cream tea.'

'We could book a wraparound cover of *The Bookseller*,' suggested Belinda.

'We should throw him a party,' I replied.

'But his new book isn't out for another nine months.'

'We had a party for his last one,' said Georgina, shaking her head. 'He had a complete strop. Told me he couldn't possibly invite Crown Prince Nicholas to Waterstones.'

'Wasn't *Nature's Feather* published thirty years ago this year?' I replied, trying to figure things out.

Georgina was busy googling it.

'Yes, it was.'

'Then let's have a party to celebrate that,' I said. 'Really, it doesn't matter what the reason is. His birthday, forty years in publishing, the anniversary of a release. What matters is the noise we make. If he is that important to the company, we have to spend to keep him. It should be a big, splashy party. Good for Simeon and actually, good for the company.'

'We could book Annabel's,' said Belinda, clapping her hands together.

Even Ian joined in with the venue brainstorm, but I just looked at my watch again. I was running really late now, so late I wasn't sure if I would make it in time.

'Ian, do you mind if I go?'

'I thought we were in the middle of something,' he said, frowning.

'I have a meeting.'

'Can't you push it back half an hour? This is important.'

'Ian, really. I have to go . . .'

He sighed deeply. I saw his lips purse, a little bit of the goodwill I had just won dying in front of my eyes.

Chapter 23

I found a taxi as soon as I left the office asked it to take me to Gray's Inn Road.

I'd enjoyed the meeting with Ian. All the talk of the party, with caterers, cake and celebrity guests had distracted me, helped me pretend that was life was normal. But out on the street, I was brought back to reality.

The law firm was based in Clerkenwell, far enough away from my place or work, Robert's Marylebone office and Highgate to feel secure that I wouldn't be spotted. But it was near enough to make my 1.15 meeting having left Edelman at a little before one.

Bill had been right about seeking help. There was no one I could talk to about what was happening to me – not Serena, not anyone at work, and I could hardly call up my NCT pals and say 'Hey! Haven't seen you in fifteen years, by the way I've just had a one-night stand and he won't leave me alone.' I certainly couldn't speak to Robert or Dylan and I knew that I was close to reaching breaking point.

The internet search I had conducted immediately after cleaning up my yard, googling 'what to do when you have a stalker', had been terrifying.

I quickly discovered that whoever was harassing me had chosen well: the law hadn't caught up with technology and consequently the authorities weren't motivated or equipped to track down offenders. The few times the police had managed to catch a stalker, they'd only really made the effort because the victim had been assaulted or even murdered, none of which was reassuring.

A deeper Google search had unearthed the website of Charlotte Callow, a lawyer who specialized in helping women who were being targeted online. Revenge porn, trolling and digital protection were all covered in her online literature and I immediately saw that this was the way I needed to go.

The sun was a weak yellow orb that cast deep shadows on the pavement. The newspapers had been calling it the warmest autumn on record, but there was no sign of balminess today. The sky was bright, but there was a vicious wind running north to south, funnelled between the tall buildings all along the Farringdon road, so that as I trotted along Clerkenwell road looking for the solicitor's office, an icy blast would cut through my thin coat at every corner. And yet, as I pressed the buzzer next to the 'Callow and Callow, Solicitors' sign, I was still sweating – a combination of exertion and nerves.

The door buzzed and I pushed into a small reception area. I stopped. There was a desk, but no one manning it and I paused, unsure.

'Rachel?'

I looked up to see a woman with curly red hair and glasses standing on the stairs.

'Hi there. I'm Lottie Callow, would you like to come up?'

I followed, edging around a few open cardboard boxes stacked on the landing and into a tiny office, barely big enough for a desk. Charlotte Callow was younger than I had expected, perhaps mid-thirties, but she had an air of efficiency that I immediately liked even though I was always fairly certain she was the only Callow in the Callow and Callow operation.

'Excuse the chaos,' she said, indicating the two chairs facing her desk. 'We need a bigger office so we're moving up to Bedford Square in a couple of weeks'

I grimly wondered if the business of advising stalker victims was a brisk and increasing trade.

'I take it you're being harassed?' said Lottie, cutting to the chase.

I looked at her sharply and she smiled.

'If you wanted to write a will, you wouldn't have come to me. I specialize in online harassment cases, stalking and blackmail – the website is very clear about that – and that's what I tend to get through the door. So . . . when did it start?'

I looked down at my hands. *It started because I cheated on my husband.* How was I supposed to say those words to a complete stranger?

'You're in a safe place, Rachel,' said the solicitor more gently. 'Everything you say in this room is completely confidential. And there's no judgement; I simply want to help you if I can.'

So, haltingly, I began to tell her. I didn't mention Chris and our night together, instead I began with the text after my night out at Le Circe, then Jemma's fake Facebook account. I told her about the postcards, the Twitter posts and the text messages by the ponds and the note rolled up inside the tin can. By the end, I felt better, unburdened. But I also felt slightly embarrassed; laid out like that, it didn't sound like much. I was sure the walls of this office had been witness to stomach-churning tales of terror and abuse and here I was, complaining about some overturned bins and a couple of postcards.

When I had finished, Lottie sat looking down at her notes, lips pursed.

'I'm sorry . . . it sounds thin, but I've been frightened.'

'Absolutely do not apologize. You have done nothing wrong. There's no doubt that you are the victim of harassment,' she said, 'And possibly a stalker too, given that the offender seems aware of your movements.'

I swallowed, not entirely sure if I liked the idea, but glad that I was being taken seriously.

'I hate it. I don't feel safe and I just want it to stop. I didn't know who to talk to.'

She reached behind her to pop a pod into her Nespresso machine. 'You're right to come and see me as soon as possible. These texts, messages, they're designed to scare you. But please be reassured that we will stop it.'

She looked at me for a moment. 'First however, you need to tell me what happened.'

'What? When?'

She tapped her pencil against her pad, reading from her notes.

'"I saw you", "I'm going to tell", "You won't get away with this". Whoever is sending these messages, they want you to think they have some power over you, some information they possess. And in this case, it all seems to be referring back to an incident, probably fairly recently.' She cocked her head. 'Do you have any idea what that might be?'

She was pushing me slowly, to reveal who it was and why it had started.

'I had a one-night stand. It was stupid, I regret it.'

'Who with?' she said, handing me an espresso.

I told her about Chris, the broad strokes of our night together and how the messages had begun soon after.

Lottie nodded as she scribbled everything I was saying down on yellow legal notepad.

'You say he's an old flame, what's your history?'

'We had a pretty intense relationship in our third year at university. He helped me through a difficult situation.'

'So there is some sort of bond between you. That can often be a trigger.'

'I suppose so,'

I didn't want to be drawn on any more of that. I didn't want to admit how much I owed Chris Hannah and how let down he must have felt when I ended our relationship.

'Why did you break up? The first time.'

'I went travelling. I wanted to move on.'

'So you ended it. What about the second time?'

'I'm married. It couldn't continue.'

'Did you let him think there could be a relationship between you?'

I'd asked myself the very same question. Had I done anything to lead Chris Hannah on?

'I don't think so. We had a connection that night, but I thought he knew the score.'

'Maybe he didn't.' She said it bluntly but it wasn't a reprimand. 'Right, down to business,' she said, sipping her own drink.

She told me there were five main types of stalker but the behaviour of mine ruled out all but two, 'the rejected stalker' and 'the resentful stalker'. Rejected stalkers often began when their partner ended a relationship. Typically, they felt as if they deserved the victim's love and were furious when they didn't give it to them in the way that they required. Resentful stalkers were a little different. Simply, they wanted to distress you, possibly because they were angry at you but sometimes because the subject was an unlucky substitute for someone who had hurt them in the past.

'I think we might be dealing with a resentful stalker here which is good news.'

'Good news?' It didn't feel like it.

'They're the least likely to be violent and tend to back off once we get legal on their ass.'

'Is that the proper terminology?'

'Sorry,' smiled Lottie. 'Very unprofessional. But you get the idea. The more quickly we act the better. The longer the stalker continues, the less they tend to respond to legal threats.'

She ringed something on her pad.

'It seems that Chris Hannah wanted to rekindle your romance and when the reality of the situation set in, he took his anger out on you.'

I knew this was possibly a good time to mention that it might not be Chris Hannah at all. That my neighbour's carer had also been acting strangely after he'd caught my husband going down on me on the kitchen table. But I felt cheap enough as it was, and didn't want to feel any worse. Besides, I wasn't sure the *who* mattered right now, just the how to stop him.

She gave me a stack of leaflets and I flicked through them.

'Hide your personal information,' it advised and I wondered how old the pamphlets were. It wasn't hard to find out personal information in this day and age. We lived our lives in public whether we liked it or not.

It didn't feel like a foolproof plan.

'You're married?'

I told her about Robert and Dylan and our life in Highgate.

'Have you told your husband?' asked Lottie briskly.

'I had a one-night stand,' I said quietly. 'I'm not sure how forgiving my husband might be about that if he finds out.'

'You should think about telling him,' said the lawyer sympathetically. 'You want allies, not secrets.'

The solicitor's face turned serious. 'It's your call, of course, but I would say we should move on this straight away. Leave Chris Hannah in no doubt that you have no interest in seeing or contacting him again.'

'But how do I do that? I met him last week and told him to leave me alone, but that's when the really scary texts started – all that "I want you, I want to touch you" stuff.'

She nodded.

'The first thing is that you don't meet him again. Ever. Delete any Instagram or Facebook posts that could give clues about your life – where you go, what you do.

'Adjust your privacy settings on social media. Avoid it where possible. If anything does get through, I want you to screenshot it and keep it as evidence.'

She opened her drawer and gave me another pack of information.

'There are also various other remedies. A cease and desist letter, for example. And we can go to the police.'

'Evidence, remedies . . .' I looked up, sure she could see the fear in my face. 'And now you're talking about the police. It's a lot to get my head round.'

'You have to stamp on this, Rachel.'

I knew she was right but I wasn't sure I could. Not after everything that had happened.

'I don't want to go to the police. Not yet,' I said, my voice quiet. 'I ruined his life once. I don't want to do it again.'

'You don't owe anyone, anything,' she said. 'Seriously, Rachel.'

I nodded but I wasn't sure I agreed.

'And there is one last thing you absolutely have to do,' said Lottie. 'You have to tell someone else. A friend, family, someone you trust. Get it out there, face it down. Because I promise you once you break the spell, this whole thing won't seem so overwhelming.'

I stood up and thanked her, shaking her hand and taking the leaflets, walking back down the stairs. It all made perfect sense: tell someone, share the burden. But tell who? Robert? Dylan? Serena? Who? And here was the real question: who in this world could I really, truly trust?

Chapter 24

I returned to the fifth floor of the Edelman building shell-shocked but strangely energized. Some of the weight had been lifted from my shoulders. I had shared my secret and the world hadn't stopped.

In my absence from the Simeon Averill meeting, Ian had put me in charge of his tribute party and decided that we needed a November date in the diary by the end of the week so invites could be sent out as soon as possible. Georgina had already made a start by the time I got back to the office, and found out that most of the exclusive venues had been booked up months earlier, given that the Christmas party season was almost upon us. The price of those places with availability was astronomical.

'It's going to cost Edelman an arm and a leg,' was Georgina's tart parting shot before she went home. I couldn't help but think they were all blaming me for the idea. Given there was the whisper of redundancies in the air, it was no wonder that an expensive party for a difficult author wasn't how some people wanted to spend company money.

I worked late to make up for my long lunch. I had a lot to think about and the upside to my troubles was that it looked as if I was fully committed to Simeon's party.

'Still here?'

I looked up in surprise. There were a handful of people left on the floor but I didn't think Ian Sinclair would be one of them.

'There's stuff to do,' I said, wishing he would leave me alone.

He came around my booth and sat behind me in Vicky's chair. I was forced to spin round to speak to him.

'I think you're settling in very well.' He crossed his legs and the heel of his loafer slipped off his foot.

'The industry loses too many good editors to motherhood. But I'm glad we've managed to tempt you back.'

'I don't think you're allowed to say things like that Ian,' I laughed as a distant cleaner switched on their hoover.

'Probably not,' he said with a shrug. He gave me a longer look. 'I'll have to count on you not to tell.'

He turned and glanced down the corridor. 'Speaking of tempting people back,' he said, lowering his voice a fraction. 'I wondered if we might discuss something.'

'Fire away,' I replied, suddenly feeling on edge and uncomfortable, alone with my superior.

'David Becker. I mean you made his career and he hasn't had a hit since *This is Your Life*. Nothing of the size of that one, anyway. I was wondering if you might drop his agent a line. Have a little word in David's own ear, if you're still in touch. See how he would feel about coming over to Edelman. Maybe we could test the waters with him over dinner.'

I didn't like to admit that I hadn't spoken to my prized author for nearly twenty years. Having guided him to a million-copy-selling hit, I had to watch him sign a new deal with another publishing house as soon as he was out of contract, a mega-bucks deal being apparently too tempting, although he did tell me it wasn't about the money, which didn't exactly make me feel any better.

'I'll see what I can do,' was my reply.

Ian nodded without taking his eyes off me.

'Good. It's a tight ship here at Edelman. Everyone has to give 110 per cent. Regroup about David Becker in the next week or so, hmm?'

Ian glanced at his watch and stood up to leave as I was left wondering if he had just issued a threat.

The few remaining Edelman staff seemed to disappear within seconds of Ian going home. No point in staying if the boss wasn't there to see you beavering away, was there? The overhead strip lights had dimmed, a recent energy saving initiative. Through the plate glass windows, I could see the outline of the city – just a series of dark shadows, black on black, punched with soft orbs of the streetlamp sodium. There was the hum of a vacuum cleaner on the other side of the floor, and I was sure I could hear scratching in the walls. Vicky had told me the day before that after six o'clock, when everyone had gone home, mice appeared out of the skirting boards and scurried across the floor. I'd never seen that in our much older offices in Bloomsbury even when I worked long into the night, but I didn't want to hang around to see it now. In fact, I didn't want to hang around much longer at all.

But there were a few things that I had to do first. I pulled out the sheet of 'Callow and Callow' headed notepaper that had been folded in half and put in my bag. All of my notes from the meeting had been scribbled on it, some of the points ringed or underlined. It was a dangerous piece of paper to keep but I decided it would be fine to stash at work. I folded it up into a smaller square, put it in an old envelope and hide it the back of my drawer.

I was glad that I had gone to see Lottie Callow. Glad that I had been able to tell another human being what was happening to me, even if I'd had to pay for the privilege. It was the isolation, the sense of being lost in a giant maze where every turn took me deeper, that was what had been killing me. Now at least, I had some sort of map.

I pulled a box out of a bag that I'd had stashed under my desk all afternoon – a new mobile that I'd bought after my meeting with Lottie. Over the past couple of days, I'd felt too vulnerable without one; even here, sat in a big office with a landline in every cubicle I knew I was unguarded and unprotected.

I'd already juiced up the battery so all that remained for me to do was insert the SIM card and follow some online instructions. When my new number flashed on the screen, I wrote it down on a Post-it note which I put in my purse.

I punched a few buttons on the mobile, checked out the camera. My contacts book was empty. Given my old phone and SIM was at the bottom of Hampstead Ladies' Pond I had no idea how to retrieve my numbers, but the idea of a fresh start was no bad thing. There was a spike of anger as I put the new phone back in my bag. I felt like a criminal, someone forced to wipe clean their identity. That's what the worst sort of monsters did, wasn't it – child-murderers and Nazis. All I did was have sex with an old boyfriend and now I was the villain.

There was a packet of Mentos on my desk. I popped one into my mouth as the phone rang.

Alexa, our receptionist, had gone for the night which meant it must have been through the security switchboard.

'Hello?'

The line was silent.

I didn't say hello again but just slammed down the phone.

I grabbed my coat and in my haste to get away I put my arm into the wrong hole.

Shaking off the coat, I picked up my new mobile to call an Uber before realizing I hadn't even installed the app.

Damn, damn, damn.

I was about to switch off the computer when I noticed I

had an incoming email from Robert. That was unusual. Robert hardly ever emailed me, preferring text or WhatsApp. I clicked on the box and the first thing I saw was a photo.

It was the front of an office block and it took a full second to realize that the anonymous brown brick facade was Callow and Callow.

There was writing before the image and I read it aloud.

I know what you've been doing.

Bile rose in my throat and I fought to swallow it. I studied the email again, forcing myself to re-read it. It was then I noticed something strange. Robert's email address: it was a Gmail account, with the username RobertReeves56925.

It wasn't his usual work email address – in fact, it felt wrong, fabricated. It felt like a chink of hope.

I stayed rooted to my chair for another couple of minutes, trying to call up some courage. I thought about people who were really going through difficult times, people who were sick, homeless, bereaved, then I shook my shoulders, told myself to get a grip and took the lift down to the deserted lobby.

I wanted to ask security about the call that had been put through to my phone, but there was no one behind the huge front desk.

I hung around for a couple of minutes, my fingers tapping impatiently on my thigh. But as the rain started to lash against the plate glass windows, I took it as a sign to head home and that it was finally time to tell someone.

Chapter 25

The black cab pulled up outside our house. I felt like I was carrying a bomb, the fuse already lit and fizzing in my hands. What damage would the explosion leave? Broken windows, shattered furniture? Or would the whole house heave and fall in around us?

Robert was home – I could see that immediately from the glowing windows and his Range Rover in the drive. What was more unusual was the white Porsche parked next to it. I wasn't aware that we were having visitors. That was something else to fret about right there. That I had forgotten about a dinner party or drinks that had slipped out of the diary. It was just worry, upon worry – a trembling Jenga tower of anxieties that was threatening to fall in on itself.

I hugged myself, cold, despite the cloying warmth of the cab. The cabbie glanced in his mirror, eager to get me out and move onto his next fare. I paid him with a decent tip and turned towards our gate like a man shuffling towards the gallows.

I had no idea if the email from RobertReeves56925 was genuine. What I did know was that I was tired of feeling afraid and alone. 'As soon as you turn a light on them, it exposes the creeps hiding in the shadows. And then they lose their power,' was how Lottie Callow had put it, and I'd turned it over and over in my head all afternoon. She was right. While Robert didn't know about *Him,* my stalker, whoever was trying to frighten and intimidate me, had me in their grip.

My shoes echoed on the drive – hollow thuds on the brickwork. Taking out my key, I ran my thumb along the ridges, feeling it slide into the lock, turning it slowly as if every movement, every moment was significant. The fuse on that bomb was running down.

'*Robert, I've got something to tell you.*'

'*Sit down, we need to talk.*'

'*I do still love you; you know.*'

There was no easy way to explain it.

Was it possible to tell him about the stalking without revealing I'd had sex with another man? I wasn't sure.

Voices. I stopped; the door was still open. I kept still, not daring to breathe. Voices, coming from inside the house, from the living room, a man whose words I couldn't quite make out.

Then Robert, his baritone voice raised.

'This is absolute bullshit.'

Fear gripped my chest.

For a sliver of a moment, I thought about stepping back outside, quietly closing the door and running into the village. Maybe get a double vodka at The Flask: a last-minute reprieve for the condemned.

But there was something about Robert's voice that stopped me. He sounded angry, yes, but something else. Anxious? Disappointed? No, heartbroken.

But who was he with? Chris, Nathan, someone else? Whoever it was that was stalking me, had they the gall to come inside my house and confront my husband? I took a step forwards to find out.

I closed the door, harder than I needed and dropped my

keys on the counter. 'Hi!' I called, cheery and upbeat, at least as much as I could manage. 'You here?'

There was a sudden silence, as if Robert and the mystery man had frozen, caught doing something indecent.

'Hey,' Robert finally replied. 'We're just through here.'

I walked into the living room and immediately saw Max sitting on the sofa. Robert was standing by the fire, but looked restless as if he had just paused from pacing the rug.

He gave me a small smile; his expression was troubled but soft and I knew right then that the RobertReeves56925 email was not from him and that he didn't know about Chris Hannah. But still I had some instinct, a sense that something wasn't quite right and that we were in the slipstream of lingering bad feeling.

Max stood up and came over to me.

'Hey Rachel,' he said, stepping over for a double-kiss. 'How's the new job?'

I glanced across to my husband and then back to Max.

'Full-on,' I said as breezily as I could. 'That's why I'm only getting home at this hour, we've got a big launch coming up. All hands to the pumps.'

'Make time to send me those running routes, yes?'

'Gosh, I'm so sorry. I forgot.'

'What's your number? I'll send you a text to remind you.'

I couldn't remember my new cell phone number. Even if I could, if I said it out loud Robert wouldn't recognize it and would know something was wrong. Instead, I gave him my old phone knowing Max could never get through. I doubted that Max needed running trails information that much.

'Can I make you something, Max? Coffee?'

'No,' he said, glancing at Robert. 'We've just finished and I've already taken up too much of his time. Got to get home. I need to make calls to Moscow before they close up for the day.'

Robert showed him to the door and I waited in the kitchen.

I strained my ears, trying to pick out what they were saying at the front door but they had gone out onto the drive and I just could feel the cold air blowing into the house.

I washed out the teapot, clank, clank, just a normal evening at home, but my antenna was tingling. What had made Robert so upset?

I heard the door close and turned. Robert was still leaning against it, as if he was considering running back out there and carrying on his conversation with Max in the street.

'Everything alright?' I said, still faking the breeziness.

He muttered something but I couldn't quite make out what he had said.

I went over to him and held out a nervous hand but he just walked past me.

'How was your day?' he said finally. He was staring into the blackness of the garden and didn't turn to face me.

'The usual,' I said.

'How come you haven't answered your phone all afternoon?'

'You called?' Anxiety collected across my chest and squeezed hard.

He faced me again. 'Twice. I sent you a few texts as well.'

I searched his voice, wondering if he was onto me.

'I've lost my phone,' I said quickly.

'When?'

'Monday. I went out for a run and it must have fallen out of my pocket. I retraced my steps, but I couldn't find it anywhere. I was hoping someone would find it and hand it in.'

'You'll be lucky.'

'That's what I thought, so I bought a new one. I have a new number. I'll text it over.'

'A new number?' He looked sceptical.

'It's a new phone. A pay as you go. Just a cheap thing.'

'Why did you get one of those?'

'In case my other one turns up.'

He poured a large glass of claret from the decanter on the countertop and gulped it down. When it left a blackcurrant rim around his mouth I didn't point it out.

'You can keep the same number, you know.'

'It's fine,' I said, rubbing my damp palm against my skirt. This was more difficult than I thought. I could barely explain why I had a new phone, let alone why I had a stalker.

He poured me a glass and handed it to me. 'I'll sort it out for you when I get a minute. You just need to get a PAC code from the phone provider, although I think you might have to speak to them.'

'I said it's fine,' I said, hearing my voice quaver.

'But what about all your contacts?'

I held up a hand. 'Robert, please, it's okay, honestly. We've got enough on our plates without sorting out crap like this. A pay as you go number will work for the minute.'

He looked at me, and then shook his head with a hint of exasperation.

There was a pause and I knew that was my moment, right there. To do as Lottie Callow had recommended. Tell my husband.

All afternoon, I'd been trying to muster up the courage to tell him about Chris Hannah, the messages, about Lottie Callow. But I couldn't.

'We should get those apps, Find My Phone. I said you should have installed it when you left your phone at the gym that time.'

I knew my window of opportunity had passed.

I poured myself a wine and held it to my chest.

'So what were you and Max were talking about?'

I wanted to change the subject. I wanted to know if it was the reason my husband was being so tetchy.

'Nothing.' There was a stiffness in this voice and I could see it in his stance, the defensive back, the level gaze into nothingness. The past few weeks had put my instincts on edge and now I could sense that there was something wrong with my husband. I suspected it was his conservation with Max. I hoped it was his conversation with Max.

'Is it Elena's gallery?' I ventured.

'No, it's not.'

'I haven't asked about Edelman supplying books to it yet, but I will, when I get my feet under the table.'

'Thanks. There's no rush.'

Things had been so good between us recently but tonight he was distance and edgy. Tonight he needed me to be the good, supportive wife.

'You can talk to me about it you know.'

'No,' he said so quietly that I could barely hear him. For a moment, I forgot about my own worries and stepped towards to touch his hand.

'It's nothing. Just business,' he said, as if he appreciated the gesture. 'You know what it's like sometimes.'

I knew I was going to get no more from him that evening. When he moved away to go and pour himself another glass of wine, I decided that the best thing was to leave him alone.

I knew better than anyone that you had to pick you moments, choose your time to open up and share what was troubling you, and right now Robert had to work through some things himself.

Chapter 26

I went home for my mum's birthday every year but this time, her annual celebration couldn't have come quick enough. I was desperate to get away.

Home. That's what I still called our little corner of Belfast, although it hadn't felt like home for a long time. The city had changed a lot in the decades that I'd been gone. The old town was on the up, a whisper of gentrification in the pizza joints and coffee shops lining Newtownards Road, even a hipster barbers advertising 'waxing' where the old pet shop used to be. A chalk board outside a café – vegan, no less – advertised spicy butternut squash and falafel. The old men falling out of O'Connor's pub would have choked on their JPS.

But there were still traces of the old Belfast I remembered – the murals on the Shankill Road, the peace walls built along the fault lines of the city – a reminder of the sectarian divisions that existed within the communities and continued to this day. My mum's house still looked the same too, save a new coat of paint on the door – red this time – mum liked to present a jolly face to the world. But aside from a few new cars parked at the kerb and the odd rust-streaked satellite dish, the rest of the street looked exactly as it had growing up, when I had dreamed of running away.

'My baby,' she cried, throwing her arms around me the moment I stepped into the hall. 'You're back.'

Her accent was still as rich and rounded as it had been when I had left all those years ago. Any trace of Northern Ireland had disappeared from my voice a long time ago, although when I had too much to drink, the soft uplift returned.

'A flying visit,' I said, following her back into the kitchen, the heart of her house. 'You know I've got the job . . .'

'Yes and I want to hear all about it. Has your man Robert finally gone and lost all his money now?'

I had to laugh. 'Not at all. He's doing well. In fact we're thinking of buying another place.'

'Whereabouts?'

'The Cotswolds.'

'Cotswolds? What's that got that we haven't got over here? You could buy a waterfront mansion in Bangor for the sort of money you two have.'

There was a faint disapproval in there somewhere about our lifestyle choices. Despite everything, mum had still not forgiven me for moving to England, couldn't understand why I hadn't wanted to come back to Belfast now the Troubles were long over.

'How's my darling Dilly? Show me some photos, I can't wait to see some of her at uni.'

'I haven't got any,' I admitted.

'None?'

Definite disapproval this time.

'They were on my phone, but I lost it last week.'

She shook her head but gave a slow smile.

'Not like you. Ach well, I'll call my granddaughter myself and get her to send some over. That's if she hasn't forgotten about her old nan.'

I watched my mother as she rattled about, filling the kettle and lining up the best china. She looked as beautiful as ever deep into her seventies; she had always made me feel dowdy and something of a disappointment as the daughter of 'the lovely Sonia O'Sullivan'. But it was good to see her looking so well; so many of my friends had begun to lose their parents to heart disease or dementia. You had to count your blessings, that's what Mam always said anyway.

'So what brings you home?' she asked when we were settled with our tea.

'I thought it was someone's birthday tomorrow.'

She waved a hand. 'Ah, I don't want to make a fuss.'

More code. She meant she wanted a big fuss to be made, especially since it was a significant birthday: seventy-five. Not quite the start of a new decade but in your advancing years something to celebrate. Not that you'd know my mum was deep into her eighth decade. Mam had always carried herself like a 1940s starlet, hair and shoes just right, never without 'whiplash red' lipstick, although I suspected they'd stopped making it years ago. Still, I had noticed a huff as she sat down and a creased brow as she lifted the teapot. It had been – shamefully – a year to the day since I had been back here and the difference was striking. Yes, she still looked ten years younger than she was, but she had diminished somehow. Less vital.

'So how are you keeping, Mam?'

She shrugged. 'Mustn't grumble.'

This was true, she never did. Not even when Dad was killed in a bomb near the Shankill Road when I was ten. He'd only gone for a drink, visiting friends he knew from the snooker circuit. And then he was gone. Mum let Auntie Siobhan move in with us for a week, but after the funeral it was business as usual, work at the post office, gin and tonics with her friends on Friday nights, ferrying me to gym class three times a week. Dad was hardly ever mentioned, except on the anniversary of his death when I used to listen through the wall of my bedroom wall and hear her crying.

In Belfast, your reputation was everything. Mum never let anything get her down, never let anyone believe she was anything other than strong. I only wished I was more like her.

'I'm taking us out for supper tonight, okay?' I said, keen to change the subject. 'I see there's a new French place down near the church.'

'Why would you waste your money on that when I have a perfectly decent meat pie in the fridge?'

'It's your birthday, Mam.'

'Sure. Why do you think I bought it?'

We compromised on the food prep with Mam allowing me to peel the carrots. Standing at the sink, I couldn't help feeling déjà vu over that afternoon at the barbeque when I had stood side by side with Dylan, mother and daughter sharing a homely activity.

'I did this with Dilly the other day,' I said, 'Only it was fruit not veg.'

There was still a small red scar from where I had sliced my finger.

'She's enjoying college, yes?'

'Loves it. She's been home a couple of times. I was worried at first. But Dylan is Dylan. She's tougher than I was.'

'You miss her.'

I nodded.

'It's hard, isn't it?'

She said it simply but with such power that I only realized how difficult it must have been for my mother, at that very moment.

Mam could never understand why I hadn't wanted to go to Queen's, our great college in the south west of the city, where many of my friends were going. But I'd wanted to get away from Belfast as soon as I could. I wanted to put it behind me, leave the memories of my father's violent death and just take away my recollections of happier times to a gentler place. I'd chosen my university simply because it sounded so quaint and lovely. Durham, with its soaring castle, and ancient traditions, its stone town with riverside meadows and tea-shops where you could while away afternoons over Jane Austen and saffron cake. I felt nothing bad could happen there, until it did.

'Do you think she'll come back?'

'To London? I don't know. I think so.'

Mam smiled. Her eyes still had that twinkle. 'That's what I thought.'

'Really?'

'No. I knew you were gone forever.'

I put down my knife and put my arms around, inhaling the familiar smell of pressed powder and Yardley perfume.

It felt so comfortable in my mother's arms, her big, warm blousy hug was like being wrapped up a thick, fluffy duvet on a cold winter's day – I almost had to stop myself saying 'five more minutes' when she pulled away.

'Why don't you move over?' I said suddenly.

'To England!'

'It's not such a daft idea.'

'I'd be on top of you.'

'The new house we've bought in the Cotswolds is big. There's lots of bedrooms, lots of space'

She glanced over suspiciously.

'How big? How many bedrooms?'

'Fifteen, I think.'

'Fifteen bedrooms? When I was Dylan's age, I had to share a bedroom with Auntie Siobhan and cousin Pat and Eileen.'

'Which is exactly why you deserve to live in Marley Hall, even if it's for just a few weeks at a time.'

'Marley Hall! Imagine me, Lady of the Manor. And what would Robert say about it?' she chided.

For once, I didn't care.

The pie was delicious. In fact, I couldn't remember the last time I'd had a real pie. Pie just didn't exist in our high-end middle-class bubble where carbs were verboten and pastry only allowed on French mini-breaks. As we ate, I sat and listened as Mam caught me up on the local gossip. Her friend Orla had lost her job in the High Street bank when it had closed to make way for a gastro-bar, Father Kenneth, the priest at All Hallows had been 'retired' over 'financial irregularities'.

By six o'clock I was exhausted with trying to keep everyone straight in my head and excused myself to have a bath. I luxuriated in the hot, bubbly water and thought about how much Robert spent on our bathroom with its retractable skylight, tropical rain-shower and the flatscreen TV inserted into the wall, deciding that all a bathroom really needed was hot water and decent bubble bath.

My mum knocked on the door and told me that my room was ready. By that she meant clean sheets on the bed and a neat pile of baby-pink towels on the chair by the door. I towelled myself down, slipped on my mums fluffy dressing down and went into her bedroom to fetch the hairdryer. I saw my degree certificate was hung above the dressing table as it had been for all these years – old and yellowing now despite the glass frame. I still couldn't look at it without the prickle of shame collecting in my chest. I padded back into my room, eyes downcast.

Most of the things pinned to my own bedroom walls had the opposite effect: they still made me smile. Posters of *Top Gun* and *Desperately Seeking Susan*, a calendar from 1988 still showing December, a kitten wearing a Santa hat. The bookshelf contained all my teenage favourites from Jilly Cooper and Shirley Conran's *Lace*, right through to Evelyn Waugh's classics and a collection of poetry by Yeats. A present from him – from Chris.

Downstairs I heard by mother laugh loudly at the television – something Simon Cowell had said, no doubt. She'd always loved her Saturday night television and I knew she wouldn't mind me stuck up here, would probably prefer it if I gave her an hour's peace.

I got on my hands and knees and reached for the shoe box that I had always kept under my bed. Back in the day I would sit cross-legged on the carpet and read everything contained within it.

Today, I climbed on the bed, propped a pillow in the corner and went back in time. The photos in their little card packets: me in untidy school uniform, me with the family at Christmas, me snapped at a wedding I couldn't remember. And there were dozens of me from my uni days looking so young – a child! Parties, fancy dress, formal balls, grinning and laughing all the way through – a whole new life, a life that had made me forget why I was there in the first place. Pictures of people I'd almost forgotten existed, suddenly brought jarringly into the present. James Harbour, Simon Winterton, Vicky Roper, all people I'd spent hours, weeks and years with. Uni friends, course mates and refugees from my long-forgotten past. And right there at my side, grinning and laughing too, was Chris.

Chris Hannah, slimmer, younger, with a droopy indie-boy haircut and a Levellers T-shirt. Chris holding up a plastic pint glass in salute, Chris and me, kissing in front of a statue. We were inseparable. Young love. Burning bright, too hot to hold.

I pulled out a folder rammed with papers: flyers for long-forgotten gigs, tickets for a Christmas Ball, the programme from a student production of Macbeth where I'd fancied the guy playing the lead, even a load of stuff from my course: timetables, tutorial groups, a form for joining the library. Why had I kept that?

The letters were at the bottom – they weren't the oldest things in the box but they were the most secret. Pink and white envelopes were ones from friends – Donna, Suze and Moira – girls from sixth form who had stayed in Northern

Ireland. I opened one from Donna. Aiden – Donna's boyfriend who had started off as a fresher's fling – had proposed during a weekend break to Donegal. She was wondering whether to accept, debating whether she was too young. I smiled sadly as I reread her letter, wishing I could have told my twenty-year-old friend to enjoy every precious moment that they had together – because Aiden would die in a kite-surfing accident at the age of thirty, not quite ten years into a blissfully happy marriage.

Moira on the other hand, spent pages pining over her next-door neighbour, Samuel, dissecting his every move, every conversation. No one knew back then that Sam was gay, that he would have to move to London to come out quietly, but that he would return to Belfast in his forties and become the perfect godfather to Moira's daughter Rose.

Suzanne's letter was the one that invited me travelling. Goa, Nicaragua, Perth, she wasn't entirely sure where she was going yet, only that she had gone to STA travel, priced up some round-the-world tickets and was I in for the ride? It was going to be a blast, she said. Full moon parties, white beaches, and did I know that men out-numbered women fifty to one in the Outback? It was going to be the trip of a lifetime. And it was, kind of.

Finally, I opened one from Chris.

Dear Rach

I hope this reaches you at your mum's – I'm guessing that's where you're spending the summer. Did you get that job at the pet shop? I still don't really understand why you couldn't stay. I'm doing double shifts at the Spotted Horse now, so we could have lived like kings!!

Seriously though Rach, I don't blame you for what happened, really I don't – it was all my own stupid mistake. I wish I could turn back time, but no use crying over spilt milk and all that.

I know what you said that night by the bridge, but I'm sure I could change your mind if you'd let me? I haven't done anything but work since you left, so I've saved up a bit of money. Give me the nod (phone me at the pub?) and I'll be straight on that ferry.

You said not to use the 'L' word anymore, so I'll leave you with the words of the great poet Morrissey: 'you're the one for me, fatty.'

I miss you though.

Chris x

With shaking hands, I slid the letter back into its envelope and squeezed my eyes tight. I felt as if I'd been punched. Had I really been that callous?

After all he'd done for me, I'd effectively cut him out of my life, moved back to Belfast without even telling him where I'd gone and then headed off to Thailand with Suzanne without so much as a goodbye. I could feel the pain behind his words, the confusion and hurt. Why have you done this? What did I do? I caught my reflection in the mirror on the dresser: dismayed and appalled. And a dawning sense of disquiet. Because over the past few weeks, I had done exactly the same thing to Chris again. Led him on, made him care and then cut him dead.

And it gave Chris Hannah two very good reasons to hate me.

Chapter 27

I was tempted to stay in Belfast. I felt insulated there. No phone, no computers. Just Mam's old house full of books and comforting bric-a-brac. A simpler life.

On her actual birthday I took her for afternoon tea at the Merchant Hotel in the city centre and we indulged on tiny scones and finger sandwiches presented to us on three tier cake stand. We had a makeover at the House of Fraser on Victoria Square, saw the Titanic Exhibition down by the docks and went for a walk by the river in Roseau Park, enjoying the crunch of dry Autumn leaves underfoot.

With Dylan gone, I knew I could have stayed here for a least a couple of days more without Robert grumbling too much. But my job at Edelman meant that I had to get back to London and it was the first time since I'd started work that I resented it.

'So what you're saying, you no want calls put through? No calls . . . at all?'

Valentina, Edelman's receptionist, looked at me suspiciously. She was gorgeous, all high cheekbones and cat-like eyes but she also had that other essential quality you needed in frontline staff: she looked like she could snap your neck if you got out of line.

'No,' I said patiently. 'I'm saying I want them forwarded to my mailbox.'

'Mailbox,' she repeated. 'Everyone's?'

'God no!' I said urgently, instantly imagining the entire office going silent with everyone's phone calls, including Ian's, being routed to my mailbox.

'No, just my calls. All calls for—' I held up my security pass so she could read my name '—Rachel Reeves.'

The girl nodded, her eyes narrowing as she compared my headshot with the wide-eyed woman in front of her. I could hardly blame her; it was a fairly crazy request. It wasn't as if I was the CEO or some celebrity likely to be harassed by fans, I was just some grunt doing sickness cover.

But I knew it was time to make some changes to protect myself, and with Ian Sinclair out of the office for three days on an international publishing conference in Latvia, now seemed as good a time as ever.

'Internal calls are fine,' I added. 'They can go straight to my desk.'

'Internal calls go to Rachel Reeves,' she nodded, writing it down as if humouring a lunatic. Which I suppose was what it sounded like.

The next conversation was with the post-boys who lived in the vast control centre in the basement. I could hear the sound of Kanye West blaring out of the sound system by the time I'd even got out of the lift. The atmosphere became immediately subdued when I walked in, the sound of loud, raucous laughter dying down and I looked for Bryan who was in charge of post.

I showed him the pile of postcards that had been collecting in my absence. I had seven of them now. *Money and Morals* by Eric Gill, *Non Stop* by Brian W Aldiss, *Fallen Star* by James Blish, George's Sava's *Link of Two Hearts*. Today's arrival was a line drawing of an angel on a blood red background – *Love* by Walter de la Mare, one of my favourite writers. I adored his poems, his gothic horror stories, but this had turned me right off them.

Bryan looked at them, puzzled.

'What are these?'

I took them away from him before he could read the back of them.

'Junk mail. Anything like this addressed to me I want you to hold back okay? Put them to one side. I will collect them at the end of every week.'

I pressed a twenty-pound note into his hand and he didn't question the request any further.

I took the postcard back upstairs. I was desperate to get rid of them but Charlotte Callow had been strict about keeping things as evidence in case we needed them for any future legal action or prosecution.

In the steely confines of the lift I took a moment to read the message that had been send to me, one word a day.

Thus the candle has singed the moth.

I'd studied enough Shakespeare over the years to recognize the quote. *The Merchant of Venice*, although I couldn't recall which character had said it. But I knew what it meant. That our helpless attraction to something glittering but dangerous could harm or destroy us.

But who was the moth? Was it him? Or me?

I rode the lift back up to the office, mentally ticking off the things I had to do today. Now even more than ever, I had to keep on top of work, couldn't let anything slip. I felt like those old-time jugglers spinning plates; if I took my eye off one, they would wobble and crash to the ground. I had the Simeon Averill party to organize and was working on cover ideas for two authors on my list. Weighed down with guilt, I had volunteered to help Jemma Kwan plan the office Christmas drinks.

I was still forming my internal to-do list as I approached my desk – to find Serena perched on the corner.

'Hi,' I said, slightly taken aback. Serena worked two floors above me, on a different imprint. She'd popped down a couple of times during my first week to see how I was going, but generally she kept away, choosing to meet me in the ground floor foyer on the odd occasion we met for lunch.

Suspicion kicked in. Had the receptionist immediately called her to report my oddball request? Had Bryan in the postroom reported me to HR about the twenty pounds I had slipped into his hand. But no, that was just paranoia, wasn't it?

'Do you have a minute?' she said. No smile, all business. Without waiting for a reply – of course I had a minute – she turned and walked back down the corridor, turning into the boardroom, expecting me to follow her.

'Shut the door,' she said, as I followed her in.

'What's up?'

She was making me nervous.

'We have an issue,' said Serena. I noticed she was carrying an A4 notebook. Something with stuff inside – a large envelope by the looks of it.

'I'm hoping it's just a prank gone wrong, but, well . . . you'd better see for yourself.' She pulled out the envelope and sat down at the desk, glancing over to the interior windows to check that no one was watching.

She took something out of the envelope – photos by the looks of it – large black and white prints, the sort you saw so rarely these days in the age of Cameraroll and Dropbox.

When she handed me one, I tried to keep calm as I looked at it. It wasn't a pornographic image, but it wasn't far from it.

'They arrived in Ian's post this morning. As you know he's out of the office, but he'd asked Lydia to handle his mail in case anything important came in. Lydia brought them straight to me. She didn't know what to do but knows that we're friends.'

Boom, boom. My heart was thudding so hard but I had the horrible sense that the knockout punch was yet to come.

The image was of a woman, standing hands on hips wearing nothing but a bondage mask, a black studded cuff and a tiny pair of leather pants cut high.

The mask obscured the model's face but the passing similarity to me was immediate – she was a similar build to me, small breasts, high waisted, with the same shoulder-length blonde hair.

'You should read the back,' said Serena.

I knew from her tone of voice that I wouldn't want to.

Rachel Reeves, Adventurer

'This isn't me,' was my initial response, looking at my friend in panic.

She handed me another one. The same model, I guessed, although the face had been cropped to the mouth. Her legs were splayed, she was naked except for the same pair of tight black pants, her hand was pushed inside the front of them, touching herself.

I turned it over, hardly daring to see what it said.

Rachel Reeves, Masturbator

The third image was off the same woman. Side-on this time, wearing a peek-hole bra and thigh-high boots. You could see her mound of nipple, the curve of buttock. A naked man thrust into her from behind, his hands gripped to her hips. You could feel the raw erotic power of desire radiating off the page even those both faces of the models were obscured.

The reverse of the third photograph contained just one word.

Rachel Reeves, Adulterer.

'And there was this,' said Serena finally.

A note. Typed.

I like taking pictures.

'I'm not sure what that means,' said Serena, sounding as if she was losing her patience. But I did.

It was a message. To me. I looked at Serena but I didn't say anything. I couldn't see for the cloud of tears smearing the front of my eyes like a film of Vaseline.

'Rachel, we've got to discuss this.'

Serena tried to catch my eye,

'Who's seen this?' I said in a thin croak.

'Lydia. Me. Obviously it could have been worse, if Ian had been in the office. Can you imagine if the postroom had opened them, if the envelope hadn't been sealed?'

I didn't want to think about that. Instead I looked at the photos again, and I knew right then, that I couldn't escape. Whatever I tried to do he was one step ahead, tightening the screws bit by bit.

'As you might imagine, the company takes anything sexual, anything contentious like this, extremely seriously.'

She sounded tight and formal. It didn't feel particularly loyal.

She'd been dragged into it and I could tell she resented it and was trying to keep her distance from any potential fallout.

'This is nothing to do with me,' I fired back.

'It certainly seems that way.'

I gulped hard.

'Lydia had better not report it to HR. I think she found them quite distressing,' said Serena, pressing ahead.

I didn't look at my friend, annoyed that she was laying it on. I could have done without the curt disapproval and conjecture of what might happen. It was almost as if she was enjoying it.

It was another few seconds before anyone said anything. I could hear the rise and fall of Serena's breath, slow and steady. For a moment I hated her, jealous of her perfect, ordered world.

'Why don't you tell me what the hell's going on?' she said finally. There was a still the element of the boss/employee

201

dynamic there, but mostly I suspected she was pissed off that I hadn't spoken to her sooner.

'Rachel, tell me,' she repeated, softer this time, more supportive, the voice I needed to hear. And I started to cry. Heavy sobs that I had been holding in for so long.

Serena touched my arm and then put an arm across my shoulder. It was stiff at first – Serena was not naturally a tactile woman – but when she pulled me tighter, I knew I had to tell her everything.

'I'm having trouble with someone,' I said, barely getting the words out.

'What sort of trouble?' she said, pulling away from me.

It was time to tell her everything. The dozens of emails, the hundreds of Twitter notifications, the postcards, texts and the silent phone calls to our house. The hundreds of pounds I'd spent on taxis because I was too scared to walk up Highgate Hill from the tube station especially now the nights were drawing in because the clocks had gone back.

She listened as I spoke and I could see her brows knit, even the two vertical lines I knew she had softened with filler became more pronounced.

'You have a stalker?'

I nodded.

'Christ, Rach, how could you not tell me about something like that?'

'It's all happened so fast. I only went to see a solicitor last Thursday.'

'You need a lawyer?'

I didn't reply.

'Who is it?'

I bit my lips to stop myself from crying some more.

'I don't know.'

'Can you hazard a guess?"

I shrugged. 'Possibly the neighbour's carer. The one who caught us on the kitchen table.'

Her eyes widened. 'The Peeping Tom?'

I shrugged.

'You did do all the checks on this guy? Followed up references?'

'Yes, I did all that.'

I had. I'd even checked again when Bill suggested he might be stealing.

I paused. I had her on-side. Now it was time to land the killer punch.

'More likely it's a guy from university.'

'What guy?' she said. She had the scent of blood. I couldn't let it go now even if I wanted it to.

I blew out some air.

'An ex-boyfriend. We bumped into each other in Soho, had a coffee, swapped numbers. I think it's him.'

Serena looked at me until I met her gaze.

'You had a coffee?' Her tone was flat, accusatory.

My cheek colour gave the game away.

'You slept with him.' She said it so matter-of-factly there wasn't even time to construct a lie.

'The night of the Emerald launch party. That's where I met him. It was a mistake.'

'I'll say.' Serena lowered her voice. 'I assume Robert has no idea about all this.'

The displeasure was back in her voice. I didn't blame her. Robert was her friend. Sometimes I felt they got on with each other better than they did with me. And although they sometimes butted heads, their egos dictating that neither of them backed down, they both recognized each other's passion and drive which resulted in respect.

'I've not told him yet. He's got two massive projects on the go and he's stressed enough as it is.'

'Rachel, you need to tell him. If this guy, the one you shagged, is sending photos to Ian, how long before he's contacting Robert? It's a hell of a risk to think he won't, and to try and keep it a secret especially when things seem to be escalating.'

'It's not that easy . . .'

Her grey eyes narrowed.

'Did you always know he was mentally unstable?'

'Who?'

'The university sweetheart. Your stalker.'

'Look, I don't know it's him.'

'Say it was . . .'

'He doesn't seem it,' I admitted.

'What does he do?'

'Something in the hospitality sector. Events, I think. He was vague.'

'Where does he work?'

'Not sure. I googled him but couldn't find anything.'

'Sounds like you don't know anything about him at all. Don't you think you should find out?'

I twisted my wedding band around my finger. It felt loose, bigger. I had lost weight.

'The lawyer said I shouldn't have anything to do with him.'

'You don't want to invite him out for another *coffee*, no. But I think you should at least know who you're dealing with, rather than trying forget about it and hope he will go away. He could be properly dangerous.'

'I have these strange feelings too. As if I'm being watched.'

'Followed?'

'I don't know.'

'Shit, Rachel.'

She looked up. Her face looked paler.

'Well, at least you've told me.'

'You prised it out of me.'

We both gave a little macabre laugh.

'You should go to the police. If you think he's following you. Taking pictures of you . . .'

'I don't want to go to the police.'

Serena was the last person I wanted to tell why I had loyalties to Chris Hannah. She never needed to know.

She looked at me with the exasperated expression she sometimes gave her teenage boys.

'I don't want to make this more complicated than it needs to be. If I get the police involved then I'll have to tell Robert . . . I can't risk that.'

Serena nodded and didn't say anything more.

'Thank you,' I said quietly. 'It feels good to tell someone I'm not paying.'

She met me with a level gaze.

'Can I ask a question?'

I nodded.

'Why?' she said simply. 'Why did you sleep with your ex-boyfriend?'

'Because I wanted to,' I said honestly. It felt good to be so blunt, so true after hiding and lying for so many weeks.

She gave a warm, low laugh.

'For a moment I thought you were going to blame it on the booze.'

When she gave me a hug, I thought I was going to cry.

Serena put the envelope back in her notebook, squeezing it tight as if she would never open it again.

'It will sort itself out. This weirdo, he'll get bored, things will get back to normal. But at some point, you need to think about your relationship.'

'I have. We both have. Me and Robert. We're trying hard to make it work. In fact, we're buying a place in the Cotswolds not too far from you'

'Really? Where?'

'Ipslow. Marley Hall.'

'Marley Hall? Wow. I know that place. It's beautiful.'

I thought I saw her mouth tighten. It didn't matter. We were all envious of something.

And besides I had bigger things to worry about.

Chapter 28

'I'm going for a ride,'

I was drying my hair in the dressing room when I saw Robert's reflection in the mirror dressed in his Lycra cycling gear. I hadn't seen this look before. An all-in-one bib shorts that looked like spandex lederhosen. From this distance I could see the undulations of muscles in his legs, finely tuned and sinewy like an athlete's and the ripple of taut stomach under his skin-tight shiny top. Of the many reasons why I slept with an ex-boyfriend, a husband who had gone to seed was not one of them.

'Why can't you have a lie-in at the weekend, like normal people,' I smiled, aware that I was flirting, trying to make an effort, trying to make myself remember that I had a perfect husband, that we had the perfect life.

'Lie-ins are for losers,' he said putting on his fingerless gloves.

I wasn't sure if he was joking.

Robert liked cycling and climbing to relax – it came with the driven, Alpha mind-set. That need to do something, often something high-octane and difficult, to wind-down was something I had never understood. Who needed Tough Mudder when you could have an oily bath and some champagne truffles? But I didn't say anything as I knew my husband needed his Ironman workouts today more than ever.

He'd seemed distracted for at least a week and I could trace it back to his meeting with Max Miskov. Robert hadn't mentioned anything problematic about Elena's gallery development, but he never really discussed the ins and out of his business with me. I imagined him turned over his problems with every rotation of the pedals, and he was keeping fit in the process. Was this what successful people were like? Driven but also efficient? Perhaps I needed to get back to Zumba.

'Why don't we go out for dinner?' he said kissing me on the top of my head. 'I'll ring around when I get back. See where can squeeze us in.'

I waited until I heard the door close behind him, then another few moments to check he didn't come back for a forgotten water bottle or his phone, then went to the upstairs window that overlooked the drive.

I watched the garage door open and then watched him steer his bike onto the path. He checked the tyres and the chain and threw one leg over the frame. A slight wobble and he was off towards the Heath.

I felt a pang of affection that hovered on pity. I knew he would hate me for that if he could see inside my head.

When I was sure he was gone I pulled my laptop from out of the dressing table drawer and took that to the kitchen. There was a tub of mango in the fridge and I took it out, but once I had ripped off the lid, I didn't feel like it. Gin for breakfast was all I craved. Instead, I made one of Robert's strong coffees.

I flipped the computer to check the new Gmail account that I had set up to contact old friends from Durham.

Most of them hadn't been too difficult to track down at all, although it had meant going on social media and LinkedIn. Things had ramped up considerably over the past few days. More fake profiles, more emails to my work address. He was using filthy, foul language now. I was an ugly mother fucking bitch and an old witch with a tight anus and a dried-up snatch. I wanted to ignore it, ignore it all, but we were past that now. Instead, I wrote everything down in a diary.

Serena had one too after she had volunteered to go through everything with me every day; as she pointed out, echoing the advice that Lottie Callow had given me, everything needed to be read in case the tenor of them became dangerous or overtly threatening. She was right about something else too. I needed to know more about Chris Hannah even if I didn't get it from the horse's mouth.

I had made a start on that project straight after Serena had taken the photographs away, deliberately targeting old friends with a connection to Chris Hannah – students from our course, or people who were in his college. Chris was friendly enough but had still been an outsider, at Durham to study not drink and party. He'd had a part-time job at the local pub – not one of the popular student bars – but I had even tracked down a couple of his co-workers from there.

My memory box in Belfast had helped jog my memory for names. Some of them I barely recognized, others instantly brought back vivid memories. When I tracked them down online, some seemed unchanged save the addition of wives and children, others had packed on the pounds or lost their hair. And some had simply disappeared – or at least, had managed to swerve the gravitational pull of social media.

I'd probed all of them gently, said I was gauging interest for a possible reunion and dropped Chris into the conversation hoping for a bite. Louise Parker, a girl from our English course had replied first, saying she was already planning a reunion at the Soho Theatre in a couple of weeks' time. One of our college mates was doing a stand-up show there, she was group-buying tickets and did I want to go along? Others were slower to get in touch and when they mentioned Chris it was to say they were 'crap at keeping in touch'. No one seemed to have seen him in years. He had simply fallen off the radar.

There was one message that looked more promising. Mike Weller had lived in the room opposite Chris in the first year and they had been good friends. By the time we had started dating in our final year, when we had dropped everyone around us to spend exclusive time together, Chris and Mike only saw each other for a weekly five-a-side match at the sports hall.

But it appeared he had some knowledge of what his friend had been up to once we had scattered away from Durham. I read his note on LinkedIn for the second time.

Hi Rachel.

Great to hear from you. Glad to hear that life is treating you well. Always up for a reunion. I work in Reading – IT. Never quite made it as a Premiership footballer or even anything faintly to do with sport. But I do enough running around after my twin ten-year-old lads to keep me fit.

In London three days a week. Love to see you for lunch or beer even if the reunion doesn't happen. Not seen Chris for over a decade. I feel really bad about everything that happened.

I stopped and read the last line one more time. What had happened to make Mike Weller feel bad? There was obviously a story there and I wanted to hear it. Instinct told me that bouncing a few messages back and forth wasn't going to get to the heart of whatever it was that went on. I suggested meeting up the following week and lunch was planned for the Monday.

My coffee had gone cold and my feet were chilly.

I wiped my browsing history clean from my computer before I closed it and rubbed my eyes.

At least some progress that been made which was more than could be said for my internet search about Chris. How could there be nothing? I'd looked once before in the days after our one-night stand – gingerly probing around the internet looking for photos, information, evidence of a girl-friend or wife. There had been nothing then and nothing now on a deeper dive, scrolling twenty pages of more into a Google search. It was almost as if he didn't exist.

I threw my coffee down the sink and watched the bronze rings bleed around the white porcelain before I rinsed them away. The doorbell rang and I jolted, spikes of cortisol rushing around my body.

I remembered once reading about the horrific Boxing Day tsunami in Southeast Asia, how elephants and birds had fled the coast minutes before the fatal tidal waves had struck, and now my sixth sense was prickling now.

Despite thousands of years of evolution, we were all animals at heart and we had still not lost our nose for danger.

I picked up my phone then walked to the door.

Although I felt as if I was being proactive, I was still constantly on edge. I hated being alone in the house. That week, Robert had gone to Geneva for the night, and I'd got another call to the house. Six crisp rings at nine o'clock. I'd picked it up, always worried that it might be Dylan, but there was no one at the end, just the vaguely audible sound of breathing. They didn't ring back but I didn't sleep a wink. At work, I'd felt sick with exhaustion and had to go home early. I'd told Serena and she said that the next time that Robert went away I had to stay at her house.

I peered through the peep hole now and sighing with relief when I saw the Barry, our regular postman in the fish-eye lens, standing on the step.

'Package for you, today,' he grinned, as if I was in for a nice surprise.

It was addressed to me, but I couldn't remember having ordered anything.

Closing the door, I took the parcel upstairs. It was long and slim, the shape of a Harry Potter wand box we had once bought for Dylan when she was mad about everything to do with Hogwarts. It was wrapped in brown paper. I used my nail clippers to snip the string and perched on the end of the bed, unwrapped it slowly, tearing back a long stripe of paper, wondering what it could be. My heart was thudding in my chest. There was a glimpse of dark grey cardboard, thick and texture – the sort of package you got in expensive stores or Net-a-Porter.

I put the box on my legs, pausing before I opened the lid. My robe had slipped open to expose a square of thigh and the box was cold against my skin.

I could hear drilling in the street – I had seen a series of cones and barricades being erected outside Bill's house the day before and obviously the road works had begun. Usually I hated the angry, monotonous sound of construction which always reminded me of the dentist, metal against enamel, but now I was grateful that it wasn't silent. I didn't feel quite so lonely. Someone was close – a builder, a workman in case there is trouble.

The lid pulled away from the box with the expensive resistance of quality. Nestled on a bed of pale grey silk was a black leather whip, stiff and thin like a riding crop.

I peeked under expecting something else to drop out, half expecting one of those notes you saw in the movies where the letters had been cut out of newspapers. For the avoidance of any doubt that I'd been sent a sex toy and not an equestrian aid, there was a small white card.

Want to play?

I recoiled away from it, unable to touch it or look of it for a second longer. I felt sick, the world was spinning, the room tilting from side to side as if I was in rough seas. I stood up but my knees seemed to buckle under me. Somehow I made it to the en-suite. I gripped the side of the basin and my body retched and a thin dribble of vomit and phlegm trickled down the sink.

211

I was shaking but I couldn't stop. I was desperate for a drink – my Devon gin, vodka, anything, but I knew it wouldn't help.

My throat was tightening.

I wiped my mouth with some tissue and threw it down the loo. I took my toothbrush from the cabinet, applied a long stripe of paste and scrubbed my teeth and my gums. When I had finished, I blew into a cupped hand and smelled my breath, still tainted with the lingering smell of sick.

The card was handwritten. It wasn't something that came in every box – it was a personal message to me. From him.

I felt as if he was getting closer, that the screws were getting tighter.

My phone was in dressing gown pocket. Where it always was these days – on me, just in case.

I pulled it out, swiped to Google and leaned against the edge of the tub.

I needed something, someone to grab onto to.

I knew which site to go too.

Of all the bits of information that Lottie Callow had given me, the web address for YouAreNotAlone.com was the best one thing. The home page was the usual checklist for stalking victims, but it was the forum that I visited, sometimes every day. It made uncomfortable reading – the stories of intimidation, harassment and threats. A barista had to put up with the same customer, a friend of the owner, who came into the coffee shop every single day and watched her. Someone else was being targeted by their dentist and had only realized it was him when he'd had his fingers in her mouth during a check-up, someone else found their ex-girlfriend hiding in their car, having slashed the back seat with a razor and threatened to do the same to her wrists. Their profile pictures offered no names, addresses but I felt as if I knew them all.

A red strip across the top of the page told me I had to sign in if I wanted to contribute to the conversation.

I gave one of the fake emails I'd been using to log in an created a post.

How do you know when your stalker is dangerous? He has just sent me a whip.

I felt better when I'd sent it and I knew there would be replies soon. It was a supportive community, and advice was often extensive. I supposed it was free therapy for everyone.

I put the phone back in my pocket, resolving to come back to it later. Robert would be back soon and my laptop was still on the dining room table.

I went back in to the bedroom and gasped when I saw Robert walking through the door.

'You're back,' I said, barely stopping myself from shrieking.

'You were complaining,' he smiled, pulling his cycling top over his head and wiping his face with it.

'I wasn't complaining. I was just wondering where you found the energy,' I said, trying to keep my voice controlled.

My eyes glanced over at the bed but Robert saw me do it. In the moment that his eyes were covered I went to grab the whip off the bed. But it was too late, he had seen it.

'What's that?'

It was too late to hide it. At that moment I decided there was only one way to play it.

I put the lid back on the box, looking down, concentrating hard, trying to force my cheeks not to blush.

'I thought it might be fun but now I think it's silly.'

Robert threw his top on the bed and came over to me.

I could smell the sweat that glistened on his chest hair.

'Come on, what is it?' he chided.

He lifted it carefully out of my hands and looked inside.

'Been reading *Fifty Shades of Grey*?'

There was a tiny smile on his face. It was the lightest I had seen his expression in days.

He took the whip out of the box, handing it carefully, as if it was made from crystal.

I tried to smile and took the box back and put it on the bed.

He'd seen the whip – that was bad enough. I didn't want him to see the message.

'I bought it on a whim. You said we should make an effort. But now I feel stupid.'

'You shouldn't.'

He moved closer. I could see his hardness beneath his ridiculous Lycra bib shorts.

Had I stopped to think about what was happening, I should have realized it was the perfect moment to tell him the truth, about the stalking, about my suspicions of Chris and Nathan. I should have realized that pretending I had bought the whip myself was only making it more difficult to finally tell him the truth. But I didn't. I'd started with my charade and it was too late to turn back.

'Where did you get it?'

'The sort of place I don't usually shop.'

I shocked myself at how convincingly I could lie but I had made the decision and I couldn't turn back now.

He pulled the belt of the robe and the thin silk fell apart quite easily.

I was naked underneath. Robert reached for the crop and brushed the end of it against my nipples. I was ashamed to feel aroused. I had always been curious about the things I saw in the sex shops. Not the sort of places that were peppered around Soho, the dark doors with little notices that said 'Poppers! And Girls upstairs'. But the smart places where mannequins in leather harnesses and lace panties stood, hand on hip, in the shop windows. But I had never done anything like this.

'Shut the curtains,' I whispered.

'No one's watching,' he said as he turned me around and kissed the curve of my neck.

'Please,' I insisted as we paused to close the blinds. Because I didn't believe him.

Chapter 29

I lay back on the bed, naked, hot and spent. My buttocks were still smarting. Robert was staring at the ceiling. He looked tired but content, a man pleased with his performance. I had hated every moment of it.

Ding-dong.

'How important do you think that is?' he asked, welded to the mattress.

'If it's a delivery they'll wait twenty seconds and then dump it at Bill's,' I replied, too sore to get up.

He sighed and sat up.

'I'd better get up then. My new cycling helmet went missing for a week the last time anything got dropped off there. Mind you, it's probably Dylan.'

'Dylan?' This time I sat up. 'Again?'

'She texted me last night to say she was coming,' said Robert, putting on his towelling robe before he went downstairs.

Of course, I was glad to see my daughter, but I didn't want her to see me like this.

I jumped in the shower and lathered myself with soap. There was no time to wash my hair. Instead, I rinsed the suds off my skin and turned off the jets. I rubbed myself down with a towel and put on some jogging bottoms and a T-shirt that were hanging on the radiator. I hid the whip, wrapping it in a carrier bag and stashing it under the bed until the time came to dispose of it.

'Dylan, sweetheart.'

I was hot and bothered, a guilty mother barely covering up her indiscretions.

I pecked her on the cheek then moved away.

'You two not up already?' she said, with a look that said *I know what you've been doing.*

'Where are your keys?' I said, changing the subject.

'Couldn't find them.'

She picked up an apple from the bowl and bit into it.

'I didn't know you were coming.'

'I sent you a text but you never got back to me.'

I frowned. 'I've got a new number. I did give it to you. Did you use it?'

'Soz. Probably not.'

Robert was already making French toast. He hardly ever cooked but that was the one thing he was good at.

Dylan disappeared upstairs to put her bag in her room.

I went back into the kitchen, got the carton of orange juice out of the fridge and poured into three tumblers as if there was nothing wrong.

'Icing sugar, berries,' called Robert, his back turned to us but a firmness in his voice like he was navigating a military operation.

'Is this what your life is like now?' grinned Dylan sitting down at the breakfast bar. 'Getting up late, French toast on tap . . . Glad to see you have finally got Dad well trained.'

'Believe me, this is for your benefit,' I smiled, washing the raspberries in the sieve and putting them in a bowl, enjoying the moment.

'What time did you leave Birmingham?' I said, glancing at the clock. I assumed the trains were regular but still the journey

216

was almost an hour and half, with extra travelling time at either end she must have been up at the crack of dawn.

'Dunno. I was half asleep. But I got a taxi from halls to New Street so it wasn't too bad.'

I looked at her. 'I thought you said you were getting the coach next time.'

'Yeah, but it would have taken a zillion hours.'

'Are you sure you're enjoying uni?' I said it casually but it was an important question.

'Yes. But I like London too and you know loads of my mates are still around.'

'Speaking of the Prodigal Daughter,' said Robert, adding some bacon to the plates of toast, and then dishing them out, 'David's coming back.'

'Has Uncle Dave transitioned?' said Dylan entirely seriously.

'Not to my knowledge,' replied Robert, licking icing sugar from his finger. 'I mean he's moving back to England. With the family.'

'You didn't tell me,' I said, glancing at my husband, surprised he hadn't mentioned it earlier. 'It's been what? Ten years? What's happened?'

'Not sure. He only emailed me yesterday. We'll find out in a couple of weeks. They're flying into Heathrow from Kuala Lumpur.'

'Just like that.'

'Apparently so.'

'Where are they going to live?'

I had no idea what their circumstances were but David didn't seem to have much money. The obvious solution, unless they had other arrangements, was for David, his wife and their twin girls to stay with us. Any other time I might have been hesitant. I liked David and his wife but entertaining a family of four for a weekend was hard work, let alone indefinitely. But now, the idea of a house full of people felt like a godsend.

Robert shrugged.

'What about here?'

'You're kidding,' said Robert with an alarmed expression. 'David's my brother but he's a total pig. He'll wreck the house and not even notice.'

Dylan hadn't offered an opinion, which was unusual. 'You look a bit pale,' I said looking at my daughter more closely. She hadn't eaten much of her French toast.

'I'm fine.'

She didn't look fine. She looked as if she was ill or had been up all night.

'Are you sure?'

'Got a bit of a headache but yeah, I'm okay.'

'You aren't studying too hard, are you?' I asked, turning my attention away from David's domestic arrangements.

'No. It's a doss compared to A levels.'

'I wouldn't doss too much,' I said as carefully as I could. 'One minute you're freewheeling in your first term, there next minute you've got too much ground to make up for a decent degree.'

She glared at me.

'God, why are you grilling me like this? If I'd known I was going to get the Spanish inquisition I would have stayed at uni.'

I held up my hands. I thought we'd passed the teen attitude phase but she was jumpier than ever.

'Sorry, I'm your mother. It's my job to worry about you.'

'Guys, calm down,' said Robert, downing his orange juice.

'Tell Mum that,' she sniffed and went to the sink for some water.

I offered to go and get some painkillers. I kept our medicines in a box in the bathrooms so I went upstairs, hoping that my absence from the kitchen would simmer down the tension. I had a root around the first aid kit, past the diarrhoea tablets from a trip to Vietnam two years ago, ear-plugs, plasters, Savlon, even sachets of Calpol that must have been seven or eight years old. Where was good old-fashioned paracetamol when you needed it, I wondered, picking up a box of Cold and Flu Max capsules which were possibly too heavy duty for the job.

I crossed into the dressing room to check my handbag to see if there was any ibuprofen lurking around in there but the only thing at the bottom were cab receipts.

As I mindlessly looked for the medicine, I wondered why our daughter was being so cagey. I was about to go downstairs with the flu capsules when I looked into Dylan's bedroom and saw her rucksack and handbag – a fashionable cross-body one we had bought from Bicester Village when she'd got straight As in her A levels – on the bed. I knew she usually carried a zip pouch around with her where she stashed her asthma spray and her headphones.

When we'd gone shopping in Hampstead on the day of the barbeque, she had fished some paracetamol out of it and given me a couple when I mentioned that I'd had a bit of headache.

I didn't like to pry through my daughter's stuff but it was just a quick peek. I saw the zip pouch immediately and opened it. Asthma spray, tiny earphone buds and a blister pack of paracetamol. Eureka. There was something else in there too. Something soft and furry. I pulled it out and a tiny teddy bear holding a heart sat in the palm of my hand.

I frowned. It was sweet enough, but who had given it to her? A friend, maybe, but the plush red heart was embroidered with the words I Love You. Were teenage girls really that gushy? I supposed they were.

I put the bear back in the bag and popped two tablets out of the blister. I saw her train tickets too and pulled them out have a look, wondering how much it had cost her to come for the weekend. We gave her an allowance, and she had never put her hand out asking for any extra, but train travel wasn't cheap and I thought I might slip her a couple of twenties to pay for it.

I looked at it and frowned. It wasn't the cost that bothered me. It was the date. The outgoing portion of the journey was dated two days earlier and the return portion was valid for a month from that date. That meant Dylan had bought her ticket forty-eight hours before she'd travelled, or more likely, given her early arrival in Highgate, that she hadn't travelled to London that morning at all, but on Thursday. And if that were true, where the hell had our daughter been for the past two days and why was she pretending she had been at college?

Chapter 30

'You know there's a reunion already happening,' said Mike Weller slicing his knife and fork into his pepperoni pizza.

It was good to see him. Mike was one of those guys that everyone liked, a big teddy bear with a broad smile and an easy way about him that made everyone feel comfortable. I wished we'd have stayed in touch, wished it was just a little bit easier to keep friends with members of the opposite sex once you left college and met partners who were suspicious about the word 'platonic' or were wary of the message you sent if you suggested meeting an old pal for a drink.

Certainly, I wouldn't have ordinarily invited Mike to lunch if I didn't have a good reason. But I did, and I was grateful that Mike had been able to meet so soon, thanks to a cabling job he was doing in Ludgate Circus that week.

'Nothing official but Ollie Brown is doing a comedy gig at the Soho Theatre. A big group is going down to see him. You must come.'

He'd exhausted all the university gossip he could remember within the first ten minutes of our lunch, but he seemed as keen as I did to know more.

'I heard about that,' I replied, not wanting to admit that

I had also been in touch with Louise Parker, and everyone else who I had considered a friend at university.

'Ollie was at my college. I turn my back for a minute and he's actually famous.'

'Are you going to go?'

I shrugged.

'Come on,' he grinned, wiping some cheese from his chin. 'I'm going. The last train back to Reading is worth hanging out with celebrities even if it's only Ollie. But I suppose you must do it all the time.'

'Hang out with celebrities?' I laughed. 'Believe me, that's not the life of a book editor.'

Still, I told him about Sir Simeon's tribute evening, the demands, the tantrums, which Mike found funny and in turn, I enjoyed feeling successful and interesting.

'Your life does sound glamorous.' He said it with the tinge of regret I'd heard in many of our forty-something friends.

'I tried to be a sports reporter, straight out of college. I'd have loved that. I wrangled a job as a runner for *Solent News* and went with them to cover Cowes. Never been in a bloody boat before, despite three years at Durham. We hit a wave chasing one of the tall ships, and I went over the side.'

'Like that scene in Bridget Jones where she goes down the fireman's pole and shows off all her knickers?'

'Not quite,' said Mike, dabbing the corner of his mouth with a paper napkin. 'It would have been funny if I hadn't taken £10,000 worth of sound equipment with me into the water. I was fired as soon as I was back on dry land. My media career was finished as soon as it had begun. I found myself in the quieter world of IT,' he said with a shrug. 'Less drama but not quite the stuff of dreams. I often wonder how my life would have panned out if we hadn't hit that wave.'

I nodded in agreement. I supposed that feeling of reflection came with our age; as we slipped into the second half of our lives it was natural to wonder if we'd made the right choices in our first act.

'It's never too late,' I smiled, sipping the second glass of wine I had quietly ordered.

I saw Mike glance at his watch; he'd said he could only have a quick lunch and I knew the clock was ticking. I couldn't wait for the right moment any longer.

'So, what was all that you mentioned about Chris Hannah? In your messages, you said you felt bad about what happened.'

He searched my face for one moment, assessing what I knew.

'Did you not keep in touch?'

I shook my head.

Mike pushed away his place and asked for the bill.

'You heard he ended up in prison, right?'

At first, I thought I hadn't heard him correctly.

'Chris Hannah went to *prison?*'

'You didn't know?'

He looked really embarrassed now.

'No. We broke up not long after we left Durham and like I said, didn't really keep in touch.'

He looked awkward.

'What was he in for?' I almost didn't dare ask.

'GBH, I think. We'd lost touch by then too, but I heard he got a couple of years for it.'

I was too stunned to speak.

'I couldn't believe it either,' said Mike, shaking his head. 'Chris Hannah had everything; he was funny, good-looking, smart. More than anything he was just a nice, decent bloke. I can't believe how things went so wrong for him so quickly.'

He stopped, as if he'd joined the dots a split second too late.

'It must have been that whole plagiarism business,' he said quickly – after all, he was too polite to blame me. 'It was idiotic, yes. But it must have knocked him for six. Can you imagine, being in line for a First and then getting a pass. To be honest, he was lucky to get that.'

I looked away, remembering every moment of that horrible week as if it was yesterday.

I remembered Chris Hannah coming to my little flat in Church Road, sitting on the bed, his head in his hands, inconsolable, and I'd been gobsmacked when he'd told me why.

I'd had no idea that he had copied his dissertation from an obscure work he'd found in a Northumberland book shop, although it turned out that the text was not so obscure. As it was, its author – an Italian priest and literary scholar – was quite well-known in some academic circles, not that a twenty-one-year-old student in the pre-Google era would know that.

Chris was heartbroken, repentant that his final thesis hadn't all been his own original work, but it hadn't been enough for the disciplinary committee, who told him that his actions had been a major infraction of plagiarism rules and breach of the university code. They'd stopped short of expulsion, but given the circumstances, the university couldn't award anything higher than a pass degree.

'He didn't leave enough time for his dissertation. He panicked and got caught,' I said quietly, surprised that I was sticking up for him.

'But did he learn his lesson?'

Mike waved for the bill. I said I'd pay for it but first, I had one more question.

'What do you know about the GBH charge?' I didn't want to hear it, but I had to know what he had done. I needed to know if he was dangerous.

My old friend shrugged. 'Not sure. I heard he fell in with a bad crowd. It's such a shame. To think he had the girl, he had his swanky graduate place with an advertising agency and he threw it all away.'

I nodded because all I could do was agree.

Chapter 31

It was only when Mike had gone and I was out in the fresh air, that I realized how ill I was feeling. The news that Chris had spent time in jail had stunned me. The two large glasses of wine I'd had before Mike had arrived at the restaurant hadn't helped. But looking back, I hadn't been feeling 100 per cent for days, and although I'd dismissed it as stress, now I thought it was something more.

Feeling dizzy, I stopped and put my hand out against a wall to support myself. A huge lorry, stationary at the light, coughed out thick, noxious fumes and the odour made me gag.

I really didn't feel well at all – my whole body ached and was tender to the touch as if I was on the cusp of a virus. But I couldn't be ill. A trip to Birmingham was scheduled for the following day, which meant that four days' work in the office had to fit into three. With everything else that was going on – Simeon's party, a manuscript to edit, and the photos that had been sent to Ian – I couldn't afford any more time out of the office, I had to be vigilant. I had to be there, I had to be firing on all cylinders to deal with everything that was going on.

I needed water. That would sort me out. It was too late

to go back to the restaurant but there was a newsagent just a few metres away. I bought a bottle of Evian, walked out without getting my change and drank half of it in one gulp.

I don't really remember what happened next. I felt as if I was floating and then I opened my eyes and I could see a little crowd gathered around me like a ring of faces.

'Are you alright?'

The voice was muffled. As I began to focus, my hearing became more acute as if cotton wool had been pulled out of my ears.

'Do you want me to call an ambulance?'

I shook my head. I realized it was being held in somebody's warm hands.

I flinched and forced myself to sit up.

Glancing behind, I saw a twenty-something woman with long black hair, kneeling behind me.

'Easy does it,' she said, holding my shoulders. She was being kind but I didn't want to be touched, not by someone I didn't know.

'We should call 999,' said another voice.

'No, no. I'll be fine in a minute.'

There was a pop as a bus ran over my water bottle that had rolled into the street. For a second, I thought I'd been shot.

Someone mentioned A&E. Someone else was going to find water.

I was helped to my feet and I wanted the ground to swallow me.

Usually it was difficult getting an appointment at my local GP but when I phoned them up and told them what had happened, they said that they had a 3 p.m. slot available with my regular doctor. I got there with a minute to spare and went straight through to one of the consulting rooms.

Dr Price was sitting in front of her computer, glasses perched on the end of her nose as she typed up the notes from her previous patient. When she turned around and smiled, I knew I had an ally. Dr Price was the closest thing there was to a family doctor when you lived in London; she'd been at the practice for years and had been incredibly proactive and supportive throughout Dylan's eating disorder.

I perched on the edge of the plastic chair, embarrassed that I felt better than I had outside the pizzeria where I had met Mike, and ran through my symptoms that I'd had over the past few days.

'Are you pregnant?' asked Dr Price without any preamble once I had mentioned that I had fainted.

For a moment, I thought I hadn't heard her properly.

'Pregnant?' I said, aghast, when what she'd said sank in. 'No, no, no,' I said, before I stopped to even to think about it.

'Fainting is a common enough symptom of pregnancy. The body goes through hormonal and physical changes. When was your last period?' she asked, trying to catch my eye.

Panic collected in my belly.

'I don't know. I hardly notice my menstrual cycle. I have a coil fitted . . .'

Dr Price looked at my file on screen.

'That's right. You've had that a few years. Probably time to get a new one. Have you had sex recently?'

My head was swimming, my cheeks were hot, my whole body consumed with a sense of dread.

Pregnant.

How could she even think it? I was forty-seven years old. The stubborn hairs on my chin, my mood swings – my body was preparing for the menopause, not another baby.

'Have you had sex in the past few weeks?' repeated Dr Price.

Images flashed in my head like strobe light. Flesh, thighs,

nipples, mouths, fingers twisted around crisp hotel sheets, hands gripping my hair as he came inside me.

We hadn't thought about contraception that night, nothing beyond a hasty assurance that I had the coil. It seemed so stupid, so reckless now but back then we'd cared about nothing but our desire.

There was no time to even squeeze my eyes tightly shut before I burst out crying.

'Is everything okay?' asked Dr Price. I could just about see through my tears that she looked shocked.

'I can't be pregnant. I can't. Not at my age,' I managed to stutter.

Dr Price handed me a tissue. I balled it up and pushed it into each eye socket one after the other.

I could feel reassurances coming about geriatric mothers and the happiness of conceiving in later life, but thankfully the doctor said nothing.

Sucking air into my lungs, I wiped my eyes with the back of my hand before I spoke again.

'I'm sorry. I've been feeling a bit emotional lately. My daughter has left home, university, I have a new job. It's been overwhelming and I'm not sure I'm coping.'

I gave an embarrassed laugh and blew my nose on the damp tissue

Dr Price didn't find it funny. 'Are you sleeping?'

'Not well,' I said honestly.

'What about your appetite. Are you eating three balanced meals a day?'

Her interrogation helped me regain my composure.

'I don't know. I try.'

'Do you drink?'

'Yes,' I admitted.

'How much?'

Her questions came thick and fast. Concentration levels, diet, mood, stress, panic attacks. As I answered them all, I didn't need to be a doctor to know that my mental health didn't sound good and that I was drinking far too much.

'You've been under a lot of pressure over the past few years. Eating disorders can affect the whole family. A child leaving home can also be difficult.'

I looked down in shame, wondering whether to tell her about Chris Hannah, the abusive texts, the cards, the whip, the fear of it escalating into something more. Then I thought about the people in the waiting room, eager to get seen. There was only so much you could get through in a ten-minute appointment, and there was certainly not enough time for tales of my stupidity. Besides which, she knew Dylan and Robert.

'First things first,' said Dr Price, her tone brisk and efficient. 'Your coil has probably stopped being effective. You should get it replaced and I suggest you do a quick home pregnancy test just to rule that out. You could have a virus and we should also address your anxiety. We should look at a holistic strategy. Make a plan for making healthy choices. Lots of people report that running is a good way to manage stress.'

'I don't want to run.'

There was a snap in my voice as I remembered my last run to Hampstead Ponds. Dr Price looked taken aback by the aggression.

'And there's various types of medication we could look at if you were open to that,' she said more slowly. 'Fluoxetine is considered safe to take even if you are pregnant. And I can begin a referral to a therapeutic service. I can also recommend some excellent private therapists . . .'

'Fluoxetine?'

'It's an SSRI. An anti-depressant.'

It felt like another punch in the guts however kindly she tried to say it. I knew that if I was a New Yorker, if I had been brought up in a culture of uppers and downers to regulate my moods, I would have had no reservations about taking them. But I was still a girl from Belfast, and I could hear my mum's voice in my head – 'what do you need those for, love?' – at the mention of anti-depressants.

'They can help,' said Dr Price, feeling my resistance. I knew she was right. I knew I wasn't coping, that my control on my life was slipping out of my grip. And that was before I had even begun to think about the consequences of being pregnant. I felt teary again. I was afraid, defeated, but the sound of a printer whirling to life and a green prescription pressed into my hand suddenly made me feel a little bit better.

Chapter 32

Robert and I had wanted a big family – we'd decided that very early on. I could remember the conversation quite clearly, on our honeymoon in Sicily, watching a group of children play on the pebble beach, their screams of laughter lifting in the heat of the warm, lemon-scented air as they scrambled into the shallows of the silver sea. We'd watched on, sipping red wine, still basking in the afterglow of our small Chelsea Register Office wedding a few days earlier. Robert had taken my hand and said 'two girls and a boy' and I had just nodded because I had understood what he wanted. As a new bride, dreaming of our future life, it was what I wanted too.

It took two years of trying to get pregnant with Dylan and we'd tried to conceive again almost immediately after she was born. But the big family hadn't happened. Not after the timetabled sex, the ovulation kits, the acupuncture, and finally the five rounds of IVF. We'd tried for more than ten years, until I was deep into my forties, until sex was just a by-word for stress and disappointment. My husband just couldn't get me pregnant. Not like Chris Hannah.

I'd got pregnant the first time I'd had unprotected sex with my university sweetheart. It was the weekend after our finals, a weekend spent in the Kielder Forest in a cabin we didn't leave for forty-eight hours, and when we'd run out of wine and condoms, Chris had said he'd go out, late at night, to find somewhere that sold them.

'It doesn't matter,' I'd told him, not wanting him to disappear into the dark, not wanting to spend a minute away from him. I loved him so much, was so sure of our future together, that I didn't even care if we had sex and I got pregnant. The truth was, I wanted to have his baby. It didn't matter when. I wanted to be connected to him forever. Not just by a ring or a marriage certificate, but by another human being.

When I missed my period a month later, I didn't even notice. There were other things to worry about. Chris had been found out by then, the disciplinary action had begun. By the time I skipped my second period, I was back in Belfast. I told my mum I had to go back to Durham to sort out the deposit on the student flat I'd lived in in my third year. Instead, I went to Newcastle and had an abortion. I had never felt more alone than on that coach journey to Liverpool to catch the ferry home. Until perhaps today.

There was a chemist in the village but I walked straight past it. Instead, I went back to the house, got in the car and drove straight to Brent Cross, to a superstore that felt big enough, far away enough from Highgate, for no one I knew to notice what I was doing.

I put a packet of butter, a can of coke, and a First Response kit into my basket, paid for it in the self-service counter and threw the receipt away before heading straight into the customer toilets to do the deed.

In a few moments I would know if I was pregnant. Less easy to tell who was the father of my child. Since that night in Soho, I'd had sex with Robert two or three times a week, more often than we'd made love in the past twelve months. He liked to come inside me and I'd let him every time. It was the least I could do, after all the mistakes I'd made. After what I had done.

But as I closed my eyes I could picture a baby with thick dark lashes, just like my university sweetheart's, and a crippling sense of dread made me feel faint.

Crouching over the loo, praying I wasn't having my one-night stand's baby, it was impossible not to think back to the moment I had found out I was pregnant with Dylan. Back then, I'd been pretty sure there was a tiny, beautiful foetus inside me. We'd been trying for so long, I'd missed my period and I just felt different. After all, a mother knows. In readiness for two pink lines, I'd bought fresh flowers for the flat and had some sparkling grape juice chilling in the fridge. I'd waited for Robert to come home, and had put on my prettiest dress, wanting the memory of it to be just perfect. Robert had waited outside the bathroom door and afterwards, we'd sat on the bed holding the urine-soaked stick, hardly daring to breathe, desperately watching the colour develop and when it did, I had never felt closer to my husband, never felt more joy.

But now the fluorescent lights were bright and stark over my head. The laughter of children washing their hands in the sinks outside the cubicle was like an angry white noise.

I wasn't thinking about baby names or local schools, all the things that had been whirling through my head that night we'd found out about Dylan. Instead, I wondered if I should kill myself.

Hesitant piss dribbled out of my body.

I sat on the damp seat, my toes clawing down into my shoes.

Those three minutes seemed to take forever. I looked down and there was a lonely single red line.

I kept staring at it, and a tear dripped down my cheek. The children left the bathroom, the light flickered overhead and started humming. There was still a single dark pink line.

I wasn't pregnant.

A sob collected in my throat and I couldn't hold it in.

I gripped the pregnancy stick so hard it snapped in my hand.

Exhausted and thirsty, I took the can of coke out of my bag and drank it all, wiping my mouth with the back of my hand, then I slid the stick into the sanitary bin, pulled up my knickers and smoothed down my skirt, ready to leave.

I didn't remember parking in the parent and child section and it took me a few minutes to find the car. I climbed into the driver's seat, locked the door and didn't turn on the engine. In the rear-view mirror, I could see two red eyes peering back at me. Only me, I told myself. Only me.

Breathe in. Breathe out. Breathe in. Breathe out, I told myself, wishing I'd have kept the pregnancy stick as a reminder that I'd been given a second chance.

If you feel your mind wandering, bring it back to the centre.

Breathe in. Breathe out. The mindfulness techniques were working and I allowed myself to feel relief. There was even a sense that my luck was finally changing.

My phone chirped. I pushed my hand into the bag, past the pointless packet of butter, and pulled it out.

Where have you been?

Only four people had my new number. Robert, Dylan, Serena and Georgina from work. I knew instantly that this message wasn't from any of them.

I started to tremble again. How did *he* have my new phone number when I had only given it to four people?

I read the message again, trying to work out if he knew that I wasn't at work or at home. That I was in a supermarket in Brent Cross doing a pregnancy test. Or was he just poking me, like a troubled adolescent, smiling as they pushed a stick into a hornet's nest?

Lottie Callow had told me I shouldn't engage. She'd told me that at least half a dozen times.

But I needed to know. I wanted to know if he was watching me and how he knew how to contact me.

How do you have this number? I asked, gripping my phone with both hands, my fingers stabbing the keyboard as I wrote out the text.

I checked that the car doors were still locked as I waited for the reply. It was instantaneous.

Bile rushed up my throat when I read the reply.

Because I've been inside your house.

Looking back, I don't know why my immediate impulse was to floor the accelerate pedal. I wasn't thinking. My only impulse was to get away.

I had to get somewhere safe.

The car was facing forwards. I slammed it into gear and stamped on the accelerator, whipping my hands around, spinning the wheel to the right, the wing of the car barely missing a bollard, the engine bucking, jerking forward out of the lane, powering towards the blue 'exit' sign.

BLAAAARE!

A car horn, a squeal and then a crunch.

The car rocked back on its suspension as I looked up into the wide eyes of a child, her face pale through the passenger window of a red hatchback.

'Oh God,' I whispered, fumbling for the door.

I fell out of the car in my haste.

I ran towards the other car, only to be blocked by a red-faced middle-aged woman coming from the driver's side, her khaki parka billowing like a cape, anger twisting her face.

'What have you done!' she screamed. 'My daughter's in there – you could have killed her! You could have killed us both.'

'I know, I'm so sorry, I didn't see . . .' I stuttered, looking down and seeing the phone still clutched in my hand. I watched as the woman saw it, saw her face harden, felt the fury as her eyes met mine.

Shoppers had stopped pushing their trolleys to watch us.

'I'd better call the police.'

Chapter 33

A rap at the window startled me.

I came out of my daze, my hand gripping the inner handle of the car door, and I looked right to see a face at the window of the car. It took a full second for me to realize it was Robert.

I didn't know how long I had been here, sitting on the drive, but it was dark. The radio was on playing Smooth FM at barely audible volume, the doors were locked.

I switched off the music and wound down the window

'What's going on? Are you okay?'

Robert tried the car door but it wouldn't open.

'I'm okay,' was all I could say, but Robert still looked concerned.

'What's happened to the car?'

'There was an accident.'

I got out of the car and just stood there.

'Honey, come here. Tell me what's happened.'

I just wanted him to hold me but I felt too ashamed to be touched. Instead I just looked down at the drive, forcing myself to keep myself together.

'Rach, what's wrong? What's happened.'

'I smashed into someone . . .'

I listened out for the sigh of disappointment and I heard a faint modulation of his breath, so slight it took twenty years of living with him to recognize it. But still – it was there. Not disapproval, but frustration and I couldn't blame him.

'You're okay?' he pressed. 'No one was hurt?'

'No,' I whispered. 'Just the car.'

We were stood just a foot apart but he came closer towards me.

'Why are you sitting outside in the dark?'

Too many questions. Not enough answers. At least not ones I could give him.

'I've lost my keys,' I lied.

Robert knew that Bill and Iris had a spare set but he didn't ask why I hadn't been round and collected them.

'She called the police,' I whispered.

My voice finally cracked and I started to cry. I felt like a criminal.

'It's only a car,' he said as my body softened into his. 'I'm more bothered about you. You sure you're okay?'

'I'm fine.'

'You don't want to get checked out at A&E? You feel cold.'

'I'm just in shock.'

'Come on. Let's get you inside.'

I was still shivering even though it must have been two hours since my accident.

Robert only let go of me when we were in the kitchen. He switched on the bank of soft lights over the kitchen units and listened as he made tea and I described what happened in more detail. It was still select information – the dent to Ruth Andrews' Zafira and my interview with the police.

'Was anyone else in the car?'

I told him about the young girl in the passenger seat and the baby in the back. My husband tried to hide his disapproval but I could still see his concern that children were involved.

237

'And everyone was fine?'

He needed me to confirm it.

'Thank God,' I said, my voice a repentant whisper.

I could hear the soft gurgle of the kettle.

'I might get points off my licence,' I admitted after a moment.

Robert put a cup on the island top and looked at me. 'What for?'

'For using a mobile phone while driving,' I said, feeling my face redden.

The mood shifted.

'You were on your phone?'

There was more obvious disapproval in his voice now.

'No. Ruth Andrews saw me with my phone when I got out of the car and she told the officer.'

'But you were using it when you had the crash?'

'No,' I repeated. Strictly speaking, it was true, although I was holding it at the wheel.

He handed me the tea. I wished it was the Sauvignon that was chilling in the fridge, but alcohol was not Robert's prop. He used it to show off and lubricate business deals, not to self-medicate, and I didn't want to disappoint him any more by showing him that I did.

I needed to sit down and walked through to the living room and perched on the edge of the sofa, my hands cradling my knees, still sore from the accident.

Robert sat on the next sofa.

'So where did it happen?'

If I thought it was the end of the matter I was mistaken.

'Brent Cross,' I said after a moment,

'What were you doing up there?'

I'd rehearsed this bit.

'I needed some work clothes.'

I only went to the big North London mall with Dylan and even then, we hadn't been for at least a year. But thankfully, it was still a believable story.

'Did you take any photos? We'll need them for the insurance.'

For a moment, I hated him for being so particular and thorough.

'My phone is in my bag. I'll get it in a minute.'

As I sipped my tea, I could feel my husband watching me.

'Rach . . .' His usually self-assured demeanour looked hesitant. 'Rach, you would tell me if something was wrong?'

I felt exposed in our bare, beautiful living room, on the couch, looking into the eyes of my husband I had cheated on.

'Why do you say that?'

'You've just not been yourself lately.'

'I've been busy, that's all.'

He shook his head.

'You never used to be like this when you were at work.'

'That was twenty years ago. How can you remember what I was like? Maybe I'm just tired. I had more energy in the old days.'

He glanced up. 'Maybe.'

The prickle in the air disappeared as soon as it had come.

'I just need a good night's sleep.'

'I think we both do. I've got a breakfast meeting at seven-thirty in the City tomorrow.'

There was no point in me telling him that we both needed to slow down. I wondered if he even remembered his big speech at Marley Hall. How we both needed to enjoy life, enjoy each other.

'Can I get you anything?'

He didn't ask this much but I could see he was trying to be supportive.

'Just stay here with me.'

I tipped my head back on the sofa and Robert moved seats, coming to sit down beside me.

'The last thing I feel like is going to this bloody literary festival in Birmingham tomorrow.'

'Then don't go. You shouldn't go.'

'I have to. It's Jemima French, one of our big authors.'

'You've been in an accident. Can't someone else go?'

I didn't reply.

'Are you going to see Dylan?'

I didn't want to tell him my plan.

'She's doesn't want her mum turning up, midweek.'

'It'll do you good to see her.'

'I thought I should stop chasing her around.'

Robert nodded in silent agreement.

'You know what I do feel like?'

'What?'

'Hot chocolate,' I smiled weakly.

'Hot chocolate?'

He looked like I'd asked for heroin. But then Robert was away so many nights, he didn't know how much Dylan and I used to love a mug of cocoa to wind down.

I tried to laugh.

'Don't worry, I'll do it,' I said, waving my hand. 'Dylan says I am the world's best hot chocolate barista.'

Robert held my hand as I pushed myself off the sofa. Stiffness had gathered across my shoulders. My left shin hurt.

I went to the kitchen cupboards and retrieved the bag of chocolate callets, the velvety cocoa pellets I had found, by trial and error, made our favourite bedtime drink. I opened the fridge, took out a pint of milk and looked for the frother, which made it light but firm, just how Dylan liked it.

My bag was on the island and I thought of my phone inside it. Not the photos of Ruth Andrews' car that my husband wanted to see, but the last incoming text message.

I have been inside your house.

I knew I should keep the message as evidence but I couldn't chance Robert checking my phone.

I fixed my eyes on the oven, staring into its dark depths, thinking, wondering, trying to come to terms with the events of the day.

It was only then that I noticed that something was inside the oven. The hum was so soft that I could barely hear it, but it was definitely on and when I looked through the glass window I could see something inside.

I tried to remember back to that morning, past everything that had happened that day, finally picturing the small bowl of cereal I'd had for breakfast. At no point had I needed to use the oven, so there was no reason for it to be on.

I flipped open the door. It was on low, and the heat that escaped was just a warm waft of air.

Whatever was cooking was on a metal tray.

Instinct told me to back away, but I needed to know what was inside. I picked up an oven glove and slid out the rack. I wasn't sure what it was at first. Some dark unctuous muscle, scored with thin, white sinews and red veins. It was only when I saw the round halo of aorta, that I realized it was a slowly baking heart, and I dropped the milk so it smashed to the floor.

Chapter 34

My body felt as if it had woken up too soon. My eyes could barely open, a deep headache throbbed from inside my brain, pressing its way out. I was a deadweight on the mattress, every muscle not quite able to lift up my bones.

I lay still, trying to adjust from the unconscious to the conscious state.

It still looked dark but my back faced the window, and besides, our state of the art blackout blinds blotted out most of the daylight whenever they were closed. I wondered if it was still the middle of the night, a blissful thought telling me I could fall straight back to sleep, but as my hands stretched over to Robert's side of the bed, fingertips creeping across the crisp sheet, I could feel nothing but a cold space that had been long vacated.

Sleep had congealed in the corner of my eye and I rubbed it away with my knuckle. I groped around the bedside table looking for my phone but it wasn't there. It was another moment before I remembered that wasn't where it lived now, when I went to sleep at night. How it had to live in my handbag, out of reach, out of view, for my own protection.

I pushed back the duvet and slid out of bed. I looked down

at my watch and as I brought it close to my face to make out the time, I swore at my ineptitude.

9.37.

The plan had been to meet Jemima French and Georgina Archer, the publicity director at Edelman, at nine o'clock outside WHSmith at Euston in time to catch the 9.23 train to Birmingham. We had advance tickets booked – first class. Not only was I late, the train would have gone.

I stumbled over to the window and opened the blinds. As they purred towards the ceiling, letting in the pale morning light, my eyes darted around the room looking for my bag.

There were three missed calls, all from Georgina, and a voicemail alert.

I couldn't bear to listen to the message. Georgina was not my favourite member of the Edelman team. Her confidence scared me, her air-kissing lovey-ness seemed insincere. But there was more to it than that. I wasn't sure she liked me. Word had it she was keen to make the leap from communications over to editorial and had seen Ginny's maternity leave as her chance to do it. But now she resented me for taking that position, resented the attention I'd received from Ian. I took a deep breath and returned the call. Relieved when it didn't connect, I texted her to explain my absence,

Problems at home, I'll meet you at the literary festival venue as soon as I can.

The panic of getting dressed, gathering my work things and booking an Uber took my mind off the night before.

The half-cooked, still bloody heart in our oven. The lies to Robert when he found me, frozen, surrounded by shards of glass.

'What's the hell is going on?'

He'd slipped, his socks not quite gripping to the tiles, when I'd screamed and he'd run into the kitchen. I'd hated seeing him fall, but it had given me enough time to close the oven and turn it off.

'I just dropped the milk,' I had said, excusing myself to find the mop, desperately wishing my only crime was being clumsy.

I tried not to think about it on the way to Euston, but it was difficult.

How had he got into the house? How had he got past the security system? In the aftermath of my accident, my distress and Robert helping me into the house, I couldn't recall us switching off the alarm, so perhaps it hadn't even been on in the first place. We weren't particularly thorough about it, although lately I'd tried to be more cautious.

As the cab stalled in traffic, I'd hopped on the YouAreNot-Alone forum again because right now, they felt like the only people I could talk to. Lottie Callow would only tell me to go to the police and I knew that an arrest for breaking and entering was likely to put Chris Hannah back in jail. Despite everything, I wasn't entirely sure I wanted that. Better to get out of town and delay any decisions. Better to keeping praying that he would go away.

I got to Euston just before half past ten. I'd just missed another fast train, but I knew the London–Birmingham times – I had done ever since Dylan had accepted her university place – and knew there would be another in twenty minutes.

I bought a new ticket and a black coffee that spilt on my lapel as I paid for it.

I glanced around as I dabbed myself with a napkin, glad that the station was busy. I knew it was possible that I was being watched. He saw me at Lottie Callow's office, he had been inside my house. The text that he'd sent in the car park had been no idle threat, or an untruth to scare me.

I checked the platform and found my train. I picked a window seat and put my bag and coat defensively in the space besides me.

We'd just started to move when my phone rang again and I steeled myself, ready to speak to Georgina, but it was a male voice, deep and unfamiliar which made my heart start pounding inside my rib cage.

'Rachel.'

It didn't sound like Chris Hannah. It didn't sound like Nathan Deer. The voice was too rich, too deep.

'Yes?'

My voice, by comparison, was small and nervy. I looked around the carriage just to make sure he wasn't close by.

'It's Sir Simeon Averill.'

'Sir Simeon. Hello,' I said, almost laughing out loud in relief. A businessman looked over. I wasn't sure if it was because I was being too loud or whether he'd guessed who I was talking to.

'How are you?'

I'd had a couple of conversations already with Averill's agent, but never with the man himself. For a moment, I forgot everything, thrilled and yet nervous, to finally speak to the literary lion.

'Rachel, Georgina gave me your number. There are a few things we need to discuss. About the party.'

'Fire away.'

I was pleased with how things were going, but soon it was apparent that nothing about the upcoming book launch was right – at least in Sir Simeon's eyes. The guest list was too short, the security was inadequate, he needed finer wines and an assurance that food was to be served on porcelain not paper plates. Most of all, he was dissatisfied with the venue, The Mark, a chic boutique hotel in Soho.

'You're not keen on The Mark?' I replied, shocked. Securing the venue at such short notice, especially during the Christmas party season, had been a coup. Currently the bolthole of choice for the fashionable and young Hollywood crowd, The Mark had the right balance of glamour and charm, plus it was right in the centre of town, meaning we stood a high chance of actually getting people to come.

'Do *you* think it's suitable?'

This was obviously a trick question.

'It's considered one of the top hotels in London, at the moment Sir Simeon. It's brand new, hip . . .'

'Hip?' He said the word with some disgust. 'My dear, this event is a celebration of one of the greatest books of the twentieth century. Not some it-girl's twenty-first. Thanks heavens I actually went to check it out. Penelope seems to think it was okay, but I was at the Garrick last night, popped in to have a look on the way home. Honestly, the Mark bar was like a discotheque.'

The line cracked and then he was cut off.

'God,' I muttered, trying to reconnect but it went straight to message and I spluttered something about speaking to Ian Sinclair and seeing what we could do.

Chapter 35

The event had started by the time I had got to Birmingham's Copthorne Hotel. I reminded myself that it wasn't vital that I come today. Editors didn't have to go with authors to talks and book signings, that was the publicity team's job. But still, as I'd emailed Jemima earlier that week to say how much I was looking forward to meeting her, it didn't seem like my finest moment.

I peered through the porthole door into the room where Jemima was doing her talk. She was sat on stage talking animatedly to a ponderous-looking moderator. I had no idea what they were discussing but I could hear the audience laughing from here. Jemima's books weren't particularly humorous, but she had the fans in stitches of laughter.

I spotted a more discreet side entrance and slipped inside, taking a seat at the far edge of the stage. I could barely see a thing, but it hardly mattered.

I could tell Jemima was a brilliant performer, even if I could only hear her. Funny, wise, self-deprecating and best of all, on brand, she up-sold her backlist, made them salivate for her upcoming release and directed the audience towards the signing table piled high with *Cage of Gold* merchandise.

When the talk finished, Jemima remained on stage to

unplug her microphone. I took my chance and went over to introduce myself.

'Rachel, I'm so glad you could make it,' she beamed. We were worried about you when you didn't show at Euston. Is everything okay?'

'I was in a car accident last night,' I confided. 'All okay, but I was still a bit shell-shocked this morning.'

It felt cheap using the crash as an excuse for my tardiness but I felt it could get me out of the fix.

'You poor thing. What on earth are you doing here?' she said touching me on the arm, a gesture that, though short and slight, let me know how warm and caring she was. How I would have liked her to be my friend.

'You were amazing today. You need your own show.'

'You're joking,' she said, tucking a sheaf of silver bob behind her ear. 'I felt sick with nerves. Either that or it was a dodgy bagel I had on the train.'

'Nervous? You're an absolute natural.'

'Believe me, this doesn't come easy,' she said as we started to walk towards the signing table. 'But I'm glad to get out of the house and I owe it to the readers. You know, I came to events just like this one when my kids went off to uni. I wasn't just a fan of the books; I came to be inspired. I came to see that authors were people just like me. If I can go out there now and connect with someone who has always put other people first, if I can make them think that they can do this too, make them see that there's life beyond motherhood, then it's worth every second of stage fright.'

'That's right,' I said, feeling lifted by my author's words. 'You started writing when your daughter left home.'

'I wrote to relieve my pain,' she smiled.

'I know how that feels.'

'Have yours left too? You hardly look old enough.'

'She started at Birmingham University a couple of months ago.'

Jemima smiled broadly. 'How wonderful. Is she here? No. Don't even answer that. I don't suppose she wants to hear some old fuddy-duddy bang on about Elizabeth of Scotland does she. Not unless she's doing History. Even then.'

We both laughed.

'Well, I hope you're off to meet for a lovely lunch somewhere. You know you have to make the effort. My three were scattered around the country. Edinburgh, Exeter, Bangor. I'm sure they did it to keep me on my toes, but I always made the effort. Met up with each of them every term to take them somewhere nice. You have to make the effort with your grown-up children or else they'll drift away. You don't want them to become strangers.'

Georgina was putting signed book plates into jiffy envelopes by the time we got to the signing table at the back of her room.

She shot me a filthy look as we approached, then switched on a bright smile for Jemima.

'You could go into the Top Ten from the sales we'll make in this room alone,' she gushed, motioning towards the queue of fans already stretched back towards the stage. She turned to me.

'Made it then?'

I was about to reply but she beat me to it.

'Ian's here.'

I didn't miss the whisper of triumph in her smile.

I felt my heart sink. I had no idea Ian Sinclair was coming to the festival. Then again, I'd been avoiding him ever since he'd returned from the Latvian publishing conference, in case he'd got wind of the porno photographs.

'Sorry, everyone. Just talking to Hilary Mantel.'

We heard Ian before we saw him. The crowd parted, and he appeared at the signing table, ignoring me and heading straight for Jemima, grabbing her before she had chance to sit down.

I got a tarter welcome.

'You've arrived,' he said, exchanging a glance with Georgina.

'Rachel was in a car accident last night,' said Jemima, popping the top off her signing pen and flashing me a look of support. 'I'm just glad she made it at all.'

Now was not the time for excuses.

'I didn't know you were coming,' I said gathering up some book plates.

'Last minute decision,' he said, polishing the lenses of his glasses with a cloth. 'I've got a dinner with Ian Rankin tonight down the road. Thought I'd come early and support Jemima.'

He put his glasses back on. 'So how about lunch? There's a great restaurant that Nigella once recommended to me, just around the corner.'

'I'm starving, so sounds good, when I've signed all these,' said Jemima.

'Rachel?'

I hesitated.

Disapproval clouded Ian's face again. Our relationship seemed to have shifted lately. Ian Sinclair was fine but only when you did everything he said.

'Got a better offer?' he said with a hint of challenge.

'Yes, she has,' said Jemima, flashing him a look. 'She's arranged to see her daughter. She's at Birmingham University and they are meeting for lunch.'

'Maybe I can pop along for a bit,' I offered.

'It's not every day we get to take Jemima out, is it?' replied Ian pointedly.

'I won't hear of it, Ian.' Jemima's tone was an undisguised reprimand. 'I don't need anyone to plump my feathers. You and I can have a quick bite and then I'd better get home. I believe I have another book to write for you and my deadline is looming. Rachel, you go and have a lovely time with your daughter.'

Ian couldn't argue. Not with his star author.

*

It was Sarah, one of the mums at the eating disorder group who had told me how her daughter, Eve, had floundered invisibly at university. No one in Eve's family realized she was skipping lectures, not eating and spending most of her time in her tiny single room on her own. How would they know? Eve had a second life once she'd packed her bags for college. A secret life.

But one of Eve's university friends had suspected something was wrong and had tipped off Sarah. When Sarah had confronted Eve, it would have been easy for her to believe her daughter that there was nothing wrong and that she was loving college. It would have been easy to believe because everything looked fine.

Instead, Sarah had staged an ambush.

'Sixth sense,' she'd said to me over lukewarm coffee at her first meeting of the eating disorder group.

She'd gone to visit Eve at university without any warning and faced with her mother in her small, lonely room, Eve had broken down and begged her mother to help her escape the cycle of starvation and isolation, which was how they'd ended up at the support group.

There was no reason for me to be particularly worried about Dylan, but the train ticket I'd found in her bag had bothered me. And so, although I'd mentioned my Birmingham trip to Dylan in passing, although I would have loved to officially combine Jemima's talk with an afternoon tea at The Edgbaston or a walk around campus with my daughter, once I'd seen her train ticket and realized she had come to London earlier than she had said, I remembered what Sarah had told me, and decided to keep my work and travel plans to myself.

I crossed the main road to a taxi rank and told the driver where I wanted to go. I'd checked the route via online maps and knew it would only take a few minutes. I was off-grid, but felt no exhilaration from my spontaneity – I was still too rattled from the day before.

I'd read enough about stalkers over the past few weeks to know that they succeeded by keeping you off balance and constantly looking over your shoulder. Mine hadn't sent pornographic photos to Ian Sinclair to tell him what a slut I was, he had done it to hurt me and to let me know that he could reach me anywhere. When he'd said he had been into my house, he was really trying to unsettle me in the one place I felt safe – my home. He wanted me cowering in a hole, and it had worked.

As I sat back, something in my coat pocket jabbed into my hip. I pulled a business card out of my pocket – the police constable's details from yesterday.

She'd been a young officer, twenty-five tops, and if she'd have been a nurse, you'd have said she had a good bedside manner. I had no idea if she had any experience with stalkers, or disturbed acquaintances who broke into your house to frighten you. I had no idea if she could help me. But I looked at the card and wondered if I should call her. If I should finally confess.

Sweat was beading at my temples. The air of the taxi was suddenly cloying.

'You want dropping off here or should I drive down the hill?' asked the driver as he slowed on the dark leafy road outside the entrance to The Vale campus.

'Here is fine,' I replied, knowing that the short walk to her block would do me good.

For a Tuesday afternoon, it was busy. Students bundled up in scarves and thick jackets walked purposefully carrying books and boxes of craft beer. I could hear music drifting from an open window, a cyclist riding past me at speed, rang his bell for me to get out of the way.

This was my daughter's world and suddenly I felt safer.

As Dylan's halls came into view, I slowed my pace trying to work out a plan. Presumably halls of residence didn't just allow random people through their doors, even if they were parents – *particularly* if they were parents – so by the time I got to the car park I wondered if I should just turn back. At least call Dylan. Tell her I was here and arrange to meet.

I pulled out my phone, deciding what I should say. She'd been so prickly, so guarded with me lately, I wasn't sure she would even pretend to be happy to see me. Even if I had a signed Jemima French book in my bag for her, I didn't suppose that would cut much ice or forgive my intrusion.

And then, incredibly, there she was. Walking out of the building, laughing. Arm in arm with a man. Stopping, turning. Kissing. She looked so happy I almost lost my breath. But who was she with? She whispered something to the man and then threw her head back and laughed so hard that her ponytail swung from side to side like a pendulum. And when they changed direction, away from me, that was when I saw his face.

The man she had been kissing was Nathan. Nathan Deer, our neighbour's carer.

Chapter 36

London was dark and I was tired. The cab was almost in Archway, but we were crawling along; the blue flashing lights ahead suggesting some sort of accident. Suicide Bridge? The old Victorian railway bridge across Archway Road had long been known as a place the despairing had used to end it all. I could sympathize, but all I wanted was to get into a hot, oily bath, and forget about everything.

After the shock of seeing Dylan and Nathan together, I had slunk back to the train station, my mind turning it over and over: my own problems with Chris Hannah forgotten.

Was Dylan too old for a boyfriend in his twenties? She was barely out of school. More to the point, why hadn't she told us about her new romance? All those years we had spent together, the bond that we had, and she had lied to my face. Did I even know my daughter anymore? Had she changed so much that she couldn't tell me something so important. Was she ashamed? And if she was, why? Was dating the neighbour's daughter a breach of Nathan's professional ethics? Or had Dylan sensed he was a bad boy, dangerous, off-limits, and that was why she had kept their relationship a secret.

Nathan Deer made me uncomfortable, I knew that much. Even though he had impressed me at first, that picture I had in my mind of Nathan looking at me that night in the kitchen was scored in my brain. Then there were Bill's accusations of stealing, Nathan's comments about my husband, calling him a 'dickhead'.

Who had he been talking to when he had said that? I grimaced at the thought that it could be have been Dylan herself.

Finally the taxi was moving and I watched the streets pass in a blur, utterly wrung out. I made sure the driver stopped right outside the house. I don't know if he sensed my anxiety but he waited until I was inside the door before he drove away.

The trees rustled and a creeping dark curl of cloud passed in front of the disc of moon. The house looked stark, deserted, just like it was designed to look. I quickly opened and closed the door behind me, double-locked it and flipped on the hall light.

I turned to switch off the alarm but it wasn't on. I'd left home in a hurry that morning. Despite my anxieties, it was possible that I had forgotten to activate the security system. Still . . .

I took a few steps inside, my footfall sounding unnaturally loud.

Robert's black cashmere scarf was on the hook, but his car wasn't on the drive.

'Robert?'

I took off my coat and hung it up. The kitchen and living room were empty and the house was still. I listened for signs of life but heard nothing but the distant purr of the boiler.

I went from switch to switch, turning on all the lights – the spots in the ceiling, the soft-glow pendant that hung over the slate-topped island in the kitchen. Outside, the garden and the cemetery were black. I felt as if I was on stage, bathed in limelight. Unlike an actor, I prayed no eyes were watching me.

I looked inside the oven but it was empty. I scanned the

room for anything else that looked out of place, but everything seemed exactly as it always looked.

I exhaled deeply, trying to shake off the sense of unease. I wasn't hungry but I opened the fridge anyway. My hand hesitated on the handle before it popped open, but there was nothing much to see under the bright lights of our Sub Zero, more sparsely stocked than when I didn't work. No bowls of freshly prepared salad straight from the Ottolenghi cookbook, no homemade pesto and hummus, just a few empty take-away cartons from a local high-end Chinese. If Robert had noticed that our house was starting to slip from its standards, he hadn't said anything, but I had and it was just another thing to feel guilty about.

There was some left-over wine from yesterday, enough for a tumbler full. I'd picked up the Prozac I had on prescription from the Boots at New St Station, but I hadn't popped my first pill. One small glass of Sauvignon to set me on my way wouldn't hurt. Then I would start the course of medication.

I poured the liquid into a glass and sipped it, my eyes trailing towards the plate glass window. As I pictured Nathan Deer's face at the window again, I shivered.

I've been inside your house . . .

We'd welcomed Nathan Deer in our home on a number of occasions. Bill and Iris had a spare key to our house and it wasn't too much of a stretch to imagine Nathan finding it. Someone on YouAreNotAlone had described how their stalker had broken into their house and deactivated their alarm by working out the code from fingerprint marks on the keypad.

At least the cow's heart was out of the house. When Robert had taken a call, I'd thrown it in the bin, and taken the black liner out of the house into the big plastic wheelies near the street. Part of me wondered if I should have kept it as evidence but I could imagine it now, smelling, rotting, uncooked blood spoiling to inedible marbled brown.

I took my phone out of my pocket and put it in my pocket – just in case – before I went upstairs.

I was on the landing, when I heard it. A sound coming from the top floor. There was only Robert's study and a spare room up there but peering up the stairs I couldn't see any light coming from either one. In fact, both doors looked closed.

I gripped my phone like a grenade.

'Robert,' I called out again but there was no reply.

I carried on walking, telling myself that I couldn't be afraid of my own house. No one was here. No one had broken in. It was just the flutter of a pigeon's wing or a rat scuttling across the loft.

I pushed open Robert's study door. It was a series of shadows, the only light was the soft blue glow from an open computer, but I could make out the tall back of his office chair that was facing towards the window and bottle of scotch on the desk.

'Robert?' I whispered.

'What?' said a voice in the dark.

The chair spun round.

'It's you,' I said in relief.

'Who did you think it was?'

I turned on the lights but he threw up a hand with a grunt of disapproval.

'Turn that off,' he muttered. I used the dimmer switch to soften it so there was just a faint distant glow from the spotlights on the ceiling.

It felt as if we were floating in space up here. I could see a white pepper spray of stars, the cemetery beneath us was like a black hole.

'I didn't think you were home. Where's the car?'

'Still in town.'

He was drunk. I could tell that much. That was why his Range Rover had been abandoned.

257

'Why are you in the dark?' I said.

'Just thinking,' he said, lifting a tumbler and taking a drink. That might have been the case but they clearly hadn't been happy thoughts. It was etched on his face, the lines and creases like Braille. He looked awful – the worst I'd ever seen him. I lowered myself onto the arm of a chair next to him.

'Do you want to talk about it?'

He shook his head, but still not looking at me.

'It's just business.'

'Just?' I said. 'What's wrong?'

Robert flicked a hand as if shooing a fly, but I wasn't going to let him push me away this time. I caught his hand and sat forward, forcing him to look at me.

'Tell me.'

He took a long swig of Scotch.

'It's Cadogan House,' he said finally with a long exhale of breath. 'The sale has fallen through.'

I didn't follow the details of Robert's transactions, but I knew that this was a big one – the huge twelve-bedroom detached in Belgravia, that he had been expecting to finalize soon.

'Okay, so you find another buyer,' I said. 'It's an amazing property.'

He snorted. Scotch didn't agree with my husband. It made him a nasty drunk.

'Do you know how much it is? Do you how many people can afford the price tag?' he said, tipping back more alcohol.

'Plenty of rich people want a place in London. Nigerians, Chinese, Russians. You seem to be plugged into that scene.'

Robert picked at his thumbnail, always a sign of stress with him.

'The market's changing so fast. I've never known it change so quickly in such a short space of time. Even during the '08 crash it wasn't like this, there were people with money.

Now . . .' He wiggled his fingers in the air like a magician making things disappear.

'I thought the high-end market was different—'

'Not anymore,' he snapped, stopping me in my tracks. 'Big private houses in this price bracket are not that easy to sell anymore. Russians are leaving, the Chinese are getting nervous about the economy and there's only so many Saudi princesses.'

'Just give it time,' I said softly.

He pulled back, his eyes intense.

'You're not getting it, Rachel. There is no time. If I can't get the money from this sale, really fucking quickly, things are not going to be great for me. It's going to be bad.'

That stopped me. I could hear the fear in his voice, in the tightness of his face. I had never seen him like this before.

'Bad how? Cash flow? Robert, tell me,' I pleaded.

'It's long and complicated,' he said, pressing his temples with his fingertips. 'All you need to know is that I need to find a buyer. I need the money from a sale as soon as possible or the wheels are going to stop turning.'

I gulped hard.

'What about a bridging loan, investors . . .'

'Maybe,' he said, barely audibly.

'If the problem is one big house, turn it into apartments.'

'And how long do you think that is going take? You think we just put up a few dividing walls and rent them to students?'

I flinched at his sudden anger.

'It was just a suggestion.'

His face softened.

'I'm sorry. You're right. Flats would have been a better idea. What I should have done in the first place. Instead, I went for the big trophy property that would put me in the orbit of the heaviest hitters. Wrong call,' he said with a slight slur of his words. 'And now it's too late.'

I reached out my hand. At first he didn't take it, then he sighed and relented. His slim fingers were cold.

'Listen to me,' I said, forgetting about everything else except helping my husband. 'I know it looks bad, but it still only needs one person to get that sale. It's an amazing house and I know you'll find that someone. Soon.'

'Sure,' he said with a weak smile. 'Soon.'

He put down his empty glass and stood up, pulling me with him.

Clearly, he didn't want to discuss Cadogan House anymore.

'How was your day?' he said, rubbing his face. 'How was Birmingham?'

I could tell he wanted to try and change the subject although I could tell his mind was still on his work.

'Birmingham was fine, but . . .'

'But?' He wasn't drunk enough to miss my hesitation. 'Rach, what is it?'

I paused. Perhaps now was as good as any time to drop the bombshell. One of them at least.

'I went to see Dylan. I went to halls and I saw her.'

'Good. How was she?'

'She was with Nathan.'

'Nathan? From next door?'

Robert seemed to sober up immediately, his own problems forgotten.

I nodded.

'Why was he there?'

'I don't know. I didn't actually speak to them. I panicked and ran off when I saw them together so I didn't confront them.'

'Are you sure they were *together* together?'

'They were kissing.'

He didn't say anything but I saw everything he was feeling in his expression – his instinct to protect his daughter, his embarrassment about her getting caught in a sexual act, the guilt about almost assaulting Nathan.

'We should wait until she comes home, next time. Discuss

it with her then. We can't do anything otherwise. If we phone her up, tell her we know about Nathan, imply we object, it will only be driving them closer together.'

Robert nodded but only barely.

'What do you think of him?'

I could hardly tell him the truth.

'I don't know. After the window thing, I guess I'm biased.'

'No, it's not ideal.'

'I enjoyed the festival. The author, Jemima French was lovely, which was good luck but I've had Simeon Averill on the phone.'

'Sir Simeon?' he said.

'You do listen to me,' I replied, feeling a wave of love.

'Tell me about Sir Simeon,' he said with a small, soft smile.

I took Robert's whisky out of his hand and pretended to take a sip, and then put it on the desk out of his reach. My husband was not a good drunk. Neither was I.

I sat on his knee and enjoyed the sensation of his arm snaking round my waist.

I sighed. 'He's having a hissy fit because Edelman didn't treat his last book as the landmark publishing event he thought it was. Not enough posters, not enough adverts, not enough glowing reviews or TV appearances. Now we're throwing him a party in a bid to keep him on our list, but that's only stirred another hornet's nest and Ian Sinclair is going to be furious when he finds out. The party was supposed to be a sweetener, not a deal breaker.'

'What's his problem with the party?'

'The venue.'

That perked him up a bit. He knew practically every building in London especially the big, grand ones.

'The Mark Hotel in Soho.'

'Nice place. Where does he want it if not there?'

'Buckingham Palace, the way he's been going on. Apparently, the knighthood's gone to his head.'

'What's his guest list like?'

'*Tout le beau monde*,' I smiled. I reeled off a list of invitees; even if I said so myself, it was a pretty impressive collection of hot names from the film, art and fashion scenes. 'There's even talk of additional security measures; one of the royals might be coming. Not sure who though.'

And then, as if a cartoon light bulb had pinged on above my head, it came to me.

'Robert,' I said, eyes wide. 'What about Cadogan House?'

My husband was only seconds behind me in the thought process.

'For Simeon's party?'

'Remember the open house you did for Portland Place?' I said, words rushing out in my excitement.

Portland Place was a luxury apartment complex Robert had developed a couple of years earlier. The market was fizzing at the time and the swish apartments had sold in a flash, all except the penthouse, sitting unloved and unviewed for months until Robert had a brainwave: throw an open house event. He had dressed the flat like a designer show home with borrowed cutting-edge furniture and art, then brought in Dylan and me – suitably styled – to play the part of the perfect British family.

Robert had three offers before the end of the day. In the end, it had gone to sealed bids.

'Couldn't we dress Cadogan House like you did at Portland Place?' I said. 'But set it up for a party instead, then we hold Simeon's launch there and add your prospective buyers to the guest list. Most of these high-net guys only want to use their London pad for entertaining anyway. Let's show them what life could be like, if they owned it.'

He looked across at me.

'Do you really think you could get all those names there?'

'Definitely. Simeon knows everyone. Besides, holding it at a fancy private residence will add to the appeal. They'll be curious.'

Robert's eyes had taken on a faraway look, as if he were picturing it in his mind.

'It would be like they were walking into the best party of all time,' he said. 'The clients would love it.'

He frowned and looked at me.

'But won't Simeon object?'

'He won't know, he'll be too busy holding court. And anyway, he's definitely the sort of man who likes being surrounded by the rich and successful. He's not going to turf a Saudi prince out, is he?'

A slow smile was spreading across Robert's face and I knew I had hit the bullseye. For once, I felt useful and wanted. I had made a mess of things but now I was going to fit it. For the first time in a long time I felt like a good wife.

'When's the launch?' he asked.

'Three weeks. Is that too late?'

He shook his head. 'I'm sure I can work it out.'

'In which case, it's sorted.'

He took my head in his hands and kissed me softly.

'I knew there was a reason I married you,' he whispered.

'Not just my good looks?'

'That too.'

He kissed me again. And he kept kissing me all the way down to the bedroom, with Nathan, Dylan, Chris Hannah and Cadogan House forgotten.

Chapter 37

'So how much is this going to cost us?'

We were in the smallest meeting room on the floor but I felt like we were in a police cell.

Ian Sinclair sat back in his chair and put his hands behind his head. I wasn't a body language expert, but I knew that the pose was meant to say 'I'm in charge'. It also communicated 'I'm annoyingly smug', but I was just grateful that he wasn't looking at me like I was some sort of sexual deviant. Word about the explicit photos had obviously been contained by Serena and Lydia.

'The party itself will cost Edelman nothing. RT Developments will provide the house and all the other entertaining costs,' I explained, looking at my notes written on the pad on my lap.

'Booze as well?'

There was still a chippiness to his voice. I suspected he was still angry that I hadn't come out for lunch with him and Jemima the previous day. He hadn't brought it up, or even mentioned Jemima French, but I could see how he might have been a bit miffed about it given he had travelled a hundred miles to Birmingham to join us. Still – I thought he could be at least a bit more grateful that I was about to salvage his Simeon Averill party.

'Food, drink. It will be all covered,' I confirmed. 'Edelman just has to get the guests there, invitations and taxis for Simeon and other VIPs. But it will be a massive saving from the cost of The Mark, who've agreed to give back the deposit because one of the banks has just taken it for their Christmas bonus party.

'What's in it for RT Developments?'

He still looked sceptical although I didn't blame him for that.

The offer was generous, suspiciously generous.

'What's ever "in it" for a sponsor?' I said with a half-smile. 'Its association with the brand, in this case, intellect and creativity. RT developments has money and property; Simeon has a global reputation. It works for both sides. Besides, it's my husband's company.'

Ian didn't respond. I thought I saw his thin eyes narrow under the blue tint of his lens.

'He might want to invite a few guests,' I said quickly.

'How many?'

'Literally a handful,' I replied, deciding that the best option was to be open about the arrangement. The last thing I wanted was for one of Robert's top investors or ultra-net worth clients being turned away at the door because Ian was being imperious. 'Don't worry. They'll certainly add something to mix.'

Ian twisted his pen around his fingers which made me nervous.

'So that's all fine?' I said, wishing we were in a bigger room and the space between us wasn't so small.

'Let's hope it's fine,' he said coolly.

'What do you mean?'

'I mean that there can be no mistakes on this event. None, whatsoever.'

'Of course not . . .'

'Didn't you say that about Jemima's Birmingham literary event?'

'Ian, I explained about that. I was in a car accident the night before . . .'

'Then you should have called Georgina. There was no excuse not to. It was unprofessional and embarrassing. Ginny Lane would never have done anything like that. Thankfully Jemima is very accommodating but Sir Simeon is more exacting. You drop the ball, even once, and it's just an excuse for him to move publishers, which is precisely what this party is trying to prevent. Am I making myself clear?'

Lydia put her head around the door.

'Rachel. Phone call.'

She didn't look me in the eye. I'd had a word with her earlier to diffuse any embarrassment but I still couldn't look her in the eye. Apparently, Serena had already told her that the envelope of photographs she had opened had been a horrible joke, but I wasn't entirely sure she believed it.

'Lydia, really. We are in a meeting,' snapped Ian, putting up a hand.

'Apparently it's urgent,' replied his assistant.

I sat up straight. I'd told Valentina on reception 'no calls', but I couldn't admit that in front of Ian.

Ian tutted, his displeasure obvious, and waved a finger.

'Go on, if it's that important. Then can you please come straight back here. There's less than three weeks to sort this out although I am not entirely sure how I have found myself as a party planner rather than the managing director of this company.'

I was on the edge of getting fired, I could tell. It would be framed in a different way, of course. 'We're not in the position to renew your contract,' would be the most likely excuse. Perhaps they'd float the rumour that Ginny Lane was due to come back, even if she wasn't.

I slipped into my cubicle and picked up the phone, at first angry at who it was that was calling, and then afraid.

There hadn't been any communication from Him for the

past few days. No postcards, tweets, emails. No presents, nothing. Was it over? Had the break-in and the bloody heart been his swansong?

Had he finally got bored as Charlotte had said or was his silence over the past few days just a hiatus before a new, bold approach?

'Hello,' I said nervously.

'It's Nathan. Thank God, you've answered. I couldn't get hold of you on your mobile number.'

'What's wrong?' I asked, my heart still thumping. Phone calls from Nathan were never good, but now I knew about his relationship with Dylan, I was even more anxious.

'It's Bill.'

I breathed a guilty sigh of relief.

'What's wrong?'

'He's acting weird. He's hot, feverish. He started lashing out and then he fell.'

'Oh no.'

'He's okay. I managed to get him up. He's not hurt but still, I don't think he's in a good way.'

I glanced towards the boardroom where Ian was waiting for my return. I saw him watching me and then turn away when he realized I had seen him.

'You should get him to the doctor's,' I said, lowering my voice.

'I think it's gone beyond that. What should we do?'

I knew what Nathan was saying. *You sort it out.* But there was no way I could leave the office. Someone else was going to have to deal with it, even though my default setting so to say 'yes' to whatever Nathan was suggesting.

'I'm not sure I can leave work straight away but I'll call Robert, see if he can help,' I said into the receiver. 'In the meantime, call the doctor's surgery or 111. See what they recommend.'

'Alright,' grunted Nathan but I could tell he wasn't happy.

*

By lunchtime I just needed some fresh air.

The office atmosphere was cloying and Ian was in a jumpy mood – according to Vicky, he was always like that when he'd been out of the office for a few days although I was now convinced that he hated me. Back in the meeting room he'd asked me if everything was okay, but he'd said it in a way that suggested he was losing his patience, even though I had thrown him a lifeline for Simeon's party.

At least Nathan also seemed to have things under control. An ambulance had been called to take to Bill to the Whittington hospital and the agency had arranged for replacement cover to make sure Iris was also okay. And when I had spoken to Robert to tell him that the event at Cadogan House had been green-lit, he too had sounded so pleased he hadn't minded giving Nathan a helping hand, given that he was on a site visit nearby in Hampstead.

The clouds were heavy and grey as I stepped out onto Aldwych, and the light was cool, giving the city a pale starkness I only ever noticed in winter. There was a wind whipping at my collar as I stepped into the street, but I didn't mind.

I just kept walking, enjoying the sense of moving forward. I went to the deli on Fleet Street and wanted somewhere quiet – but not lonely – to eat my sandwich. I knew just the place. Middle Temple. I crossed the road and entered the complex of lanes and courtyards.

A man hurried past in a navy chalk-stripe suit, swinging a worn leather briefcase like a metronome. An unfamiliar sense of calm settled over me. For a moment, I was a time-traveller in this strange, beautiful little hidden corner of London, a character in a Dickens novel watching other people's daily life happen around me.

I sat on a wooden bench in a place called Fountain Court, according to the cast iron sign and took out my lunch. I was grateful for the barristers young and old that hurried past. I didn't want to be alone.

'Do you mind if I sit here?'

I looked up and saw a woman, around thirty-five, holding a similar paper bag to mine. She looked familiar and then it struck me that I'd seen her just a few minutes before, in the deli where I had bought my sandwich.

'Sure. Go ahead,' I said, sliding along the bench.

Something in my baguette got stuck at the back of my throat. I coughed hard and drained the last of my water.

When I carried on coughing, she handed me her unopened plastic bottle and I gratefully gulped down a few more mouthfuls.

'Cress,' I stuttered.

'The devil's food,' replied the woman.

'I wasn't aware of that.'

'It's not. In fact, it's the blandest food known to man.'

'Barely food,' I smiled, handing the bottle back.

She was still looking at me and it put me on edge.

'Have we met?'

'No.'

I crunched the paper bag in my hand with a sinking dawning realization.

I'd always assumed that the texts, the letters were from Him. What if it was a *Her*?

When I had finally regained control of my lungs, I gave her a longer look. Slim, attractive, blonde hair tied back neatly with a shrewdness in her expression. She could have been a barrister or a clerk in the legal offices behind me, but I suspected she was neither.

'Katherine McCauley,' she said finally. 'And you're Rachel Reeves?'

'I don't mean to sound rude, but have we met?'

'I know your husband.'

'Really?'

Neither of us said anything for a few seconds. I was too busy piecing my own thoughts together.

Over the past few weeks I'd tortured myself with the memory of my infidelity. There was part of me that even believed that I deserved all the texts and the photos and the filth that had been sent. I was being punished for my actions. But perhaps I was wrong. I remembered a story I had once read on the YouAreNotAlone forum. A woman had been intimidated for months; had been sent a dead toad through the post, had her car windscreen graffitied on with a Sharpie and been subjected to a three-month-long barrage of texts and crank phone calls. Her stalker turned out to be one of her husband's colleagues, someone he'd slept with at an overnight conference. He'd cut the affair short after just a few weeks, but his fling hadn't been able to accept it and had turned all her frustration and resentment onto his wife.

My blood felt cold. After all this, maybe Robert had also been unfaithful and this was payback – for both of us.

'Could we talk?'

I scrunched the bag up tighter in my fist.

'What do you want to talk about?'

'I have a few questions. About Robert.'

'What questions? What's this about?'

'Your husband's business.'

'What about it?' My voice was stiff and defensive.

She didn't speak for another few seconds.

'What do you know about money laundering in London?'

I almost laughed with relief.

'Money laundering? I'm a book editor, not MI5.'

'But you read the papers?'

I nodded stiffly.

'So you'll know how much dirty money flows through this city,' she said simply.

'Do you want to get to the point?'

'Let's walk.'

We stood up and I followed her. I would have preferred

to have gone in the direction of busy Fleet St, but instead she headed in the direction of the river.

'What do you want?' I asked, staring out on the steely water of the Thames.

'I wouldn't mind your life,' she shrugged. 'From the outside, it looks pretty good. Your husband is the sole director of RT Developments. You live in Highgate. His current developments include a fifteen-bedroom house in Belgravia, and an apartment block by Regent's Park. The penthouse in that one is being marketed as one of the finest homes in London.'

She knew so much about our life. Like a stalker.

'Where do you think the money comes from, Rachel? To buy, to develop these properties.'

'Banks, investors, the same as any business,' I replied sharply.

The truth was I had no idea. Not for sure.

'His investors. What do you know about them?'

'I don't know anything about them. We hardly talk about his business.'

'But you know he has Russian business associates.'

'So that's where this is going.' I nodded.

Katherine McCauley didn't say anything.

I stopped and turned to face her.

'Do you know how small-minded this sounds? I'd go so far as to say racist.'

She ignored me and carried on talking.

'We have a number of ongoing investigations into money laundering in the capital. Money is being washed through a variety of high-end properties, residential and commercial. Billions of pounds worth, all bought by offshore companies. Beyond that, it all gets murky who the real owners are, the origin source of the money.'

'You obviously have an idea.'

Katherine paused.

'The money is washed because it's dirty. It's the proceeds

271

of crime, corruption. The offshore companies are just a registered base, it allows the real owners to be anonymous.'

I gave her a hard look.

'What's all this got to do with Robert?'

'Your husband is working with Elena Dimitrov.'

My gut instinct told me not to say anything.

'I have to get back to work.'

'He is helping her source a premises. A gallery.'

I was about to tell her that she was being ridiculous. Elena's gallery was Robert's smallest development. Barely a development, more a property sourcing mission. The sort of work you saw Phil and Kirsty get up to on *Location, Location, Location*. And Elena was lovely, friendly, kind. Not an oligarch's moll – at least as far as I could tell. But for the moment, I held my tongue. She was fishing for information and I wasn't going to give her any satisfaction by giving her something she wanted.

'Who are you Miss McCauley, and what do you want?' I replied.

'What do you know about Elena, about her family?'

'As I said, I know very little about my husband's investors.'

'Elena's father is Dmitri Anotov. She's married – hence the different surname.'

Another long pause.

'Dmitri is the director of the Zengset bank. Officially that's his job. He is also the head of one of the most prominent crime syndicates in East Europe. A conservative estimate is that he has washed in excess of one billion dollars through London alone.'

'Crime syndicate?'

'We have reason to believe that the Anotov family have been using high-end property developments to launder large sums of money generated by their real business interests – drugs, prostitution, people-trafficking, extortion.'

I gaped at her.

'Organized crime, Mrs Reeves,' said McCauley. 'They are the Russian mafia.'

'You're wrong.'

It was the most instinctive thing to say.

She gave a low laugh.

'I'm supposing you've met Elena. Liked her. We're not even sure how much she knows about her father's line of business. But the gallery is a front, make no mistake. If Anotov's associates are seen in London – there's a legitimate excuse. A small gallery in the East End is a believable investment for a pampered daughter of a wealthy man. But a huge development worth hundreds of millions . . . That's going to raise more questions.'

She paused before she spoke again.

'Their real business interest in London is the Regent Place development. They are providing the finance for it. Max Miskov is Dmitri's man in London. His consigliere, if you'd like.'

I shook my head violently.

'I don't believe you. My husband is a legitimate businessman. He would only deal with legitimate businesspeople. I'm not saying anything further to you,' I said, turning on my heel.

'You know it's true.'

'Why are you telling me all this?' I asked.

'Because we need help,' she said more slowly. 'We know things but we can't prove them. If we can't prove it, we can't stop it.'

'I can't help you,' I spluttered. 'I barely know where my husband is from day to day, let alone the ins and outs of his business.'

I stopped, feeling my chest collect with emotion. Of course it all made sense. Robert's black moods, the cloud of unease that had hung over his head the past few weeks. His friendship with Max Miskov, the argument with Miskov at our

273

house. Panic gripped my thoughts, my own problems temporarily forgotten.

If Max was in London to do Anotov's bidding, that put Robert in danger if he put a foot wrong. Perhaps Robert had finally felt that fear. Perhaps he had finally realized what sort of people he was involved with.

I sank down onto another bench feeling wiped out.

Katherine sat down next to me, closer this time. Her expression had softened, was more conciliatory.

'Best case scenario is that your husband has been prepared to turn a blind eye to the accounts from Cyprus, British Virgin Islands, Malta. Who cares where the money comes from unless it stops flowing? The worst case . . .' She paused and our eyes locked. 'The worst-case scenario is that he's more complicit in Anotov's business deals.'

'What are you suggesting now? That my husband is an actual criminal?'

'Mrs Reeves. These people are dangerous. There's a word for the grand properties that they buy. Blood mansions. Bought with black money which directly stems from pain and suffering. They need to be brought to justice and for that, we need evidence.'

'You've still not told me what you want.'

I could hear the panic in my voice.

'We want him to co-operate, and that's where you come in. We want you to ask him.'

'You ask him,' I shot back

'Too risky.'

'Risky?'

'We need to know if your husband will co-operate. If he will, then we can deal directly with him. If he doesn't, we will have to assume that he is complicit with Anotov and we will have to try and get the information another way. You'll need to tread carefully. There's a strong chance that he'll let Anotov know of our interest – knowingly or otherwise. And that would jeopardize our investigation and potentially put him in danger.'

My stomach dropped.

'Danger?'

'Last week, a Russian lawyer was gunned down in Moscow. He worked for Dmitri. Word has it, his death was an assassination.'

I didn't reply.

'Rachel, these people are ruthless.'

For the first time in our meeting I thought she was with me, not against me.

'If they think Robert is a weak link, people are easily disposable,' she continued. 'You, however, are above suspicion. And I'm guessing you might be able to find things out for us.'

My hands were trembling. 'But why on earth would I want to do that? Even if Elena and Max are providing dirty money, which I don't believe they are, if her father is some warlord, why on earth would I want to get involved? You've already said that one of Anotov's associates had been killed.'

I was trying to breathe in and out.

'I can't do this.'

'Yes, you can.'

She opened her bag and handed me a magazine.

'Open it,' she said, looking straight ahead.

There were four or five photos slotted between the pages. They were small 7x5-inch images – the sort you used to slot into a photo album – but still I was reminded of the images that had been sent to Ian Sinclair, that Lydia and Serena had intercepted.

This time the pictures were of me. Not explicit but equally revealing. Me and Chris Hannah. Photos of us disappearing into the Soho hotel, of me emerging, the next day, bleary-eyed in yesterday's clothes.

I gulped hard.

'How do you have these?'

'We don't want to use them.'

'That wasn't the question,' I said, my voice lifting a note. 'How do you have these?'

'Sometimes you need leverage.'

'You've been following me?'

It was all making sense, a fog in my mind lifting so I could see the shapes and colours of what lay beneath it. When I felt as if I was being watched, I was. At Le Circe, on my run on Hampstead Heath. It was Katherine McCauley. It was all her.

There was a long silence.

'I assume your husband doesn't know about this?'

Another thought. This one made me want to vomit.

'My friend. The man in the picture. Did you send him to meet me?'

'You made that mistake on your own,' she said, not taking her hard eyes off me.

'Messages, texts . . . I've been getting stuff from him. Was that you too?'

Katherine buttoned up her coat and pulled a card out of her pocket.

'Think about it and let's talk again,' she said without answering my question.

'Please, tell me,' I pleaded but she had already got up to leave.

'Don't worry. You can keep those. I have another set,' she called back to me as she disappeared into the ancient warrens of Middle Temple.

Chapter 38

Deep down I had been expecting something like this to happen. That one day I would be approached by a Katherine McCauley, or someone just like her, and our world would one day come tumbling down. And now it was, now the day was here – and I had no idea what to do.

Trying to put it out of my mind, I wiped a hand across the cold window of the bus, cutting a hole in the condensation to see where we were. Just another identical shelter, another dark London street, another line of workers shuffling home to their interchangeable houses. I squeezed my eyes shut.

Was Robert mixed up in something illegal and dangerous? It was certainly plausible, I had to admit that.

It had taken my husband less than twenty years to go from a one-man-band, renovating a small flat in St John's Wood, to being head of a property firm that had forty-five employees and bought and sold homes to ultra-high net individuals. If I was honest, I'd shied away from thinking about how Robert had managed such a rapid climb, just content to upgrade from the Holloway Road maisonette we'd lived in as newlyweds, to a terrace in Crouch End, to our concrete masterpiece in Highgate. I was content to feel financially comfortable, to take increasingly opulent holidays with kids' clubs and spas without thinking too much about where the money came from.

Yes, he was smart and focused but I had also attended enough of Robert's business dinners to get a sense of the people he dealt with; under all the handmade shirts and the gold Breitlings and the smooth charm, there was always the feeling that these men and women were skating on the edge of legality. And I'd read the newspapers of course, read about the money men who moved in the grey areas of the law, the shady margins where pay-offs and 'sweeteners' went in and out of Swiss bank accounts.

But was that just his clients? Or was it Robert too?

It was one thing to suspect that your client's money was less than clean but it was quite another to get actively involved in money laundering or illegal deals.

And yet . . . and yet I still wanted to believe in my husband. Our marriage wasn't perfect, but I still saw my husband as a good man, a fair man, a slick operator, a tough negotiator, not a criminal.

Was it me, who lacked the morals? Katherine McCauley knew that. She had seen the pictures of me with Chris Hannah and assumed I would help her, because I had already betrayed my husband once. When you've already crossed that line, what was one more knife in the back?

The bell dinged and the 'Stopping' light came on. I knew why I'd taken the bus – because it would take longer, the equivalent of a child dragging her feet on the first day of nursery. But glancing out of the window, I saw the sign for the hospital.

Fearing we were about to glide past it, I scrambled to grab my bag and clattered down the stairs, just squeezing through as the bus doors hissed closed.

A steady drizzle was coming down as I walked up the steps towards the Whittington. I pulled out a Post-it note and tried to match the directions I had scribbled down to the baffling map on the wall in the entrance. In the end a friendly lady in a sash marked 'Can I help?' had to direct me: up a flight of steps, along the corridor, turn right, then left, straight on until you see the nurse's station.

'William Neville?' I said to the woman at the desk.

'Ah yes, Bill,' she smiled. 'He's on the left, bed four by the window.'

I stepped forward and lowered my voice. 'How is he?'

'Physically he's on the mend. Urinary infection, that's all. Happens to men his age, I'm afraid. We've given him anti-biotics and plenty of fluids and the doctors are pleased with his progress. Nothing broken in the fall, either. He should be out in a day or two, all being well.'

I thanked her and walked onto the ward: eight beds, four each side, a dark window at the end. Bill was sitting up in bed, a drip attached to his arm, face turned towards the blank window.

'Hello there,' I said as cheerily as I could. 'You're looking better.'

It was a lie. He looked wan and drawn, as if he'd aged five years overnight. For a moment, Bill didn't respond, then he slowly turned to face me.

'Ah,' he said. That was all.

'How are they treating you? Looks like it's pretty cosy here.'

Cosy in the sense that the beds were uncomfortably close together. Across the room from Bill, there was a red plastic bucket evidently put there to catch drips: the ceiling tile directly above was bulging and stained copper brown. Functional yes, cosy no.

'I spoke to the nurse,' I said. 'She says you're doing really well. You might be home tomorrow.'

Bill gave a one-shoulder shrug, as if he wasn't bothered one way or the other, then turned to look out the window again.

'You look deep in thought, Bill,' I said.

'Not much else to do in here,' he replied.

I pulled up my bag.

'I brought you something,' I said, pulling out a handful of CDs. 'Audiobooks,' I said, offering them to him, then when he didn't raise a hand, placed them on the bedside cabinet. 'Hearing impaired version. There were a couple lurking around the office.'

It was only now as I looked at the boxes that I realized what a useless present they were. CDs needed a CD player and headphones and with Bill's sixty per cent hearing loss in each ear I wasn't even sure they were going to work.

'I'll bring in a CD player tomorrow if you haven't been sent home,' I said lamely. 'I know Dylan has one I can borrow.'

There was another pause, then Bill looked back at me.

'He didn't take the book, you know,' he said.

'Who?'

'Nathan. He'd only borrowed it to read. We had a good chat about Spitfires.'

'Well, that's good. I'm glad you've found some common ground,' I said, but didn't mean it.

I didn't want to hear nice things about Nathan Deer. In fact, if he had been a thief, it would have been a handy reason to get rid of him. My daughter's relationship with him had changed all that.

'Robert came this afternoon. Said he's going to sort me out with a private room.'

'You might not be here long enough for that.'

I sat down on a chair next to the bed. He was as pale as the greying sheet under which he lay.

'Thank you,' said Bill so quietly I could hardly hear him.

'What for?'

'For everything. You've been very good to us. If you hadn't been there, I'm not sure what we'd have done. Don't tell my nephew but we're changing our will. I think it's only right that you and Robert should get recognized.'

'Bill, that is absolutely not necessary,' I said, still pleasantly surprised by this acknowledgement. That was enough – more than any bequest of Iris's favourite earrings. 'But, can I ask you something?'

He turned towards me, interested. Perhaps my tone hadn't been as even as I had hoped.

'Remember when I asked you about people in the street?'

'What people?'

'When my bins had been turned over. I asked you if you had seen anyone strange in the street, or perhaps driving past?'

He nodded. 'Why do you ask? Is something wrong?'

'Oh, nothing like that, I was just wondering if you or Iris had seen anyone visit our place recently. Coming to see Robert, business associates, that sort of thing?'

'Hello, hello.'

We both turned at the sound of a cheery voice.

It was Nathan, the shoulders of his anorak soaked, a bag for life hanging off one arm like low slung fruit.

There was a long pause but it was not the time or the place for awkwardness.

'I thought you'd gone home,' I said stiffly. I tried my best to be civil.

'I'm going out in Islington. Thought I'd pop in on my way down there and bring some goodies.'

I wondered who he was meeting in Islington, remembering he lived in Finsbury Park.

He raised his eyebrows at Bill. 'Don't think the food in here would worry Gordon Ramsay, eh? So, I brought you some bits.' He unloaded the bag – grapes, biscuits, fruit jellies.

I couldn't deny it was thoughtful.

'They told me something at lunchtime was soup,' said Bill, pointing to a far bay. 'But I think it came out of that bucket over there.'

We all laughed and Bill poked at the jellies, holding them close up to his face so he could see them properly.

We made some chit-chat about the weather turning cold and hospital food and how Islington's Upper Street had changed so much over the past fifteen years.

When I stood up to leave, I asked Nathan for a quick word.

'Be back in a minute, Bill. Okay?' said Nathan, before following me.

I walked back past the nurse station and out into the corridor. I waited until he caught up.

When he did, he didn't look me straight in the eye

There was no easy way to say it.

'I know, Nathan,' I said. 'About you and Dylan.'

I had expected embarrassment, shame or outright denial. Instead, I got a shrug.

'She's a great girl,' he said. 'Did she tell you?'

'No,' I said. 'Which is the part I don't like. Why did you keep it from us?'

He looked more contrite. 'Dylan wasn't sure you'd approve.'

'Why not?'

'My age, my job,' he said simply.

I was angry but I found it difficult to be too hard on him.

'Nathan – I admire what you do. Really. You've been great with Bill and Iris. But what I'm upset about, is that you haven't been honest with us.'

'With respect, Mrs Reeves . . .'

I suddenly felt less charitable. People only began sentences with the phrase 'with respect' when they were about to irritate you.

'Dylan and I are both adults and neither of us require your permission to be in a relationship with each other.'

Nathan was right, of course. They didn't need my permission and if I tried to come between them, it would only make the whole thing more appealing and romantic. But I was damned if I was going to make things easy.

'That may well be true,' I said, straightening my back. 'But it would have been a lot more "adult" if you had told us from the outset. As it is, it feels like we've been deceived.'

Nathan looked at me, his caring bedside manner more steely now.

'Why not say, you just don't like me,' he said flatly.

'Pardon?' I said, shocked at his resistance.

'You've been avoiding me since that night, that night your husband had a go at me.'

'He did not have a go at you. You invaded our privacy watching us like that. We were understandably upset.'

I hadn't planned to ever discuss the kitchen table with Nathan Deer, but now we had, I was glad to get it off my chest.

'I was only there for a second. As I told your husband, I didn't see anything and even if I did, it's your business. I'm not embarrassed if you aren't. I've seen some things in my time. Bodily functions and all that. We should just let it go and don't use it as a cross to beat me with about Dylan.'

His frankness and maturity took me back. There was nothing I could shoot back at him without looking petty.

'Fine,' I said, clasping my handbag to my side.

'Don't worry, I have no plans to do anything other than treat Dylan exactly the way you'd wish me to.'

'Then we don't have a problem,' I replied. But somehow, I didn't believe it.

Chapter 39

Robert's office looked like a spaceship. Of course it did; how else would the 'king of modernism's' HQ look? If he could have lived in the Death Star, I'm sure my husband would have; in fact, that was probably the source of his love of all things slick and minimalist. Then again, most little boys want to be Luke Skywalker, not Darth Vader.

At this time of night, the fluorescent lighting glinting from the glass and chrome, the RT Developments office did look otherworldly, especially here in Marylebone among the Georgian terraces and Victorian mansion blocks. I pushed through the revolving door and into the chic marble lobby.

'Hey Mrs Reeves,' said Martin, the receptionist, raising a hand. Martin was in his sixties, grey hair, always dressed in a sharp blazer with a dark tie. He looked more like a hit man than a receptionist; given the revelations from Katherine McCauley, I'm guessing that came in handy.

'Shall I call up? Or is it a surprise?' he asked, buzzing me through the security door.

'He knows I'm coming,' I said. 'We're late for dinner.'

'Uh-oh,' Martin grinned a happy arch of yellow teeth. 'Leave me out of it.'

I ran up the stairs, my going-out heels clacking on the

marble steps. This was supposed to be a date night, a trip into Mayfair for sushi and expensive cocktails. It was the one upside of my night with Chris Hannah. Trying harder with my husband. Trying to get it back to how we once were.

Robert had texted me at work saying he was running late. Suggested I go to Selfridges and meet him at the restaurant. But I had other ideas.

Petra, Robert's assistant, was leaving her office as I slipped past the empty reception. The rest of the place was empty, which for a Friday night didn't seem unusual.

'You're here late,' I said, kissing her on the cheek.

Petra was twenty years younger than I was and smelled of the hairdresser's and make-up. She'd been my husband's right-hand woman for over three years, and it was hard not to feel anxious and suspicious when I saw her working side by side with him, deep into the evening.

But despite my concern I had never seen any evidence to suggest she was anything other than a brilliant, hardworking PA.

'Party planning,' she smiled, slinging her leather tote over her shoulder.

'I'm so grateful for everything, you've done,' I said honestly.

Robert had suggested she get involved with Simeon's party and she had managed to arrange the catering, staff and deco inside a week single-handedly. If it had been left to the Edelman marketing office, the same task would have taken a whole department a month and a stack of paperwork for overtime.

'Knock knock,' I said, putting my head around the door of his office. It was sleek and Spartan, just a glass-topped desk, a phone and a silver laptop, moodily lit with an apricot glow of down lighters. One uncomfortable leather couch and an angular coffee table stood isolated by the windows and there was nothing as ugly or utilitarian as a filing cabinet or, God forbid, a kettle; all the practical stuff was hidden away in another room.

'I thought you were going shopping,' he said, glancing up from the computer screen.

'Thought I'd come and pick you up en route.'

'Just give me a few minutes, got something important . . .' He trailed off, his mind clearly elsewhere. His hair was mussed and he looked harassed. Experience told me there was no point in hectoring or hurrying anyway. I'd managed to get a table at Miso2, the hot new Japanese place on Mount Street, and we were originally due there in ten minutes, but it wouldn't do any good to point that out. With Robert, work came first.

I walked across to the couch, but didn't sit. I'd run out at lunch to get this dress, a beautiful blue silk number with an eye-watering price tag.

'Maybe we should just ring ahead. Say we'll be late,' he said, finally looking up. He ran a finger along his collar, as if it was too tight.

'How long do you think you'll be?'

'I don't know. Twenty minutes. Half an hour. It's still early on the West Coast,' he said, as if that explained everything.

I watched him, dark eyes focused on his laptop, brows knitted together in a thick black rope above his nose. I could feel and smell his anxiety and knew he wasn't going to enjoy small talk over dim sum.

'We can always not go,' I offered and he had the good grace to skip a beat.

'Do you mind?'

'We can get a take-away,' I shrugged. 'You can make your calls from home, and there's a new BBC thing I want to see starting at nine. We'll enjoy the restaurant more when we're not rushing.'

He shot me a grateful half smile, then turned off his computer and glanced at his watch.

'Just let me nip to the bathroom, then we can go.'

I didn't know what I was looking for. There was a Regent

Place sales brochure on the table by the sofa. That was to be expected. But why else had I come to his office rather than meet him in Mayfair? What was I hoping to see? What did I expect to find? Hammer and Sickle pamphlets, a Kalashnikov machine gun, a McMafia DVD? I was hardly Columbo.

I went behind his desk and opened the desk drawer but there was nothing of any note. Just a notebook, a few pencils and a pack of chewing gum.

His computer was still on. I glanced towards the door but could hear no noise from the rest of the floor. Licking my dry lips, I clicked onto his emails and typed Max's name into the search bar. Dozens of emails filled the screen. I read one, then another. They were both work-related, nothing out of the ordinary for correspondence between business partners.

Distant footsteps echoed in the corridor.

I was starting to sweat, puddles of moisture pooling on the turquoise silk beneath my armpits.

I clicked back onto his inbox, then closed it down, just as Robert appeared at the door.

'You okay?'

I was still standing behind the desk.

'Yes,' I smiled, wondering if he could hear the tremble in my voice.

'Let's go home,' he said, taking his cashmere overcoat out of the cupboard where it was hanging on a single metal coat hanger.

As I followed him out of the office, down into the garage to collect his car, alone in the concrete, pillared basement of the building, I knew that I would have to return another day.

Robert was quiet for most of the journey home. I stared out of the window, staring at the black, sooty skies, trying to enjoy the warmth from the heated seats under my thighs. The balmy summer nights, when it didn't get dark until ten o'clock and it seemed safe to let Dylan hang out with her friends until the pubs closed, felt a long way off, another lifetime ago. My old, carefree life seemed a very long time ago.

'Elena called this afternoon,' he said as we drove up Highgate Hill, leaving the congested city centre behind us. 'She wanted to know if she could bring some friends to the party.'

He glanced across. I knew what he wanted me to say, what I had to say.

'Of course she can. It's a big house, so there's lots of room,' I said, secretly wondering what Ian Sinclair would say.

'How's the guest list coming on?' He asked me every day, always casually, always with that undertone of worry I could detect after twenty years of marriage.

'VIPs can be hard to pin down,' I told him.

'Why? Are they waiting for better offers?'

'There are no better offers on the night of our party. They'll come,' I smiled, trying to sound confident.

'I could do without David coming here,' he said as we arrived in Highgate. 'What are we going to do with them? And it's the girls' birthday that weekend.'

'How about London Zoo? Dylan always loved it when she was the twins' age.'

He glanced across. 'As if I don't spend enough time in Regent's Park . . .'

'Of course. It was just a suggestion.'

He put a hand on my knee. 'I was joking. We haven't seen them for ages and we should make the effort. The girls will love the zoo and we can go to Feng Shang afterwards for dinner.'

'How is Elena?' I asked as casually as I could.

'Fine,' said Robert, pulling into the drive.

'And the gallery?'

'There's delays. They are quite specific about the contractors they want to use.'

'They? I thought it was just Elena.'

'Max is involved too,' he said, looking across. 'You know that.'

'Where does Elena's money come from then?' I asked as we pulled into the drive. 'Is it family money?'

'The money? Her husband's rich.'

'What does he do?'

'Telecoms, retail . . . quite a diverse portfolio.'

He stopped the car. I couldn't stop though. Not now.

'Is it kosher?'

Robert frowned, his hands still on the wheel.

'What do you mean, is it kosher?'

I tried to keep my voice light. 'There's been so much in the news lately. These Russian oligarchs who are connected to the Kremlin and the mafia.'

'You read too much.' He clearly didn't want to talk about it. Neither did I, but I knew I had to ask.

'Seriously Robert, are they legit?' I lowered my voice. Even in the confines of the car, I didn't know who was listening, who was watching us. Everything put me on guard.

'Legit? Where has all this come from?'

'You know what I mean. Are they dangerous?'

'Max and Elena?' He didn't miss a beat. 'Rach, I know you've been back in the land of fiction, but this isn't some John le Carré movie. Yes, there is some illegal money flowing through London, but most people are legit and to think otherwise is a bit insulting. Max and Elena would be mortified if you even thought this.'

I knew I had to keep pushing. I'd come this far and I couldn't stop now.

'So you think you'd know if they were dodgy?'

He threw his hands up in frustration.

'Yes, I'd know. Don't you think there are checks for this sort of thing, compliance you have to do? This isn't the bloody Wild West, Rachel. It's all regulated.'

I'd been told. I wasn't even sure I wanted to report anything back to Katherine McCauley. One thing was clear, it wasn't going to be easy getting any information out of my husband, even if I did.

We got out of the car. Robert turned off the alarm. The high-pitched beep disturbed a wood pigeon in a nearby tree.

He was angry. I could tell from the thin line of his lips.

I glanced over at Bill and Iris's where all the lights were off.

'Should we check on Iris?'

Bill was still in hospital. Nathan had the day off and although I had arranged with the agency for someone to pop in to visit Iris first thing and at 8 p.m. to check that everything was switched off, it still left a long time for Iris to be left alone given her unpredictability. I glanced at my watch and knew it couldn't hurt if I was there when the temp came to drop by.

'I suppose,' said Robert.

'Come with me?' I replied.

It felt pathetic to ask but the street was dark and my nerves were on edge. Besides, I wanted to soften the mood between us.

He gave a quiet sigh but closed the door and followed me towards Bill's.

There weren't many streetlamps on our road. The cemetery wall lined one side of it, a thick bank of trees the other. At night, I doubted there were fewer blacker spaces in central London, especially when no light spilled from our house or Bill's.

Their gate creaked open. Even in the dark I could tell how overgrown the garden was. It was just another job that needed doing, a reminder that their home was just too big and demanding for them. Two bright eyes peered at us from the undergrowth. I gasped and grabbed Robert's arm.

'What was that?' I said. My breath made tiny white clouds as I spoke, as if I was breathing fire.

'It's a badger,' he said as it rustled away from us.

Robert inspected a loose tile in the porch and muttered that he should fix it as I fished out my key fob which contained Bill's spare.

The house was in complete darkness and there was a musty smell which hit me in the face when I opened the door. The place needed airing and probably a good clean. We'd been told at the start that carers could help with bathing and cooking, but housework was out of the remit. Although I'd arranged for our cleaner to go to Bill's once a week it was clearly not enough.

'She must have gone to bed,' I said, hoping she was asleep, hoping I wouldn't have to deal with anything like urine-soaked sheets or a naked Iris, who had recently developed a fondness for taking off all her clothes.

'I just hope she's here,' said Robert, no doubt remembering a story that Nathan had told us at the barbeque: how one of his previous clients, a retired naval captain who lived in Dartmouth Park, escaped on a regular basis, and on one occasion, he'd exited his locked house through a window and was eventually found at his former golf club over seven miles away.

'Where's the light?' asked Robert, touching the wall.

'Just here,' I said, reaching behind the coat rack.

It was so quiet that the click of the switch seemed to echo around the room.

I blinked when the overhead dusty chandelier lit up the hall and adjusted my vision.

I saw her fingers first, pale and splayed on the floor.

Robert had seen it too. We gasped in tandem.

Iris lay motionless at the foot of the stairs, her white hair fanned out around her thin, ghoulish face like a halo. One spindly leg was bent up against the steps. Her slipper had fallen off and lay upturned by her hip. Her eyes and mouth were open. There was not a flicker of movement anywhere on her face.

'Don't look,' said Robert, pulling me into his chest.

I buried my face in his shirt, then stopped myself from glancing back. I didn't need a second glimpse to know that she was dead.

Chapter 40

The rain held off, at least. As we walked from the cars down the gravel path towards the chapel, the slate sky seemed to be sitting on top of the trees, long, gloomy shadows laid across our path. But funerals weren't supposed to be happy, upbeat affairs, were they?

Bill leaned on my arm as we shuffled along, upright and stoic. He was wearing a dark navy suit with a striped tie and had been silent and pale all morning. He had left hospital the morning after Iris had been found at the bottom of their stairs and I was seriously worried about his health, given his own stay in hospital.

'She didn't want to be cremated.'

Bill's voice was so quiet I could hardly hear it.

'Her father was Jewish, you see,' he said. 'She wasn't brought up in the faith, but still. It's not allowed in Judaism. Iris didn't want to be cremated.'

I nodded with sympathy. Bill had been telling me this story since he had grasped the fact that his wife was dead, repeating it over and over like a mantra. Like it would keep evil away. I looked up at the cross over the door of the chapel as we walked inside. *It's a little late for that*, I thought.

The vicar greeted us with two-handed shakes and a smile pitched perfectly between warmth and sincerity as we drifted towards the front. Waiting as the pews filled. Or rather, waiting until all the mourners had arrived: the pews were mostly empty. It was not a large church, but still, it was less than a quarter full, perhaps thirty people. The sad reality of old age; too many of your friends had already passed or had scattered to the four winds. And in London that was multiplied. Aside from their direct neighbours – myself and Robert, and I was glad that Dylan had come back to pay her respects – Bill had almost no one to invite.

Then again, I was almost half Iris's age and how many real friends did I have left? Before Serena had forced it out of me, I'd had no one I could confide in about my stalker – I'd had to pay for the privilege of that confidence.

We sat and we waited some more and finally, the service began with 'Bread of Heaven', Iris's favourite hymn. I knew this because I had put the order of service together on my computer at work. John, Iris's nephew, had been next to useless and it had fallen to me to arrange the funeral and the wake in my lunch breaks.

Bill sat with his hands neatly folded in his lap as the vicar began a eulogy.

'Perhaps many of you will not be aware,' he said, 'that Iris was a refugee. Her father, an arts journalist critical of the Nazi regime, fled Munich for Switzerland with his young family – Iris was a young child then – before settling in England after the war.'

I glanced around as there was a murmur of surprise throughout the church. I supposed that, like us, most people had only known Iris as an old lady. We'd asked them if they wanted milk in their tea, whether they needed anything from the shops, but how often did we probe into the tapestry of their lives? Because they were old, did we simply write them off as dull and uninteresting?

'Something else many people don't know about Iris,' said the vicar, 'is that she was an artist. Iris won a scholarship to the Slade School of Art and was one of the first women to have a solo exhibition at the prestigious Stirling gallery in London.'

I glanced across at Bill and was surprised to see he was smiling. And why wouldn't he be? Yes, we were saying goodbye, but right now people were seeing Iris how he saw her, as a real woman who had lived. The vicar continued about Iris's love of Italy, how she and Bill had lived in Tuscany as newlyweds. Her talent for design and her job creating sets for a theatre in Soho in the Sixties. I was amazed. For five years, I went to their house most days and all we talked about was the weather or their various medical complaints.

'Bill and Iris were never blessed with children,' said the vicar. 'But when they moved to Highgate, Bill's nephew Johnny lived with them and Iris always regarded that time as the happiest of her life. She was immensely proud when Johnny became a prefect at Highgate School, even though he was not her son.'

I turned to look at John, but he was staring down at the Order of Service in his hands. I could barely believe it: Bill and Iris had raised him as their own and yet he couldn't manage to organize the sandwiches for his aunt's funeral? I felt bad the moment I thought it. Right now, Iris's nephew must be struggling with both grief and guilt, given the circumstances of her death. And that was the real reason for my outrage: I felt the same way. What if I hadn't gone back to work? What if I had stayed looking after Bill and Iris? Would I have been there; would Iris still be alive?

'Tragically Iris was affected by dementia at the end of her life, but I'm sure we will remember Iris as the vivacious, vital and remarkable woman she was.'

We stood to sing another hymn and I wondered whether that was true. For Bill, it certainly was; Iris would forever be the girl he'd fallen in love with and chosen as his partner through life. But the rest of us? Could we see beyond the slightly batty, mostly grumpy old woman Iris became? And more importantly, was that a fate waiting for all of us? Would the things we had done be remembered? How would people remember us? I glanced up at Robert, so serious and solemn. In twenty, thirty years if he was standing here alone, what would he feel? How would he remember me?

We listened as the vicar committed Iris's remains to the safekeeping of the Lord. One by one, the mourners hugged Bill and we all filed back to the cars. The sky was even darker now, but that seemed right.

The wake was held in the restaurant area of a local pub, all trestle tables covered in white paper tablecloths and buffet food. We'd paid per head, but even as I had agreed the price, I'd known it was a waste. No one ever ate much at funerals; even if you were ravenous, it seemed disrespectful to be enjoying your sausage rolls when people were suffering. Bill, of course, was top of that list. He held his head high, but he was so choked up, he could barely speak, just nodding and grunting as friends and acquaintances muttered 'Lovely service', or 'She was a fine woman.'

Robert stood close by, running interference or jumping in whenever things became awkward. I was proud of how solicitous he was. I was also grateful that Dylan had come, not that it had taken much to persuade her. Dylan was old enough to remember Iris as she had been. She'd still been at prep school when we moved to Highgate and back then Iris had been more sparky and fun, always insisting on baking her a cake for birthdays and letting her climb the big oak tree in their garden. I supposed her boyfriend was the other reason she wanted to come.

She walked over and watched as Nathan helped Bill into a seat.

'He's so good with Bill,' said Dylan, looking over adoringly.

I'd never heard her say anything like that when I went around to the Nevilles'. When I shopped and cleaned for them, when I paid their bills, and cut their hair and toenails.

But now was not the time for feeling jealous and overlooked.

'Yes, he is,' I said, putting a hand on her shoulder.

'Nathan's been brilliant,' she said, not looking at me.

She was right, although she only knew what he had told her. But even I could admit that Nathan had been a rock over the past few days. Helping out with the arrangements for the wake, running around to the supermarket, library, chemist, to make sure that Bill had everything he needed.

I didn't reply.

'You're not still being funny about him, are you?' she said with a sideward glance.

I'd told her that I knew about their relationship when she'd come home the night before. I'd said it simply, without any disapproval. She'd already known, because Nathan had told her.

'Of course I'm not being funny,' I said, taking a sip of mineral water from a glass.

'He told me you warned him to be good to me.'

'That's what any parent says to the new partner of their child, particularly when they are six years older.'

Dylan turned to face me head-on.

'Look, we both know Nat's older than me. But it's a good thing, Mum. Honestly. He's mature. And he's the only boy I've ever met who actually has food in the fridge, who actually calls when he says he will. There's no angles with Nathan, no posing. So many boys play games with you, but he's straightforward. Super honest. That's what I love about him.'

Love? She had casually slipped it in, but I knew it was deliberate. I wanted to tell her about young love, about *my* first love. How at eighteen, everything seemed certain and forever, how you thought you knew someone, when in fact you knew nothing about them at all, and certainly didn't know to what extent they could change.

But I said nothing.

The pub manager came to speak to me to discuss closing the open bar and Dylan went to talk to her dad.

When he had gone, I crossed the room to the buffet table and stood on my own, nibbling a mozzarella stick.

Dylan and Nathan were stood by the window, late afternoon light washing over them. They were talking about me again; I knew it and I didn't like it. He glanced over at me and there was a look, just a hint of triumph, that put me on edge. For all his help and support with Bill, I still wasn't sure I trusted him.

'Drink?' said a voice at my shoulder.

I turned and saw Robert who handed me a glass of wine.

I shook my head.

'I don't feel like drinking,' I said, not looking him in the eye. I hadn't told him about the Prozac but I doubted he would find my abstinence strange on a day like today.

I motioned towards the window. 'We had another word.'

He knew I was talking about Dylan and Nathan.

'We've got to tread carefully.'

'She's seen the inside of his fridge.'

'It could be worse.'

I glared at him.

'How could it be worse, Robert? She's been to his house.'

'Didn't you go around to your boyfriend's place when you were at university?'

I took too big a sip of water and it spilled down my blouse.

'Poor Bill,' said Robert after another moment.

Our gaze changed course from our daughter to our neighbour. He was sitting in the middle of the room, half slumped on a chair, seemingly listening to the vicar – the one man, I noted, who was tucking into a plate of food – but Bill didn't seem engaged, his eyes were distant, his brow furrowed.

'He's grieving. You can't expect him to be at his best, especially when he's just come out of hospital himself.'

Robert nodded, still looking at Bill. 'I think we've got to consider you going back.'

'Going back where?'

There was an awkward pause.

'Bill needs us,' said Robert finally.

'Us?'

'Someone. Someone more than a carer.'

I knew what he was saying. He thought I should give up work, stay at home, and look after Bill.

'Then speak to his nephew,' I said, feeling my temper flare. Even so, I said it quietly, through my teeth, not wanting to be heard. I felt guilty challenging Robert's proposal, after all, the situation did seem too much for Nathan to cope with alone. But I also knew that people would let you take the responsible if you didn't push back.

'I have spoken to John. He's retiring next month and moving to Gibraltar.'

'That's handy,' I huffed.

Robert's voice took a more diplomatic tone. 'It would only be for a few weeks. Let Bill grieve, get back on his feet.'

I wasn't sure my husband understood my reticence.

'Robert, my job is just for a few months.'

'Exactly. It's temporary. So it's not the end of the world if you have to pull back.'

That smarted.

'How about you take a sabbatical?' I snapped.

'Rachel, don't be silly.'

'I'm not. You're the boss of your own company. Make it work if it means so much to you.'

'Don't you care about Bill's welfare?' he said, making me

feel even more shitty. 'Is Simeon Averill's party really more important than our friend?'

'Don't make this sound altruistic, Robert. You've never wanted me to go back to work, that's the truth of it.'

Robert's small shake of the head spoke volumes.

'Rachel, what's wrong with you these days?'

'What do you mean.'

'You're so wound up. Angry, sensitive, stressed and it's since you started at Edelman. Maybe it's a good thing if you stopped. If you're not doing it for Bill, do it for yourself. For us.'

I gulped hard. I'd started taking the Prozac and it was definitely kicking in. Over the past few days, I was less teary, hormonal, less like I was trapped in a perpetual cycle of PMS. I felt more equipped to cope no matter what the universe was throwing at me. But the emotion of the day, and Robert's suggestion about giving up work, the fact that he had noticed my anxiety, had me in its grip and it was squeezing tighter.

I glanced around. No one had noticed our disagreement.

I was embarrassed we'd had it. Ashamed that we were arguing at a wake.

'I'm sorry. I don't want to put pressure on you,' he said, more quietly as if he had felt my distress.

My body was tight and rigid and I didn't reply.

Robert sighed, a hint at relenting. 'Look, I know you like work.' He paused as if he was still thinking it all through. 'We can get around it. Throw some money at it if we have too. It's probably time he had a live-in carer, or at least one that can stay overnight.'

I felt ashamed that Robert thought all my problems stemmed from work.

'I do care about Bill,' I said honestly. 'But there's only so much I can do. And I don't need my husband making me feel like the shittiest person in the room.'

'You are the kindest, most lovely person in any room, Rach

and that's what I'm worried about. I hate seeing you like this. Stress. It's a viper, Rach. It sneaks up slowly and then it squeezes the life out of you.'

'I'm fine,' I whispered.

'Maybe you should see someone . . .'

'A therapist?'

My voice had a bark.

'Just think about it. This is your mental health we're talking about . . .'

'I don't need a bloody therapist.'

He stopped as if he had just changed his mind about saying what he was going to. Instead, he just took my hand and I breathed in, relaxing to diffuse my frustration, enjoying the warmth of skin, the solidity of his palm as it pressed against mine.

'I'd better go and rescue Bill from the vicar,' said Robert letting go. And as my eyelids fluttered open and I saw my husband cross the room, glad-handing the vicar with charm and grace, I said a silent prayer, thankful that we had someone to look after us.

Chapter 41

Shaftesbury Avenue was throbbing. The pavements were five people deep with the pre-theatre crowds, the roads clogged with tourists, cabs and Deliveroo cycles. I took a left up Dean Street into the bowels of Soho, turning up my collar to stop the chill running down my neck. Smokers stood in solidarity outside pubs and dark doorways. I'd never smoked but right then, wished I could join their secret club.

It was Robert who'd insisted that I go to the reunion. I'd mentioned that my old Durham gang were meeting up to watch our college-mate's stand-up show and he'd said it would do me good to go. That seeing old friends, watching two hours of comedy with them and having a laugh was just what I needed. Not moping around at the house, feeling sad about Bill, angry about Dylan and Nathan, and stressed about work, and part of me agreed with him. My lunch with Mike Weller had been one of the highlights of the past month, at least until he had told me about Chris Hannah's jail sentence. But still, I was nervous. Nervous about being in crowds, nervous to never quite know who was out there watching me. Nervous about seeing people I did know – people I hadn't seen in over twenty-five years. In the end I had sent Mike a message, saying I would go to the reunion if he did.

I slowed my pace as I approached the theatre. It was weird seeing Ollie Brown's name in lights in the plate glass window. At Durham he'd been a medic, so no one had ever expected him to get into showbusiness. I'd bought his book – *Confessions of a Junior Doctor* when it had been released a few years earlier. One of the hundreds of thousands of people who bought it, it had turned out, as it became the non-fiction sensation of the year. The book became a hit Edinburgh Festival show, that show morphed into a two hundred date sell-out tour. Ollie no longer worked in the A&E department of a West Midlands hospital.

My phone vibrated in my pocket. I hadn't got around to buying a new one or changing my number again. I knew it could be him, but I thought I should answer it as I was due to meet Mike in the foyer at any minute and we'd swapped details in case either of us was running late.

Having a nightmare. Still stuck on a job in Holborn. Not sure I'm going to be able to make it. So sorry. Mike

My shoulders slumped as I silently cursed my friend. Stick or twist. Stay or leave. Could I go through this on my own – I wasn't sure.

I was about to turn on my heel when I saw someone was waving at me from the door and came out onto the street.

'Rachel!'

I recognized Louise Parker immediately. She looked less intimidating than she had at university; a few pounds heavier, her face more moon shaped and her glossy beige hair was flecked with grey. At Durham she was a show-pony, a striking home counties blonde who joined every committee and seemed to know everyone at college, but today she looked like another school gate mum.

I was genuinely thrilled to see her and my pace picked up to meet her.

'I didn't know you were coming. I haven't got you a ticket,' said Louise, looking absolutely panic-stricken. I guessed she was a woman who thrived on drama – eleven-plus exams, slack cleaners, Ocado being out of avocados – and I was just another thing on her weekly list of things to worry about. I knew it, because although I was not from Louise's world, I'd joined the affluent middle-classes and lived her life.

'Last minute decision and don't worry, I bought my own,' I said, holding up the ticket I'd bought at an inflated rate on a resale site.

Louise sighed. 'I can't believe you paid for one. Ollie's got us house tickets, right near the stage.'

'He's confident there's going to be no heckling from the old crowd then,' I smiled.

'It's so good to see you,' she said, giving me another hug. As she pulled away I saw her quietly clocking my Anya Hindmarch handbag and watch, then linked her arm into mine as if we were better friends than we had been at Durham.

'So you work in publishing,' she said, voice raised as we were sucked into the venue, into a fug of good-hearted noise and blue and red light.

My palms were clammy. I reminded myself that this was supposed to be fun, that many of the people here tonight would be lovely old acquaintances, if not exactly old friends.

I told her about my job and didn't let on it was temporary.

'You should sign Ollie! That would be so funny if you worked together. If you were the editor of his new book.'

I started to laugh. I hadn't told Ian Sinclair where I was going that night because he would have tasked me with that exact mission. I could only guess how many brownie points it would earn me if I did speak to Ollie tonight, arranged a lunch, make a pitch for him to join the BCC group. I knew that's exactly what Serena would do. Serena would have already done as Ian Sinclair had asked and brought David Becker into the fold with a giant cheque and a bucket-load of charm. Then again, I wasn't Serena.

Our crowd were on a long table by the bar. There was nowhere for me to sit. I said hello to everyone, relaxing when they were all so welcoming. Potted CVs and stories from the frontline of parenthood ping-ponged around the group. I was glad to be able to join in with stories of Sir Simeon and Jemima French. I wasn't sure I would have come if I hadn't been working.

Someone handed me a beer and I'd barely had a chance to refuse it when the bell rang and everyone started to mill around upstairs to watch the show.

'Drink up,' said Louise, waiting for me. She had one eye on the door, another on her watch; as the de facto leader of the reunion she wanted to make sure that everyone was here. 'Are you sure Mike's not coming?'

'He was vague but I don't think so. There was a problem at work.'

'Maybe he can join us for dinner afterwards. I know it's a school night but most of us are keen to push through. Apparently Balan's is open twenty-four hours.'

She spoke quickly as if there wasn't enough time to get her words out, but then she stopped.

'I don't believe it. Is that Chris Hannah over there?'

I spun round and at first I couldn't see him.

'Where?'

'Just walked in. Did you invite him? Still bloody good-looking, I see. How come men our age can still look like that and I ended up with someone who became fat and bald as soon as I married him?'

She smoothed her hair, a subconscious preen.

'Come on, let's go and say hello.'

She felt my resistance and gave a complicit smile.

'Come on, Rachel. Don't be shy. I had a teeny tiny thing with Ollie in Freshers week and *I'm* here,' she said, lowering her voice. 'I wonder if he remembers.' She giggled. 'I hope so.'

She tugged my sleeve and led me over. I was stiff and hestitant.

'Chris!' she said, tapping him hard on the shoulder and he spun round looking startled.

'What are you doing here?'

He directed his words at Louise and when he kissed her on the cheek, I saw her flush just like I had done at the Ham Yard Hotel.

'A big group of us have come down. Ollie's first London night and all that. He's going to try and come for a drink with us later.'

I could tell he'd only been half listening to our university friend.

'Hello Rachel,' he said with little enthusiasm.

'Chris.'

Louise obviously hadn't detected any awkwardness between us.

'Did Mike Weller tell you we were coming?'

I had to ask it.

'Mike Weller?' He shook his head. 'No. I work close by. I saw the What's On poster in the window and wanted to see the show.'

'This is such a coincidence,' gushed Louise as the bell rang again. 'Ooh. Curtain's up. We should go and grab out seats. You go ahead. I'm just nipping to the loo.'

We both watched her go.

'How are you?' he said when she'd gone.

'Good. Fine. Okay,' I said feeling my pulse quicken, from dread not sexual attraction.

'Which is it?'

'I'm okay,' I replied.

'Just okay?'

He could always read my mood.

'Actually, my neighbour died a few days ago. She was a good friend. It was the funeral on Friday. I've had better weeks.'

'I'm sorry.'

I just nodded.

'I've been worried about you.'

I didn't say anything.

'I keep thinking about those emails and messages you've been getting. I felt bad about our meeting last time. I was going to call, find out if I could do anything to help, but I didn't think you'd take the call. I sent you a letter. Did you get it?'

'No. I had a stop put on my post.'

He looked at me, right into me. 'Did you find out who it was?'

I was too tired to play games with him. I just wanted to leave, although I knew it would look churlish if I did and I didn't trust him not to follow me.

'I didn't, no,' I said, not looking at him.

'Is it still going on?'

I glanced up the stairs where an usher was trying to get everyone in the auditorium.

'I don't know. I've taken steps to protect myself.'

Neither of us said anything for a couple of seconds.

'It wasn't me, Rachel.'

'Can we not talk about it?'

My chest felt tight. I could barely breathe.

'We should go in. Which row are you?' I said quickly, just wanting to get out of there, get away from him.

'Balcony. Row Z. Serves me right for not booking sooner. I was lucky to get a return.'

'Well, I'm this way. Row F. Stalls.'

'Right then.'

I thought of my car, with the still smashed bumper, the bloody heart in the oven, the photographs addressed to Ian Sinclair and the Prozac in my handbag I had been driven to take, and I felt a surge of fury so strong I could feel it prickling in every nerve ending of my body.

I looked right into his eyes, those extraordinary green pupils, but their beauty was now hard and cold.

'Did you really see Ollie's poster in the window?' I said crisply.

'Yes. And I saw it on Facebook.'

'I thought you weren't on Facebook,' I said, determined to catch him out.

He frowned. 'I wasn't but I've dragged myself into the twenty-first century.'

I was still holding my tumbler of beer. The glass was feeling warm against my skin. I took a last sip before I put in on a ledge and my hand was trembling.

'You still think it's me, don't you? You think I'm the one hassling you.'

The bell rang again but it hardly registered.

'I saw Mike Weller. He told me,' I whispered. 'He told me about . . . prison.'

I had to force the word out and I watched his expression crumble – crestfallen, ashamed. I couldn't help but feel sorry for him.

He rubbed his hand across his mouth. 'I suppose you can understand why I didn't bring it up,' he said, looking away.

'We spent three hours talking about the last twenty-five years,' I said, my mind rewinding to more thrilling times – our night in that Chinese restaurant. 'I'd have thought it would be a defining moment.'

'It's not exactly something I'm proud of,' he replied.

'What happened?' At that moment I just needed to know. It was as if, for a second, the world had settled, stilled, and I wasn't scared anymore. I didn't even care about the texts and the messages and the pervy photos he'd sent to Edelman. I just wanted him to tell me how the smartest guy in college could end up in jail for a violent assault. Was I really such a poor judge of character?

'Things unravelled for me after college,' he said finally. 'I drifted, got by with a string of casual jobs. I lived in a house in Brixton, the rent was cheap and it was near the tube. My flatmate Jed was a low-level weed dealer. Fun guy but a magnet for trouble.'

He paused. Upstairs I heard the door to the theatre close. We had missed the start of the show but I could only listen to Chris.

'One night we went out drinking. Jed got into an argument, he owed money to someone you shouldn't mess with. We saw him in a pub. There was a dispute. They followed us home, picked a fight. They would have killed him,' he said, his voice trailing off at the memory of it all. 'I tried to break it up at first, but it escalated. I was an angry young man and every ounce of fury I had got directed at this one guy. One punch and I'd broken his cheekbone. Next thing I knew I was up on a GBH charge.'

'How long were you inside for?'

'Twelve months.' I watched his Adam's apple rise up and down in his throat. 'When you're twenty-four it feels like twelve years.'

'I'm sorry.'

I really was.

'You don't sound it . . .'

'I am. Maybe things would have been different if . . .'

'It's not always about you, Rachel. People make their own shitty choices.'

'I know all about that.'

Our words were beginning to feel like chemistry and I wanted to kill it dead.

'The show will have started,' I said, looking down.

Chris didn't make a move.

'Look, I get that you're pissed off that I called your home and I'm sorry for that. But I didn't think I was speaking to your daughter . . .'

My anxious mind could still knit that piece of information together with another.

'You spoke to Dylan?'

'When she answered the phone. The day you said you had the barbeque. I thought she was you. You sound the same. It was just a few words and then I realized . . .'

I tried to rack my brains. I couldn't remember exactly what she'd said when she'd handed me the phone, when I had sliced open my finger. I was sure she'd said that she'd passed the phone straight over to me.

'You know I'm always here for you. If ever you need me.'

We both looked at each other but I was too stunned to speak.

'The show's starting. You'd better hurry,' said an usher, tapping me on the shoulder.

Chris Hannah shrugged.

'I don't think I'm sitting anywhere near row F so I guess this is goodbye.'

I let him walk away. My brain was trying to make connections with everything that had been said, everything that had happened over the past few weeks, but I forced myself to shut all the thoughts down.

Chapter 42

Bill's front room was transformed. Where once had stood a sideboard, there were now only marks on the carpet and in place of the plastic-covered sofa, was a single bed complete with brand new duvet and linens. A chest of drawers replaced a Welsh dresser that was now in the garage along with the plates and china ornaments which had stood on it, now wrapped in newspaper and safely stowed in a cardboard box marked 'Iris's Treasures'.

'I'm not convinced,' said Robert, hands on his hips as he appraised our morning's work. 'Would you want to live here?'

'Look, I know it's weird having a bedroom downstairs, but it's what Bill needs.'

'What about the night carer? Where are they going to sleep? Not Iris and Bill's old room, surely.'

'Obviously not,' I said wiping my dusty fingers on my jeans.

'What about the cupboard under the stairs? Harry Potter style.'

'Robert!'

'I was joking!' he said, holding up his hands.

'Why don't you go and have a look around and see where's best. And don't even think about making any improvements,'

I smiled, imagining him calling in his architects before you could say *Changing Rooms*.

'What are you going to do?'

'I'm going to work out where all this stuff is going to go. The garage is full of crap as it is.'

'We've started so we'll finish,' I said, kissing him on the cheek and we pressed on.

It had been a week since Iris's funeral and support arrangements for Bill had been stepped up. Nathan was still coming during the day, which was good news for Bill, not that you'd be able to tell – he just sat in his chair, staring out the window, barely moving, just mumbling his wife's name, but Nathan's 8-5 p.m. hours were to be beefed up with an additional sleeping night service so that Bill had round the clock care.

John the nephew had power of attorney over Bill's affairs but had been predictably elusive when it came to any practical discussions. Sick of it all, we had offered to sort it all out and Robert had gone through Bill's finances. From the outside, Bill and Iris were a wealthy couple – at least on paper. Their beautiful home was mortgage-free, and was worth, on the open market, a great deal of money. But it wasn't the time for a discussion about selling the place and anyway it wasn't yet needed – having been through Bill's accounts, Robert estimated that his savings would cover at least eighteen months of round-the-clock care.

I had resisted Robert's suggestion that I stop work and help Bill, but there was still so much to do even with beefed up help from professional carers.

But I was starting to feel stronger, brave enough to believe that my harassment had stopped, hopeful enough to think that I could finally start to move forward with a clean slate, that a simpler life was tantalizingly within reach.

'Where am I going to put all this?' I sighed, looking around the hall. It was one thing changing the front room into an ad hoc bedroom, but a lifetime of stuff – all the furniture and knick-knacks the old couple had collected over the years had to go somewhere. There was an old cathode ray television, a family of china dogs, a pile of *Radio Times* dating back to the Nineties and dozens of framed pictures of Bill and Iris, all smiling, all full of vitality and life. I made sure the best of those had pride of place where Bill could see them.

Robert had returned to the garage, having identified the attic as the best place to put a granny flat and was rearranging the boxes around 'so we don't kill ourselves the next time we walk through that door.'

I swept the ground floor rooms, tidying as I went, the mother's default setting. A cushion under one arm, a vase clutched to my chest, I opened a cupboard under the stairs looking for more space. No such luck; there was a sports holdall crammed inside.

'Bill?' I called. 'Can I move this bag?'

No response. I walked through to the front room, but the old man hadn't moved. 'Bill?'

'I don't want to sleep downstairs,' he said without turning around.

'Bill, it's for the best. The stairs are dangerous. The fewer times you go up and down them, the better.'

'They were fine for sixty-five years. Wide tread. Iris never missed a step on them. Ever.'

His eyes stared out of the window, his world shrinking on so many levels. I made him a cup of tea but he didn't want to talk anymore.

I drank my own half a cup of builder's brew and went back to the hall, pulling the bag out of the cupboard under the stairs so we could store the hoover and the brooms in there. A scarf and a book poking out of the top of the bag dropped to the floor. The scarf was a red one I'd seen Nathan wearing so I assumed the bag must be his. The book was a copy of *The Old Man and the Sea*. Frowning, I bent to pick it up and as I did, something fluttered out on the carpet like a butterfly landing on a flower. As I bent down to pick it up, I froze. Lying there on the worn carpet was a postcard, a vintage book cover postcard just like the ones sent to me day after day.

'Rachel?'

I heard Robert calling me from the garage, but I still couldn't move. Was it a coincidence? It had to be. But at the same time, something fit.

My phone was in my pocket. I had already worked out that the postcards sent to the office were all from a boxset of a hundred Faber book covers. What about this one? The cover was pink and purple – *The Scruffy Rafferty Dog Stories* by Roy Johnston, a book I wasn't aware of. It certainly didn't have the sexual or relationship connotations that the other postcards had.

I googled the box set containing my postcards and found it on Amazon. The box had every postcard in the collection printed on the back. I enlarged the picture and there it was – *The Scruffy Rafferty Dog Stories*.

'No,' I whispered.

I felt weak, cold. I couldn't stand but there was nowhere to sit. The nearest room was the small study, opposite the stairs. There was a leather club chair by the door and I sunk into it.

'Rachel! Can you give me a hand?'

I flipped the door closed with my foot. I didn't want to see Robert or Bill. I didn't want to see anyone.

It wasn't Chris Hannah. It was Nathan. My stalker was Nathan Deer. The postcards, the whip, the text messages.

The suspicion had always been there but I had always tried to push it away – he was too close to our life. But it all made sense. He knew everything about me. My number, my address, where I worked, lived. He had been in my house, he hadn't lied about that, he had access to a key, and he was dating my daughter – God only knew what she had told him.

Was it even why he had started dating my daughter? I closed my eyes trying to remember the first time we had met – the first day we had left Bill and Iris alone. I remembered a shared smile, the light touch of my hand on his shoulder. I remembered something Lottie Callow had said too. How a bond could trigger a dangerous attachment. And I remembered his face at the window of our bifold doors, waiting, watching, as Robert licked and kissed the space between my thighs and his impatient tongue slipped inside me.

Somewhere, my body felt relief that it wasn't Chris Hannah. But that thought was snuffed out by the importance of another. Dylan. My daughter was dating Nathan Deer, sleeping with him, I couldn't bear the thought of her with that man.

I didn't even hear the soft swish of the study door open.

'I didn't know whether we should throw this in the tip?'

Robert stood feet away from me holding a battered suitcase.

I knew he could tell I was upset, even though I was trying to hold my emotion in.

He dropped the case with a thud.

'Rachel, what is it?'

It wasn't until I felt his arms around me that I realized I was shivering. But I wasn't shivering from relief – the release from finally knowing who my stalker was. I was shivering out of fear, fear for my daughter's safety.

'Tell me,' said Robert gently.

'I just . . .' I was sobbing now, my voice thick.

I knew I had to tell him. I knew it was the only way it could be truly over.

'It's all been so hard. I should have told you; I know I should have but you've had enough to worry about.'

The words rushed out. I knew it was time. I clutched my knees to my chest and began to speak. I told him about the postcards and the texts and emails and it was as if the boot that was pressing down on my chest was lifting, my rib-cage suddenly felt free and I could breathe in air all the way down to my belly, rather than it being trapped in my throat.

'That's the real reason I changed my phone,' I said. 'If I ever acted strange over the past few weeks, it was because of this.'

My husband didn't say anything for a moment. Silence seemed to tremble between us for a minute.

'Why didn't you tell me?' asked Robert finally. He was crouching down but it still felt as if he was towering above me as I remained in the chair. Every inch felt like a mile of distance between us.

I shook my head. 'I don't know. At first, I thought it would just go away. When it didn't, I felt dishonest that I hadn't told you immediately. It just got worse and worse and I felt more trapped and alone.'

I wasn't telling him the whole truth but I knew it was better to protect us.

'And you're sure it's Nathan?'

I could see the cogs of his brains turning around. He was a sharp as a whip, never easy to deceive.

'Yes. I thought it might be Nathan who was harassing me, who was sending me those postcards at work. Now a card from the same set turns up in his bag. It's too much of a coincidence. Everything fits.'

Not quite. *I saw you . . .*

The jigsaw wasn't entirely slotted together. What had that first text meant? Where had Nathan seen me? Had he followed me to Le Circe or had he been watching me from afar somewhere else? And I still wasn't sure what Katherine McCauley had done in her attempts to get some leverage against me. She'd got those photos from somewhere, so someone had been watching me. But Nathan Deer had sent the postcards and that was enough to connect the rest of the dots.

'Why?' He seemed to be asking the question to himself.

'I don't know.'

I could taste sick in my mouth. Although I had wondered if my stalker might be Nathan Deer, now I had proof, all I could think about was him, sitting in some tiny flat in Finsbury Park with his full fridge and my daughter on the sofa, writing tweets and texts telling me I was an ageing slag and a cock-sucking whore.

Robert glanced up.

'I said he was a fucking pervert.' His voice was low, and barely controlled. Robert never swore but I could see his fury in the tightness of his jaw. 'I'm going to kill him.' Robert stood back up.

For a split second I thought he might.

'Robert no,' I said, rising to my feet and placing a hand on his chest. Despite everything, I wanted to see the best in all this. I didn't want to think that my daughter's boyfriend was mentally ill.

'There is enough upset going on around here as it is. It was nothing. I was scared, but it all stopped anyway.'

It was true. The postcards had stopped and I hadn't had a text from him in days. Serena was still monitoring my old social media, my post at work. If anything sexual or threatening had been sent recently, she hadn't told me. It was just as Lottie Callow had predicted. That he would get bored, move on.

One thing is for certain, it will stop.

'Rachel, he is going out with our daughter. He might have stopped stalking you but the bloke is a sicko and he's dating Dylan.'

He paused.

'We have to tell her,' said Robert, his eyes wide.

'And how do we have that conversation?'

Robert was always so sure of everything but now, his feelings echoed my own. A sense of helplessness, that there were some things you just didn't know, how to deal with, even after eighteen years of parenting.

Robert rubbed his hands over his face.

'We should call the police,' said Robert after another moment.

I didn't want to. He had put me through hell, but whatever was driving him, whatever issues had led him to such obsessive behaviour, now he had been unmasked, Nathan no longer seemed like a threat. He just seemed pathetic. Besides, I didn't want the police asking too many questions. I didn't want anyone to shine a light on my night with Chris Hannah. A smart lawyer, like Lottie Callow, could punch holes in any accusations in a harassment case if they knew about my affair. No – it was over. I didn't want the police involved at all.

'We need to talk to Dylan first,' I said, hoping he would forget any talk of criminal charges.

Robert was still shaking his head.

'I can't believe you didn't tell me,' he said, his voice low. 'I thought we were a team.'

I felt guilty again but then I thought of Katherine McCauley. The secrets that we were both keeping.

Would you tell me everything, I wanted to say. But I didn't.

'I want to leave here,' I said, my voice was cracked and tiny.

'Let's go home,' he said, putting his arm around my waist.

'I mean Highgate,' I said looking at him. 'Let's just sell up. Start again. Move into town. Or get a place by the sea.'

'Give me some time. I'll work out buying Marley Hall.'

A big stately home, too far out of our financial reach, didn't seem as appealing as it once had. I didn't want the risk. I just craved security and safety.

'Do we really need a fifteen-bedroom mansion?' I asked, trying to search for answers. 'Why do we have to strive so hard for more when we can just let ourselves be happy with the level that we're at.'

I expected him to challenge me but when he didn't, I nestled into his chest to just let my husband hold me. For a moment I felt safe. I think we both did.

We didn't speak for at least a minute. Robert lifted his hand to my cheeks and I closed my eyes, enjoying the coldness of his wedding band against my skin.

'I'd better go and check if Bill is okay,' I said finally.

'And I've still got to Marie Kondo the garage.'

'You know Marie Kondo?' I was beginning to feel lighter.

'I'm not a complete Neanderthal,' he said. He smiled and it pricked the tension.

We stood opposite each other, our gazes not flinching. 'Let's just sort Bill out. Then we can decide how to deal with Nathan,' he said and it felt like a pact.

I was glad to be left alone. My body felt wrung out, but still something stirred inside me.

For weeks I'd avoided looking at my phone, but I wasn't going to be bullied anymore. I had Nathan's number in my new phone. I clicked on messages and began to type.

I know what you did. If you come near me or my daughter again, I will rip out your throat. And consider yourself fired.
Rachel Reeves

Straight afterwards, I rang the care agency and explained that the situation in the Neville household had changed. Bill needed a fresh face, a new full-time carer, and although I considered telling them that Nathan Deer was unsafe and unstable, I had something more pressing to do first.

Tapping out Dylan's number, I took a deep breath and I pressed 'call'.

Chapter 43

Dylan was screaming. Not just venting her frustration, but actually wailing, like she was in pain.

'Why?' she yelled. 'Why don't you want me to be happy?'

'I do, of course I do,' I said as sympathetically as it was possible to sound on the phone. I should have waited to speak to her face to face. Should have guessed she'd have been with Nathan who'd read the text during our call and obviously told her.

'If you want me to be happy Mum,' she shouted, 'then why are you trying to break us up? Why have you fired him?'

I was short of breath, on the back foot.

'You don't know him, sweetheart. I hate telling you this but I'm your mum and I care about you more than anything. Which is why I've got to tell you this.'

'Of course I know him,' she screamed. 'I love Nathan, Mum and I know him better than you do. And if you loved me as much as you say you do you will back off and let me be with him.'

I glanced back at my husband who was standing in the doorframe.

'Just meet her,' he mouthed.

'Where are you?' I said quickly.

'Finsbury Park.'

'Of course,' I said it bitterly.

It made sense. It was Sunday and Dylan had obviously been coming back to London from Birmingham every weekend, possibly ever since the barbeque, and going to Nathan's flat.

'I need to speak to you. In confidence.'

'What for? To lecture me?' She clicked her tongue. Dismissive, like she doubted I had anything she'd want to hear. But at the same time, I also detected unease.

'I think you might understand a little bit more once I tell you what's been going on,' I said.

'Why not just tell me now, get it over with.'

'Please Dylan.'

There was a long, drawn out sigh meant to communicate impatience and irritation, but simply served to remind me that my daughter was still a teenager.

'Alright,' she said finally. 'There's a café on Holloway Road. The Barn. I can be there in an hour.'

'I'll be there,' I said and rang off.

Dylan was at a table in the corner. She didn't look any less angry than how she sounded on the phone. Her eyes were ringed red as if she had been crying and her cheeks were blotchy circles of pink. I reached out to touch her, but she shrank back.

'You always do this,' she said as I took my coat off to sit down. 'Always trying to control me, you always think you know what's best for me.'

'Why don't we keep the hysterics down,' I said, lowering my voice and glancing at the waitress who was hovering for our order. The café was busy, twenty-something hipsters and millennial couples with babies and Bugaboos sipping smoothies. The last thing I wanted was a scene, but clearly Dylan had no such qualms.

'You are controlling, Mum,' she continued. 'You try and micro-manage my life. Ever since all that crap with my diet.'

'Diet? Dylan, you were hospitalized!'

'See? Again, you're rewriting history. I went to a hospital to see a shrink – that's not the same thing. And I was fine, I was just being a teenager.'

'Dylan, you were anorexic,' I said, whispering the last word.

'I was on a crash diet. When did anyone actually say I had anorexia apart from you? You are always seeing problems when there aren't any.'

She crossed her arms. Defiant. 'So, what is it this time? What have you dreamed up about Nathan?'

'I haven't dreamed anything up . . .'

'He's a good guy. You'd find that out if you gave him a chance and spent some time with him. Instead you've decided Nathan's some sort of pervert because you're feeling guilty about screwing Dad in full view of the street. And now he's showing interest in me, you're looking for any reason to get rid of him.'

I was mortified that my daughter knew about the kitchen table. Of course he'd told her. And of course she wanted to talk about this in public, to shame me into silence. But we were here now and more importantly, Dylan needed to hear what kind of man her boyfriend was.

'Alright Dylan, just listen,' I said.

She sat back in her chair and folded her arms in front of her.

'Around six weeks ago, I started to get cyber-stalked.'

'Stalked?'

I nodded.

'Texts, social media, postcards. Photos were sent to my boss. A . . . sex toy was sent to the house. It was scary. At one point I was getting thirty, forty messages a day. I had no idea who it was.'

Dylan red eyes grew wider. She knew what I was implying immediately.

'Don't say it. Don't even suggest it,' she snarled.

'Dylan, it was. It was Nathan.'

'Bullshit. You're making it up.'

'I wish I was, but I'm not.'

I could see the disbelief on her face and the hurt. Why was I saying this? Why would we stoop so low? She simply didn't believe me and I wished Robert was here to back me up. He had offered to come but I knew two of us together would be overkill. After all, she was just a girl in love, or at least thought she was.

'What makes you so sure it was Nathan?' she said tightly.

I took a deep breath.

'He sent me a series of cards, one a day. Suggestive cards. I found one of the cards in a bag he kept at Bill's.'

'That's it? Cards? This is ridiculous.'

'I know you don't want to believe he's capable of anything bad,' I said. 'But it was him, Dylan. They were a very specific set of postcards. Nathan's actually lucky we're not going to the police.'

'Police?' she hissed. 'You are joking, aren't you? With what evidence? Some postcard you found snooping about in his stuff?'

'What are the chances that Nathan had the same cards from the same set that were being used to intimidate me.'

Dylan sat back in her chair.

'So what did they say?' she demanded, sitting forward. 'What was written on them?'

I looked away, feeling uncomfortable.

'It doesn't matter.'

'Well, it does to me,' she said, banging her fist on the table. 'Tell me!'

The couple with the baby and the toddler on the next table stopped eating their avocado on toast but pretended

323

they weren't listening. The mother put a crayon in her daughter's hand and told her to start colouring.

I sighed. 'It was a quote from Shakespeare.'

'Terrifying,' she snarled sarcastically.

'Dylan, he broke into our house and left a heart in the oven.'

'Why the hell would he, would anyone, do that?' She looked at me in disbelief.

'He's had some sort of fixation . . .'

'What are you are suggesting? That Nathan is in love with you?'

'No, I don't think that . . .'

'I suppose you think the only reason he is with me is because of you?'

Her voice was quavering but I could still pick out each individual emotion. Distain, anger, hurt.

'Oh yes, I've read about this: a woman gets older, she gets jealous of her daughter . . . but I thought you'd be above that.'

It was a like a slap across the face.

'Dylan. There isn't even a grain of truth in that. I'm just trying to protect you. Nathan has issues and I think he needs help and until he gets some sort of assessment or treatment, I don't think you should see him.'

'It's not him,' she said with steel.

'Dylan, I'm sure.'

She didn't say anything and when she looked up, a hint of defiance in her eyes.

'What about Southern Electric then?'

Her voice was low and controlled. I almost envied her, how she could be so strong and so sure in what she believed.

'Southern Electric?'

I heard the stutter in my own voice.

'Who was that, Mum? The day you cut yourself with the knife?' It wasn't the electricity people, was it?'

She gave a hard laugh but I could see her eyes were pooling with tears.

'A friend at uni told me she was two-timing her boyfriend back at home. He was controlling. A total nightmare,' she said, talking quickly now. 'She met someone in halls, someone else. Jed. Third year. But she hadn't finished with her boyfriend yet so, you know what she did? She said that she's got Jed's number stored under something else, and when she told me that, it rang a bell. I thought about Southern Electric and I remembered, it was a man's voice saying your name. It wasn't a call centre. It was someone who wanted to speak to you. Someone who sounded like he *really* wanted to talk to you.'

I stayed silent. I didn't want to lie to my daughter. I didn't want to lie to anyone ever again. I felt the blood drain out of my face. I rubbed at my finger, and could feel the roughness of the almost-healed scar from my cut.

'Are you cheating on Dad? Are you shagging someone else?'

'No, I am not.'

'Look me in the eye and swear on my life.'

I couldn't do it.

For a moment, I saw fury in the dark depths of her pupils.

'I don't believe it . . .'

I reached out my hand.

'Dylan, please.'

'Why?' she whispered, her voice quivering with hate.

'I'm not having an affair. I love your father.'

All of it was true, if you thought the few snatched hours I had with Chris fell short of an extra-marital relationship. Where did you draw the line? In my own mind I'd written it off as a drunken mistake, barely a betrayal yet alone at night, I knew exactly what it was – cold-hearted treachery.

Her face looked hot and rigid. A tear trickled down her pink cheek but I knew she hadn't softened.

'You're lying. That's who's been sending you the postcards and the texts and the sex toys. Southern Electric. Your fucking boyfriend,' she spat.

She was lashing out, angry. I was struggling to stay calm. 'He's not my boyfriend,' I said with more passion.

'Well, it's not Nathan,' she said, matching my own volume.

'Dylan, I love you,' I said, my voice cracking.

'Then don't make me choose you or him . . .'

I was frightened at how quickly this was escalating. I knew we were just a few ill-chosen words away from losing each other.

'Dylan, please . . .'

But she wasn't paying attention to what I was saying. I followed her gaze over to the entrance and stopped with a jolt. Nathan was making his way over to our table.

'You invited him here?' I gasped.

'I didn't know what you were going to accuse us of, but we wanted to tell you straight, that we've done nothing wrong.'

We, we, we.

My daughter was united with my enemy. She had made her choice and she had chosen him.

Nathan looked stony-faced. I almost admired his gall for turning up here. He pulled up a chair and Dylan immediately turned to him.

'My mum thinks you're a stalker,' she said. 'Her stalker.'

'Dylan, keep your voice down,' I hissed.

'What are you talking about?' said Nathan.

He had the confused expression down pat.

I'd read about this. Stalkers could be clever manipulators.

'That's why she got you fired,' said Dylan, her slim finger stabbing the air.

'Dylan,' I snapped. 'This is not the time or the place.'

A prickly heat rash pooled at my neck. I knew I shouldn't be the one who felt shame-faced but I felt as if I had been ambushed.

'Stalker?' said Nathan.

I scrambled around my bag for my purse and threw a twenty-pound note down on the table.

'We'll talk about this another time,' I said, grabbing my coat and pushing my way out of the café. My heart sank as I heard footsteps behind me on the pavement.

I spun around, desperate to see my daughter. Instead, I came face to face with Nathan. I hated him so much and wanted to dig my fingernails into his cheeks until they drew blood.

'What do you want?' I screamed.

'Calm down,' he said. Nathan put up his hands like he thought I was going to attack him.

I took a breath.

'What were you talking about in there?' he said.

I looked away towards the busy road, letting the roar of the traffic and the exhaust fumes from the traffic consume me.

'You've got a stalker and you think it's me?'

'Think?' I shouted; my anger drowned as a bus growled past. 'I don't think it's you, Nathan. I know.'

'Mrs Reeves. I've done nothing wrong. You've got the wrong guy.'

'Then explain the postcard in your book,' I said, spittle flying out of my mouth.

'Which postcard?'

'The Faber postcard used as a bookmark. I saw it, Nathan.'

He pulled an exasperated face. 'I really don't know what you're talking about.'

'The bookmark. In a Hemingway book I found in the bag you keep under the stairs at Bill's?'

'Yeah, I stash some stuff there, but what postcard do you mean?'

I chopped my hand through the air in frustration. 'I'd respect you more if you just admitted it Nathan. You do know there are laws against this sort of thing?' I said. 'The Protection From Harassment Act. You realize you could be prosecuted?'

'But I haven't done anything!' he said defiantly.

'Nothing?' My voice was shaking and I could feel tears coming, but I was damned if I'd give him the satisfaction.

'You didn't stand outside my house watching me? Is that what you're telling me? You didn't send all those texts . . .'

His face contracted into a truculent scowl.

'We've been through this. I wasn't watching you . . .'

I snorted in disgust.

'Alright, who wouldn't look for just a few seconds? But I'm not a stalker.'

'Then who is it, Nathan? Who has been following me, watching me, sending me postcards?'

My throat was hoarse, my head was spinning. I was beginning to doubt my own sanity. Desperately I tried to remember the white pamphlet that came with the Prozac tablets. Was paranoia, madness a side-effect? I didn't think so.

He frowned, his lips moving, as if he was talking to himself.

'Iris,' he said quietly.

'Iris?' I said, not sure I had heard correctly. 'You're telling me Iris was my stalker?'

'No, no, Iris said something. That she had seen something.'

I put a hand on my hip.

'What?'

I was intrigued but I tried to stay stern.

Nathan frowned as if he was trying to retrieve a fragment of memory. 'She said, "I saw you. She won't be happy." Something like that, anyway.'

His eyes opened wide.

'I didn't think anything of it back then, but maybe Iris saw whoever it is creeping around after you.'

I saw you. That's what the first text had said.

'Iris said that?'

'I assumed she was just talking rubbish. She was an old lady with dementia. She said all sorts of things.'

'When?' I said, intrigued despite myself. 'When did she say it?'

He shrugged.

'Try, Nathan,' I snapped. 'For someone who could have the police knocking on their door any minute, you could give me a bit more than that.'

He sighed. 'A few weeks ago? I don't know. Maybe the same week Bill said you went around to their house. He said your bins had been attacked by foxes.'

I shook my head in disgust. It was just a pathetic ruse to shift the blame – he knew we couldn't exactly ask Iris to corroborate his paper-thin story.

'Just stay away from us, Nathan,' I said turning away. 'And stay away from Dylan.'

'I won't do that, Mrs Reeves,' he said simply. 'You can't blackmail me to stay away from her either. You can go to the police for all I care, because I've got nothing to hide.'

Chapter 44

I drove around for an hour after I left him.

Round and round the streets of Holloway and up towards Crouch End. I hadn't planned to go back to our old house, but when I found myself outside, I pulled over and just sat there. I saw a family come through the front door – once red, now painted a serious, fashionable dark grey. Mum, dad, and a child in a buggy that looked so high-tech compared to Dylan's old Maclaren. How things changed.

They weren't the couple we'd sold the house to. They were younger. She wore skinny jeans and Birkenstocks, her face was still fresh and ripe with youth and unlined with worry. Nothing bad had ever happened to this woman yet. For a second, I had never felt so old, watching the snapshot of someone I once was, a happy young couple in a starter house with a glittering, hopeful future ahead of them.

'I was going to send out the search party,' said Robert when I got home. He'd sent me two texts but I hadn't replied.

'I went for a drive to cool off.'

'You could have told me.'

'I'm sorry,' I said, slumping into the sofa.

'So? How did it go?'

By the time I had arrived home, I just felt drained, but Robert predictably wanted to go over everything.

'He denied it, of course,' I said, throwing my head back so I looked mindlessly at the ceiling.

Robert came and sat down next to me.

'So I've spoken to Tom, our IT guy at work.'

'IT guy?' I said. 'What about?'

'About the emails and texts. I suspected Dylan might not believe you.'

I could see my husband had gone into problem-solving mode. 'Apparently, there's a way of finding out for sure where they were sent from. Like a digital fingerprint – which device they came from, which server they passed through, that sort of thing. If they came from a phone or a laptop, you can even pinpoint where he was when he sent them.'

'Rob, maybe we just leave it,' I said, putting my face in my hands. My palms smelled of sweat and the leather of the steering wheel.

'Leave it? How can we just leave it?'

There was a veiled question in the way he said that, along the lines of 'What are you not telling me?' which was a road I didn't want to go down.

I looked at him, framed against the floor-to-ceiling windows where the sky outside was beginning to darken. 'She doesn't believe Nathan's capable of anything like this. She started saying things like "don't make me choose".'

I started to get emotional again. If I thought I'd lost my daughter when she went to university, that was nothing. I knew how hot-headed and wilful Dylan could be – she was capable of pushing the nuclear button and not seeing us for six months, a year, blowing up our hearts in the process. Empty nest was one thing, estrangement was another.

'Which is why we need hard evidence,' said Robert. 'Right now, it's us or him, and she is going to choose Nathan unless we can convince her that he sent those messages and postcards.'

I nodded in agreement. Robert was a doer, a man of action who hated having to sit on his hands. And I did want to know who had been stalking me. I wanted it confirmed so we could move on and I could reboot my life, forget about everything that had happened.

'So, should we do it? See if we can get hold of his phone? Check Bill's computer at the very least. Then we've got something to go to the police with.'

I felt trapped, checkmated by my opposition. To move forward with the police risked angering Dylan even more. It risked her telling Robert about Southern Electric and all the messiness that entailed. A messiness that could end in divorce if my husband found out about my one-night stand.

'Let's just leave it a few days. She'll be back at uni tomorrow night. Maybe we can go there and speak to her in private.'

It was the only solution I could think of.

'And in the meantime, you're happy for her to be in a house, alone with him?'

'No, I'm not happy about it at all. But what choice do we have? Robert, she hates me. We have to tread carefully or we'll only push her further away from us. She already thinks I'm controlling; she's even started believing we made up her eating disorder.'

'When did she say that?'

'Today.'

Neither of us spoke.

'So she's not coming home?'

'I don't think so,' I said, shaking my head.

'I'll give her a ring. Try and talk some sense into her.'

He wrapped his arms around my waist and as we pressed together, I could feel the thud of our hearts, beating in time.

'Am I a bad parent?' I whispered.

It was a question I'd asked myself every day after Dylan's eating disorder. Why hadn't I noticed sooner? Had I done enough to help her. Had my daughter properly recovered, or had I missed signs that she wasn't properly well? Had I been foolish to let her go off to university so soon, when she was still fragile underneath that tough shell? Why hadn't I noticed that she was involved with someone – that she was dating Nathan? I was overwhelmed by the sense that everything was my fault.

'You're a wonderful mother,' he said quietly.

'I'm scared,' I whispered.

'I know,' said my husband.

I could feel his fear too as we held each other. The fear of pushing away our child, the fear that knowing what the right thing to do felt just out of our grasp.

I thought about my husband sitting in the dark, drinking his whisky and I knew that I was not the only one who was vulnerable. Me, my husband, Dylan – we all were. And it made me very sad.

Chapter 45

'We should have got the bloody tube.'

Robert pushed the sleeve back on his coat and looked at his watch. I didn't reply. I'd spent the past half an hour trying to psyche myself up for being sociable, but the traffic on the way to London Zoo hadn't eased my anxiety. A cycle race going through Regent's Park meant closed roads and vehicles backed up at virtually every junction. Then once we were close enough to walk, we had been forced to circle almost back to Euston in search of a parking space. And now, as we half-trotted towards the Zoo's entrance, laden down with heavy bags, we were getting impatient texts from his brother David.

Where are you? Didn't we say one?

I quickened my pace to catch up with my husband and caught sight of David Reeves on the far side of the zoo's turnstiles, peering down at his phone, presumably in mid-text. His wife Cherry was standing four paces to his right.

'Hey,' said Robert, giving his brother a manly back-patting embrace. 'Sorry, traffic in London . . .'

David stepped across to me for a standard air-kiss. 'Good to see you too, Rachel.'

He looked around.

'No Dylan?' He stopped. 'I forgot. Empty nesters now. Fancy trading places?' he smiled, glancing over at his two girls who were fighting over a Chupa Chups lolly.

'How are you, Cherry?' I asked, turning to the tiny woman with long black hair. 'It's been such a long time.'

Cherry hadn't seemed to age a day since I had last seen her on a pit-stop visit to Kuala Lumpur what – three? four? – years ago. David on the other hand looked about a decade older than Robert.

A thick paunch had settled above his trousers and the stubble on his jowls was grey. I would have thought living in Malaysia in all that sunshine might have made him look younger, browner, leaner, although I had to admit, he had a happy mellowness to him that I envied.

'Too long,' smiled Cherry. 'You won't recognize the children.'

'Yes, where are the twins?' asked Robert, unshouldering his backpack. 'We've brought presents.'

'Don't say twins in front of Cherry,' David whispered theatrically. 'It's Madeline and Veronica. Apparently, we have to treat them as individuals.'

I grinned, suddenly looking forward to the day. David was always good fun, didn't take life too seriously, but I'd forgotten what a laugh he actually was. In many ways, I wished that Robert could be more like his brother. My husband's drive was a financial blessing; I knew that life with an alpha man had its rewards – the beautiful house, the luxury holidays, the freedom from never having to worry about money. But it was also a curse. The hundred-hour working week, the constant Keeping Up with the Joneses. Certainly, Robert would never be able to drop out like his brother. Scour the world for a place where you could rent a nice place for five hundred dollars a month and spend weekends at the beach with the woman he loved.

I glanced over at Robert and saw that he was finally

smiling, the stress from our tortuous journey to Regent's Park gone. We needed a fun day because the previous evening had been awful. We'd tried to watch a movie but barely got past the opening credits. We couldn't touch a takeaway that we'd ordered. Twice I'd had to stop Robert from tracking down Nathan's address and going around there to wrestle back our daughter. Finally, I had gone to bed alone, waiting for Robert to come upstairs and hold me but instead I heard him go upstairs to his study, returning an hour later, his tense, rigid body, a sign of someone plagued with multiple worries.

'I've got something for Madeline and Veronica,' I said, delving into the huge shopper hanging off my shoulder.

'Girls!' shouted David. 'Come and see what Uncle Robert and Auntie Rachel have brought you.'

Veronica and Maddie came running over, shockingly tall and overdressed in designer teen gear, I suspected was all fakes. Although they were only nine, they had changed into young women in tiny T-shirts emblazoned with 'Gucci' picked out in sequins. I immediately knew I had messed up with their presents.

'Here you go,' said Robert, handing them a bag each. 'Rachel picked these out herself.'

I winced. I had bought them Disney backpacks and filled them with books, films and fun, glittery nail polish-type accessories appropriate for girls just turned nine – or at least they were appropriate for Dylan when she had been that age. One look at these girls and you knew they'd only be pleased with Chanel or Prada or whatever deluxe brand was hot with teenagers that summer. Veronica held her bag away from her like I'd just handed her a dead pigeon. There was a similar disgusted look on Madeline's face as she unzipped her backpack and peered inside.

'What do you say?' prompted David.

'Thank you, Robert and Rachel,' they said in a harmonized sing-song, then handed the bags straight to Cherry, before sprinting off again. 'We'll be by the monkeys,' shouted Maddie over her shoulder.

'Well, they've grown up,' said Robert with admirable understatement.

'It happens so fast, doesn't it?' said David, as we all followed in the twins' wake. 'Madeline is grade seven in violin already. And Veronica's number six synchronized swimmer in her age group. National, of course.'

'I never had you down as a Tiger parent,' I teased him.

'I've made such a fuck up of my own life, thought I'd better help the kids channel more of their Uncle Robert.'

'They don't want to turn out like me,' he said with a snort, but I could tell he was pleased.

We walked through the zoo, bouncing from elephant house to feeding pen, exchanging all the news that had happened since we had last seen one another, relaxed small talk about our respective families. We filled David in on Dylan's progress, leaving out the fact she was shacked up with a madman, and David told us his IT business was doing well, which seemed to surprise even himself.

'Can we get pizza?' chorused the girls when we caught up with them near the tiger enclosure. 'Can we? Can we?'

It was already getting dark now, a soft gloom collecting in the air, and the zoo was emptying – no one was ringing a bell, but there was the distinct feeling that it would be closing soon. We had booked the smart, floating Chinese restaurant to the north of the park for supper, but I suspected the girls would prefer a slice of margherita before the zoo shut.

'Better be quick then,' said Robert, pulling out his wallet and leading Maddie and Veronica towards the café like the Pied Piper, with Cherry in their wake.

I took a moment to watch my husband, feeling the grip of longing that told me how much I still loved him.

'How are you?'

David's question brought me back to the present.

'I'm good,' I lied as we slowed in front of a coffee concession. 'What about you? I want to know what's bringing you back to England?'

I ordered two Americanos and paid for them.

'Age, nostalgia. It's definitely not the weather,' he quipped, zipping up his jacket.

'It's definitely permanent?'

David nodded.

'I think so. We've got a long-term rental in Dorset so we'll see how that goes.'

'Dorset?' It was where Robert and David were brought up. My husband hardly spoke about it. 'What's wrong with London?'

David shrugged. 'Besides the cost?'

'Robert knows where the good deals are. He'd love you to be around.'

'Would he?' answered David a fraction too quickly. 'He never bloody gets in touch.'

I took a sip of my drink.

'Don't take it personally. I'm his wife and I barely see him from one day to the next.' Robert, Cherry and the girls had disappeared out of view into the café.

'How is Bobby Dazzler?' said David as we lingered. He didn't need to say that he was worried about him. I could read the patterns in his voice.

'Same as usual,' I said, blowing on my drink to cool it down.

'Work crazy as ever?'

'You know the score.'

'And that's all?'

I glanced over at my brother-in-law.

'Come on, Rachel. I might live halfway around the world but he's still my little brother. I always did know when he'd nicked my favourite Panini stickers and when he'd got a detention at school for smoking fags. And I know he's got something on his mind.'

It wasn't my place to tell David about Cadogan House and Marley Hall but I was curious to know what he'd think, what he'd do. Although Robert was more successful than his older brother, I could recognize that David Reeves had the street-smarts of someone who had survived hard knocks. I didn't doubt that if I told him about Nathan Deer he would have some off-the books idea about how to get him off the scene.

'Look after him, won't you?' he said with surprising soft-ness.

'Why do you say that?' I said, starting to get worried.

David had gone into the City straight out of college, but had lost his job in the early Nineties recession, leading him to pack in corporate life altogether to go and live in Malaysia. But I knew he still understood the world Robert moved in and recognized the pressure he was under.

He knocked back the dregs of coffee and threw it into a bin overflowing with crisp packets and paper cups.

'Maybe it's something to do with turning fifty, but I've been getting worried about everything lately. Probably because of our dad . . .'

Robert didn't talk much about his family. I'd met his mother once, but she had passed away soon after and he mentioned her rarely since. He did go down to Dorset every year on the anniversary of his father's death to lay flowers at the church. I'd been with him once or twice but I could tell he preferred to do it alone. A picture of Robert and his dad climbing Snowdonia was the only other picture in his office along with a family portrait of me, himself and Dylan but he didn't talk much about him either.

When we first met, when we had started opening up to each about our dreams and aspirations, he had told me how his father had killed himself with a shotgun when Robert was just eleven. In return I had told him about my dad, how he'd been blown up on the Shankill Road, and from that moment on, I had known that we would never be apart. The violence of our fathers' deaths was something we had in common and it created a bond between us so tight, that I knew, as soon as he had told me about it, that I would marry him. But at the same time, it also became the great unspoken thing. Privately, I knew how it had shaped Robert, and he'd even confided it was part of his drive for success, but once admitted, he didn't discuss it any further.

'What about your dad?' I said, sensing I needed to probe David while we were alone.

'He was fifty when he killed himself. My age,' he said bluntly. 'It was depression. Sometimes I wonder if it runs in the family.'

I had never really got to the bottom of why he escaped to Malaysia. Robert had told me with a roll of the eye that it was one failed business and relationship too many and that the equity from his three-bedroom house in Salisbury would go a whole lot further in Kuala Lumpur. But perhaps it was something deeper.

But as his eyes trailed towards his brother, I could tell his concerns were for his brother, not himself.

'Rob's got a few work worries but I'm not sure he's depressed,' I said, not entirely convinced I was right.

I thought of him sitting at his dark office with his tumbler of whisky and although I had always seen Robert as the toughest of nuts, I knew enough about mental illness to know that anyone could feel the black dog.

'No one knew that Dad was depressed,' said David, glancing over at me. 'Looking back, things were tough. I was a bit older than Rob. I guess I picked up on more things than he did. I heard whispers around the house that Dad's job was in the balance, heard my mum and dad arguing about it. But I'm not sure you were allowed to think you were depressed in those days, let alone talk about it.'

'There were no signs?'

David shrugged.

'Not really. Dad loved his wife, his kids, his friends. We didn't have much money but he seemed to have so much to live for. It's hard to know what people are really thinking or feeling isn't it though. Who knows where worry stops and depression begins?'

'Maybe I should book us a nice mini-break,' I said, thinking out loud. 'Somewhere where we can talk.'

David gave a soft snort. 'Good luck with that one. Rob would never admit that he needed help even if he did. I remember when Dad died, I used to hear him crying in his room every night for six months but by the morning, he'd be dressed, ready for school before me and Mum were even up as if he didn't have a care in the world.'

I nodded, thinking about hearing my own mum through the thin walls of our Belfast terrace.

'Robert never talks about it, not even now. Maybe he should.'

David nodded.

'We didn't lose one parent the day that Dad shot himself. We lost two. Mum was never the same afterwards, that's when the drinking really began. I had to help bring Robert up, make sure mum kept on the straight and narrow. I think I lost my focus, lost my way a little. Maybe it was why I underachieved. Robert on the other hand, he became driven. But sometimes you can't keep going. Sometimes you just run out of gas.'

'I don't want anything to happen to him,' I whispered.

It was the one upside of everything that had happened over the past few weeks. I loved my husband more fiercely. I swallowed hard.

'Come on. This conversation has got way too maudlin,' said David, suddenly perking up. 'How about I power-walk race you to the pizza place?'

'Rachel!'

We looked up to see Robert running out of the restaurant, his phone in his hand.

'We're about to be told off for loitering,' grinned David as we broke into a trot.

But Robert was racing towards us faster. As he got closer, I could see the frantic expression on his face and I knew immediately that something was wrong.

'What's happened?' asked David, trying to force his heavy frame into a sprint. 'Is it the girls?'

Robert shook his head, his eyes fixed on mine.

'No,' he said, his voice shaking. 'It's Dylan, she's in hospital, Rach. She's been run over.'

Chapter 46

Robert's Range Rover screeched to a stop outside the entrance to A&E.

'Park up. I'll run in,' I said, yanking the door open and tumbling out of the passenger seat.

I saw him almost immediately: Nathan Deer standing to the left of the double doors, smoking a cigarette.

I ran up to him and lashed out, thumping him on the chest. Nathan dropped his cigarette and stumbled back.

'I knew I shouldn't have left her with you, I knew it,' I screamed, feeling my features disappear into a tight knot in the centre of my face.

But I already knew it was too late. I heard the car's door slam behind me and saw it all unfolding in slow-motion, Robert crossing towards him, his jaw clenched.

My husband looked even angrier than I did. Despite my own upset and frustration, I knew that more violence was not the answer.

'Robert, don't,' I screamed as he ran up to Nathan and grabbed him by the collar of his hoodie.

'I told you to leave our family alone.' He roared spit and fury into Nathan's terrified face.

'It wasn't my fault,' he cried, throwing up his hands. 'We were just crossing the road.'

'Just?' yelled Robert. 'My daughter is in the hospital because of you!'

There was the blare of a siren and we all turned to see an ambulance pulling up right behind the Range Rover.

'You're blocking the way, get the car out of here,' I yelled, grabbing Robert and pulling him off. To my relief, he backed off, stabbing a finger towards a cowering Nathan.

'It's been nothing but trouble since you arrived. Unless you disappear, I will have you arrested.'

He jumped back into the car and roared off and I turned to Nathan.

'Where is she?'

My voice was trembling. I didn't care what he had done to me. All I could think about was my daughter. I tried to control myself. All that mattered now was Dylan and finding out how she was.

'Inside, in the treatment area. She's okay. She's got some cuts and bruises, maybe a fractured wrist but she's okay.'

He put a reassuring hand on my hand but I shook it away. How could he think that broken bones were okay?

'You were supposed to be looking after her,' I said through my emotion. 'She trusted you,' I said, my final words loaded with meaning.

He looked like he'd been stung. It had been Nathan who had called Robert at the zoo telling him about the accident so I assumed he had come with her to hospital in the ambulance.

'Where were you? Where did it happen?'

'In Dalston,' he said, voice low. I could tell he was upset and that his cigarette had been to calm himself down. 'We were coming out of a bar and Dylan ran on ahead to check out the menu at a restaurant across the road. Honestly, there was nothing I could do, it all happened so fast.'

His voice cracked with emotion. Despite everything he had done to me, my instinct told me he had nothing to do with Dylan's accident.

'I need to see her,' I said, running into the hospital. 'You should just go,' I added, looking back. 'Please. Just go.'

To my surprise, he nodded.

Homerton had been the closest hospital to the accident, but it looked much the same as the Whittington where I had visited Bill. The same bright corridors, the same squeaky floors, the beds and curtains and cardboard bowls all interchangeable. Even the doctors and nurses seemed to blur into one, which I supposed was the point of the white coats and uniforms. I wondered if they felt the same way about their patients? When Dylan was born, there were complications and I'd spent a week on a recovery ward in an intense relationship with the nurses and midwives gliding in and out, day and night, kind and caring and super-professional. A few weeks later, stir crazy from the endless swirl of feeding and changing, I took Dilly out for her first long ride in her pram and ran into Sammie, one of our maternity nurses on the other side of the street. I waved, but either she didn't see me, or she simply didn't recognize me. We'd had such intimacy; she'd had my blood on her hands, wiped away my placenta, been there at the most important moment of our family life, but I knew I had been instantly forgotten. It didn't matter. The important thing was they had done their job, and now the doctors and nurses were here for our daughter again.

I was whisked through to meet the reassuring A&E consultant, Dr De Silva. He had calmly told us what had happened. According to an eyewitness, a car had come out of nowhere, knocked Dylan sideways before accelerating away and disappearing into a back street. She'd been clipped, rather than tossed into the air, but had still broken her wrist in the fall. Had the car been going faster or if Dylan had landed in a different position, her injuries could have been much worse. Regardless, she was still badly shaken, and the doctors wanted to keep her in overnight for observation.

'You can go in and see her,' smiled the doctor. 'But go easy. She's had quite a scare.'

I gently pulled back the screen to her cubicle and choked back a sob. She looked so small and vulnerable, as if no time had passed between that week in the incubators eighteen years before. My movement must have registered as her pale eyelids fluttered open.

'Mum?'

'It's me. I'm here baby,' I said, leaning across to gingerly stroke her bruised forehead, not knowing where it was safe to touch, which part might hurt.

'How are you feeling?'

'My neck hurts,' she said quietly.

'The doctor said that's common when you've hit your head,' I said, pushing the hair back from her face. 'The skull's solid, so the neck takes the strain.'

She gave a weak smile. 'You calling me thick?'

I smiled; that was more like the Dylan I knew.

'Where's Dad?'

My heart sang that she wanted us.

'Just parking the car, he'll be here soon.'

That car journey east from the zoo had been horrible, Robert and I both silent, each in our own private hell, each recounting all the things we could have done differently, each praying for our little girl to be okay. No wonder Robert had gone off like a bottle rocket when he'd seen Nathan lurking by the door. Not that I would be telling Dylan about that. I supposed when she did hear about it with Nathan's added victimized twists, it would give her yet more reasons to hate us, but right now, she seemed happy to see me. And for now, that was enough.

'Sweetheart, what happened?'

I touched her hand as gently as I could.

'It all happened so quickly . . .'

A tear dribbled down her pale cheek.

'I know. Apparently one of the police officers is still here, so I'll go and speak to him in a minute.'

'I wasn't pissed,' she said, her voice small. 'I'd had a drink at lunchtime but I was fine. I didn't run into the road or anything like that. All I remember is this black car. Boom. Into my side. And then I fell and I was shaking in the road and I think I might have peed myself. It was so embarrassing.'

Fat tears leaked from her eyes and I wiped them away with my thumb.

'All anyone cares about is that you are okay.'

Dylan nodded but I could tell she didn't believe me.

Everything wrong in our life was because of me. Without my job there would be no Nathan, without Nathan, Dylan would not have been in Dalston. My selfish need to 'have a life' had led us here to this hospital.

As if she were reading my thoughts, Dylan's eyes met mine.

'He's here, Mum. Nathan,' she said. 'Don't make a big deal of it, please?'

'I wasn't going to.'

'He just went to see if the coffee shop was still open.'

'Coffee shop?' I smiled. 'I think we could all do with a double vodka right now.'

Dylan laughed and then clutched her ribs.

'Bruised?'

She nodded. 'Not broken though, they said. Just the wrist. It might get me out of my tutorial essay.'

She gave a wan smile and I mirrored my expression with hers.

'Don't worry about any of that. And I don't think you'll be going back to uni. Not yet anyway.'

'The doc says I'm fine.'

I nodded, swallowing back a sob.

'They're keeping you in overnight though.' I didn't really

want to think why. The danger of internal bleeding, or some other overlooked nasty that might need sudden surgery.

'Mum, there's still two weeks of term left.'

'I'll call your tutor and the halls tomorrow. You can't go back like this.'

'But I want to. It's only a broken wrist.'

I admired her, despite everything, I could see her love of university shining through. Despite her love for Nathan, she still wanted to get back there.

She paused, looked up at me as if she wanted to clarify that.

'Nathan said he'd come back to Birmingham with me,' she said.

I was expecting an additional tart remark, some reference to Nathan's availability and free time because I'd had him fired, but there was none. Just a simple affirmation of her love for him.

'I've been thinking . . .' She was so drained her voice was barely a croak.

'Don't do too much of that,' I said, trying to make light of it. 'You need every ounce of strength you've got. Sleep and eat chocolate for the next twenty-four hours. Mum's orders.'

'No, Mum. I was thinking about your stalker.'

I frowned. I was trying hard to block it out of my mind – at least for now.

'You don't think this is him, do you?'

I almost admired her blind devotion to her boyfriend.

'What? This?'

'You get harassed. Then I get run over. Mum – it didn't feel like an accident. I heard the car accelerate towards me.'

I looked at her, aghast. I hadn't even thought of connecting the two.

'You think someone tried to hit you. *Deliberately*.'

She nodded again.

'I couldn't really see who it was in the car. I only got a glimpse. But I'm sure . . .' She tailed off.

'Dylan, darling. Tell me.'

'I'm sure they were smiling.'

Rain started to rattle against the dark window next to her bed.

'Sweetheart, who was it? What did they look like?'

I willed her not to describe someone with green eyes and dark eyes, but she just shook her head.

'I'm scared, Mum,' she said, touching my hand.

I was too, but I didn't want to show it.

'Darling, the doctor said the police think it's joy-riders, just some random thing. Nothing else. If the driver was smiling, he was probably high.'

'What about your stalker?'

'Dylan, sweetheart. Please leave it.'

'It's not Nathan. I know it in my heart.'

'Just rest,' I said, stroking her head, careful not to touch – or look at – the thin line of congealed blood near her hairline. 'It's all just a coincidence. Just coincidence, nothing more.'

But I wondered who I was trying to convince. Dylan or myself.

Chapter 47

Cadogan House was magical. There was no other way to put it. The snow, in particular, had been a masterstroke. The road, the pavement and every windowsill on the house was covered in a cloak of sparkling white, the party-goers footprints leading to the open door. I wished I could claim credit, but it had been Petra from Robert's office who had waved her glittery wand over the street. It turned out she was 'having a thing' with a movie art director based at Shepperton Studios who had access to a snow machine, a silver-screen version of those snow-blowers they have on the piste in Klosters. It looked like a Dickensian Christmas dream, a month early. I assumed the neighbours of Cadogan House were enjoying it too. There had been no complaints, although Robert said most of the road was owned by wealthy Saudis and Nigerian's who were never there.

'You're here!' said Serena, draping an arm around my shoulder. She was holding a glass of champagne and I felt a few cold droplets spill on my shoulder.

'Of course, I'm here.' My eyes darting from corner to corner, the good host, making sure everyone was having a good time.

'How's Dylan?'

I'd had to tell Serena about the hit and run. After all, she was Dylan's godmother and it felt strange not to. But I'd played the events of Sunday afternoon down – my friend had shared enough drama with me over the past few weeks and I didn't want her to think my life was a total train crash.

'Fine, thank goodness. In fact, she's insisting on going back to Birmingham tomorrow. I've pleaded with her not to go, there's barely a fortnight of term left, but then I caught her on ASOS shopping for party dresses, and thought it's probably what she needs.'

'Where is she tonight?'

'At home. Robert's brother and family are over from Malaysia so I've got them to go round and keep an eye on her. I really didn't want to leave her but she was looking forward to hanging out with her cousins and I've just sanctioned a hundred pounds' worth of Domino's Pizza so I'm guessing they're having a good time.'

Serena smiled. 'Did she get my flowers?'

'She did. They cheered her right up.'

'Well, I have to say, this is pretty bloody good, Rachel,' said Serena, lifting her glass expansively around the room.

'The party or the champagne?'

'Both,' she said. 'This place is astonishing.'

Cadogan House did look amazing, a perfect balance between the period features of the terrace and the modern, with mid-century furniture and abstract art on the walls.

'Most importantly the great author is happy,' said Serena, nodding towards the fireplace where Simeon was seated in a high-backed leather chair, grandly receiving guests as if he were the Pope.

'He should be,' I said. 'Have you seen who's turned up?'

Among the well-wishers were some genuine A-listers: a Hollywood actor, a couple of musicians and a supermodel who was deep in conversation with a man in orange robes.

'Who's that with Summer Sinclair?' I said, leaning into

Serena. 'I don't remember seeing any Buddhist monks on the guest list.'

'Her "plus one"?' suggested Serena. Her eyes darted around the room like a particularly vigilant cat. 'Then again, there's a lot people I don't recognize. I suppose you don't expect the usual publishing crowd when it's a party for Sir Simeon.'

'Expect the unexpected,' I smiled. 'When I called up asking for his final guest list that's what he told me.'

'I hope you didn't mention that to Robert. It must be a security nightmare tonight. One drunk editorial assistant and a hand goes through that Bridget Riley right there.'

'Don't say that,' I replied, shuddering as I looked at the expensive artwork that lined the walls, Robert's window dressing to make his guests imagine what it would be like living here.

Serena gave a deep sigh. 'I keep having to remind myself that you actually own this place.'

'I don't own it. Robert's company does. And even then, it probably has all sorts of charges and mortgages all over it.'

'Can't you persuade him to keep it?' said Serena, a glint of coquettishness in her eyes.

'What? You think we should live here?'

'Don't you want to feel like Emma Wodehouse – handsome, clever and rich?'

'This place would be way too big,' I smiled, admitting to myself that I had rather felt like a Disney Princess – perhaps Elsa or Anna – when I had drawn up to the front door in the fake snow.

'Says she, moving to Marley Hall,' replied Serena, raising one eyebrow.

'That's not a done deal,' I said with a sip of my mocktail, not wanting to discuss our financial situation here.

'I thought you had exchanged on it?'

'I'm . . . we're still not 100 per cent convinced it's a good idea.'

'Good idea? Rachel, it is one of the finest buildings in the entire south of England,' said Serena seriously. 'Places like that hardly ever come onto the open market. I had no idea it was for sale.'

She said it with a touch of indignation, as she should know everything that went on in her neighbourhood.

'You know Robert.'

'I do. And I can't believe I gave him to you. It could have been me, living in Marley Hall with that view down the avenue of limes, having tea under the dovecote with a view of the river.'

She knew an awful lot about Marley Hall. I expected she had googled it given that we were going to be neighbours, but still it unnerved me how much she knew about it.

'Since when did you give Robert to me?' My tone was light, but it was a serious question. Had I missed something?

'You remember, the night you two met,' said Serena, with an edge to her voice. 'I was there too. You almost ran for the hills when he asked us if we wanted a drink.'

I had forgotten that detail of the evening, but now I could see us, in the Moroccan-themed basement of Po Na Nas in Chelsea, our regular haunt at the time. I lived in Clapham but Serena's Fulham Road flat was a stone's throw from the clubs and bars favoured by the young, affluent Sloane Set. Every Friday after work, we'd go for drinks and then weave our way to Chelsea, ending the night at Serena's, giggling about what had gone on in the previous few hours. It was one of those nights when I'd met Robert, standing at the bar, loudly debating the relative merits of a cosmopolitan or a mojito, both of which had seemed incredibly exotic at the time. Robert had heard our conversation and offered to buy us both to try.

I remembered looking at him for the first time and freezing. Obviously good-looking and super-confident men – true alpha males like Robert Reeves, always made me nervous.

A fragment of memory, lost for so long, was suddenly

crystal clear in my mind. I'd been about to bolt to the loos, when Serena had whispered 'you have him' in my ear and disappeared to the dance floor.

In that moment, I could smell her perfume as she came close – the sweet, rich scent of Calvin Klein's Obsession. The smell of it had made me giddy, it had allowed me to claim a little bit of my friend's sexy inner confidence when I'd spoken to Robert.

'I remember,' I said, although I hadn't thought about that night for years.

I noticed that her speech was starting to slur, her eyes were open just a fraction wider than a sober person's.

'I'd met Alan the week before, hadn't I,' she continued. 'He'd been bloody handsome himself, in those days. He'd invited me to a wedding in Scotland – the Duke of Moray's daughter, if I remember rightly – and I was rather excited about it. So excited, I'd sort of taken myself off the market temporarily. I wonder what could have happened if I hadn't.'

She looked round again, tipping her head up to elongate her slender neck. 'Where is Robert anyway?'

I shrugged, watching her. There was a definite edge to the way she was talking.

She looked back at me, as if demanding an answer.

'Schmoozing probably,' I said finally.

'Oh yes, he'll definitely be schmoozing. That's what he's like, isn't it?'

I didn't like the way she said it, but I held my tongue. I knew that Serena was the driven, competitive sort, much like my husband – sometimes I had thought they would be the better match. But I had detected a tension since I'd mentioned Marley Hall and idly wondered if she was jealous or even resentful. It was just the sort of family seat that Serena had always wanted for herself and I suspected she felt I didn't deserve it. And on that account at least, she was probably right. But before I could say anything more, Serena was moving away, waving at a tall blonde on the arm of a man in a velvet suit.

'Rachel . . .'

I spun around as I felt a hand on my bare shoulder, it felt a touch familiar and I turned expecting it to be Robert. Instead, it was Ian Sinclair. Immediately I could see he was in a good mood, slightly drunk and bubbling over.

'Are you coming over to talk to Simeon?'

I glanced across at the author.

'Ian, there are two Academy Award winners lined up to talk to him. I'm not sure there's room for me in that heady social orbit.'

'Au contraire,' smiled Ian, looking at me directly. 'He asked for you by name. He's thrilled by the way the party has turned out. *Entre nous* – Penelope, Simeon's agent wants to meet for lunch tomorrow to discuss a new offer.'

'That's great news,' I said, genuinely pleased. 'Mission accomplished.'

'We should also have lunch,' he said in a quieter voice. 'Discuss your position in the company. Something more permanent. See how your role could evolve.'

I had to say I was surprised at his offer. Ian had barely contained his disapproval at my professional behaviour for weeks and I'd felt in constant threat of being fired. As early as that morning, he was still muttering his doubts about the party. Certainly, he had not been happy at the start of the week when I had asked for two days compassionate leave to look after Dylan, and had only allowed it after I had agreed to Skype calls with Vicky and Lydia on the hour to check everything was in place for the party. Had anything gone wrong, I felt sure I would have been sacked on the spot.

But although I wasn't even sure a full-time, contracted job was what I was after, it felt good to be asked and made to feel valued. It also meant that Serena obviously had not breathed a word about the erotic photos to Ian. It would have been so easy for her to do so and damage my reputation; instead, she had contained any gossip or rumour and for that I would always be grateful.

'I'm just glad everyone thinks it's gone well.'

'So how about I book The Ivy for Friday?' he smiled. I noticed he had a flake of pastry on his tooth.

'I'd like that,' I said.

He touched my arm for a fraction too long and I tried not to flinch.

'So would I,' he replied and weaved back to Sir Simeon.

Chapter 48

With no one else to immediately talk to, I walked a circuit of the ground floor, checking the bar and the waiters carrying trays of canapés: everything seemed to be going smoothly with the party. Ian was right – the party was going well, but Serena's words were still ringing in my ears: I didn't know where Robert was and had no idea how the other part of the operation was going. I threaded through the crowds and up the staircase. The house was fully dressed as a home, and the upper rooms were all bedrooms, sumptuous emperor-sized beds the centrepiece of each. Too tempting for drunk or frisky guests to resist; it wouldn't do for Robert to lead a potential buyer into the master bedroom and find someone en flagrante in the en-suite. I moved across the carpet lightly, but with purpose. I'd been nervous about tonight, but now I felt strong. Ian was right; the party was a glittering success and failing some disaster, I was a success too.

Surely Robert's clients could not fail to be impressed by Cadogan House and the potential it had for their own lavish entertaining.

I checked the bedrooms to the right of the staircase – all clear, as was the huge master bedroom, decorated in iridescent ivories and pale gold like the inside of a pearl. I moved back to the stairs and I finally heard Robert's voice coming from the room furthest away from the landing.

'Serena, no. Please.'

I hovered outside the door, holding my breath as I peered through the crack. A glimpse of Serena's red silk dress, like a warning flag, then Robert's blue shirt.

I didn't breathe as I took a closer look. Robert was backing away from her.

'I just want to show you how proud I am,' she said, her words slurring, tossing her bouncy blonde hair back like a matinee star.

'Thank you, but it's not necessary,' said Robert, both hands up in a 'stop' gesture as Serena tried to put her arms around my husband's neck.

I could barely stand to watch and yet my eye remained glued to the sliver of space between the door and the frame.

'Serena, go back downstairs,' he said firmly. 'I don't want guests up here.'

She took an unsteady step backwards.

'Is that all I am? A guest?'

'Right now, Serena, yes you are,' he said, unabashed, and right then I was fiercely proud of my husband. Proud of how he dealt with her advances. So much prouder of him than I was of myself.

I backed away before I was seen, silently slipping back downstairs, grabbing a flute of champagne from a waiter and gulping it down in three swallows, keeping one eye on the stairs, then slunk into a corner, watching the top of the stairs, waiting for Serena to come down. And there she was, descending with a smooth, liquid movement, like a catwalk star. I felt a flash of hatred. She'd been rebuffed, but you'd never have imagined it; Serena looked like she was having the time of her life. I watched her pass, trying to process all I had seen and heard. My cheeks felt hot with anger. Had my best friend actually tried it on with my husband?

How could she? Why did she? Had I ever really known her?

Just as I was thinking it all through, I spotted another familiar face, but one I hadn't been expecting. Max Miskov walked over, a plate of canapés daintily balanced in one hand.

'You certainly look the part,' he said, 'very Gatsby. What was the wife called?'

'You mean Daisy from the book or Zelda from real life?'

I tried to act normal, but I could tell I was being guarded. I could certainly feel my whole body switch into stiff, defensive mode.

'Whichever one was the most beautiful,' said Max. He said it playfully, just a friend paying a compliment to a colleague's wife, but I still felt uncomfortable and exposed. I had dressed for the occasion in a shimmering gown and ridiculously high heels and I could feel Max's gaze running over me. I wanted to cover myself with a blanket.

'I didn't know you were coming,' I said. As in: *you weren't on my list*.

'Robert invited me. I'm not exactly a fan of Simeon Averill's – I find his stuff too floral, too pretentious. But I always like to see Robert's projects brought to life.'

'Is Chloe here?'

Whatever Katherine McCauley has said to me, I'd found some reassurance in Chloe. She seemed like a lovely girl, certainly not the type to be mixed up with Eastern European gangsters.

Max shook his head.

'Tonight is business,' he said, taking a bite of a savoury choux bun. 'Where is Robert, anyway?'

Instinctively I wanted to protect my husband from this man. I didn't want him here and felt irritated that he'd been allowed to step behind the velvet rope, but it was more than that, but I couldn't exactly say why.

'I'm not sure,' I said, my heart drumming at the lie.

'And how's your daughter?' he said, suddenly changing tack. 'Robert told me what happened – poor thing.'

'Yes, she's fine, which is such a relief,' I said. 'She stayed in hospital overnight, now she's back home.'

'No long-term damage then?'

'Hopefully not, it was just a broken wrist. She's got a cast on that and it should be fixed within six weeks.'

Max nodded.

'Just shows, doesn't it? Accidents can happen to anyone at any time. Just step out into the street and . . .' He clicked his fingers. 'Gone.'

There was something about the way he had said it that wasn't just an observation. A warning? Or was that just paranoia rearing up after Serena's behaviour tonight?

'Glad that it turned out okay this time though,' he said.

This time? I looked at him, searching his face. There was a smile there, but it was ice cold.

'I should go,' I said. 'Check no one's stealing the silver.'

'It's all work for you, right? Then again, what did Camus say? "Without work, all life goes rotten."'

Max began to leave but then stopped, turning back in a very deliberate movement.

'Oh, and if you do see Robert,' he said, 'tell him I need to talk to him about the money he owes me. Although I'm sure after tonight, he'll be in a position to pay it.'

I was trembling, but I forced myself to hold it together, giving him a non-committal nod.

'And send my love to Dylan,' he added, giving me a little two finger salute. It was a friendly gesture, off-hand, throwaway. But as I turned away, I realized that he was pointing two fingers at me. Like the barrel of a gun.

Chapter 49

We were the last to leave. Ian Sinclair had gone, Serena had gone, Simeon had left with two supermodels, one on each arm. Even the waiters and the caterers had packed up; there was barely a trace of the champagne cocktails and thousands of tea-smoked duck rolls that had rolled continuously from the kitchen since seven o'clock.

The only people left were Robert and me, but I didn't even know where my husband was. I took off my heels and padded up the stairs, half-hoping to find a stray bottle of prosecco to mine-sweep, but the caterers had left the place spotless and I knew that any serendipitous alcoholic discovery was unlikely.

I found Robert in the pearlescent master bedroom. The lights were off and he was looking out of the long windows onto the backstreets of Belgravia. I could see his reflection in the glass, long and pale like a primitive mask. I walked across the carpet, my toes sinking into the thick pile. I was almost on top of him when he turned around.

'Bloody hell. The silent ninja.'

I stood next to him, our hips not quite touching, and we just stared out of the picture windows, watching yellow lights disappearing into the night air, dark and matte as artists' charcoal.

'I think it went well,' he said finally and I could see his shoulders soften in relief.

'Simeon's happy,' I said. 'Looks like he's signing on with Edelman again. I hope he doesn't expect a party like this every year.'

'Well I'm glad,' he replied quietly. 'Now, how about we go home.'

I nodded, eager to get back to our daughter. 'I'll text Dylan and let her know we're on our way back.'

Robert paused.

'Before you do, you should see this.'

He took his phone out of his pocket and clicked on mail. 'I got a message from Tom, my IT guy an hour ago.'

I peered over to see what was on the screen.

IP addresses from a couple of messages match your neighbour's computer. Call me.

I wasn't a techie but I understood.

'The horrible emails? They came from Bill's computer?'

Robert nodded.

'Some of them did.'

I closed my eyes and felt sick. It had been a risk letting Tom and Robert access my work laptop and my email, but after seeing Dylan in hospital, I knew I had to do everything I could to protect my daughter.

I'd spoken to Tom, a twenty-something computer whiz kid based in Robert's Marylebone office, and he'd explained that an IP address – where it was sent from – is coded into every message sent, like the serial number on the bottom of a kettle or the back of a TV. Unless you are high-level law-enforcement with a court order, there's no way of finding out where the message came from, unless you could physically match the IP address with the computer used to send it. Without breaking into Nathan's house, the only device we had access to was Bill's ancient PC which lived on the desk in his study.

'I think we can be pretty certain they weren't sent by Bill or Iris,' said Robert, breaking into my thoughts.

'Dylan,' I moaned softly, thinking about the safety of our daughter.

'Don't worry, I've already called David. He's under strict instructions to kill Nathan if he comes round to the house.'

I could tell he wasn't really joking.

As my toes curled deep into the pile, my fingers followed suit making a tight, anxious claw.

'What's wrong?' said Robert trying to catch my eye. 'I thought you'd be glad we've nailed the little bastard.'

Suddenly the filthy messages didn't even seem important. I certainly didn't feel better knowing that Nathan really was my cyber-stalker.

'We have another problem,' I said quietly.

'What now?' he frowned.

I'd been storing it all up in my chest for the past hour. I'd been outside, tried to force cold air into my lungs, I'd downed at least two glasses of champagne, hoping it would take the edge off what I had been told, waiting for the right moment to discuss it with Robert.

'I think you know,' I said finally.

'Know what?'

He looked at me and I instinctively knew, but I needed to say it anyway.

'I spoke to Max Miskov earlier.'

'Did you ever send him that running information?'

I wasn't sure if he was going to try and deny anything, but he pressed his lips firmly together, like he did when he was anxious or upset.

'He told me you owed him money.'

A tiny pulse started beating hard under Robert's left eye and I wanted him to deny it. I wanted to feel some reassurance even if it was a lie. I wasn't sure I could take the truth tonight.

Robert didn't flinch. 'Max? We're business associates. We're certainly financially connected but I'm not sure you could say that I owe him money.'

'Robert, tell me. Just tell me the fucking truth.'

My raspy, alcohol drenched voice echoed around the room. I had no idea any if any of the catering staff who were still here heard me. I didn't care.

I waited until the room seemed to stop vibrating.

'Do you owe Max Miskov money?'

I glared at my husband, willing him to answer me.

It was another few seconds before my husband spoke. 'He thinks I do,' said Robert, looking away.

There was a tightness in his voice – I couldn't tell what it was at first, but then I knew. It was fear.

'Please Robert, you have to tell me what's going on,' I said, forcing myself to be less hysterical. 'I think Max might be responsible for Dylan's accident.'

I watched his Adam's apple go up and down.

'What makes you say that?' he said.

I heard the tremor in his voice. I never heard Robert sound anything other than completely self-assured. But he was definitely frightened.

'He said something to me at the party. He was threatening me.'

'Threatening you?'

'He didn't admit he'd had Dylan knocked down, but he asked about Dylan and then said he was glad she was alright, *this time*. It was just the way he said it. Knowing, menacing. He meant to frighten me, not console me.'

There was a long silence, then Robert looked at me. In the cold moonlight streaming in through the window, he looked pale, bloodless like a jellyfish.

'You didn't tell him about Dylan's accident, did you?' I whispered.

It was a few moments before he shook his head.

I grabbed his arm, clutching at the crisp fabric of his sleeve.

'Robert, what's going on? Who is Max Miskov?'

He sank down on the edge of the bed, hanging his head, like a man defeated.

'Tell me!' I screamed, still clawing the cotton into my fist. Slowly, he began to speak.

'Three years ago, right around the time I met Max, I got wind that the owners of Regent Place were in financial trouble. I knew them, I knew it was a special property. I said I'd help them get out of a hole and broker a fast deal.'

'Did you?'

'I bought it myself.'

I wasn't sure how these things worked and I had no idea how Robert would have been able to raise the money for that sort of transaction.

'What with?' The sale must have been worth tens of millions. 'How did you afford it?'

'Leveraged debt, loans, I scraped enough together – just. It was a risk, a big risk, but I knew that if we could get the right planning permission, it would be the bargain of the century.'

He licked his lips as if he was parched.

'So where does Max come into it?'

'Max is the investment manager for a very wealthy Russian family.'

'Elena's family?'

He didn't reply.

I prodded him further. 'When you say investment manager, what's that in the real world, Robert? Consigliere?' I remember it had been the word that Katherine McCauley had used; my husband looked up with some grudging admiration for my savvy and understanding of what was going on. He nodded.

'Max told me he was looking for an investment. I told him about Regent Place. His fund wanted in.'

I noticed how careful he was being with his lexicon, using terms like 'fund' and 'investment manager', as if this was all professional and above-board, not a money laundering racket designed to wash the proceeds of drugs, violence, and people trafficking.

'So Max and these Russians joined you as an investor?'

It made sense. I could see how Robert's company might scrape together the purchase costs of Regent Place but then there were huge development costs to think about.

Robert took in a sharp breath.

'No, I sold the building to them.'

I tried desperately to piece it all together.

'But Max told me that you owed him money. How come, if they bought the building from you?'

'I bought Regent Place using an offshore company. There's lots of advantages to doing it like that. Anonymity is one of them.'

'So Max and the Anotovs didn't know they were buying it from you?'

Robert shook his head. His knee was bouncing up and down. I could tell he was as desperate for a drink. So was I.

'I found that property, Rachel. I had the balls to buy it when there were no guarantees for planning permission. I took the risk. Finally, it was my turn for a big pay day rather than working for commission or a miserable slice of equity.'

'So why is Max unhappy?'

Robert didn't say anything for what seemed like an eternity. It was as if he was chewing it all over, debating whether or not to tell me.

'He thinks I stitched them up.'

I could see why Max might see it that way, and how his bosses might agree. Robert had claimed he'd found an invest-ment property and negotiated a price, presumably taking a commission to boot. If it turned out that he was the owner all along, the Russians would assume Robert had lied at every stage in order to squeeze the maximum money from the deal – and from them. The Anotovs, if they were who Katherine

McCauley claimed they were, didn't sound like they had much of a sense of humour. I could only imagine what they would do to people who they believed had screwed them over.

'How did Max find out?'

'I don't know,' he said, shaking his head bitterly. 'He must have met someone involved with the original owner, maybe they told him about my involvement in the sale. It doesn't matter, the point is he put two and two together.'

Robert's eyes were glistening now. I had never seen him cry. Even when our daughter had been born, or when she had first wrapped her tiny fist around his finger. And that scared me more than anything.

'Tell me Max had nothing to do with Dylan's accident, Robert.'

Tears dripped down his Robert's cheeks, leaving dark circles on his collar.

'I don't know what he's capable of,' he said honestly.

'Have a guess.'

He glanced around from side to side, as if he was looking for someone to help him.

'That night he came around to the house . . . the night you saw him. He came to tell me that he'd found out that I had owned Regent Place originally. He knew how much I had bought the property for and obviously knew how much the Anotov investment fund had paid for it. He wanted me to refund the difference or else . . .'

'Or else what?'

I took hold of my husband's hand. It was stone cold.

He eyes were staring at the wall, at if he were almost catatonic.

'At first, I thought I'd be able to pay him. I mean, we had this place. I bought Cadogan House, with the profit from the sale of Regent Place to Dmitri. This place was always meant to be a quick flip, just cosmetic work and cash it in. I don't want to give Max any money but I knew I could pay the bastard if I had to. If he got difficult.'

The tremble in Robert's voice told me that everything Katherine McCauley had said was true. Max was dangerous, the Anotovs were dangerous, and my husband was completely out of his depth.

'How much money are we talking about?' I asked, with a coolness that surprised me.

He told me and I gasped. My brain was quickly joining the dots.

'Which is why you need Cadogan House to sell quickly. Why you were drinking in the dark the other week when the sale had fallen through.'

I was angry, scared, incredulous that my whip-smart husband had been so reckless in his pursuit of money. Then again, I knew how foolish we could all be if we followed our desires without too much thought for the consequences. *You stupid, stupid, stupid idiot.*

That's what I wanted to say, but I knew there was no point screaming at him. It was time to be smart. I wasn't going to let anyone destroy my family. Not after everything we'd been through.

I forced myself to think. 'Max is blackmailing you. But surely he is being duplicitous too. Do you think Elena's father is ever going to see any money that Max extracts out of you? Can't you turn this back on him? After all, this is a play by Max for money and power. And you could play hardball back. Threaten to tell Elena's father what his right-hand man has been up to.'

'But it's a risk I just can't take,' said Robert, his voice smaller and weaker than my own. 'I need to pay him the money. Cadogan will sell after tonight, I know it.'

'What makes you think Max isn't going to tell the Anotovs after you pay him off?'

'He won't do that. The second he takes the money is the

second he's screwed the Russians too. The best thing to do is pay him. That's my leverage.'

He was shivering now. My husband was six foot two with the lean body of an athlete, but sitting there on the emperor-size bed he looked as small and lost as a child.

I put my arms around his and stroked the back of his head, where I could feel sweat collecting on his scalp.

I sat next to him on the bed and took his hand.

'The best thing we can do is get help,' I said softly. 'From people who know more about these sorts of people than us.'

'Help from who,' he said with the hard laugh of the defeated.

I took a breath.

'I've been approached by someone.'

He turned to look at me. 'About what?'

'I'm not really sure who she is. She's called Katherine McCauley.'

I told him about our meeting in Middle Temple. I didn't tell him about the photographs she had of me but I told him everything else. What she had told me about Max and Elena's family, the bloody money and the assassination of the lawyer in Moscow.

Robert stood up and started.

'Why didn't you tell me this sooner?'

'Because I didn't believe her,' I said with feeling. 'I didn't want to believe her. It was only when I spoke to Max Miskov tonight that I did. What do you think?'

'I think I have to sort this out on my own.'

'Robert, please. At least just sleep on it.'

'Who is she again?'

'I'm not sure.'

He looked out of the window again as if he was thinking.

'Do you know how to contact her?'

'I've got her card at home.'

'Does it not say who she works for?'

'It's just her name and contact details.'

'You'd better give it to me.'

I nodded. I supposed that was what Katherine McCauley wanted anyway.

'I'll sort this, Rachel. I will.'

I closed my eyes and said yes, desperately wanting to believe him.

Chapter 50

Dylan hadn't said two words since we'd stopped for a coffee at Oxford services. I didn't blame her. We'd been on the road since 7 a.m. and up late the night before talking.

We'd told her about Nathan and IT Tom's email as soon as we'd got home from Simeon's party. She needed to know about it sooner rather than later, and it was a calculated decision telling her while David and the family were staying over, figuring it might keep a lid on any histrionics and hysterical accusations that we were ruining her life.

As it was, she was eerily calm and rational. She wanted proof, but when Robert showed her the email from Tom, who'd sent a very comprehensive report about IP address matches, she just said she was going to bed, which freaked me out more than if she'd spent the entire night screaming.

I'd crept up to her room every ten minutes to check on her, until she got annoyed with me and then the next time, I went up she was asleep. I'd stood by her bed and looked at her, her pale face on the pillow, the crescents of lashes and tell-tale pink cheeks on a pale exhausted face that proved she'd been crying and I'd said sorry, over and over again.

'Did you enjoy hanging out with your cousins?' I said, smiling, keeping both hands on the wheel. Robert and I had stayed up another hour debating whether she should go back to Birmingham at all. Until Max Miskov was deported or imprisoned, I didn't want to let Dylan out of my sight. But as Robert pointed out, Max wouldn't be a problem while he thought Robert was pushing hard to sell Cadogan House with the intention of giving him the profits from the sale.

'The twins? They're sweet,' said Dylan, her eyes trailing out of the window towards Spaghetti Junction.

'I noticed they signed your cast.'

'Vanessa is really good at art. She wanted to do a full cast tattoo with those felt-tips you bought her.'

I laughed loud, artificially so. I was just so pleased we were talking. I wanted her to feel it every minute I was with her.

I concentrated on the road as I came off the motorway. I wasn't a particularly confident driver at the best of times, content to let Robert do most of the long car journeys. When we were on a long, straight A-road, I glanced over at her.

'About last night,' I said quietly.

'I don't want to talk about it,' she said, eyes looking straight ahead.

'I didn't want it to be Nathan, you know. I didn't want it to be him who sent those emails. I thought he was a nice guy. I thought he was kind.'

'So did I,' she said. Her words had a tartness but it wasn't directed at me. 'People disappoint you.'

'You can say that again,' I said, remembering Serena trying to seduce my husband at Cadogan House. Even though I understood infidelity because I had done it myself, there was no way I could ever forgive my friend.

'Looks like I can sort out that work experience your tutor was after for her third-year students,' I said, wanting to change the subject. 'I've got lunch with Ian, my boss tomorrow. He's really happy with how the party went. He talking about offering me a permanent role at the company.

I can make sure the work experience is one of my terms of employment.'

'Thanks.'

I didn't know what I was expecting. I could hardly expect to be her favourite person right now, or that she would be happy after the painful conversation we'd had the night before.

We were in Edgbaston now, close to the halls of residence. Just a few weeks ago I had felt sick as we had driven this same stretch of road, but now I only wished that term-time was a little bit longer. I longed to see nice Amy from Mech Eng and Instagram photos of my daughter having a brilliant time on campus. I just wanted her to be safe until we sorted everything.

'Not even ten o'clock,' I said, glancing at the clock on the dashboard as we pulled into the halls car park. 'You might even make your first lecture.'

She got out of the car and asked me to pop the boot to get her backpack.

'You don't have to come in,' she said, already a few steps away from the car. 'Not unless you want a quick coffee to pep you up for the trip home.'

She grinned sheepishly and her dimples looked like two smiles. I knew then that our relationship would get slowly back to where it was.

'Tempting as it is to experience Birmingham's very own Central Perk, I should probably get going. Unless you want a lift down to campus, that is.'

'You go,' she smiled. 'You need to get back to Edelman for your Simeon Averill victory parade.'

I stood motionless.

'You aren't going to contact him, are you?'

'No,' she said, looking down.

I tried to catch her eye.

'If he gets in touch with you, be polite, but firm. You don't want to aggravate him,' I said, repeating some tips from Lottie Callow, who I had called after I'd found the Faber postcard at Bill's. She'd sounded genuinely relieved that I'd discovered his identity but hadn't mentioned sending the bill, which led me to believe she wasn't quite sure it was over.

'Nathan's not dangerous,' said Dylan quietly.

Despite everything, I could feel her loyalties were for him. She reminded me of myself – still wanting to make excuses for Chris Hannah even when I thought he was tormenting me. It reminded me how messy and complex love could be.

'Goodbye honey,' I said, stepping forward to hug her. 'I'll be back next week to pick you up. In the meantime, if you need anything, anything at all, just call me. If you are worried about anything just message me and I will come and collect you straight away.'

Dylan gave me a squeeze and it was as if life was being pumped back into my body.

I could feel her chest tremble against mine.

'I'm sorry,' she said into my ear.

'What for?' I said, pulling back in surprise.

'For upsetting you. I know you've only ever had my back. I love you.'

A tear dripped down her cheek.

'Sweetheart, why are you crying?'

'I just think it was all my fault,' she said and I could see her throat trembling.

'What's your fault?'

She looked away, her shoulders sunk and I could hear anxious staccato breathe stutter out of her breath.

'I told him.'

'Told who, what?'

'I told Nathan I thought you were having an affair. I wanted to talk about it, get it off my chest, so I told him about the Southern Electric call and what I thought it meant.'

'Darling, just forget about it.'

'No. I need to talk it through. What if he made a judgement about you? What if he thought you were promiscuous?
What if it was my allegation that started the unwanted
attention?'

'Darling, I'm sure that's not the reason. It doesn't matter
anyway. It's over.'

I held my breath, waiting for her to ask me more about
that phone call, ask me who Southern Electric really was and
what he meant to me. I'd already prepared a little script in
my head. That I'd been sad and lonely and neglected and an
old flame, my first love had come along and swept me off
my feet and I'd been foolish enough to think he was worth
it.

But she didn't ask.

After all, she was the adult in the family.

I was back in the office by one-thirty. Half the office was out
for lunch but I could tell that the mood was still giddy from
the party the night before. Pictures of Cadogan House were
online on *The Bookseller* website already. They'd gone big
on the story and I wasn't surprised, given it was the starriest
literary bash seen in years according to the Books Editor of
the *Mail*. There were half a dozen diary pieces in the broad-
sheets, even the tabloids had a quarter page pap shot of
Simeon, flanked by the supermodels, whose clothes seemed
to have gone semi-transparent overnight.

Serena had also obviously been down and left a Post-it
note on my keyboard with 'TRIUMPH! CALL ME!' written
on it underlined twice. I screwed it up and tossed it in the
bin, glad that I had missed her, although secretly I was willing
to accept the compliment.

The previous evening didn't feel so much a triumph as a
turning point.

The party was a success, my one-night stand forgotten.
My cyber-stalker was vanquished, and my relationship with

my daughter was back on track. Ian Sinclair had already let slip that he had a couple of new authors lined up for me – two debuts that he'd just bought in a little acquisitions flurry before the Christmas lull. The sense that things were slowly moving forward was palpable, I was no longer trapped. Even the fact that I had driven to Birmingham and back already that morning felt like an achievement. And yes, there was just the shadow of Max Miskov hanging over everything and he needed to be dealt with, but my husband always found a way to get what he wanted and I was sure he would see off the problem of Max Miskov.

'For you,' said Ian, thumping a manuscript on my desk. 'Simeon's new book. About to crack on with the edit but I wanted to know what you thought of it.'

'Thank you,' I said, looking at the six-inch doorstop. I wasn't sure why he hadn't just sent me the digital file but I knew it was a compliment asking me to read it. 'I can't wait. I'll make a start this weekend. I'm sure I'll burn through it.'

Ian loitered by my desk.

'So, are we still on for lunch tomorrow?'

'I am if you are.'

'I've got breakfast with Simeon first so we should probably just meet at The Ivy at one.'

I smiled, suddenly reminded of an industry urban myth. That once Simeon's manuscript had been so late, his publisher had been sent to his house to do the edit on-site. The idea had been to speed up the process, but it had achieved quite the opposite as the Edelman employee had so enjoyed living in an outhouse of Simeon's grand Hampshire manor house, taking advantage of his extensive wine cellar while waiting to be drip-fed pages, the publication date had had to be put back a whole six months. Although it wasn't the Nineties anymore, I still had a feeling that Simeon's editing breakfast might run on and that our meeting would be cancelled at the last minute.

I yawned and heard my jaw click. I'd hardly had any sleep and it was beginning to catch up with me. I opened a bottle of water on my desk and took a long swig. I heard my stomach rumble and realized I hadn't eaten anything all day, just getting by on black coffee and Evian.

I pulled on my coat and took the lift downstairs. There was a Pret two minutes away which I usually avoided because it was so busy. But the lunchtime rush had died down so I grabbed a tuna baguette and a cake and turned to go back to the office.

'Rachel! There you are.'

'Serena,' I said, clutching my Pret bag close to my chest like a lift-belt.

'I came down to see you earlier. Wasn't entirely surprised you weren't in. You absolutely deserved the morning off.'

'I wasn't having a lie-in. I was taking Dylan back to Birmingham,' I said crisply.

'You never stop.' She paused. 'I meant to tell you . . .' She was waving her hands around as if she was nervous. Another liar's tell. 'Alan won a holiday in some charity auction last week. I say won. He paid through the bloody nose for it. But it's seven nights in Tuscany. Beautiful villa. Can't take it in the school holidays but then you're not tied to those anymore, are you? Anyway,' she said, curling her mouth around the word with relish, 'we were wondering if you and Robert would like to come with us? Apparently, there's a butler and an in-house chef if you needed any more excuse to say yes.'

It would have easy to say yes, very easy indeed but I felt something snap inside me.

'Don't pretend you're my friend, Serena.'

I wasn't sure where it came from. I was just sick of people pretending, sick of liars and cheats.

'Sorry?' She literally took a step away from me on the pavement.

'I saw you with Robert at the party. I saw you in the bedroom.'

She frowned as if she was thinking.

'The bedroom? Of Cadogan House?'

'You know what I'm talking about, Serena.'

'Robert was just showing me around the house.'

'You were all over him like a rash,' I said, determined to say my piece.

'That's ridiculous. I was just admiring the decor.'

'Is that what they call it now . . .'

'Rachel . . .'

'I was there, at the door. I know what I saw. Robert had to push you away.'

Her eyes narrowed.

'Well, you'd had quite a lot to drink,' she said tartly. She might as well have said 'as usual'. She was certainly thinking it. 'I can assure you it was all perfectly innocent.'

I tried to keep my voice level.

'Don't invite us on any holidays, Serena. Don't invite us out for dinner, just stay away from us.' It was hard standing up to people like Serena. Even her presence, in four-inch heels, was so much bigger than mine. But when you had stood at the edge of a cliff, when you have experienced the very real fear of losing everything, you weren't afraid of anything anymore because you had got used to the idea of falling.

'How dare you,' she hissed, her face contorted with such contempt that I could barely recognize her. 'How dare you suggest that I'm the enemy when I've done so much for you. Without me, you wouldn't even be back in publishing. You'd still be sat at home, drinking gin and reading romance novels. Without me, you'd have been fired by Ian Sinclair weeks ago, your reputation shot, the entire company talking about the promiscuous, alcoholic editor with the S&M fetish.'

She was lashing out. I knew it was a sign of her guilty conscious.

'Nothing happened between me and Robert,' she said, calming her own voice down.

'But you wanted it to?' I said quietly.

The air was cold but still her cheeks burned pink.

'I trusted you, Serena,' I continued. 'You knew what I was going through, but you took advantage of my weakness. Friends don't do that. Friends don't stick the knife in when you're floundering.'

I didn't think I'd ever seen Serena stuck for anything to say. Not in the twenty-five years that I'd known her. But after I'd said my piece, she just turned on her spiked high heels and scuttled back to the office.

As I stood there watching her go, my own words kept repeating themselves in my head, as if on a loop.

I knew I was guilty of one thing I had just accused Serena of.

I hadn't been a good friend either.

I watched the cars on the busy street go by, colours blending into one another like a paper streamer rippling down the road as I went back in time.

If it wasn't for me you wouldn't even be in publishing . . .

I pulled out my phone, ready to send a text but then I realized I no longer had his number. That it was at the bottom of the Ladies' Pond.

'But he's joined Facebook,' I muttered to myself, downloading the app.

He wasn't hard to find. Chris Hannah with his forty-seven friends and a profile picture that made him look like Gerard Butler. I knew he wouldn't have just forty-seven friends for long.

I kept my message simple.

We found the cyber-stalker. I'm sorry. For everything.

I wasn't looking for a reply. It was just something I had to say. Despite everything that had happened, it still felt as if it was the right thing to do. For all the Serenas in the world, the fake friends who were with you out of convenience, or because you served a purpose – there were others who cared for you and always wanted to help.

But he sent a message back before I'd switched off my phone.

I'm glad. I hope you can put it all behind you. Friends?

I was tempted to send back something trite. A smiley face emoji or a thumbs up sign. But I knew I just didn't owe him an apology. I finally owed him the truth.

Chapter 51

He suggested we meet in the Crown pub in Soho. I knew it from my early days in London – a lively, noisy sort of bar where twenty-somethings congregated outside in the summer and rowdy birthday parties were held in the first-floor function room. Now it was where couples met on Tinder dates before the night took them wherever the breeze blew, and heavy drinkers came to take advantage of the cheapest lager in the W1 postcode.

I was aware it wasn't entirely appropriate to meet Chris Hannah in a pick-up joint, but I didn't see him in that way anymore. Since the pregnancy scare, it was as if that whole side of me had been switched off. I had tried to put it down to the perimenopause, although deep down I wondered if it was shame.

It was dark in the pub, thin winter light dribbled in through the windows. I asked for a soda water at the bar and went to sit on the banquette in the corner. When Chris arrived, I saw him peer anxiously around the bar and could almost hear his heart jump when he saw me. I also felt a flurry of nerves. After all, I'd waited twenty-five years to have this conversation.

'Sorry I'm late,' he said, slipping into the chair opposite me.

'Don't worry,' I replied, fiddling with my straw.

'Let me get you another drink.'

I knew the situation called for vodka, but I knew what happened last time I hit the spirits with Chris Hannah. Besides, I was determined to stop drinking. Last night's champagne was my last, Prozac or not. It just wasn't good for me.

'Just another soda,' I said as Chris motioned to the man behind the bar and mouthed our order to him. There was a familiarity between the two men that made me look again.

'Do you know him?' I asked.

'I work here.'

'Here?'

'Bar manager.'

He looked at me, waiting for me to say something.

'I thought you had a hospitality company,' I said, immediately on my guard.

'Not quite a lie.'

'Not quite the truth.'

We both smiled awkwardly.

'I guess it sounded better.'

'I thought you knew me better than that.'

'I know you're not a snob, Rach. But I was just a boy who wanted to impress a girl. To be honest, I was probably doing it more for myself. For one night only I was the man I wanted to be when I was twenty. The successful businessman with the most beautiful girl at college on his arm. I guess I was lying to myself.'

Our drinks were brought over and Chris nodded to the barman but didn't smile.

'So you found out who it was? The harassment?'

'I'm so sorry for accusing you,' I said with purpose. 'I'm absolutely mortified and I just wanted to come and say it in person.'

'I'm just glad you sorted it all out. Who was it?'

I ran my finger around the edge of the glass.

'Our neighbour's carer. Actually – it's more complicated than that. He's also in a relationship with my daughter.'

'Does she know?'

I was grateful for his calmness. I always was.

'I'm not sure she believes it, but she's agreed to stay away from him. For now. I'm so sorry,' I said again.

Chris gave a laugh.

'You don't have to be sorry to me.'

'Chris, I'm sorry for everything,' I said more quietly.

'What do you mean?' he said, looking more serious.

'You had your whole life laid out before you. The job with the ad agency, a life in London. And then it all changed because of me.'

'It changed because of two stupid decisions I made. I plagiarized a book and I hit a bloke who deserved it too hard.'

'But one led to the other. And I lit the touch-paper.'

We looked at each other and we were both remembering that day in Durham. The day that changed the courses of our lives forever. The day he said he'd write my final dissertation for me.

I knew now that I probably needed Prozac even back then. Dark thoughts lived in my head, my moods, my energy would slump without any reason. Chris Hannah was like a drug. He pepped me up, and made me fizz. But love alone wasn't quite enough to keep me afloat.

I was also struggling with my course. I loved books, but I lacked the confidence to articulate what I felt about them, especially compared to my thoughtful, self-assured contemporaries. I believed that my opinions were less valid than other people's and the longer I felt it, the more insecure I became. By my third year, I felt completely out of my depth – on track for a third-class degree, with no motivation to go to any of my tutorials.

I admitted my struggles to Chris one night when we were

huddled up watching a video on the small portable in my room.

'Let's study,' he suggested as he made us cheese toasties on my little grill. Fuelled by the four-pack of lager, it had all come out. My inner fears that despite my good A levels, I was stupid, and I worried that the third-class degree I was on course for would be worthless.

He'd held me for at least an hour while I cried. Looking back, being so miserable about my course didn't sound rational. But depression isn't rational.

'We'll fix this,' he'd said in a way that made me believe him. And the next day he helped me. We picked the subject for my final thesis, due in six weeks' time. We'd spent hours in the stacks, then back at my student digs, I'd lie on the bed munching crisps, curled up under a blanket, barking the occasional academic thought at Chris who would sit by the window with a notebook, writing it all down. Not my words it turned out. His own interpretation of what I had said, what we'd found out in the library, on the microfiches, from the academic and experts.

The day I'd read my dissertation, I'd wept. It was brilliant; insightful, erudite – a first-class thesis, which, it turned out it was. I knew it wasn't mine, barely one word of it, but by then it was too late to turn back.

'You never held a gun to my head, Rach,' he said, rubbing a spot on the table with his fingertips as if he was sanding down the grain. 'I wrote your final dissertation because I wanted to help you. It was my fault I didn't leave enough time to do my own essay, my fault I copied someone else's work and passed it off as my own. My fault I drifted, got in with a bad crowd, and ended up serving time. I did all that to myself. It was nothing to do with you. I'm not a victim of anything other than my own stupidity.'

I swirled the melting ice cubes around my glass.

'If it's any consolation, I got my punishment. For years I'd sit at my Edelman desk and feel like a fraud. It doesn't leave you, that sense of shame. Even when I started back at work after eighteen years, I still felt it. I was still the girl who cheated.'

He looked at me with those green eyes.

'Maybe the thesis wasn't all yours. But you still loved books, words, stories. You became a successful editor because of those things not because of one thing you didn't do.'

'But I still lost you,' I said quietly.

Chris looked at me. After everything, I owed him an explanation.

'That night in Soho. You asked me why I ended our relationship. Why I just disappeared without a word. The truth is . . . I had to. Every time I saw you, spoke to you, or received one of your letters, it was a reminder that I wasn't good enough and no matter how much I adored you, how much I loved you, it could never quite compensate for the fact that I didn't really like myself. That's why I went travelling. Why I just disappeared. It just seemed like the easiest way to finish it but I knew, even back then, how shitty it was.'

'It's fine. I survived.'

'I know. But I still want to apologize. For everything.'

He looked away, deep in thought.

'My turn for a confession. You want to know why I turned up to Ollie's show?'

I shook my head, although I remembered what I had thought when I had seen him at the Soho Theatre. I thought that he was following me. I thought that it was the final conclusive proof that he was my stalker and he was finally revealing himself from out of the shadows.

'I went to see the show, because I wanted to see what success looked like,' said Chris quietly. 'And I saw it. Heard it. The laughs and the standing ovation and the T-shirts in the foyer with his name on them. I was thrilled for him, you know. Ollie's a good guy and a massive talent. But I'd be lying if I said it doesn't make you think about your own life, what you've got, not got, where you've ended up, especially when you're faced with someone who started out at exactly the same point at you.'

'Chris, you're not even fifty. If you're not satisfied at the pub, then do something new. You're talented too.'

He gave me a half-smile.

'Ollie went home in a blacked-out Mercedes, that night. I came back here to cash up. But I realized something. I love my job, my life. I have great friends, work with fun people. My flat is small, but it's home. I have enough money to go surfing in the summer weekends, and I still write the odd bit of prose and poetry.' He grinned and he looked lit from within.

'Still dreaming you could be Morrissey,' I said with affection.

'I could have done without time inside, but I'm happy with the way things have worked out. One day I might even go back to college and do another degree. The only thing I really regret is losing you.'

He put his hand on top of mine. It wasn't sexually charged but affectionate and tender.

'Friends now?'

'Friends,' I nodded. And I felt that we were.

He smiled back at me. 'I still think the moral of the story is no cheating.'

I couldn't help but think of Robert and Max Miskov and the underhand Regent Place deal and nodded.

'I'm always here to help you, Rachel,' he said and for the first time in a long time, I didn't feel quite so alone.

Chapter 52

'Fancy going out for dinner tonight?'

Robert came into the kitchen fastening his cuffs, and I could just about hear what he was saying over the noise of the juicer.

I'd got up half an hour earlier than usual, determined to make us a delicious breakfast, determined to set positive new routines around the house, or at least revert to the old ones we had when Dylan was here, when I'd work really hard to make stuff that might tempt her to eat – omelettes stuffed with cheese and peppers, smoothies crammed with berries and superfoods, eggs benedict dripping in homemade hollandaise. I had quite the repertoire in those days and I was pleased with the spread I'd laid out on the table today. Crepes with caramelized pears, cinnamon toast and fruit salad all to be washed down with a mango and kiwi super juice.

'What did you have in mind?' I smiled, pouring the thick, yellow liquid into two glasses.

'Dinner. Cinema. I thought we could go back to the rib place on the Holloway Road,' said my husband, sitting down at the table.

'Chuckies?' I laughed, looking at my husband's surprise suggestion. He generally didn't like to eat in anywhere that

J.L. Butler

didn't have at least one Michelin star, but Chuckies was a cheap as chips BBQ shack populated by teenagers in massive trainers. 'We haven't been there for years. In fact, it's probably luxury student accommodation these days.'

'It's not,' said Robert, drinking his smoothie. 'I drove past it the other day and it's still there. There's even a special offer on the baby back ribs. Come on, we should go.'

He was trying hard. I was trying hard. For the first time since Dylan went away this felt like a future I could enjoy, it felt like I could fall in love with my husband again.

'These are great,' he said, sliding a fork through the pancake.

If he'd noticed I didn't cook for us much lately, he hadn't said so. But I could tell by the way he was shovelling the food into his mouth, the way he licked his lips after he sipped the smoothie that he was enjoying every minute. I was a domestic goddess once more. A domestic goddess and a career woman and boy it felt good.

'By the way, I've got a viewing on Cadogan House,' he said, wiping the edge of his mouth with a napkin.

'That's brilliant. You should have told me.'

'I've only just found out,' said Robert, pushing his plate to one side.

'Someone from the party?'

'Actually no.'

I laughed. 'You see. You don't need me.'

'He's an American financier. Forbes list rich. House fits his exact specifications. He's having a personal tour from yours truly and lunch afterwards at Scott's. I've googled him and found a *New York Times* interview with him. He relaxes listening to Steely Dan and reading Simeon Averill novels so I think he might enjoy hearing about the party even if he never went. Coffee?'

We grinned at each other as Robert walked round the breakfast bar to select something from his coffee capsule holder.

He was halfway there when he stopped and bent down. At first, I thought he was tying up his shoelace, but I heard him mutter.

'What's that?' I couldn't really see what he was doing. Just the curve of his head and the arch of his back.

When he stood up, he held out his hand. I could see him looking at something in his palm and I knew I wasn't going to like whatever it was.

Robert held it up between his thumb and forefinger and held it to the light.

'Shit.'

'What is it?' I asked, but I'd recognized the sea green capsule immediately.

He handed it over and I felt my jaw clench, my good mood evaporating.

'Prozac, by the looks of it.'

I watched the expression on his face change, from puzzlement to concern, a dawning realisation of what the discovery could mean.

He flashed me a look.

'Did you know?' he said.

I didn't reply because I didn't know what to say. I was too busy wondering how the hell a Prozac capsule had found itself on the kitchen floor.

'What are we going to do about it?' he said, not waiting for my reply. 'We've got to speak to her.'

I took it off him and closed my fist around it, feeling more powerful than I had felt over the past few weeks.

'It's not Dylan's,' I said, squeezing the pill, feeling the powder explode in my grip.

Robert didn't say anything.

'So, whose is it?'

I supposed I could have passed it off as David's easily enough but I'd had enough of secrets.

'It's mine.'

'*You're on Prozac?*'

I nodded.

'Why didn't you tell me? How long have you been taking it?'

'Not long. I was going to tell you, but I was embarrassed. I thought you'd think I wasn't coping and make me quit the job.'

Robert stepped forward and put his arms around me.

'Oh, Rach . . .'

'Honestly, I'm feeling better all the time,' I said, starting to babble. 'It was stupid of me not to say anything. You know I wasn't thinking clearly I was so bogged down with everything that was happening.'

'We need to be honest about how we're feeling.'

I stepped back and looked at him.

'And I mean all of us.'

'I'm fine,' he said with an air of self-importance. I could tell he was niggled that I might even suggest he need anti-depressants.

'Have you called Katherine McCauley?' I asked.

'Yes,' he replied, still sounding irritated.

'What did she say?'

'We're meeting next week,' he said, adjusting his tie. 'Although at this rate we won't need to.'

'Why not?'

He turned back to look at me as if it was obvious.

'If the sale of Cadogan House goes through quickly, I can deal with this. We won't need any help from Katherine McCauley or anyone else.'

I waited a moment, and used the opportunity to clear away the plates.

'You know, I think we need a holiday. Dylan suggested it, actually, which was a surprise, seeing as after the Ibiza trip I was convinced she never wanted to go on another family holiday again. Maybe we could go somewhere for Christmas.'

Robert nodded, looking mollified. 'It's a good idea. If the American puts an offer in for Cadogan. Where do you fancy? Barbados? Turks and Caicos? The beaches are so white out there you can even pretend it's snow.'

My husband liked to holiday where rich people went. Where men in two-hundred-quid swimming shorts had an air of self-importance, and their wives with tiny heads and SoulCycle bodies ignored tanned, beautiful children playing at the foot of their sun lounger. I would take a beach house in Cornwall anytime over the Caribbean but I had to admit, even though I usually loved the magic of London in December, the idea of going somewhere far, far away for the long Christmas holidays was an appealing one.

'Should I start looking at flights?'

'I'll get Petra to sort it out.'

He looked at his watch. 'I should go.'

'Good luck with the viewing. What time is it?'

'Ten o'clock.'

I kissed him on the cheek.

'Good luck,' I said and I meant it.

I can spot a liar now. I have the experience. The way that Chris Hannah was vague about his job at the Chinese restaurant should have been a giveaway that he didn't have his own successful corporate events business. Serena's gentle probing about my marriage and how happy we were weren't just the concerned questions of a friend, but someone with ulterior motives. As for Nathan's generosity – the fruit jellies, mangoes and grapes all bought on a meagre salary, should have been a sign that he was guilty about something, not just the fact he was dating our daughter. I knew what a liar did, how they behaved, because I had also been a liar myself and right now, I was fairly sure that Robert hadn't contacted Katherine McCauley. He hadn't looked at me when he said he had, had fidgeted with his tie, the way he had snapped at me, was someone who wanted to cut dead the conversation because they didn't want to carry on lying.

As I scrapped the detritus of breakfast into the waste disposal and loaded up the dishwasher, I mulled over the reasons why he wasn't being honest. The most obvious was that he wasn't convinced that we should involve Katherine McCauley at all. She'd said she could help us but even I doubted that protecting our reputations or liberties was top of her priority list.

I still had no idea who she was, even though I'd spent hours googling her. I suspected she was a journalist, and I felt sure they could be incredibly ruthless to get the story they wanted.

I washed my hands and went upstairs to the bedroom. I had a meeting with an agent at eleven and the office wasn't expecting me in until the afternoon. Outside, the world had been stripped of its colour. I wasn't sure when autumn and its splendid colours had disappeared, but it was well and truly winter now. The plane trees still had some of their leaves, but looking onto the cemetery I could see more gravestones now, rotted teeth jutted up from the wild, overgrown woodland.

I pulled my phone out of my bag and lay back on the mattress for a minute staring at the Alexander Calder mobile.

Max and Elena liked art. It wasn't worth what Max Miskov wanted from Robert, but I would happily give it to him as a down payment if he would just leave us alone.

Still lying on my back, I looked at my phone and scrolled through my photos. Robert had asked for Katherine's card, and I had given it to him. But not before I had taken a photograph of it, just in case.

WhatsApp was safer to communicate with, I remembered that much. I tapped in a message:

Has my husband contacted you?

I sat up, put Katherine's details into my phone and pressed

send. I almost felt gleeful. Dylan thought I was a dinosaur but suddenly I felt like James Bond.

The reply was almost immediate.

No, he hasn't.

I took no pleasure in being right.

Chapter 53

'He said he was going to call you,' I said, pacing around the koi carp pond in the garden.

Katherine McCauley had called me minutes after she had sent her message. I imagined her pouring over *The Guardian*, drinking her coffee, when my WhatsApp gave her a hit of adrenaline more than any mug of Kenyan blend.

She told me to go outside before I said anything sensitive over the phone. I thought it sounded a bit paranoid but I was happy to take her lead.

'It can take a while, before people make the decision to move things forward,' she explained. 'I wasn't sure I'd ever hear from you again, but here you are.'

'Believe me, my husband has all the incentive he needs to challenge these bastards,' I said after telling her about Dylan's accident and Max Miskov's threats. 'But the fact that he hasn't called you, means he's worried about getting you involved. He needs to be convinced.'

'You need to persuade him to meet us, Rachel. I work with various authorities. We can help you. You don't want to try and deal with these people alone.'

'We should probably meet again,' I said slowly.

'Good idea. How about the same place we met last time,

and we can find somewhere from there? One o'clock tomorrow?'

'Do you mind if I bring a friend?'

I listened carefully as Katherine McCauley gave me strict instructions about what to start looking out for – account numbers or account details, particularly those from overseas accounts – Malta Cyprus, Cayman Islands, Jersey. I was looking for spreadsheets that could be analysed – inflated fees, commissions, or other purchases that could be set against development costs. Art work bought for double the going rate, furnishings that looked suspiciously expensive – apparently that was one well-known laundering scam, persuading store owners to invoice well over the odds – a £10,000 sofa could be billed for £30,000 and the difference refunded in cash in a win-win situation where everyone was making money.

When she rang off, I went back inside the house, into the bedroom and fished out the business card Chris Hannah had given me the day before from my coat pocket. I paused before I sent him a message. I knew it was making a massive presumption. Just because Chris had been in prison, it didn't make him Tony Soprano, but I suspected he had more guile than I did when it came to dealing with people like Katherine McCauley.

I gave him barely any details of what it was about, but he agreed to come with me to meet Katherine and our appointment was fixed for the next day.

Robert's study on the top floor of the house was as good a place to start as any. Cold morning light filtered through the window. Outside, the views of the cemetery added to the mood. Stripped trees stretched into the pale grey watercolour skies.

True to form, Robert's study was sparse and sterile, with everything put away. On one wall, was a uniform bank of cupboards and when I opened them, something I had rarely done, I was still shocked by the level of order. Pen pots, box files and piles of folders all facing the correct way, spines of books all neatly aligned. It was impossible not to compare it with my desk at Edelman: although I had been there less than two months it was already chaos, a forest of overflowing manuscripts, trial book jackets and press releases. Even the paperclips were untidy.

I started with Robert's computer, nervously turning it on. As it hummed to life, I drummed my fingers anxiously, wondering if he could tell I had been snooping. It was password-protected but I worked out what it was quickly enough – the same code we used for our joint bank account with his year of birth added on. Everything looked in order, but how was I supposed to recognize what I was looking for? I took a picture of a couple of Word Documents but it all seemed completely innocent.

'What am I expecting to find anyway?' I murmured, logging off and snapping the computer shut. Half-heartedly, I rifled through his drawers, but there was nothing there either and I hung my head in despair. I was flailing around, like a non-swimmer in the deep end desperate to scramble to the sides. Maybe if a forensic team was let loose on the house, they might find something incriminating, but I was just a book editor and one that was late for work. I looked at my watch. Nine-thirty already. I quickly sent a text to the agent post-poning our meeting by an hour and slipped my phone into my pocket. I knew I should leave for the office, but I couldn't let it go, not yet.

'Where would *I* hide something?' I said out loud. A better question might be where *did* I hide things? I strode down the stairs towards our dressing rooms. I hid my gin there because it felt safe – because it was my territory, who was to say Robert wouldn't have the same instinct?

We had his and hers dressing rooms. Mine was accessed through our bedroom, while Robert's, a larger space, was reached from the hall.

As my feet padded softly on the soft, grey carpet, it already felt as if I was doing something wrong, even though the house was empty – even though it was *my* house.

I took a moment to look around. Floor-to-ceiling shelves and hanging space lined all four walls. There was an exercise bike at one end, a huge leather ottoman in the centre of the room and was every bit as neat and ordered as his office. His crisp ironed shirts hung on expensive steel hangers, graded by colour from stark white through baby blue down to the dark grey he sometimes wore with his black Huntsman suit. I ran a hand along them just to hear the light swish as they swung. A couple of bare hangers jangled, but there was no other sound. Solid walls, oak shelving – obviously Robert hadn't skimped on particle board – and thick carpet meant it was practically silent inside. Too quiet. I stopped, cocking my head and listening. I could hear nothing, of course. Why would I? And anyway, why shouldn't I be in here, in part of my own house? Even so, I stepped up the pace, carefully lifting the knitwear neatly folded on the shelves and feeling underneath, picking up shoes and checking inside, then placing them back exactly as before. All I found was perfection. Perfect clothes in perfect rows, even the socks in his drawers were paired and rolled together in colour-coded symmetry. I opened the narrow cupboard at the back, the one area of 'freeform' storage Robert had allowed into the design. In my dressing room, I used the closet for suitcases, shoeboxes and random detritus which hadn't quite made it to the halfway-house of the garage: some little-used yoga gear, our wedding photo albums and a high tech set of scales I'd found too complicated to use. Robert had a similar collection: a fly-fishing rod, an Arctic-grade parka from a ski trip that had been too expensive to give away and various fitness gadgets from Robert's previous sports crazes. All neatly boxed and stacked, of course, and nothing hidden behind them.

The only item that didn't fit Robert's set-square uniformity was his climbing bag, casually dropped inside the door.

I knelt down and unzipped it, finding some rope, finger tape, a balled-up T-shirt and a single sock – even Robert couldn't maintain his tidiness when dashing out of a crowded changing room. I dug deeper, hating myself for doing it. Yes, I wanted answers, but even so, it was still a violation of his privacy, an unseen accusation that he had something to hide. And yet, I carried on, knowing deep down that I had to do it to keep our family safe.

Trying a side pocket, my hand hit something hard, plastic. I pressed my lips together, holding my breath. It was a phone.

Katherine had said that WhatsApp messages were another good place to start. Because of the app's sophisticated encryption it was often where illicit business was discussed. Criminals were the same as anyone else – they had to communicate – and a simple WhatsApp message was a good a way as any.

But this was a cheap, analogue mobile, the kind of SIM-free back-up you could buy from any supermarket. Hands trembling, I turned it on, excitement rising despite myself. I doubted this thing was a hotline to the Russian mob, but still, it seemed significant – and a strange thing for Robert to have too. The interface was basic – I went straight to messages and clicked on the inbox. Nothing. Literally nothing; the inbox was empty. Which was odd in itself. I went across to the 'Sent' folder. And that was full. I clicked on one – and my heart stopped.

I want to touch you

I want to feel you

I want to taste you

I am watching you

'No,' I whispered, head shaking. 'No, no.'

I clicked on another and another, trying to make sure I was seeing them right, that my eyes weren't playing tricks on me. But it was true. The messages from my stalker weren't from Nathan Deer at all. They were from my husband. It all made sense. He knew where I worked, where I went running. I didn't leave the alarm off that day I thought I was pregnant, the day I found the half-cooked heart in the oven. No one had broken in. Nathan Deer hadn't used a key. It had been the person who lived in the house with me all this time.

'Well, well. Finally.'

I whirled round and Robert was standing at the door, his face as hard as stone.

Chapter 54

I once read that in a hierarchy of our anxieties, the fear of the unknown is one of our most fundamental terrors. And yet, standing in front of my husband, his eyes dark, flat, impassive, I knew that the fear of the known was just as frightening. I barely recognized the man in front of me, hate coming from him like heat from a bonfire. He held out a hand: steady as a rock.

'Do you want to give it to me?' he said. No denials, no excuses, no 'this isn't what it seems'. There was no need for pretence anymore. Because we both knew. Robert was *Him*. Robert was my stalker.

'Now, Rachel,' he commanded, reaching for the phone. But for some reason, I pulled it back, cradling it to my chest.

'First, tell me why,' I said, not recognizing the calm in my voice. 'Tell me why you sent those texts. And I assume the Facebook messages, the Twitter notifications, the whip, the postcards . . . I assume they were all you too.'

He took a step closer towards me, his eyes shining.

'Everything could have been so good, Rachel. It could have been perfect. Dylan gone, back to just the two of us again, back when we were so in love.'

Another step towards me.

'I came home from Paris that night because I missed you, do you realize that? I missed my wife. I wanted to wake up next to you, not next to a cold space in another corporate hotel suite, so I got the last Eurostar home with that box of Fauchon eclairs you wanted. But you weren't at home when I got here, were you? You were still at your stupid party. So I got undressed, got into our bed and waited to hear the turn of the key of the lock, waited for you to come home. But you didn't come, did you Rachel?'

'Robert, let me explain . . .'

'I woke up alone,' he snapped, cutting me off. 'Next to a cold, empty space, just as I would have done if I have stayed in the hotel room. But *you* weren't alone that morning though, were you, Rachel? You were with that fucking barman.'

He spat the last word, his cool cracking.

'It was a stupid, drunken mistake . . .' I began, but it was clear Robert wasn't listening, wasn't interested in hearing anything I had to say.

'So I made the bed,' he continued. 'I smoothed it down so it looked unslept in, then I went out for a coffee. And do you remember, Rachel? When you finally did slope in, I gave you the chance to admit that you had stayed out all night, but you didn't.'

His mouth twisted to one side. 'And at that moment, I knew. I knew what you'd done. I knew my wife was a dirty little slut.'

'Robert, I made a mistake but it was one night. It meant nothing.'

His eyes clouded with emotion but he blinked it away.

'I didn't get where I am today without doing my due diligence. When I knew you were fucking someone else, I followed you when you went to work. I saw you go into Edelman. I watched you come out. I saw you meet that loser on Waterloo Bridge. I saw you give him the flowers. Flowers.'

His nose wrinkled, as if he were smelling them now, wilted and rotten in the vase.

'And I saw him stroke your cheek. I followed him too, after you'd got into a taxi – you didn't know that, did you? I followed him to that crappy pub where he works. I have to say; I didn't think you'd sink so low.'

I hated him for his cruel dismissal of Chris, but I knew that was the least of my worries right now.

'You've got the wrong end of the stick. Those flowers – he sent them to me and I was giving them back to him. Because I didn't want them.'

Robert snorted.

'I would have found out about it anyway, you do know that, don't you? Serena told me about the enormous bouquet that was delivered to your desk on your first day at work. She told me how sweet it was of me to send them, how I was the perfect husband.' His lip curled into a sneer. 'Not perfect enough, it seems.'

I put a hand out to him.

'I was lonely, Robert. I'd had too much to drink and I . . . I met someone from college. One thing led to another . . .'

There was pleading in my voice and although I regretted everything that had happened with Chris Hannah, I hated having to beg for forgiveness when he had been tormenting me for weeks.

'It's not that hard to say no,' said Robert through thin lips. He was right about that and I lowered my head.

'Serena wants to fuck me, you know that?' he said, coming up close to me. 'That weekend we went to her house. You'd gone to bed early and she followed me to the bathroom. She lifted up her dress, took my hand and put it on her cunt. She told me how much she wanted me, how much she'd always wanted me. Told me how she wanted me to do it to her. But I said no, because that's what you do when you're married. I said no and then I took you to Marley Hall because I wanted things to work between us, because despite it all, I love you. And I was prepared to forgive you, even then.'

'You've got a funny way of showing it.'

'But before I forgave you, I had to teach you a lesson.'

Anger suddenly rose up in my chest and I stepped forward, pushing him back.

'A *lesson*?' Although Robert was scaring me, I growled with fury. 'How dare you take the moral high-ground. You almost got our daughter killed so don't lecture me about family values.'

'Max only wanted to scare us.'

I wasn't sure he believed that bit, but his face was still like stone.

'Just like you wanted to scare me. Well, it worked, Robert. I saw a lawyer, a doctor. You drove me to anti-depressants. You say you love me but you sent me to the edge.'

'I did it for us.'

'You really believe that, don't you? Just like you think that this house, Marley Hall, and all your big, shiny property developments – it's all for us. But it's not Robert. It's all for *you*. If you really cared about someone you wouldn't psychologically torment them just to teach them a *lesson*. You wouldn't humiliate them by sending naked photos to their workplace, or postcards or a heart burning in the oven.'

'You're a disgrace.'

'Coming from the man who stalks his own wife. From a man who was happy to set up poor Nathan Deer.'

'We both wanted him out of the picture.'

I blinked at him as a sudden thought occurred to me.

'That message from Tom in IT. Was that you too? Another throw-away phone sending a message to yourself?'

He gave a hollow laugh.

'No, that that was real, although you're right. In hindsight a fake message, even a fake IT manager would have been easier than going around to Bill's and using his computer.'

My eyes opened wide as I remembered something that Nathan had said. The words were coming out of my mouth before I could stop them.

'Iris saw you, didn't she?' I said, the implication hitting me like a punch.

I could only think of my conversation with Nathan outside the Holloway café. What had Iris seen? Robert pulling over the bins and leaving a message for me – 'SLAG' – amid the rubbish. But she'd seen him again. She'd seen him on Bill's computer.

This time Robert didn't reply.

'Oh my God. What did you *do*, Robert?' I said, my hand going to my mouth, the full horror finally sinking in. Iris hadn't just fallen down the stairs because she was old and infirm. She had fallen – or been pushed – because she had caught Robert in the act of framing Nathan. I tried desperately to remember if I'd got an email or a tweet on the day that Iris died. I couldn't remember, but I was certain that there would have been.

Suddenly this cramped room felt far too small.

'Iris,' he said, his voice lowered. 'That was unfortunate. It was a shame she caught me.'

His expression was emotionless. It was only then I realized how damaged he was.

'You know how my father died,' he said, almost to himself. 'Derek Reeves was a fine shot, the best in Dorset they used to say. He had six shotguns, game guns, sporters, a twelve-bore short barrel he used for vermin control. That twelve-bore was the one he used to blow his brains out,' he said, louder now. 'He killed himself when he found out my mum was having an affair. With Will Durrell, the local solicitor. David still thinks it was because of money troubles, but I know the *truth*.'

The last word was sharp, vicious, and I looked at him with rising panic, saw the muscles clenching at the side of his jaw, the fists opening and closing.

'I saw it *all*, you see,' said Robert. 'I heard the moaning coming from my parents' bedroom when I came home early from school one afternoon. I hid in the garden and through the back window of the house I saw Durrell coming down the stairs zipping up his trousers. I saw my mum kissing the back of his neck, just there,' he said, touching a spot on his own skin, just beneath his ear. 'And you know the worst part? Dad knew about it too.'

He clenched his hands again.

I was afraid now. Afraid of my husband and what he could do.

'Robert, you need to calm down. Let's talk about this.'

He wasn't listening to me.

'I don't know when he found out,' he continued. 'But when I heard him crying in the shed a few days later, I knew he knew about Durrell. And a week later he was dead. That's what infidelity does, Rachel. It destroys people.'

When he looked up at me, I barely recognized him. It was Robert, but different, altered. His features had changed, twisted, the light gone from his eyes.

'And now this,' he said with menace, his hatred hitting me like a blow. 'Now I see you've been snooping again. Haven't you? You want evidence? For Katherine McCauley? Is that what you're trying to do? Ruin me?'

I swallowed, trapped in this windowless room.

'Let's go downstairs,' I said, trying to keep calm. Now was not the time for blaming one another. I took a step forward but he moved in my way, teeth bared.

'You're not going anywhere. Not until you've given me the phone.'

My stomach clenched as he held out his hand again.

'Give me the phone, Rachel. Don't make me take it from you.'

'Robert, stop this,' I whispered in panic. 'I know you're under a lot of stress, but if we just get help . . .'

As he tried to grab the phone I fell back against the shelves, my head cracking against the wood. I collapsed to the floor, stunned. The phone clattered to the carpet and he picked it up.

'Robert, please . . .'

He bent down towards me, so close I could see the open pores on his nose.

'You've tried to take everything from me,' he snarled. 'You're trying to take my business. Next, you'll want a divorce. Well, that's not going to happen, Rachel. I've not worked so hard to let my life be destroyed by someone like you.'

I crawled onto my hands and knees and tried to stand.

'You should probably stay in here, Rachel,' he said, his voice hard and cold.

There was a Cire Trudon candle on the dresser. I'd bought it for him the previous Christmas because I loved them so much. It was a masculine scent, leather and cigars, but it sat unlit, untouched under the mirror.

He picked it up, put it in his pocket and started edging out of the room.

'I'm sorry, Rachel. I really am. But I'm afraid you brought all this on yourself.'

There was a mat underneath the shoe rack and I watched him gather it up and throw it into the hall.

He's crazy, I thought with terrible clarity. *He's completely lost his mind.*

'Robert!' I screamed, scrambling to my feet, but he moved across the room with shocking speed, blocking the doorway to the hall.

'Please Robert,' I said, trying to squeeze past him, but he was too strong. 'What are you doing?'

'What needs to be done.'

With a strength I'd never imagined he possessed, he gripped me with both hands and flung me back across the floor. I toppled back, landing on my hands, pain in both arms seared from wrist to elbow.

I was dizzy, my vision not quite in sharp focus.

'You're troubled, Rachel,' he said, taking the Cire Trudon back out of his pocket. 'Your doctor knows it, Dylan knows it, Nathan Deer knows it. I suspect even your little fucking barman waster knows it. No one will be surprised when they find out you've done something stupid like leaving one of your candles unattended.'

It began to dawn on me what he was planning to do. I forced myself on my hands and knees and tried to stand.

'Robert, no. I'm your wife. This is your home.'

'I'll do what I always do. I'll rebuild. I'll start the dream again, from the ground up. Just like I did after Dad died.'

He slammed the door shut.

I was on my feet now, still dazed and took shaky steps forward, forcing myself to run, forcing myself to get out of there.

I could hear scuffling against the door. He was doing something but I wasn't quite sure what.

I pushed hard against the door but it wouldn't open. It seemed unlocked but it was jammed and wouldn't budge an inch.

The mat. He'd jammed it with the mat.

I pounded the wood with my fist.

'Let me out,' I screamed.

'What about Dylan. What about Dylan . . .'

I said her name over and over again. I wasn't sure if he could hear me. I wasn't sure if he cared.

'Robert!' I yelled, slamming my hands against the wood. 'ROBERT!'

Chapter 55

After a minute I was exhausted. My wrists, sore from the fall, were crying out in pain from all the banging.

It was another few moments before I smelled it. The acrid scent – not of candles, but of fire itself. I looked around wildly, hoping for another exit, but it was hopeless. Robert's dressing room had one way in and one way out and that door was shut. I patted my pockets, desperate for my phone, but pictured it on the bed after I had messaged Chris Hannah. I turned back to the door and pushed as hard as I could: nothing. It didn't move at all. For now. That mat would burn eventually, but I supposed that would be too late.

The door was hot now. I could imagine the flames on the other side. Smoke was beginning to spiral in through the thin crack between the door and its frame.

This room was going to be my tomb unless I could do something quickly.

I pressed both hands over my mouth, willing myself not to cry. I had no time to wallow in self-pity, staying put was not an option unless I wanted to bake. Robert was right. No one would look too hard for an alternative narrative, especially when the deceased was on Prozac, with a messy home life and a long list of bad decisions.

For a moment, I thought about Dylan. I thought of the bruise on her hip softening, I thought about her happy with Nathan. She'd miss me of course, but she'd be okay. She was strong.

'And so are you,' I said out loud. I wasn't going to give in. I wasn't going to let Robert win, allow his jealousy and pain destroy me and everything I held dear. And suddenly I thought of Iris, imagining her spotting Robert in their study, on their computer, sending the messages that implicated Nathan. Had she confronted him? Had he tried to push past her on that narrow landing, accidentally toppling her down the stairs? Or had he pushed her, seeing her as a loose end he couldn't risk? Perhaps I would never know, but I wasn't about to let Robert get away with it.

I'd spent long enough poring over the blueprints for this building; the walls were reclaimed vintage brick, expensively and expertly laid, it would take a wrecking ball to move the outside walls. But Richard's dressing room adjoined mine on one side, and they were separated by nothing more than a stud wall, still two sheets of plasterboard and a framework of solid timber, but still my only chance.

I pushed a row of suits to one side and kicked at the panel. It dented, but that was all. I tried three more times as hard as my toes would allow – barely a crack. It was hopeless. I needed some leverage. I grabbed a hanger, looked at it, then immediately threw it aside. Far too light.

I knew we had kettle bells somewhere in the house, relics from a short-lived enthusiasm for at-home fitness when the subscription at my gym had gone up twice in six months, but they weren't in here.

Panic collected in my throat. What was heavy enough to push through plasterboard?

And then I saw them, on a shelf above his sweaters. Ski boots.

I jumped up to grab them and hooked one hand inside. It

was heavy. My wrist was aching. 'One, two, THREE!' Two practice swings and I crashed the boot against the wall.

There was a satisfying crack and I swung the boot again, over and over as if it were a sledgehammer, as chunks of plasterboard fell from the wall and fine white dust settled over Robert's suits.

There was a decent-sized hole now and I could see into my smoke-filled dressing room.

I gasped. The fire was spreading quickly. I swung again and again, kicking at the plaster, raking at it with my hands. I smarted as shards of sharp plaster tore through my skin.

I grabbed Robert's thick Arctic parka and put it on, then ran at the wall with my shoulder, the thickness of the durable fabric protecting me from pain.

There was just a small gap between two metal poles but it was enough to squeeze through. I tumbled onto the carpet of my dressing room. I scrambled to my knees and immediately began coughing: the whole room was full of thick smoke. Vomit fired up my throat and trickled out of my mouth. I wiped it away with the sleeve of the parka and looked around. Fire was licking into the bedroom from the hall which was completely ablaze.

I ran out of the dressing room but I was still trapped. I dropped back down and began to crawl forward blindly. At floor-level, at least I could breathe, but the heat coming from the hall was unbearable.

My phone was still on the bed. I grabbed it and called 999. I could barely bark out my address.

'Just help me,' I screamed as the Calder mobile above my head whirled furiously.

Think Rachel, think. But it was getting harder to think, harder to move. I was coughing so hard now there were spots dancing in front of my eyes.

There was a wall of light ahead of me. The bank of windows in our bedroom.

There was only one way out.

I pushed the lamp off our bedside table and picked it up. The expensive carpentry was heavy and I was weak. I staggered to the window and threw it at the glass. Over and over until I had made another hole.

I looked down. Down below was the koi carp pond. I had no idea if it would sufficiently break my fall, I had no idea if the shards of glass in the broken window would tear me to ribbons. But jumping was the only option.

I pushed the parka over my head and, bracing my feet, counted to three.

I couldn't breathe now, and tears were pouring down my cheeks. I thought of happier times. The delight of watching Dylan running through the shallows of a pale blue sea, the joy of a walk in the park with my mum, the quiet pleasure of sitting alone with a book and a cup of tea.

Angry fire curled up the walls. The crackling of the flames was deafening.

I took a deep breath, and then I jumped. A blast of winter air hit me in the face, and then I went cold. Somewhere I registered the muffled sound of a siren and then everything was black.

Epilogue

'It's not bad,' says Simeon Averill, dropping the manuscript onto the starched tablecloth with a thud. The other diners at Scott's look up from their Dover sole, then start discreetly whispering. Which of course was exactly his intention.

'It's better than that actually. It's quite good. Remind me, where did you find this little *prodigy*?'

His plummy drawn-out delivery makes the word sound faintly obscene.

'Just tell me Sir Simeon,' I say, reaching for the Sancerre. 'Will you give me a quote for it?'

The Great Writer strokes his little beard like a cat. 'On one condition,' he says finally.

'And what's that exactly?'

'Your story,' he replies, with a hint of a smile I know too well. Superior, gleeful. He's enjoying this. 'Your husband stalker thing. I've been thinking, and I believe that the world needs a new *In Cold Blood*. I always found Capote a little overrated myself, but true crime is having a moment, and frankly I should probably be in on the action. I'd loosely fictionalize it, if I have to.'

He's nothing if not an operator, The Knight, piggy-backing on my brief notoriety, I'll give him that.

He's also right that there might be some interest in everything that has happened to me. The story of arson and attempted murder in one of London's most exclusive neighbourhoods was catnip to the tabloids when it happened all those months ago, the embers of scandal coming back to life when it was Robert's trial a few weeks earlier. But although I've had a few direct offers to tell my story, the gilded cage that became a sprung trap, my cautionary tale for lonely empty nesters and anyone tempted by the lure of an old sweetheart, I hadn't taken any of them up – yet.

Simeon arches an eyebrow. 'I have to say you seem to have taken it all very well. I mean, your husband tries to kill you, you are alive only because you jumped out of a window and a koi carp pond broke your fall and then Judge Cambourne only gives him eight years. Many women would have fallen apart at the injustice of it all.'

'Many lesser women,' I say, leaning forward to tap the manuscript, not wanting to dwell on the details of Robert's trial, not wanting to admit that the stress of the past few months had taken its toll.

I'm thinner, greyer, harder than I once was, but if Simeon Averill has noticed, he doesn't say anything. He can't see the physical wounds from that cold December morning either – the long scar that runs down my leg is hidden by trousers. He doesn't know the emotional trauma that I'm still trying to work through during twice-weekly sessions with a therapist.

I'm not sure I'll ever get over the PTSD, whether the nightmares about being trapped in a burning house, will ever stop, whether I will finally stop imagining Robert setting fire to the voile at our landing window when I close my eyes, but I certainly don't want to talk about it with one of our authors now.

'Listen Simeon, if you really want the inside story, then you need to give me a quote for the cover,' I say, pressing the point home.

Sir Simeon purses his thin lips, considering. He hates giving quotes, hates giving anyone a leg-up. 'The greatest new talent this decade,' he says impulsively. 'Now tell me what *really* happened in that dressing room. What made one of the most respected developers in London go mad? And is it true about his connection to those dodgy Russians? That exposé in the papers was fascinating.'

Simeon's questions are endless and I don't even blame him. Picking up my pen, I hand it to him and slide Chris's manuscript back to him. 'Write it,' I say, 'with a signature. Then you get . . .' I glance across at the next table, dropping my voice. '*Then you get everything.*'

For a moment, Simeon stares down at the gold Caran d'Ache ballpoint – a present from Robert, ironically – then with a groan, he writes, spitting the words as he does.

'Greatest . . . new talent . . . decade. There.'

He shoves it back and looks up at me, eyes greedy.

'Now tell.'

A smile seeps onto my lips.

'Some other time,' I say, pushing the manuscript into my tote. 'Right now, I'm late for an appointment with my daughter.'

Simeon looks at me, his face a picture of utter surprise.

'You . . . you,' he splutters. 'You *cow.*'

It's such a well-mannered insult that I actually laugh.

'It has been said. By my husband, mostly. Oh, and you can keep the pen.'

Swinging my bag over my shoulder, I walk out into the late afternoon sunshine. Mount Street feels the bounce in my stride as I wave down a cab and canter across to jump inside.

'Soho, please,' I say, falling back into the leather. I can only imagine the quivering fury I have left behind in Scott's, the hissing phone calls to Ian Sinclair denouncing me, demanding my head. A year ago, I was scared of Sir Simeon Averill and his kind, a year ago I would never have dreamed of tweaking the rules in my favour. A year ago, I might not have been a good girl, but I tried to do things the right way.

It's already getting dark as the cab drops me on the corner. Days barely have any light in December, just like my own life this time a year ago. I look at my watch, knowing I can hardly afford the detour. Dylan and Nathan will be waiting at the Curzon, some arty nonsense Nathan's persuaded Dilly to try; but he's been good enough to include me too – I know she wouldn't have asked – so I'll gladly sit through ninety minutes of monochrome dirge if it means she's happy. It isn't easy for my daughter, right now. Soon Robert will no longer be my husband, but he will always be her father and I know that Dylan has hated every minute of the scandal. I've tried to protect her from some things, the National Crime Agency investigation into money laundering, and my private fears that Dmitri Anotov might target Robert in jail, but the simplest thing I can do for Dylan is be there for her. Like others have been there for me.

I stand in the street, and walk towards the pub, pulling up the collar of my coat to protect myself from the cold. For a moment, I watch my friend through the window. Chris is leaning on the bar, his face bright, his skin golden in the soft light, laughing with a group, who are lapping up what he is saying. Charm was always Chris's superpower, the thing that set him apart. He touches the attractive brunette he is stood next to on the shoulder and her hand flies to her mouth, trying – failing – to hide her pleasure. A gesture I know only too well. Jealousy flares; I can't help myself either and I picture myself pushing in through the door, diverting his attention. Then I'd pull out the manuscript, show him Simeon's scrawl and – boom – everything would change. For him, for us. We'll stop pretending that we are just good friends and he will love me again. In that moment, at least. He *would*.

But I don't take that step. Instead I stand there, watching him laugh, content on his path, unaware he's about to take a sharp right turn.

I knew this time would come the moment I read the first page of his novel, *The Tar Pit,* the story of an ordinary man sucked into the black sands of the British correctional system. It was so lyrical, so heartfelt, so poignantly relatable. From that first page, it was obvious Chris Hannah would have had a career as a writer.

'But not just yet,' I whisper. Chris can wait a few days. And so can I.

My divorce will be finalized any day now.

I haven't seen Robert since the trial, we communicate only through our lawyers.

The slate might not be completely wiped clean but my second act is finishing. I can be someone new. Someone better and my stomach flutters at the idea of what might happen.

Chris's manuscript feels heavy in my hands, heavy with the weight of its power, *my* power. I know these four hundred pages can change his life when I hand it over to a favoured agent who will find him the publishing deal it deserves.

But as the wind licks my cheeks and sharpens my thinking, I wonder what my own turning point was, the one thing that changed the direction of my life. Was it going back to a hotel room with Chris Hannah or was it before then? Meeting Serena at Joules, or giving up my job all those years ago? Was it a big decision, like marrying Robert Reeves in the first place, or a small one like staying for one last cocktail at Clint Porter's book launch, something that seemed so random and inconsequential at the time but set in motion a rippling chain of events that brought me here.

They were big questions, but right now, there are more important things to attend to. I turn from the pub window, checking my watch again, swearing softly under my breath. I map the route in my head, picturing Dylan's anxious face. I don't want to be late but if I hurry, I'll still make it. My heels click-clacking on the pavement, I break into a run. And just for a moment, I'm flying.

Acknowledgements

Thanks to Kim Young, Sophie Burks and all the team at HarperCollins who have made publishing so seamless under the strange conditions of lockdown. To Caroline Kirkpatrick and Dushi Horti, and Philip for the property chats at the gin bar. Thanks to my tireless agent Eugenie Furniss, also Emily MacDonald, Alex Bloch and Alexandra Cliff. To Bella Andre for our Burgh Island writing retreat (working on a thriller on the tidal island where Agatha Christie used to come to write has been one of my career joys to date.)

Much love and thanks to my son Fin who is a huge reader, movie buff and is a brilliant soundboard on everything from characterization to covers. And to John for everything.

Keep Reading . . .

Make sure you've read the previous
books from J.L. Butler . . .

Francine Day is a high-flying lawyer about to apply for
silk, ambitious and brilliant. She just needs one headline
grabbing client to seal her place as Queen's Counsel . . .
Martin Joy. The attraction is instant. Obsessive.

They embark on a secret affair and Francine thinks she
can hold it together. But then Martin's wife, Donna, goes
missing. And Martin is the prime suspect.

As the case unravels so does Francine, because the last
person to see Donna Joy alive, was her.

My **client**. My **lover**. My **husband**. My **obsession**.

'A gripping, thrill-a-minute ride through London's dark
side' *Erin Kelly*

'Gripping, intelligent, thrilling' *Adele Parks*

Read on for an extract of MINE

by J.L. Butler . . .

Prologue

I don't remember much about the night I was meant to die. It's funny how the mind can block out the memories it no longer wants to store, you must know that. But if I close my eyes, I can still hear the sounds of that night in May. The howl of an unseasonably cold wind, the rattle of the bedroom window, the rasp of the sea against shingle in the distance.

It was also raining. I remember that much, because the thin scratch of water against glass is still vivid in my head. For a minute it was hypnotic. For a minute it disguised the sound of his footsteps outside: tap, tap, tap, soles against flagstone in slow determined steps.

I knew he was coming and I knew what I had to do.

Lying under the duvet on the iron bed, I willed myself to keep calm. A faint glow from the string of bulbs on the coastal path leaked into the room. Usually this spectral darkness soothed me, but tonight it made me feel more alone, as if I were floating in space without a tether.

I balled my fist, hoping, praying that the comforting twilight of the new day would present itself at the window. But even without looking at the clock, I knew that this was at least four or five hours away and I didn't need to tell myself that it would be too late. The footsteps were right outside the house now, and the faint metallic grumble of a key being pushed into the lock echoed up the stairs. It was hard to disguise sounds in the big, old building, it was too tired and weary for that . . .

How had I let myself get into this? I had gone to London for a better life, to improve myself and meet a more interesting set of people. To fall in love. And now here I was: a cautionary tale.

I heard the front door creak open. Chilled air seeped through the cracks in the window pane and pinched my nostrils shut. It was as cold as a mortuary; a macabrely apt simile. I was even lying like a mummy, arms by my sides, trembling fingers tucked under my thighs, as heavy and immobile as if they were dead weights, anchoring me to the bed.

As the footsteps reached the top of the stairs, I pulled my hands out from the warmth and settled them on top of the cool cotton duvet cover. My fingers were clenched, nails pressing against my palms, but at least I was ready to fight. I suppose that was the lawyer in me.

He hesitated outside the bedroom door, and the moment seemed to compress into a cold, suspended silence. Coming here had not been a good idea. Closing my eyes, I willed the single tear not to weep on to my cheek.

A soft push of wood against carpet as the door opened. Every instinct in my body told me to leap out of the bed and run, but I had to wait and see if he would, if he could, do this. My heart was hammering out of my chest, my limbs felt frozen with fear. I kept my eyes shut, but I could feel him looming over me now, my body retreating into a menacing shadow. I could even hear his breathing.

A hand pressed against my mouth, its touch cold and alien against my dry, puckered lips. My eyes opened, and I could see a face only inches from mine. I was desperate to read his expression, desperate to know what he was thinking. I forced my lips apart, ready to scream, and then I waited for things to run their course.